AGENT X

ALSO BY NOAH BOYD

The Bricklayer

AGENT X

NOAH BOYD

WILLIAM MORROW

An Imprint of HarperCollinsPublishers

HarperCollins books may be purchased for educational, business, or sales promotional use. For information please write: Special Markets Department, HarperCollins Publishers, 10 East 53rd Street, New York, NY 10022.

FIRST EDITION

Library of Congress Cataloging-in-Publication Data

Boyd, Noah.
  Agent X / Noah Boyd.—1st ed.
    p. cm.
  ISBN 978-0-06-182698-6
    1. Private investigators—Fiction. I. Title.
  PS3602.09326A74 2011
  813'.6—dc22

                             2010029413

ISBN 978-0-06-206420-2 (international edition)

11 12 13 14 15 OV/RRD 10 9 8 7 6 5 4 3 2 1

For my wife, Patti,
who has always grown stronger the more impossible things become

BEFORE

KATE BANNON THOUGHT SHE WAS HAVING A NIGHTMARE, BUT ACTUALLY SHE WAS dying.

Only her nagging self-awareness, even in this somnolent state, was forcing her to remember that she didn't have nightmares. The frightening images had always been there—people shooting at her, falling endlessly from towering buildings, running through thicker and thicker sand to escape something unknown—but her reaction to them had always been as an indifferent observer, curious and analytical. If the "danger" persisted, she would simply tell herself it was a dream and wake up. And that's what she had to do now, wake up and find out what was causing the chaotic images in her head.

She sat up and felt dizzy, the blood pounding in the top of her head. It hurt too much to be a dream. She felt nauseous and remembered driving home after the Thanksgiving Eve get-together at one of the local FBI watering holes with a large group of people from headquarters. She remembered having a glass of wine, and then a good-looking guy she didn't know brought her a small glass of—what did he say it was?—Drambuie. She had never tasted it before and took a mouthful. Finding it too bitter for her liking, she set it down and didn't touch it again. It must have been strong, because she soon started feeling woozy and decided to leave.

Throwing her legs over the side of the bed, she worked her feet into slippers and stood up. As soon as she was fully upright, she felt lightheaded and had trouble balancing herself. With a hand on the wall, she started toward the kitchen. Walking left her short of breath. That couldn't be from alcohol. That's when she heard the low rumbling. She continued to the kitchen and saw that the door to the garage was open. Now she could clearly hear her car running.

Without warning, her knees started to buckle, and she realized that she was not suffering from what she had drunk but from carbon monoxide poisoning. Carefully, she stepped down the three stairs into the garage, which was filled with the haze of exhaust fumes. The car door was locked, and she could see the keys in the ignition.

The garage's outside door was only a few feet away, and she lurched to it. Taking hold of the knob, she tried to turn it, but her grip failed her. She pushed on the door clumsily with her body weight but couldn't rotate the knob far enough to open it. Even using both hands, she couldn't get it to release. Next to the door, in a holder fastened to the wall, was a remote-control unit for the overhead door. She pressed the button, but nothing happened.

Beginning to panic now, she pressed it repeatedly, but still the door didn't rise. She tried to remember the last time she had changed the battery, but her mind refused to focus on anything requiring memory. All at once she crashed to the floor, knocking over her small gardening caddy and scattering tools in every direction.

She tried to get up but could only manage to roll over on her back. *Is this it?* she asked herself. After all she'd been through as an agent, this was how she was going to die? Then she saw a white light coming from the six-inch-square window in the door and wondered if it was what so many people who approached death had reported. She fell back and let her eyes slide shut. Even with her mouth closed, she could taste the thick fumes in her throat.

The actual source of the light was a small flashlight held by a man standing outside, dressed in black. When she collapsed, he turned it off and pulled the two wedges from under the door that had jammed it closed against her efforts. Then he went to the front door of the residence and removed two more. Calmly, he put his hands in his pockets and walked back to a waiting SUV.

Lying there felt pleasant, euphoric, but then it occurred to Kate that the light was gone. Shouldn't it be inside her head, too? She opened her eyes, and it was still gone. Did that mean the death sentence had been revoked, or at least delayed? Whatever it meant, she decided that she was going down swinging.

Next to her was a rake, its wooden handle thick and straight. Pushing up on all fours, she crawled to the rear of the car, dragging the rake behind her. The fumes were completely suffocating. She peeled off one of her slippers with its thin rubber sole and crammed it into the tailpipe. She was familiar enough with cars to know that the obstruction alone wouldn't stop the engine as the movies depicted but would eventually be blown out by mounting pressure. So she stuck the rake's handle into the tailpipe, forcing the slipper even farther into the exhaust.

Then she maneuvered the wooden shaft, finally wedging the steel raking tines against one of the patterned grooves in the overhead garage door, which was a foot and a half away. One of two things would happen now: Either the pressure would build up and kill the engine or the rake would blow a hole in the door and provide fresh air. One or the other could save her. Of course, it was more likely that the handle of the rake would simply snap. She reached up and held the rake in place before crumpling to the floor to wait.

Something with a sharp edge was underneath her. She realized it was a gardening trowel that had been knocked across the floor when she first fell. Inching closer to the garage door, she shoved it under the rubber cleat that sealed the entire length of the door and, using both hands, turned it up on edge to make a small triangular opening. Placing her mouth as close to it as possible, she breathed in the sweet, cold, late-autumn air.

Just before she passed out, her hand slipped off the rake and she thought she heard the car's engine sputter and die.

AFTER CLIMBING INTO THE BACKSEAT OF THE SUV, the man in black nodded to the two men in the front that it was done.

The driver, in his early fifties, was tall and slender, his suit expensive and American. His hair was full and carefully cut. His face might have been described as elegant if it weren't for the splayed, crooked nose, which gave his appearance a vague warning of violence. He looked over at the man sitting next to him to see if he was satisfied.

The passenger reached over and turned off the radio-signal device that had jammed Kate's remote-control door opener, the limited markings on it written in Cyrillic. He, too, was tall but powerfully built, and his age was difficult to estimate; he could have been in his fifties or in his sixties. His hands were thick and crisscrossed with dozens of thin white scars. His face was drawn and slightly exhausted, his eyes irreparably sad. Although his skin appeared a permanent gray, his lips were thick and an unusual shade of dark red. He looked back at the driver with eyes that never seemed to move from side to side. It was as if they were frozen in their sockets, making whomever he was talking to feel that turning away would be perceived as evasive, even when telling the truth. He searched the driver's face for any indication that he and his man hadn't been successful and then leaned his head back on the head-rest and closed his eyes. The SUV pulled away from the curb.

KATE BANNON OPENED HER EYES and wondered if she was dreaming again. Bob Lasker, the director of the FBI, sat next to her hospital bed. Struggling to recall what had happened, she wasn't sure she really could. "Am I dreaming?" she asked loudly, almost as if trying to determine if she was actually awake. She went to scratch her nose but then realized that an oxygen tube was pinching her nostrils.

"This is real, Kate." The director smiled warmly. "You gave us a scare, though. But you're going to be all right."

"I remember being in the garage and not being able to get out."

"One of your neighbors was taking his dog for a late-night walk, and I guess in the cool air he smelled the exhaust from the opening you made. He dragged his owner closer, and then the guy broke in, dragged you out, and called 911. Any idea how you left your car on?"

She told him about being bought a drink and not feeling well, then waking up to find her car running and not being able to get out of the garage. "I can't imagine doing that. And then locking the car door with the keys in the ignition? Who locks a car that's in a locked garage?"

"And this guy who bought you the drink, you never saw him before."

"Not that I remember. I would have remembered him from head-quarters. He was nice-looking."

"Maybe he was just someone at the bar and saw a pretty girl."

"Maybe," she said vaguely, her mind searching for other possibilities.

Lasker stared at her as though there were some question he wasn't asking.

"What?" she demanded.

"Kate, don't take this the wrong way, but have you been feeling okay lately?"

She gave a short laugh. "Wait a minute—are you asking me if I've been depressed?"

"Yes."

She thought for a moment. "You think I tried to kill myself?"

The question was asked with such self-assurance that Lasker couldn't help but say, "No, I don't."

"But others do?"

"A deputy assistant director almost dies, there are questions that have to be considered."

"Meaning what?"

"OPR is going to look into it. Very routine, very low-key."

"I didn't try to commit suicide."

"You know I can't call off procedure. I wouldn't for any other agent, and since everyone knows how much I think of you, I can't in this instance either." He smiled. "Please cooperate and try not to shoot any of them. As soon as you feel well enough to get out of here, you'll be returned to full duty while they conduct their investigation."

"This is ridiculous."

"I know it is. If it does get to be too much, come and see me." Lasker patted her on the arm. "For now, get well. Everything else will take care of itself."

She was staring down at her hands but finally looked at him. "I guess I should be thanking you instead of arguing."

"Just get better, Kate."

Soon after the director left the room, an agent whom Kate recognized as being from the Office of Professional Responsibility came in. "Hi, Kate. I'm Roger Daniels from OPR. How are you feeling?"

"Nonsuicidal."

He laughed. "I know this is a lot coming at you all at once. I can wait to take your statement."

Kate sat up and took a sip of water from a cup on the table next to her bed. "Don't be *too* offended, but the sooner we get started, the sooner I'll have OPR out of my life."

The agent chuckled. "Well, that carbon monoxide didn't damage your sense of humor."

"Who said I was trying to be funny? Roger, I'm sure you're a very capable agent, and maybe even a nice guy, but I did a stint at OPR, so please don't waste any of the artificial sweeteners on me. Just ask me your questions, and I'll give you my best answers."

"Fair enough, Kate." He opened his notebook. "Did you attempt suicide?" His tone was noticeably less friendly.

"I'm the one who stopped the car engine and wedged a trowel under the door to save myself. Does that sound like I was trying to commit suicide?"

"It's not uncommon during a suicide attempt for people to have a change of heart. They take pills and then call 911. Move the gun at the last moment and just wound themselves. It happens more frequently than you think."

"Yeah, well, I happen to like my life quite a bit."

"Don't take this the wrong way, but some people do it for attention."

"How could I possibly take that the wrong way?" she said, sounding more than a little sarcastic. She took a moment and then said, "If you knew me, you'd know I really don't care what people think. Why would I want to get their attention?"

"Not people—*person,*" he said.

"Person? Who?"

The agent flipped back to another page in his notes. "Steve Vail?"

"Where did you get that?"

"Answers, Kate, remember?"

"Okay, what do you know about him? And me?"

"We know that he was fired as an agent more than five years ago. That the director brought him back to work on the Rubaco Pentad case in Los Angeles—with you—and that you guys have dated. Recently it ended abruptly."

"Sounds like you got a running start on this while I was still unconscious. Okay, I'll tell you about Vail on one condition—that you don't contact him."

"If you're forthcoming, there'll be no need to."

"One of the hardest things I've had to do in my life was tell him I didn't want him in it. If you've read the Pentad file, you know he was responsible for solving that case almost single-handedly. He would be an incredible agent, but he cannot conform to anything, and that includes a relationship with me. We've seen each other three times since L.A. The first time was—I hate to use the word, but it was—pretty much perfect. The last two were absolutely awful. So I told him it would be best if we didn't see each other again. And that was a week ago. So no, I wasn't trying to get his attention."

"Trying to find out exactly who he was, I ran his name through some of our contacts at other agencies and got a hit with the State Department. Seems you and he are going to the Irish ambassador's reception on New Year's Eve."

"Boy, you have been busy. But you'd better check with them again. It should show that my escort is now Eamon Walsh."

"So you changed it."

"What's today?"

"Wednesday."

"I spoke with him Monday. He's with the Irish embassy and was the one who called me originally with the invitation. When I phoned him back to tell him Vail wasn't coming, he asked if I'd do him the honor. I didn't want to go alone, so I said yes. Maybe he hasn't gotten around to changing it officially yet. You can call him."

Daniels was making notes. "So it's definitely over between you and Vail. You told him not to come for New Year's Eve."

"Not in so many words, but I think 'We shouldn't see each other again' carries that assumption."

"That's helpful about Vail. It gives you one less reason to . . . you know."

"Off myself."

"Tell me what you remember about the night that this happened to you," Daniels said.

She repeated what she'd told the director about the stranger's buying her a drink that didn't settle well with her, then her coming home and going to bed. Then waking up and trying to get out of the garage.

He asked, "You said he told you it was Drambuie?"

"Yes."

"Hmm," Daniels said more to himself than to her.

"What?"

"I've had Drambuie, and it has a definite strong sweetness to it."

The OPR agent started making additional notes that she guessed were more than just about Kate's response. As she watched him, she remembered her time in OPR, how investigations were not about the incident but about the employee's involvement in it. They weren't criminal investigators, they were personnel investigators. As Daniels looked up from his pad ready to ask the next question, she knew that he was not going to get to the bottom of this. If anyone was going to find out what had happened, it would have to be her. "If that guy did put something in the drink, maybe he had some other intentions, and when he saw I drank only one sip of it, he got scared and took off."

"Your blood didn't show any kind of drug in it, but if you didn't drink much, maybe it dissipated before you got here."

"Are you going to try to track him down?" she asked, trying to judge just how far he was going to pursue what had happened to her.

"I'll have to see where everything takes me."

Right, she said to herself, becoming lost in thought. There was just something about a near-death experience that brought Vail to mind. And she couldn't decide whether that was a good thing or a bad thing. She knew that he would never just "see where everything takes me." A small smile creased her lips.

"What is it, Kate?"

"Oh, no, nothing. Did you need anything else?"

"That's enough for now." Daniels stood up. "Take care."

He closed the door, and after a moment her smile disappeared.

She was sure she was never going to see Vail again.

ONE

KATE BANNON OPENED HER DOOR. "WHAT ARE YOU DOING HERE?"

With mock surprise on his face, Steve Vail recoiled slightly at the level of protest in her voice. He stepped inside, setting down his suitcase and, for the briefest moment, allowed his eyes to trace the flawless symmetry of her face. "I've got the right day, don't I? This is New Year's Eve. Is it the wrong year?"

"After that last time, when I told you this wasn't going to work, I assumed you understood that included tonight."

He smiled crookedly. "Come on, Kate, it's the twenty-first century. What woman wants to have to admit that she's never been stalked? It's become an accoutrement, like Italian shoes or one of those little purse-size dogs."

"We tried, Steve. Three times. And the last two, if you remember, were not pretty."

"That means statistically we're due."

Kate shook her head slowly. She really couldn't believe he was standing there. "You know as well as I do that we're a disaster. We're too different. Or too much alike. I don't know. Every time we try to get close, we wind up driving each other crazy. You don't know how much I wanted it to work, but it can't."

Vail looked at her dress. "I guess you were planning to go to whatever this was tonight without me. Why don't we go together and see what happens? What's the worst that can happen? So I ruin your career. That would probably be the best thing that could happen to us."

"I have to go to this. It's a command performance. And you know exactly what it is—an ambassador's reception. Why else would you have a suit on? Even though the proper dress is a tuxedo. Which I'm going to guess was your way of letting all the *phonies* in the room know that you're a lowly bricklayer."

"A man has to seek amusement wherever he can."

"I'll never understand you. You could be whatever you want. You have advanced degrees. The director has offered you complete autonomy if you'll come back to the Bureau, but instead you choose physical labor just so you won't have to take orders. If that's who you are, fine, but you don't get to rub everyone else's face in it simply because they're not like you." She looked at him sternly. "It's called hypocrisy." She could see that her words had stung him, but she couldn't find anything inaccurate in what she'd said.

He reached up and traced the small L-shaped scar high on her cheekbone and then smiled gently. "You don't have to wonder anymore, Kate, whether we're too much alike. There was a time, and not very long ago, that you would have thought they were phonies, too," he said. "But you're right, I've been a phony myself. The only defense I can offer is that you make my compass go haywire. The only reason I'm doing any of this is you."

He turned and opened the door. "Like you said, we gave it a shot," he said. "When it was right, it was like nothing I've ever experienced. That's why I had to try one last time."

"You can't just walk out like that. Not after everything we've been through."

"This is the best way to leave it. Then we won't have any lingering doubts."

"At least let me drive you to the airport. It's freezing out."

"I live in Chicago, remember? This isn't cold."

"I'll feel better about this if I can take you. It'll give us a chance to talk a little more. Right now I feel like we're supposed to hate each other."

"It'll be fine, Kate. I'll get a taxi."

"It's New Year's Eve—you'll never find one."

"You're probably right." He picked up his suitcase. "Okay, I'll take a ride, but only if we don't talk. I don't want to say anything that'll make this worse."

For the briefest moment, she considered telling him about the night before Thanksgiving and asking him what he thought about the guy in the bar. The day she got home from the hospital, she'd gone into her garage to change the battery in the remote for the overhead door. But it had worked fine. She thought that maybe she'd just pushed the wrong part of it in her semiconscious state. But three days ago she'd realized that it had been over a month and she hadn't heard anything from OPR. So she'd gone back into the garage and retraced the events from that night as best she could. That's when she realized that she couldn't have opened the inside door to her condominium if her keys were locked in the car.

Then she'd bought a bottle of Drambuie and tasted it. It had a honey-sweet taste to it, nothing like what she remembered from the bar.

The next day she'd checked with the Metropolitan Police, and they'd said they hadn't had any recent drug-facilitated rapes reported. Since she was sneaking around behind OPR's back, she didn't want to start asking questions of people who were at the bar and have it get back to Daniels. Vail, who saw these things on a different level, would have been the perfect person to ask. But under the circumstances, giving him a reason to stay would be counterproductive.

"If that's the way you want to leave this," she said.

The phone rang. "You'd better get that," he said. "The Bureau probably thought we actually had a date and needed to ruin it one last time."

"That isn't fair."

"Probably not, but you can't say it's inaccurate."

"This is exactly why it would never work between us. Not everyone who takes orders for a living is a mortal enemy of Steven Vail."

Vail held up his hands in apology. "I told you I'd say something that would make it worse."

As she walked to the phone, she decided to lighten the mood and try to initiate some sort of interim peace. "I know it's been a while since the FBI fired you, but nobody gets called out on Thanksgiving, Christmas, or New Year's Eve. It's in our latest contract." She picked up the receiver. "Kate Bannon. Oh, hi, Tim. Happy New Year." She listened and after a few seconds turned her back to Vail.

He sat down on his suitcase and waited for the inevitable change of plans.

She hung up and said, "A seven-year-old boy was abducted in Reston, Virginia, which is two towns over from here."

When she didn't offer any other details, he said, "The FBI doesn't have jurisdiction for twenty-four hours in an abduction. Why did they call you?"

"The Reston chief is a retired agent from the Washington Field Office. We go back a lot of years. He's a good guy, but something like this, he's probably in over his head. His entire career was working applicant cases, asking the same handful of questions about character and loyalty. Would you mind if we stopped there on the way? It shouldn't take long. He just needs some reassurance—you know, what help the Bureau can give him. Maybe a little direction."

In a cryptic tone, Vail said, "I wouldn't miss it for the world."

"You wouldn't miss what?" she asked suspiciously.

"You pretending not to get involved to prove to me, and yourself, that your career isn't what's come between us."

"If you're trying to ensure that there'll be no talking on the way, congratulations." She handed him her keys. "There's one more call I have to make, would you mind warming up the car?"

Vail gave her an inquiring look and then started laughing. "No wonder you're able to resist my charms. You have a date."

"It's not actually a—"

Vail held up his hands. "Kate, it's fine. I was hoping you weren't serious about it being over. That's why I came. Obviously I was wrong. I'll go start the car."

Five minutes later Kate walked into the garage and climbed behind the wheel. As soon as they pulled out, Vail asked, "How long has the boy been gone?"

"So we *are* going to talk."

"I'm just trying to establish the parameters of your *momentary* detour."

"Why?"

"So I'll be able to mark the exact second you violated the estimate of your involvement."

"You really think you've got me figured out, don't you?"

"Not that it matters anymore, but oh yeah," Vail answered.

She turned to him, wanting to look indignant but knowing she couldn't pull it off. Then she told him, "Tim said about five hours."

"You do understand that the chances of him being found alive are not good."

"Then I guess you do understand that's why I have to go."

Vail stared straight ahead for a moment. "I do."

KATE FLASHED HER CREDENTIALS at the police officer behind the glass, and he opened the door for her and Vail. They were led to a small conference room where more than a dozen police officers and detectives sat crowded around a conference table designed for half that number.

The chief, Tim Mallon, rose anxiously and shook hands with her. She introduced him to Vail. One of the officers got up so Kate could sit down and Vail backed up against the closest wall.

Mallon handed Kate a sheet of paper and a photo. "That's the boy, Joey Walton, and the BOLO we put out along with the Amber Alert. He and his parents were at a local New Year's Eve 5K run. It also had a half-mile race for the kids. The parents watched the start, and by the time they got to the finish line, he was gone. No one's seen him since."

Kate said, "Okay, Tim, what can the Bureau do for you?"

"I was hoping you could tell me. Obviously, we could use a profiler and anything else along those lines you can think of."

"As soon as we're done here, I'll make some calls. I assume you're looking into registered sex offenders in the area."

The chief nodded at a detective sitting halfway around the table, who said, "I'm expecting a list any minute."

"I guess that's going to be the best lead for now."

"What else?" Mallon asked.

"Put out a plea to the media, along with the boy's photo."

"That's been done, Kate. And we have the parents doing interviews, trying to personalize the boy for whoever took him," Mallon said. "Isn't there anything else we can do?"

"Sometimes you just have to give the public some time to respond. There's a chance somebody knows who did this."

"I'm sorry, I don't want to sit and wait. There must be something we can do to be more proactive. What would you do if it were a Bureau case?"

She hesitated a moment, glancing back at Vail. "Tim, I'm sorry. I've never worked kidnappings, but I can make some calls and see if we can get someone out here from the Washington Field Office."

Mallon looked confused. "Kate, I spent twenty years at WFO. If I thought someone there had the answer, I wouldn't have called you." He looked around the men at the table, hoping someone would offer an idea of what to do next.

Kate said, "I misjudged what you needed, Tim." Then she got up and, with an apologetic grin to him, handed Vail the photo and the BOLO. "How about it, Steve? Can you give them a hand?"

Somewhat surprised, the chief said, "I'm sorry, Steve, are you with the Bureau?"

"Actually, I'm a bricklayer. From Chicago." He handed the items back to Kate. "In fact, I'm on my way back there now."

Mallon shot a confused look at Kate. "Steve's a former agent who has helped us in the past. Take my word, right now you want him in the room."

"Sorry, Steve," Mallon said. "You're both dressed up. I thought you were just Kate's date."

Vail smiled disarmingly. "Funny how easy it is to make that assumption."

Sensing some rift between the two of them, the chief said, "Steve, if you can help, we'd be grateful. This is a seven-year-old boy's life we're talking about."

Vail pushed himself off the wall with obvious reluctance, his eyes locked onto Kate's, purposely without emotion. "Sure." Vail looked around the table. "Any of you ever work a child kidnapping by a stranger before?" One older uniformed officer raised his hand unconvincingly.

Vail took a moment to consider something. "Chief, I'd recontact all the media outlets and have them put out a plea for help from anyone at the race. It being a kids' run, a lot of people are going to be taking pictures with both their cameras and their cell phones. Ask everyone to immediately e-mail all their photos to the station. Every one of them, whether they think they're connected or not." Kate watched as Vail became silent, lost in some other thought. "I assume that race officials also took photos. Have them do the same, including those from the adult race. Have you gotten a list of runners from them?"

The chief pointed at one of the detectives, who said, "They're supposed to be forwarding it."

"You'll want that right now. Also from the kids' race," Vail said. "That it's a holiday and twice as hard for the police to get anything done may not be a coincidence. Whoever's responsible for this may have learned by past mistakes. As in *convicted* child molester. Which, as Kate suggested, makes the sex-offenders list a top priority."

"What else?" Mallon asked.

Vail stepped forward to better engage the men around the table. "I know everybody is trying to think positive, but after this amount of time, statistically, there's only a slightly better-than-even chance that the boy is still alive. Not a pleasant thought, but you're police officers—you're paid to approach things from a clinical and, maybe more important, a cynical perspective. There's also a fifty-percent chance the boy's been sexually assaulted. And the longer this goes, the worse those odds become. So if cars are stopped or your instinct tells you to search someplace, don't get it in your mind that you're going to hear the victim pounding on doors or walls to be freed. Assume you're looking for a body. And remember, in a situation like this—I'm sorry, Chief—it's better to do something that's wrong than it is to do nothing at all. If someone won't allow you access, politely search anyway. Just remember: Be polite and explain the situation. Whoever took the boy is one of the few people who won't cooperate in an instance like this."

Mallon stood up and addressed his officers. "Don't any of you worry about liability. Like Steve said, explain, be polite, and then do what you have to do. All the heat is on me." To Kate and Vail, he said, "We've already got more than thirty tips. The media has been running the story every half hour. Each time they do, we get more. We're going to start chasing them down." He turned back to the officers and detectives around the table. "Any questions?" There were none. "Okay, I'll be here. If you run into anyone who's reluctant to help, and there's time, call me and I'll make the decision." The officers got up and started filing out. "Kate, you can use my office to make those calls."

"Okay."

"Steve, can I ask you to give us a hand with the tips? Sounds like you know what to look for. Maybe you'll see something we're missing."

"If I can get one of your people to run me to the airport when we're through. Kate's already late for something she needs to get to."

"Sure." Mallon glanced at her. "Kate, if you need to go, I'll understand."

Kate could tell that Vail hadn't said it maliciously. "It's nothing that can't wait, Tim. And if I don't make it, it's not a big deal. I'm here because we're friends. I'll stay until you don't need me any longer."

Vail said, "Chief, if you have a desk somewhere with a computer, I'll start on those tips. And a map of the area if you have one."

"Great. And I'll make sure you get copies of anything new that comes in."

Kate said, "Tim, could you give us a minute?"

"Sure." Mallon walked out and shut the door.

She put her hand on his arm. "I appreciate your keeping me from looking like a fool."

"No use both of us feeling that way."

She started to say something, and he placed his hand over hers. "It's okay, Bannon." He leaned forward and whispered in her ear. "I really do hate New Year's Eve parties."

He turned to go, and she said, "And don't think you can sneak out of here without saying good-bye."

Vail gave her a silent but formal salute.

While Kate started making phone calls, trying to track down agents from the Behavioral Science Unit and the Washington Field Office, the chief led Vail to a detective's desk and showed him how to access the department's different databases. He settled in and started reading the tips.

Unlike the officers and detectives, Vail had the luxury of looking at them from a different perspective. The Reston Police Department had to investigate all the tips offered. Vail didn't. So he was able to start making judgments about the callers and the individuals they were reporting on.

He checked each suspect's name in the computer to see if there were any previous contacts with the department. He also checked the callers' names—if they gave one—to see if they were chronic complaint makers, which could lessen the priority of their information. After reading all the tips, he hadn't found any he considered worthwhile. That wasn't necessarily a bad thing. Tips were a double-edged sword. While they frequently solved a case, a false lead that looked promising could be distracting, take the entire department in the wrong direction, and burn precious time. A uniformed officer walked in and asked, "You Vail?"

He stood up and shook hands. "Steve, yes."

The policeman put three more tips on the pile. "These are from the last half hour. We're also starting to get photos from the races e-mailed in. Do you want me to forward them to this computer?"

"I'd appreciate it." Vail picked up the newest tips. "Anything interesting?"

"Nothing we'll need lights and sirens for."

Vail continued searching the names through the computer. Still nothing jumped out at him. When he finished, he got up and wandered around until he found someone who directed him to a coffeepot. He filled two cups and went looking for Kate.

The chief's office was small but well ordered. Bureau memorabilia neatly lined the wall behind the desk. Kate was on the phone, so Vail placed the cup in front of her and sat down.

She rolled her eyes as she listened to the latest excuse as to why nothing could be done tonight, taking a sip of coffee. He watched her and was reminded of one of the things that he liked most about her: She thrived on work. The more difficult the case, the more focused she became. He listened as she urged cooperation. Her tone was compelling, and Vail couldn't tell whether it was actually cajoling or threatening or both. Finally she hung up midsentence. "Come January second, there'll be a number of Bureau employees who are going to be at least as unhappy as I am right now."

"Makes me almost sorry I won't be here."

She gave him a small, sad smile through pursed lips and leaned back in her chair. "Anything in the tips?"

"Not so far. The photos are starting to come in, though."

"Do you actually think we'd get that lucky?"

"I just thought it would be better to have them than not. You never know, something could come up later that a photo might help with," Vail said. "And the pendulum is due to swing the other way."

"What pendulum?"

"What most people call luck. To me it's nothing more than a temporary statistical aberration. So far tonight I've had an unbelievable amount of bad luck, so maybe I'm due."

"Sorry." She stared at him for a moment before taking another sip of coffee. "Do you know what I find to be the most confounding thing about you, Steve?"

"That doesn't sound like a question a judicious person would want to hear the answer to."

"That you're so good at this and refuse to do it for a living."

"Don't start."

The chief knocked on the door and came in. "Sorry. We may have something. From the sex-offenders list, there's one, a Frank Dillon, who kidnapped and molested a six-year-old boy twelve years ago. He was paroled in September, and he lives in Vienna, which is fairly close. We got ahold of his parole officer, who said Dillon recently changed his residence and stopped reporting. As far as the PO is concerned, he's AWOL, and he'll violate him if we want. We just made a call to his last employment, and he was at work until noon today, when he just up and quit. He did leave a cell-phone number so they could call him when his last check was ready. We're going to try to put the grab on him. You guys want to come along?"

"Sure," Kate said. She looked at Vail.

"You won't need me, Chief. I'm a civilian. If something happened, my being there would just give some defense attorney a little more smoke to blind a jury with. Besides, somebody should stay here and keep checking on the tips in case this guy doesn't work out."

Kate turned to the chief. "Tim, I'm coming with you. I'll be there in a minute." Once Mallon left, she said, "I seem to remember something about you always keeping the best lead for yourself. That's not what this is, is it?"

"Like the chief said before, we're talking about a child's life."

"Sorry." She took out her car keys. "When's the last time you ate?"

"Ah . . . breakfast."

"Please go get something. Those tips won't miss you for fifteen minutes. And I really do appreciate this, Steve," she said. "Hopefully, this won't take long. *Hopefully,* this is our guy."

When Vail got back to the detective's desk, there were four new tip sheets. He checked the e-mails and was surprised to see that the department had already received eleven messages with photos attached. The lists of runners for both races had also been forwarded. He opened the first set of pictures; they were all of the adult race. He scanned the faces, looking for the Walton boy. There was a subtle difference in quality between the phone pictures and those taken with cameras. As long as they didn't have to be blown up to provide detail, it really didn't matter.

Because of the cold weather, most of the runners were bundled up, especially the children. The kids' race seemed more crowded, with all those parents waiting at the finish line. Vail went through them three times, trying to spot Joey Walton. According to the runners' list, the sandy-haired seven-year-old was number 034. There were a couple of possibilities that looked like him physically, but the numbers pinned to their chests indicated otherwise.

An angry knot of frustration turned in Vail's stomach, and he started to regret not going with Kate. The fugitive pedophile sounded like a decent lead. If it wasn't him, Frank Dillon had certainly picked an odd time to stop reporting to his parole officer and disappear. By staying behind, Vail knew he was trying to make something happen, create some insightful discovery. Apparently he did miss the chase, but at the moment it seemed little more than useless self-indulgence. Or maybe he just wanted to impress Kate.

He started to get up to refill his coffee when the e-mail tone sounded again. There were three new messages, which had eight additional photographs attached. He took his time and looked through them twice. Then, realizing that he had no idea what he was looking for, he got to his feet and waved at the monitor in disgust. He was trying to look at the case from too many angles, a sure way to not find anything.

Outside the department's front door, he stood without a coat, trying to use the cold to redirect his thoughts. He stayed there until he could feel the bite of the wind, letting the discomfort distract him from his failing approach to the investigation.

Then one of the latest photos flashed through his mind. But the image did not last long enough for him to figure out why it had risen out of his subconscious. He hurried back to the desk and pulled the picture up on the screen. After studying every little detail, he still couldn't see anything. He closed his eyes and then slammed his fist on the desk.

The image was that of a boy, about eleven years old, breaking the tape at the children's race. There were a number of adults standing on the side-lines looking back up the course, trying to find their children in the onrushing pack. It was crowded, and people were walking in all directions. Vail could see how easy it would be to lure a seven-year-old away without anyone's noticing. By the race numbers pinned to their chests, Vail could see that some of the adults had competed in the 5K run, while the rest were apparently just observers. Then he saw what he had missed.

One of the adult runners seemed to be looking at the camera as if he were measuring its danger. His arm was in front of his number so it couldn't be read. Vail couldn't tell if he was blocking it intentionally. But what he'd initially missed was that there was a smaller square of paper attached to the lower left corner of the man's race number. It had been safety-pinned on so it could be collected at the end of the 3.1-mile race to document finish place and time. Unfortunately, because of the angle, Vail couldn't make it out either. The man was dark-complected and burly, not a runner's build. Most people who would run in the cold air of New Year's Eve were probably not novices. That the number tag was still there suggested he had not run the adult race. His registering could have been a ruse calculated to get him close to the children without seeming suspicious.

The e-mail tone sounded again, and Vail glanced at the monitor. It was from the race officials. Attached were all of their photos. Still lost in thought, Vail ignored it, trying to find a way to determine if the individual in the photo was involved in the boy's disappearance. Then it hit him. The photo was taken the moment the race's winner was crossing the finish line. Logically, the official pictures would cover that moment and then beyond.

Quickly, he opened the e-mail and began studying the images. The first twenty or so were of the adult race. He looked for that same individual, thinking the man might have initially been in that area. Vail couldn't find him. Then the chronologically sequenced photos started documenting the beginning of the children's run. Vail carefully searched each of them. He knew what the man was wearing and was hoping for a clear shot of his number, which he could match to the runners' list. There was another one of the young man winning, but Vail's suspect was not in it.

A half-dozen photographs later, there was one of a man in the distance who appeared to be the right size and with the same clothing as in the earlier photo. He had his back to the camera and stood next to a van. Vail couldn't tell whether he was stopped there or walking by. The van's plate was visible, but it was too distant to make out.

Vail found the computer's Photoshop program and opened it, pulling up the picture. Because the image had been taken with a quality camera, the pixel density was high and allowed him to blow up the license plate to where it could be read. He made a note of it and then centered the photo on the individual. In the space between the man's legs, unseen before, was what looked like the leg of a child wearing red pants. Vail called the dispatcher and had her run the van's plate.

While he waited, he shuffled through the growing stack of pages on the desk until he found the BOLO that had been sent out originally. Joey Walton was last seen wearing a black hooded sweatshirt and red sweatpants. The dispatcher came back on the line and advised that the plate came back to a George Hillstrand with a Herndon, Virginia, address.

Vail found Hillstrand's name on the adult race roster and then checked him in the Reston PD computer. Four years earlier, he had evidently worked in Reston, because the department had gotten a call about him from the Maryland State Police, who were conducting an investigation of a child who had disappeared in Colesville, Maryland. They had called to see if Reston had had any previous contact with Hillstrand. They hadn't.

The seven-year-old, Edward Stanton, had disappeared during a party at one of those pizza-and-game places that specialized in letting the kids run all over while the parents drank pitcher beer and doled out tokens to keep them busy. Hillstrand's name had somehow come up in their investigation, but no specifics were listed.

Vail called the dispatcher again and had her run Edward Stanton's name to see if the boy, or his body, had ever been found. After a short wait, she told him that the missing-person notice in NCIC was still active. Vail asked for the boy's description. It was not unusual for serial offenders to seek victims who were physically similar. The two boys' ages when kidnapped were close. She said, "At the time of incident, he was seven years old, four feet one inch tall, and weighed sixty pounds. Medium-brown hair, blue eyes. Under distinguishing marks, he has a crescent-shaped scar on the crown of his head." A lot of things were matching up, but Vail had seen it before. "Proof positive" that turned out to be a series of impossible coincidences but were in fact just that.

With time so critical, the lead had to be checked out now. He found the dispatcher's office and went in. "Hi, I'm Steve Vail. How're they doing?"

Before she could answer, a request to run a plate came over the air.

She turned to the computer to type it in and said, "They're sitting on three places right now, waiting for this guy to come back. Did you want me to tell them something?"

"No, they've got their hands full. I'll catch up with them later." Vail also knew that if he waited for them, investigative protocol would have to be followed. First, the Maryland State Police would have to be contacted to see if Hillstrand was actually a suspect in the case or, instead, if his name had come up as the result of some other "shotgun" approach, which was not unusual in that kind of case. Hundreds, even thousands of names could be generated and never be fully investigated because of sheer volume. The fact that the state police had never followed up with a more detailed query indicated that Hillstrand was probably not a strong suspect at the time. And in all likelihood, due to the holiday, specific details from the MSP probably wouldn't be available until sometime tomorrow at the earliest. Then, if Hillstrand had been a suspect in the Maryland abduction and somehow could be shown to be involved in the Walton boy's disappearance, a prosecutor would have to be contacted for a search warrant while the police went out to surveil Hillstrand's residence. And finally, finding an accommodating judge on New Year's Day might prove to be a small miracle in itself. By then, in all probability, it would be too late.

Or Vail could just go there now and have a look for himself.

He opened the drawers to the desk he'd been working at to see if the detective kept a backup weapon. The only thing he found was an extra badge with a clip-on backing. He snapped it onto his belt and left Kate a note, telling her he'd gone to check out Hillstrand, along with the address and how Hillstrand's name had surfaced. Although the information should prevent her from accusing him of hiding leads, he knew how she would interpret it. He added a P.S.: *This is a long shot, so I didn't want to bother you with it.* He reread it and shook his head. The only way that he wasn't going to be accused of deception was if

Hillstrand was one of those false leads in which only Vail's time had been wasted.

In the parking lot, Vail opened the trunk, hoping that Kate's Bureau car might have been equipped with a shotgun. It wasn't. He got in, started the engine, and pulled out into the light traffic.

There was an advantage to not involving Kate or any of the Reston PD. As long as he acted on his own, as a non-law-enforcement citizen, he had greater latitude for gathering evidence without a search warrant than sworn officers did, especially if the police didn't know what he was doing. If they did, then he could be legally considered an agent of the department. In fact, under these circumstances his room to maneuver was almost limitless. While the exigent circumstances of a young boy's life could mitigate violations of the Fourth Amendment, Vail was still worried that a pedophile might escape justice because the drafters of the Constitution hadn't foreseen the downward-spiraling depravity at the fringes of the American male population. At least that would have been his explanation if it weren't for Kate. She'd heard all his rhetoric for working alone before. In fact, it had created an almost irreparable rift between them the only other time they'd worked together. But at the moment it looked like she was, at best, his ride to the airport, so why not?

Glancing at the map again, he turned down a street and watched as the houses became more and more isolated. It then became an unpaved road that disappeared into the woods.

Vail came to a stop and lifted his foot from the brake, allowing the vehicle to advance at idle speed. It was another fifty yards before he saw any lights. He stopped again and switched off the engine. The car was still hidden by the thick evergreen woods. He got out and walked quietly toward the house. It was a single-level dwelling and bigger than Vail thought would be built in such a remote location.

He walked around the tree line at the edge of the clearing, trying to determine the exact size and layout of the structure. There were no outbuildings on the property, so if Hillstrand did have the boy, he had to be inside the house. As quietly as possible, Vail hurried back to the car, started it, and drove up to the house. The older paneled van from the photo was parked in front. Enough lights were on inside to indicate that someone was home.

Vail got out, walked directly to the front door, and knocked. The exterior of the house needed paint, but the property immediately around it seemed fairly well maintained. A bright light overhead came on, and the man in the race photo opened the door. His eyes were dark like his hair—possibly Mediterranean, Vail thought. His stare never left Vail's as the two men sized each other up. Finally Hillstrand said, "Can I help you?"

Vail pulled the detective badge from his belt and held it up. "I'm with the Reston Police. Detective Vail. We're investigating a missing child. Do you have a minute?"

"Sure," he answered, and stepped back, inviting Vail in. Once he was inside, Hillstrand shut the door. "That's an awfully nice suit for a detective." His voice had a trace of suspicion in it. "Do you mind if I ask to see your photo ID?"

Vail patted his chest pockets as if looking for his identification. He then reached under his coat and searched his pants pockets. "Sorry, I don't have it with me. I'm afraid you caught me, Mr. Hillstrand. I was on my way to a party when I got the call. Didn't even get to go into the station. They just gave me some people to go and interview. The people who were at the race tonight where the boy disappeared. I don't know if you heard about it. We're hoping someone saw something."

"You must have been caught short. I can see you're not carrying a gun either."

"That's why they gave me just the people who were in the race, I guess. The friendlies. Any chance you saw anything?" Vail could hear the television on in another room. "I'm assuming you've seen it on TV."

Hillstrand didn't answer right away but instead stared at Vail as though contemplating something he'd said. "Yes, it's hard not to have. If I had any photographs, I would have sent them. And I'm sorry, I didn't see anything out of the ordinary. Not that I can remember."

"How'd you do on the run? Three miles is a fair distance."

Hillstrand smiled uneasily. "I finished. I'm not an avid runner, so my goals are modest."

"I don't know how modest three miles is. I don't think I could make it. Did you get over to see the children's run?"

Hillstrand hesitated, and Vail suspected that he remembered looking into the camera that had taken his photo. "It was on the way to where my van was parked, so I stopped and watched the winner finish."

The voice of a young boy came from another room. "Dad, who is it?"

"That your son?" Vail asked.

"Yes, it is." Hillstrand led the way into the living room. A boy whose age Vail guessed at ten or eleven sat on the couch watching TV. He had medium-brown hair and was at least a foot taller than Joey Walton was reported to be.

"David, this is Detective Vail from the Reston Police Department. He's investigating that missing boy from the race they keep talking about."

The boy stood up and offered his hand. "How do you do, sir."

Vail took it and looked into his pale blue eyes. "Your parents letting you stay up to bring in the New Year?"

"My dad is. My mom passed away when I was born, during childbirth." Vail noted that he pronounced the words mechanically, without any sadness, his language a little too mature to be his own. The boy pointed to a nearby shelf. "That's a picture of her with my dad." Again the words seemed practiced.

Vail looked at the obviously pregnant woman in the photo standing next to George Hillstrand. Her coloring was even darker than her husband's was, her eyes almost pitch-black. "I'm sorry, David. That's really tough. I lost my mom early in my life, too. I know how hard that can be." Vail reached up and tousled the boy's hair.

He pulled his hand back carefully so as to not reveal what he had discovered. It is genetically improbable that couples with brown eyes will have a child with blue eyes, and David's hair and skin were nowhere close to the darkness of his "parents'." When Vail ruffled the boy's hair, he felt the crescent-shaped scar on the crown of his head. Unbelievably, David had to be Edward Stanton, the child abducted four years earlier in Maryland. Which meant that, in all likelihood, Joey Walton was somewhere in the house. Talk about the luck pendulum swinging in the other direction.

The boy started to sit down in front of the TV again when Hillstrand said, "That's enough for tonight, son. It's time for bed." Without any argument, the boy got up and said, "Good night, sir."

"Good night, David," Vail answered.

"Let me get him tucked in, Detective. I'll be right back. Please make yourself comfortable."

Vail went over to the photograph of Hillstrand and his wife and carefully examined it, trying to determine how old it was. By the clothing and the faded color of the picture, he guessed it was at least ten years old.

Suddenly Vail felt Hillstrand's presence behind him. He turned around and found Hillstrand holding a .45 automatic on him. "Four years and you're the first one to notice that his coloring didn't fit. I guess

I should put away that picture of my wife. I keep it there for my son. It took a while, but now he remembers her as his mother."

"I was hoping you wouldn't notice me noticing."

"It's something I've always been afraid of. When you ran your hand through his hair, I knew."

"And Joey?"

"He's fine. Downstairs in a locked room. He'll be restricted until he learns he's better off here."

"Than with his parents?"

"Since I'm the one with the gun, you don't get to be judgmental," Hillstrand said. "Besides, if they were good parents, they wouldn't have left him alone in a crowd like that."

"You mean with the pedophiles and all."

Hillstrand raised the gun and pointed it at Vail's face. "I am not a pedophile."

Vail took a closer look at the gun and said, "That thing looks pretty old. Sure it still works?"

"It was my grandfather's and it works just fine."

"That particular model is military. It has a number of safeties. Are you sure it's set to fire?"

Hillstrand smiled. "I've shot it enough times since my father left it to me to be positive."

Vail was trying to determine how familiar Hillstrand was with the weapon. Because it had been designed for the military, it had four separate safeties. Not many people knew about the disconnector safety. If the end of the barrel could be pushed back a fraction of an inch toward the person holding the weapon, the hammer wouldn't release. Since Hillstrand didn't seem to know all that much about the mechanics of the gun, Vail thought if he could get into position and push it toward him—with the body's natural tendency to push back—it would keep the safety engaged for the split second it would take to disarm him.

But right now Hillstrand was standing just far enough away to prevent that. "Can you at least let me see the boy, then?" Vail asked.

"Sure. With the carpeting and all up here, it'll be less messy downstairs."

"Call me cynical, but that doesn't sound like a very happy New Year to me."

Hillstrand's only response was to wave the gun toward the basement door. Once they were downstairs, he pointed to a heavy steel door with a thick lock and hasp. "He's in there." Carefully he tossed Vail the keys. Vail opened the lock and turned back to Hillstrand, holding the keys in his outstretched right hand. Hillstrand took a cautious step closer. Vail knew that this was it.

As Hillstrand reached for the key ring, Vail half turned back to the door and, appearing distracted, drew the key ring back about six inches. Hillstrand leaned slightly forward to get it. Vail spun quickly and stepped into him, placing his hand over the muzzle of the gun and pushing it into Hillstrand.

For a split second, Hillstrand pushed back against Vail's hand, pulling at the frozen trigger frantically. But as Vail turned to get a better grip on the weapon, Hillstrand drew it back and pulled the trigger. The .45's explosion echoed slowly through the basement.

KATE AND THE RESTON CHIEF, Tim Mallon, sat behind his desk watching the interrogation of their sex-offender suspect, Frank Dillon, on a closed-circuit monitor. "What do you think, Kate, is it him?"

She watched the suspect's body language closely. "It's hard to tell with these sociopaths. And I'm certainly no expert. I promise you that someone from Behavioral Sciences will be up here tomorrow. This detective seems to know what he's doing, though. As soon as Vail gets back, he may be able to figure it out."

"Where is he? The desk officer said he went out."

"I think he went to get something to eat."

There was a knock at the door. A uniformed officer stepped in. "Chief, the parents are here."

"Bring them back." Mallon turned off the monitor.

"You want me to leave, Tim?" Kate asked.

"God, no. That the FBI is involved is the most reassuring thing I can tell them right now."

The door opened again, and Mr. and Mrs. Walton walked in. Mallon introduced them both to Kate, and everyone sat down. Confusion and grief distorted Mrs. Walton's face. Her makeup and hair were disheveled. Her husband, whose eyes were slightly red, tried to strike a calmer pose, more to keep his wife's teetering hysteria in check than as a reflection of his own feelings. "Any news?" he asked.

"I'm sorry, not yet. But we've got the entire force following up on leads. We have brought someone in, and he's being interrogated right now."

"Is he the one? Is there something you're not telling us?" Mrs. Walton asked anxiously.

"No, no, nothing like that."

"Well, who is he?" the husband asked. "Why him?"

Mallon knew that there would be no comfort in the answer. Kate said, "He's a convicted sex offender. This is routine. There's nothing to indicate that he has anything to do with Joey being missing."

"Oh, no," Mrs. Walton said, and collapsed onto her husband's shoulder.

There was another knock at the door, and the desk officer leaned his head in again. "Chief, there's someone here that you're going to want to—"

"We're busy right now, Nelson," Mallon all but snarled.

The officer got a strange look on his face and opened the door fully, smiling as he stepped aside.

Mrs. Walton looked up and bolted to her feet, her mouth gaping in a soundless scream.

In the doorway stood Steve Vail. In one arm he held Joey Walton wrapped in his topcoat. His other hand was gently cradled around the back of Edward Stanton's neck.

Joey's mother rushed to him, pulling him into her arms. His father hugged them both, no longer hiding his tears. The chief sat dumbfounded, and Kate just looked at Vail, shaking her head.

Mrs. Walton asked Vail, "Was Joey . . . Is he all right?"

Vail nodded at her knowingly. "He's fine."

She tightened her arms around the child.

Vail turned the Stanton boy toward them so he could get the full impact of the reunion. Then he squatted down and looked into his eyes. "Now do you see why it's important to go back to your real parents? This mom and dad have only been separated from their son for a couple of hours, and look how they feel. Your parents have been without you for four years." The boy nodded dutifully, but Vail could see it still wasn't registering fully.

Kate came over to them and smiled. "And who is this good-looking young man?"

"This is Edward Stanton," Vail said. "He was taken in Maryland four years ago."

Kate's head snapped toward Vail. It took her a few seconds to comprehend that this boy was another kidnapping victim. "The same guy had him? How'd you find him?"

"I'll tell you later."

Kate sensed that her questions were interfering with Vail's attempt to have the Stanton boy realize that he belonged with his real parents, but, like Mrs. Walton, she couldn't help but ask about his well-being. "And he didn't . . ." She bobbed her head back and forth euphemistically so the boy wouldn't know what she was talking about.

Vail pulled Kate back away from the eleven-year-old. "Apparently not. This guy who abducted them, George Hillstrand, his wife and son died in childbirth just before he took Edward, here. He just wanted some part of his family back. As far as I can tell, Edward's been raised well. He's having a little trouble comprehending it all, figuring out where his loyalties lie, but otherwise he seems okay."

Kate watched the boy carefully. She knew that it was not unusual for long-held kidnapping victims to identify with their abductor rather than their family.

For the first time, Kate noticed that Vail's hand was wrapped in a white handkerchief and was damp with blood. "Are you all right?"

"That depends. Do you believe in sympathy dates?"

"Obviously you're fine." She looked closely at him and then back at his hand, as if putting off some argument until they could be alone.

The chief came over and asked Vail how he'd found the boys. Vail explained about the race photos and how Hillstrand's name had come up in the Maryland investigation. "Where is Hillstrand?" Mallon asked.

Vail took Kate's car keys out of his pocket and tossed them to Mallon. "I didn't have any cuffs, so I duct-taped him and put him in the trunk."

"What happened to your hand?"

"In all the excitement, I must have cut it."

The phone rang, and Mallon picked it up, listening for a moment. "Okay, give us a few minutes." He hung up. "The media is on the way.

Straighten your tie, Steve, you're about to be a hero." The chief nodded at the Stanton boy. "And wait till they hear about this young man also being safe and sound after all this time."

Kate looked at Vail and knew what he was thinking. "Tim, we appreciate it, but this is your time. Just mention that the FBI assisted in the investigation."

"Are you kidding me? I can't take credit for this."

Kate cleared her throat, signaling Vail that she was about to tell a lie. She nodded for Mallon to follow her and Vail out of the room. In the hallway she said, "Tim, I'm sorry, but I wasn't being straight with you when I said Steve wasn't with the Bureau. This is classified. You'll have to tell your people and the Waltons not to say anything about his involvement. He's been working a major municipal corruption case undercover in Chicago as a bricklayer. His name or face in the news will blow two years of hard work. Just tell the media what I told you: An undercover agent found them and is involved in an ongoing investigation. Except lie about Chicago. Since Edward was taken in Maryland, tell them it was Baltimore. That'll keep them running around in circles until this calms down. And don't be too modest—you are the one who called us."

"Kate, I may have worked applicants my whole career, but I was in the same FBI as you. Plus, I know what a terrible liar you are. I don't understand why Steve wants to duck this, but I'm too indebted to you both to question it. I'll just assume it's necessary." He gingerly shook Vail's hand, just interlocking fingertips to avoid the wound. "Whether you're an agent or not, Steve, I am most grateful." Mallon hugged Kate. Then he walked back into his office and said to the Stanton boy, "Edward, what do you say we go call your parents?"

"Yes, sir," the boy answered, his voice starting to gain some enthusiasm.

Kate unwrapped Vail's hand, revealing the grazing wound. Fortunately, the round had hit only the fleshy edge. "You're going to need some stitches."

Vail tightened the handkerchief back around his hand. "I've been here less than four hours and you've already gotten me shot."

"Me? You're the one going off on your own. *Again.* How is this my fault?"

"I don't know. Every time I get near you, something like this happens. It's like you're crime's version of Typhoid Mary."

On their way out, Vail remembered something and detoured back through the detective bureau. He picked up the note he'd left on the desk and handed it to her. "Before we have an argument, I just wanted you to know that I wasn't cutting you out. When I left here, I was cursing myself for not going with you, because your lead looked so much better."

Kate glanced at the note. "You're getting a lot better at covering your tracks."

"From your tone, apparently not good enough. Just remember who unleashed the hounds. I am a simple mason who was looking forward to free liquor and unsuspecting maidens." Vail checked the clock on the wall. "Happy New Year, Deputy Assistant Director Bannon." He kissed her lightly on the cheek, trying to determine if they were back on a date. Her response was disappointingly neutral. "Pace yourself, woman, we've got the whole night in front of us."

This was how it was with Vail, she thought. If there was a mystery in front of them, he was amazing, but once it was over, difficulties between them were inevitable. "Just because you rescued a couple of kids and got a little shot up, don't think that I'm waving you in for a landing, Vail."

When she called him "Vail," it was a good sign. She used it only when she wasn't mad. As they walked out into the parking lot, she took his arm, her touch sending electricity through him.

By the time they left the emergency room less than an hour later, dawn was coming up. Vail had taken four stitches in his hand, and the doctor had told him there shouldn't be any permanent problems.

"Well, what's your poison?" Kate asked. "I guess I owe you some sack time—on the couch. I can get you to the airport later."

"Why don't you just drop me there now."

"If you'll let me buy you breakfast first."

Then Kate noticed a familiar black Lincoln Town Car idling in the parking lot, its white-gray exhaust disappearing into the icy air. It belonged to the director of the FBI. As they approached the vehicle, the driver got out.

Kate said, "Hello, Mike. What's up?"

"The director sent me to get you."

Kate looked at Vail with a mixture of apology and apprehension.

One corner of his mouth lifted sardonically. "Ever notice how seldom the really good dates start out in the emergency room?"

The driver turned to Vail. "He sent me to get both of you."

TWO

THE BLACK TOWN CAR PULLED UP TO THE CURB IN THE 1100 BLOCK OF SIXTEENTH Street in northwest D.C. They parked in front of an old mansion that had a tall wrought-iron fence surrounding it. "Where are we, Mike?" Kate asked the driver.

Vail pointed across the street to a large tan and gray four-story residence. "That's the old Russian embassy over there."

"They're waiting inside for you," the driver said, ignoring Kate's question and Vail's observation.

As they got out, Vail pointed at the building they were about to enter and said, "This is the old observation post where the Bureau used to monitor who came and went across the street, but then the Russians built that big compound up on Tunlaw Road, so this place was no longer necessary. Apparently they've found some new use for it."

When Kate and Vail walked up to the entrance of the huge old dwelling, an agent who was not wearing his suit coat opened one of its heavy, ten-foot-tall oak doors. Along with his sidearm, two magazine pouches were clipped to his belt. He studied both of their faces briefly and then, in a voice that was neither welcoming nor overly official, said, "The director is waiting for you upstairs."

THEY FOLLOWED A CURVED STAIRCASE to the second floor, and Vail took a moment to appreciate the craftsmanship of the elegant structure, which he estimated to be at least seventy-five years old. The staircase was constructed of Spanish black marble that was almost without any impurities to distort its ebony gloss. A large but delicate glass chandelier hung down through the helix of stairs. "Okay, I'll ask first," he said to Kate. "What's going on?"

"Not a clue," she said. "But considering that today's a holiday, the smart money is that it's not going to be good news."

"Next time *I'm* planning the date. Someplace without telephones or emergency rooms. Or FBI directors."

"Do you think if you use the word 'date' enough times, we'll actually be on one?"

"I'm hoping you'll admire me for my perseverance."

"Isn't that the stalker's official mantra?"

On the second floor, they could hear low voices coming from a room that faced the street. They walked in, and Vail could see that it had once been an oversize bedroom but was now filled with equipment that looked dated. Metal tables, recording equipment, a small telescope on a long table at the window—which was covered with what he recognized as a one-way shade. A second telescope stood on a smaller table at an adjoining window, also shaded.

Aside from the director, there were five other men in the room sitting on a couch and chairs. As they entered, Vail was surprised that most of their curiosity seemed to be directed toward him. A room full of men invariably turned their attention to Kate when she entered, even if they already knew her.

Bob Lasker got to his feet and shook hands with Vail. "Steve, how's the hand?"

"It's fine."

The director nodded to one of the men, who got up and closed the door. "Good morning, Kate," Lasker said.

She looked at the faces of the other men. "Is it a good morning, sir?"

"We're about to find out. Please, both of you, have a seat. Kate, I think you know everybody here." The director then introduced the others to Vail. "Bill Langston is the assistant director in charge of the Counterintelligence Division. His deputy, John Kalix. Tony Battly, Jake Canton, and Mark Brogdon are unit and section chiefs within the division."

The director watched as Vail gave them each a snapshot evaluation. It was something Lasker wanted him to do, something that would help convince Vail to grant the request Lasker was about to make, that these men, while adequate administrators, were unqualified to do fieldwork.

The three unit and section chiefs were startlingly nondescript, reminding Vail that at FBI headquarters individuality was rewarded only with suspicion. Each of the men was overweight, as if even that shortcoming also met some sort of Bureau standard. Their suits varied little in color or quality and had become too small due to burgeoning waistlines. The sleeves on Battly's jacket were too long, covering half of his thumbs. Judging by the wear on the elbows, it had fit him that way since its purchase years before, and he'd never felt the need to have the minor tailoring done, probably because he took it off at his desk.

Brogdon's suit was equally fatigued, the pant cuffs frayed, the lapels wilted and beginning to curl up. Canton's shirt collar was too tight and had been left unbuttoned. Dusty spots dotted his tie where he had apparently scraped away food particles. The apprehensive expressions on all three faces, aside from their momentary curiosity about Vail, were those of men who were much closer to retirement than to taking on anything remotely associated with the unpredictable rigors of the street.

John Kalix, although not overweight, had a round, doughy face that was aged prematurely by a receding hairline that he made more prominent by combing over what was left of his mousy brown hair. Sitting to his boss's right, he somehow managed to mimic the assistant director's slightest movements. He wore the ageless uniform of an FBI manager: gray slacks, navy blazer, white shirt, and a striped tie that had been knotted too many times between cleanings.

On the other hand, Bill Langston, the assistant director in charge, looked like the second most important man in the room. In his mid-fifties, he was trim, even thin. He had a full head of brown hair that was going gray at the temples. His suit was moderately expensive, and he sat with his legs carefully crossed so as to not wrinkle the sharp creases along the front of his trousers. His posture was unusually erect, as though he were waiting for an "unexpected" photo. The expression on his face, somehow inappropriate for the moment, was one of patrician stoicism. Vail guessed that it was an effort on his part not to be easily read.

"Steve, I never did get a chance, face-to-face, to thank you for what you did during the Pentad investigation in L.A.," the director said. "I've told everyone here about your involvement in the case."

Waving his hand in the direction of Kate, Vail said, "As a result you offered this one a promotion—some thank-you."

Lasker smiled. "Speaking of which, nice work last night on those abductions, Kate. We're getting a ton of good press for a change."

"Since your driver knew to pick us up at the emergency room, I assume you talked to the chief in Reston. To be honest, sir, the only thing I had to do with finding those boys was driving Steve there."

"Looks like you were going somewhere nice before you got sidetracked."

Vail spoke first so that Kate wouldn't have to be embarrassed by trying to explain the circumstances of their failed date. "The Irish ambassador's reception. Just as well. I don't speak the language."

The director laughed. "You and Washington's elite in the same room, Steve? That would have been worth the price of admission."

"You might have been disappointed. I was under strict orders to keep my shirt on and not arm-wrestle anyone for beer." Vail cocked his head to one side to let the director know that he was becoming suspicious of the small talk. "But then I doubt we're here to catch up on my lack of social breeding."

"Sorry," Lasker said. The single word seemed genuine. "We've got a major problem. There's no way to make this sound like it's not hyperbole, but it is legitimately a matter of national security. The people in this room are the only ones who know what I'm going to tell you."

"Classified, I got it."

"I've been through your old personnel file again, so I know you've been trained in counterintelligence." Because of a master's degree in Soviet history, Vail had originally been hired to work the Russians. Out of training school, he'd been sent to Detroit to work general criminal cases in order to develop broader investigative skills, but he was frequently sent back to Quantico for in-service training. That's how he knew about the old embassy across the street and the building they were now in. "Other than the technology, not much has changed. It's still pretty much cloak-and-dagger. Actually, more cloaks than daggers. Have you followed any of the recent cases?"

"I've always been interested in anything American-Russian, so I read a lot of what's published."

"Good, then we won't have to waste time explaining every nuance of how all this works. Bill, can you fill him in?"

The assistant director stood up, went over to a laptop computer, and tapped a key. The wall above the fireplace, which was being used as a makeshift screen, lit up. A photograph of grainy surveillance quality appeared, showing a man with the flat, pale features of an Eastern European, his sideburns and mustache a little too bushy to be stylish in the United States. "A month ago this individual contacted our Washington Field Office and requested a meeting. He was guarded in the information he supplied but said that he was an intelligence officer with the Russian embassy here in Washington. He would not identify himself by name but instead used the code name Calculus. At this meeting, to qualify himself as legitimate, he turned over five classified documents. When we asked him what he wanted from us, he said he had a list of Americans, some employed by the government and some by corporations with defense contracts, who were supplying information to the SVR, which if you've been keeping up, know is the new KGB. He wouldn't say how many were on the list or where they worked. However, one of the individuals, he was certain, worked in the U.S. intelligence community. He didn't know which agency."

"The documents he turned over—how critical was the information?" Vail asked.

"Nothing earth-shattering, but enough to convince us that he could have access to what he claimed. Why do you ask that?"

"Just curious."

Kate watched Vail carefully. She detected a note of discovery in his voice.

"I assume he wants money," Vail said.

"Why else would someone betray Mother Russia and risk the executioner?" Langston said. "The way he set it up was quite clever. He would give us, in his words, the 'smallest fish first, the largest, last,' which we assume is the intelligence agent. Once we identified the first one, we were to wire-transfer a quarter of a million dollars to a Chicago bank, for which he provided an account number. He said it's a large bank and that the account, which was opened by one of his relatives who works there, is in a dummy name. He warned that if the Bureau tried to find out who it was or trace the funds, the relative would be alerted and all contact with us would be severed, because if he couldn't trust us, he was as good as dead. Once the relative notified him that the money had been deposited, we would get the next name. He wanted a quarter of a million for each of them and a half million for the last one, because according to him it's a *highly placed* intelligence agent."

"Did he say how quickly after payment you would get the next name?"

"In fact, he made that quite clear. We would get it, in his words, 'immediately if not sooner,' because he felt the longer this dragged out, the better the chances of his being exposed. He said the SVR had been given strict orders by Moscow that it must never become public knowledge that the Russians were spying on the United States again. Although their agents are extremely cautious to start with, apparently that directive has made them completely paranoid. Even the faintest hint of disloyalty launches an all-out probe."

Vail said, "So he gives you a name, you arrest that person, and then wire a quarter of a million dollars to the Chicago account. Once it's deposited, you get the next name, and so on until the intelligence agent is caught, and then you send a half million."

"Right."

"Does that mean he's given you the first name?"

"More or less," the assistant director said.

"As far as spycraft goes," Vail said to the director, "this sounds pretty paint-by-the-numbers. Why am I here?"

"A couple of reasons," Langston said. "Two days ago we got a short, cryptic text message from him. He has been recalled to Moscow unexpectedly."

"Uh-oh," Vail said.

"What?" Kate asked.

"When someone is suspected of spying, the Russians find some routine excuse to get them back to Moscow. Once there, they're interrogated, for months if necessary. Should they confess or if the SVR develops any proof, the suspected individual is usually executed for treason. And since it's not something the Russians are likely to make public, you'd never know," Vail said.

Langston continued, "Since the first letter, we've been trying to identify Calculus. And now we think we know who he is. The CIA has a fairly high-level source in the Russian embassy. In a rare act of cooperation, they've identified an individual for us. If they've given us the right name, he's an electrical engineer by training and is extremely cautious, even obsessive, which in the spy business is a good thing. His job is what we call a technical agent. He's sent all over the United States to their safe houses to wire them for sound and video and record meetings in case any of their double agents should get cold feet. Then they could be threatened with exposure, a foolproof way of keeping an asset's attention. The rest of it we're guessing at. We think, after meetings between American sources and their Russian handlers, he would collect the recordings and store them at the embassy. We think that with his financial future in mind, he started making a list of their identities. Maybe even keeping copies of the documents they turned over or other information we could use as corroborating evidence."

Vail said, "You got to love a communist who appreciates capitalism more than we do."

"Exactly."

Vail asked, "Well, let me ask you—hopefully for the last time—why me?"

"The only ones who know about this are the people in this room. If we gave this to any of our agents, I guarantee it would leak out. Your discretion has been established more than once. You have a certain reputation for getting things done despite obstacles that our agents would find . . . well, procedurally insurmountable."

Vail laughed. "You mean none of you want to get caught."

The director said, "The rest of us here are not exactly street-ready, and this has the potential to get *challenging*. The men in this room haven't been out there in decades." Lasker glanced around to see if anyone objected. "Sorry, guys."

Vail glanced at Kate and then back at the director. "When you offered me this kind of arrangement before, I said no."

The director pursed his lips. "That was because I thought your not being an agent was a waste of talent and I was hoping you'd eventually realize it. When you were vehement, I accepted it. But this is different. This is vital."

Vail got up and walked over to the window. He raised the shade and stared at the old Russian embassy across the street. "Funny, five years ago I thought this was exactly what I'd be doing right now. Instead I'm a bricklayer." He turned back and looked at the men. "While you may find that ironic, I find it unjust."

"Steve, we have to assume that Calculus is being interrogated in Moscow right now. If the Russians break him, there will be no list and all those spies will go on selling our secrets."

"I'm sorry. I'm going home."

Everyone in the room was silent. Finally the director said, "Could you come with me for a minute? There's something you need to see."

Vail followed him downstairs and then through a series of small, unfurnished rooms.

Once Lasker was satisfied they were completely out of earshot of the others, he said, "Did Kate tell you what happened to her just before Thanksgiving?"

"No."

"She almost died."

"*What?*"

"She left her car running at her place as well as the door to the garage open. She'd been drinking. Wound up in the hospital for a couple of days."

"You think it was a suicide attempt?" Vail's voice was accusatory.

"No, I don't. But it was a couple of days after she'd gone to see you in Chicago, which OPR tells me did not go well."

"Kate's way too strong for anything like that. And as up and down as we've been, I've never seen her depressed for a second."

"I couldn't agree more."

"She dumped me. I'm the one who's supposed to be suicidal."

"I thought you guys made up. Isn't that why you're here?"

"That was a lie. She didn't know I was coming. I was trying to patch things up. She was driving me back to the airport when she got the kidnapping call."

"Like I said, I know it wasn't a suicide attempt, but I can't call off the OPR investigation just because I think so. I'm sure you can remember how petty people can be in this organization when it comes to someone else's problems. When somebody is as successful as Kate is, they want to believe it. She's got people looking at her like she's a time bomb. I want her to work with you on this Calculus thing. If you two did half the job you did in L.A., all that petty whispering would come to a screeching halt."

Vail laughed. "Are you blowing this out of proportion to hook me?"

"When you and she walked into that room upstairs, did you notice that none of those men would look at her? When's the last time you saw that happen?"

Vail took a moment to consider what Lasker had said. "I'd be a fool to say yes to this." There was something in Vail's tone that told the director that was exactly what he was about to do. "Fortunately for you, it's not exactly construction weather in Chicago."

Lasker clapped him on the shoulder. "Thanks."

When they walked back into the upstairs room, the director said, "Steve's decided to give us a hand, and Kate will work with him."

Kate's eyes locked onto Vail. She had heard the surety in his tone when he'd said no to the director. She'd never seen him change his mind once it was so firmly set.

Vail looked back at her. "However, this time, if you're going to saddle me with Deputy Assistant Director Bannon, she has to understand that I am working *with* and not *for* her?"

Kate took a moment to recover and then said, "Yes, those were the two big disruptions in L.A., me giving orders and you following them."

The director looked slightly distracted by what he was about to say, missing the humor in Kate's response. "I know how you feel about answering to anyone, Steve, but because this is so potentially explosive, I'm going to need you or Kate to report to Bill at least once a day so he can keep me advised."

"Define 'report to,'" Vail said.

"This is extremely complicated, so I need everyone to work together. Whatever other intelligence agency might be involved, add in the Russians and our own State Department and it's going to be a diplomatic high-wire act. The potential for disaster is incalculable. You have to keep Bill advised."

"Is that actually what you want us to do, or are you giving me one of those orders that when you're called in front of some congressional subcommittee, you can say I disregarded your instructions? If it's the second, I have no problem with it."

"I'm sorry, Steve, I need you to report daily. I wouldn't be much of a director if I didn't keep a very close eye on this one."

Vail knew that because of Kate he had no choice. "You do realize how this is going to end."

"I'm hoping it doesn't."

"Which means you can see exactly how it's going to end," Vail said. "Kate, I've got to tell you that this is the worst date I've ever been on." She just shook her head. "Guys, consider yourselves warned: This is not who I am, but I'll do what I can."

"Thank you," Lasker said.

Vail turned to the assistant director. "Bill, I don't know you at all. What I'm about to say is based on my personal history with Bureau bosses. If it doesn't apply, ignore it."

His face expressionless, Langston said, "Go ahead."

"If you try to obstruct me simply because of your ego, I'll be on the first available flight to Chicago, and I'm going to guess that won't make the director happy." Langston still showed no reaction. Vail turned to the others. "Okay, then, does anybody have any ideas where to start?"

The deputy assistant director, John Kalix, said, "The second time we met with Calculus, we had finished analyzing the documents that he had turned over to us and knew that he was legit, so we gave him a special phone. He was supposed to use it only to contact us. It's a miniaturized satellite phone, very ordinary-looking. That's all we told him about it. It had other capabilities, one of which was to constantly track his position, even when it was supposedly turned off. He used it only once, to text us about being recalled to Moscow. Six words, that's all. That was the last time we heard from him." Kalix got up and tapped the computer keyboard. A photograph of the message appeared.

To Moscow unexpectedly. Find CDP now!

"We're guessing 'CDP' are the initials of the first person on his list," Kalix continued. "We've checked them through every available database, most of which don't have middle initials, and have no clue who it is. Not everyone lists a middle initial. There could be hundreds, even thousands of them across the country. It's not much to go on. The only other thing we have is where he traveled. It's all documented in the dark blue file on the table there."

Vail took a moment to process what he'd been told and then looked over at the folder and nodded. "And where is the phone now?"

"As soon as that message was sent, we could no longer determine where it was. Somehow the GPS must have been disabled."

"The last location?"

"Inside the Russian embassy."

"That doesn't sound promising. Anything else that might help us?"

"That's it. Like I said, it's not much to go on."

The director stood up. "Thank you, guys." The men understood that the meeting was at an end and they were to leave.

After everyone filed out, the director closed the door behind them. "Steve, you two should probably work out of here. It's secure, and there's some equipment you might be able to use. The computers are current and have complete Bureau access. The building is alarmed, and there's a stocked kitchen, a shower, and some cots for sleeping. The briefcase on the table is for you. Gun, credentials, credit card, cell phone are all inside. Parked out front is a blue Chevy sedan. The keys are in the case, too." He took out a blank business-size card and wrote down a number on it. "If you need anything else—*anything*—call this number."

Vail said, "Any objections if I move in here?"

The director glanced at Kate. "If that's what you prefer, sure."

"It'll eliminate travel time from the hotel," Vail said, and Kate understood that he had offered the reason so she wouldn't be embarrassed at whatever way the director interpreted their relationship.

"And I'm only about fifteen minutes away," she said.

Vail said, "If we round up any of these people, aren't you afraid it'll point the Russians in Calculus's direction? If they're not already onto him."

"We do have an obligation to try to protect him as best we can, but we have a greater duty to protect this country. Actually, we have discussed our options for keeping this quiet as long as possible. Through legal and bureaucratic foot-dragging, we figure the whole thing could be kept quiet for about ten days. So if you do bring someone in, that ten-day clock will start ticking. After that, I'm afraid Calculus's anonymity could become tenuous."

Kate said, "Ten days isn't much time to get from A to Z. Especially since we're not sure where A is or how many letters there are in the alphabet."

"No, it's not. And to compound the problem, we don't know if we'll get any more information from Calculus. Steve, you have no idea how much I appreciate this. Between keeping everything secret and the idea of a bunch of traitors running around Washington, it was an impossible challenge. But now we have you. I'm sorry about handcuffing you with reporting daily, but this is a completely different situation from Los Angeles. If you have any problems, you've got my number."

"'Abandon all hope, ye who enter here!'"

The director smiled. "Dante, right?"

"Rather than who wrote it, it's more important to know where it was posted."

"Which is?"

"It was the inscription at the gate to hell."

THREE

AFTER KATE HAD WALKED THE DIRECTOR OUT, SHE CAME BACK UPSTAIRS.
"Thank you for doing this. And for protecting my reputation with
the director."

"Oh, how I wish your reputation actually needed protection."

"Me, too, Vail."

He stared at her for a few seconds and then went back to the window, again staring at the old embassy across the street.

She said, "What exactly did the director show you downstairs that
changed your mind?"

"A large sum of money."

"Vail."

"Okay, he played 'America the Beautiful.'" She scowled at him.
"Metaphorically. He knew that if he got me out of that room, and away
from all that *management,* my decision would be less knee-jerk. For
being the big boss, he gets a pretty good read on people."

Kate studied Vail's face for a few seconds, looking for deception. "I
wish I could get a good read on you."

"That's the other reason we have trouble getting along. You think I always have a secret agenda."

"Where would anyone get an idea like that?"

"See, that's why I think there's hope for us. If our relationship didn't have a healthy foundation, you would've taken a cheap shot right there."

Kate smiled and shook her head. "Where do you want to start?"

"It's been thirty-six hours since either of us slept. I'm going to get a few hours' sleep. I suggest you do the same."

"I need to change, too. I'll take the car back to my place. I'll bring up your suitcase when I come back."

"I'm starving. Let's see how we're set for food first."

As he started for the kitchen, she said, "This time I need to be on the inside of the investigation, Steve."

"Okay, but just remember it comes with a lot of liability."

"Have I ever denied you when you wanted to commit a felony?"

"I said you're in, Deputy Assistant Director Bannon."

"Then explain your question about the classified documents Calculus gave up. What was that about? And don't give me that 'curious' stuff. I've seen that look before."

"Well, isn't this getting off to a familiar start?" Vail said, laughing for a moment. "Sometimes in the spy business, your opponents will run a game on you. They'll salt the mines with borderline information to convince you that they're on your side. It's just something to be wary of. And if they're good, they can wind up getting more information from you than you get from them."

She stared at him for a few seconds. "That *sounds* like a reasonable explanation, but it always does—and then suddenly I'm being shot at."

"There are worse things than being shot at."

"Like . . . ?"

"Living a life where you're never shot at." He went into the kitchen and yelled out to her. "These are spies. They don't shoot at people. But

I'd be careful what I ate." The refrigerator was stocked with food, including a carton of eggs. He took them out and checked the date. "These eggs are fresh. How about I make some breakfast?"

"I assume that you have no desire to poison me."

"Sure, we'll say that."

"Do you want me to do that?" she asked.

"I'm just going to scramble some eggs. Why don't you have a look through those files they left us."

Ten minutes later he walked out with two plates loaded with eggs and toast balanced on top. She looked at the plate he set in front of her. "Make enough?"

"With you I never know when I'm going to get to eat again." He picked up his fork. "Anything in the files?"

She took a bite of toast and pulled a photograph from the back of the file. "Here's that shot of Calculus's message."

She watched him carefully as he laid it on the table next to his plate and studied it while he continued to eat.

To Moscow unexpectedly. Find CDP now!

Finally she said, "Do you think CDP is our 'little fish'?"

Vail continued to eat, staring at the message. "It has to be. He uses only three words to notify us of his possible impending death: 'To Moscow unexpectedly.' Someone that economical wouldn't waste the last three words on something meaningless. He used exactly the same number of words to indicate that they're as important as the first three."

"Why would he care whether we found the spies if he knew he was going to be taken back there and tortured, and probably worse?"

Again Vail was lost in thought. She took a mouthful of eggs and watched him as he ate absentmindedly. Finally he said, "This is good. Very, very good."

"The eggs?"

"Your question about him caring. It could be the key to unlocking this. He shouldn't care. Yet he sent us the first mole's initials. Why?"

"Maybe he figured since he was being sent back to Moscow, he'd give us the first name hoping we'd send the money to the Chicago bank and it would get to his family or whoever."

"That's a possibility. Here's another one: What if he planned for this contingency? He knew that if the Russians get it out of him about the list and recover what he's hidden for us, they'll have all they need to convict him of treason and execute him. But if he can get us to whatever evidence he left for us, before the Russians can recover it, they won't be able to prove a thing. Maybe he's in Moscow right now enduring torture to give us whatever head start he can."

"It's urgent, I get it. But first we have to find this CPD. How do we do that? Like Kalix said, there's got to be a lot of people with those initials."

"Another good question. Unfortunately, one that is going to require a little sleep to answer. I hate to waste the time sleeping, but it'll be a good investment." Vail picked up his plate and asked her, "Are you done?"

"Yes, thanks."

"Can you be back here in four hours?"

"Seeing how the alternative is to let you go wandering off with a new set of credentials and a gun, and then having to answer to the director, I guess I'll have to."

ALMOST TO THE MINUTE, four hours after leaving him, Kate pulled up in front of the old Bureau observation post. It was midafternoon, but the temperature was still near freezing. She took his suitcase out of the trunk and carried it upstairs. He was in the room where the meeting with the director had taken place. He had shaved and showered and was reading one of the files that had been provided.

"It didn't take you long to get back at it. Anything in there?" she asked.

"There is one interesting thing. The cell phone they gave Calculus, it tracked him twenty-four hours a day. We have detailed coordinate charts telling us where he went and when."

"Nothing else?"

"Not yet, but I'm already getting the feeling I'm missing something." He stood up and went over to a computer that was on. "Take a look at this. You've probably seen it before."

She peered over his shoulder. "Sure, that's a spy satellite we have access to. How'd you know about it?"

"I kept reading in the file about transverse tracking. When I turned on the computer, I saw the icon on the desktop." She sat down in a chair next to him. "I looked through those cell-phone GPS logs. I think they're important."

"Important how?"

"Take a look at his message again." He handed her the file. "How do the last three words differ from the first three?"

To Moscow unexpectedly. Find CDP now!

"The exclamation point?"

"And . . . ?"

She looked for a few seconds and then shook her head in frustration. "I don't know, what?"

"Look at my hand," he said, holding it with the fingers spread as wide as possible. "Now look at the message again."

She did and then said, "It looks like there's an extra space between the 'CPD' and the word 'now.' " She thought about it a little longer. "I still don't get it."

"I made some coffee. Would you mind getting me a cup?" His voice was more instructional than demanding.

Her face shortened into a knot of confusion. "Oooo-kay." She went into the kitchen and started pouring coffee into a mug. "Black?" she called out to him. Before he could answer, she yelled, "The last sentence contains a message within a message!" Forgetting the coffee, she hurried back into the room. "If he didn't mean anything by it, the exclamation point would been after 'To Moscow unexpectedly,' to emphasize the danger he was in. But using it with 'now' and isolating it with an extra space indicates that there are two messages within those last three words: Find CDP and an instruction to do it *now,* at that exact moment." She grinned, realizing that Vail had sent her to get coffee so she would stop staring at the forest and be able to isolate one of the trees.

"And what are we in possession of that can quantify 'now'?" he asked.

This time Kate let her mind go blank before trying to figure out the answer. "The exact time he sent the message."

Vail said, "And since we have his exact longitude and latitude when he sent it, he might have been giving us a clue to who CDP is."

"But he would have to know that the phone we gave him was capable of tracking his movements."

"First of all, he's an engineer, an engineer in the spy business—don't you think he would assume that? Why would we give him just an ordinary satellite phone? Plus, the phone was turned on. He'd have to know we could track him then." Vail handed her the file; it was opened to the GPS charts. He turned back to the computer and the satellite imaging. "The call was made on December twenty-ninth at 4:18 P.M. Give me the coordinates listed for that time."

As she read them, Vail maneuvered the mouse over a map of the United States until the digits in the small display windows were the same as those she had given him. He locked them in and then used the on-screen control to zoom down to the location, which could be seen with incredible detail, close enough to capture the address from an adjoining map on the screen. "It's some sort of business. There are dozens of cars in that front parking lot alone."

"Here, let me," Kate said.

Vail got up, and Kate sat down at the computer. She went to a different search engine and typed in the address. A corporate profile popped up on the screen. "Alliant Industries in Calverton, Virginia." She clicked on another icon and was shifted into Bureau indices and searched the name. "There it is, Alliant Industries. They're in our files because we've done quite a few background investigations on their employees for security clearances. Evidently they have some defense contracts."

"Can you pull up the list of names that we've investigated?"

"Hold on." She typed some more, waited until the results came up on the screen, and then started scrolling through the alphabetical list. "Believe it or not, there are two with the first initial C and last initial P: Claudia Prinzon and Charles Pollock. Let me see if I can find middle initials."

She started to open the background report on the woman when Vail said, "Don't bother. It's Pollock."

"How do you know?"

"Pollock is a North Atlantic food fish. *Our* little fish."

She shook her head and laughed. "This isn't going to make the Counterintelligence Division very happy."

"Why not?"

"How do you think they're going to take it when I tell them that you found the first mole in less than four hours, not counting sleeping, showering, and shaving time? I know you're not trying to make them look like idiots, but . . ."

Vail laughed. "Maybe that's why I keep getting fired."

"Maybe?"

"Then let's not tell them."

"You know that's not possible. Now that we know who Pollock is, we'll have to start twenty-four-hour surveillance and get up on his phones and computer ASAP. And eventually search warrants. Are you going to do all that by yourself?"

"Okay, we'll wait a couple of days before we tell anyone. That way it'll look like it was a lot more difficult."

"Hi, I'm Kate Bannon. We met last year. Apparently you don't remember me because you're trying to run the same scam on me as you did then. You're still trying to end-run everyone. And in case you're counting, 'everyone' includes *me.*"

"It doesn't include you. Wherever this takes me, it takes us. It's just that the more *they* get involved, the farther away the answer always seems to get. They're like moths."

"Moths?"

"They keep flying into the light simply because it's the brightest thing in front of them, even though they're slowly beating themselves— and any chance to solve this case—to death."

"Give it up, Vail. At some point even you are going to need Bureau help."

"As clever as Calculus has been with this, maybe he's hidden evidence somewhere out there, and if we're equally smart, we can find it without wasting all that time and manpower."

"You're not worried about wasting Bureau resources. If anything, you like burning them. You're just dreaming up excuses to cover up whatever you really have in mind."

"Come on, Kate, we're ahead of schedule. Let's poke around a little and see what we can find. It's New Year's Day. There are hangovers to nurse, there's football to watch, resolutions to fake. Nobody wants to hear from us."

"Define 'poke around,'" she said, with even more caution than usual.

"It's a holiday. We have a car, a credit card, and all of Calculus's locations for the last two weeks he was here. Let's take a ride and see if he left anything else to find."

She shook her head with mild self-contempt. "You make it sound so simple, so right, and even though I know it's neither, I'm going to go along with it."

"Am I a good time or what?"

"I'll admit that it always seems like it's going to be a good time, but it usually turns out to be 'or what.'"

FOUR

WHEN THEY GOT TO THE CAR, VAIL SAID, "YOU KNOW YOUR WAY AROUND HERE A lot better than I do, so why don't I drive?"

While he drove, Kate made a list of everywhere Calculus had traveled on the day he sent his last message. "Okay, but you've got your work cut out for you. He drove over two hundred miles outside the D.C. area."

"In one day? That seems like a lot, but then maybe he wanted us to notice."

"Where do we start?"

"How about at his clue, Alliant Industries in Calverton."

She found the address in her notes and entered it into the GPS unit on the dashboard. "Do you have any idea what we're looking for?"

"What we always look for, those wonderful little failed attempts to hide the truth—anomalies."

When he offered no further specifics, she said, "These anomalies, any idea what form they might take?"

"Not a clue. I was just hoping that being philosophically vague would impress you into quiet contemplation."

"I'm a little surprised that you're still trying to impress me."

Vail couldn't tell whether the comment was meant to be sarcastic or whether she was offering some sort of truce. "Just because I can be an idiot, that doesn't mean you're not worth impressing. Who knows, maybe I could change."

"If you did, you'd probably bore me to death."

"Do you know why male moths fly so close to the flame of a candle?" he said mischievously, knowing she would object to any more moth references.

"Oh, so you *are* trying to bore me to death."

"The flame gives off a vibrational frequency similar to the female moth's pheromone. The male moth is powerfully attracted to it, even though it's extremely dangerous."

"In other words, even setting yourselves on fire won't deter you guys."

"I'm here, driving into who-knows-what, if that answers your question."

"You want me to tell you what I think? I think you're bored right now and hoping you'll drive into exactly 'who-knows-what.' "

For the next three hours, they traced the route the Russian engineer had taken through Virginia, stopping where he had, according to the Bureau charts. Each time, Kate would get out and take photos of everything in sight, making notes about the corresponding locations. Halfway back, they found a diner and he pulled in.

Inside, they sat in a booth, and after the waitress had taken their orders, Kate asked, "Well, any anomalies?"

"Not yet. But I want to spend some time with everything back at the off-site. Kind of let it all percolate a little."

"It sounds like you want to be alone."

"You're welcome to stick around, but a lot of it is going to be just busywork—printing out photos, matching them with the maps and timelines. I'm not sure you want to spend your evening like that. By morning I'll have everything a little more organized and we'll be able to figure out what our next move is."

"So in the morning there won't be an article in the paper about you breaking into the Russian embassy or involved in a shooting some-where?"

"I can't make any promises about the embassy, but you have my word I'll never get involved in a shoot-out without you."

"In that case I'm going to go home, get out a pad of paper and a pencil, and retrace my life as far back as I have to, to try to determine what seemingly innocuous, small turn in my life caused it to intersect with yours."

"You know, there's an old Chinese proverb that says if you try to learn the source of your good fortune, you will destroy it."

"What I know is that if the Chinese actually do believe that, it's because they've never met you."

THE NEXT MORNING Kate let herself into the off-site and could smell coffee brewing as she started up the stairs. She found that Vail had pushed all the furniture away from the longest wall in the room and had taped up all the photos from the day before. Below them were the time-place maps that had guided their trip.

"Did you get any sleep?" she asked.

"Enough. Did you eat?"

"I just need some coffee."

"I think it's done. Grab a cup and let's go."

"Where to?"

"Pollock's bank in Calverton."

"For?"

"I want to look at his account records."

"For?"

Vail pointed at the wall. "Remember where we stopped in Denton?"

"I'd have to look at the photos." She stepped closer to the wall.

"It's a small intersection. There's nothing there but that house."

She looked at the photo of a small, white wood-frame structure pinned to the wall.

"According to the map, Calculus was there for about two and a half hours at night. None of his other stops were anywhere near that long."

"Wait a minute. How do you know which bank is Pollock's?"

"It's in his security-clearance investigation."

"And how do his bank records tie in?"

"If he visited his bank within twenty-four hours of Calculus's stop at that house, then I think there's a good chance that Pollock made an exchange with his handler there and Calculus recorded it. So the next day Pollock would have to deposit the money, unless he keeps it under his mattress."

"Does that mean we're going to let the assistant director—or any-one else—in on this?"

"Not yet."

"Then how are you going to get bank records without some sort of court order?"

"With this." Vail held up a standard information-release form filled out and signed by Pollock.

"Where did you get that?"

"We did a background investigation on him, didn't we? And isn't part of that process for him to sign information releases?"

"How did you get into his file?"

"You let me watch your hands when you logged into the Bureau database yesterday, so I thought you were giving me your password."

She just shook her head. "But Pollock's background was almost five years ago. Those forms would be out of date." She looked closer. "It's dated a week ago."

"A little Wite-Out, a copying machine, and everything's up to date in Kansas City."

"You'll have to excuse me if I seem a little slow. I've been back here for six months, you know, following the law and stuff. Throws a girl off."

AN HOUR LATER Vail pulled up to the Denton Savings and Loan. "Since you're apparently too chicken to violate both the national banking laws and the Privacy Act, you can wait here." He got out and walked inside.

In another twenty minutes, he came out, and Kate said, "Well?"

"The morning after Calculus's stop at the little white house, Pollock deposited eighty-nine hundred dollars into his checking account."

"Eighty-nine hundred is a nice number. It keeps it under ten thousand so the IRS isn't notified, but not as noticeable as ninety-nine hundred, which is a bigger flag than if he had deposited the entire ten thousand."

Vail started the car and pulled out. "I think I know what that house is now."

"What?"

"For Calculus to be there and record the exchange, it has to be a Russian safe house. Maybe he left something there for us."

"So now we're going to Langston with this, right?" And then, pretending to be talking to herself, she said, "Oh, Kate, you are cute but so naïve. That's Steve Vail sitting next to you, and you're asking him about going to the AD?"

Vail laughed. "If you were the assistant director in charge of coun-terterrorism, what would you do?" When she didn't say anything, he said, "Come on, Kate, that was almost your job. What do you do now?"

"I'd probably black-bag it."

"And how long would that take?"

"To line up all the techs and the lock guys, do the site work, I sup-pose a couple of days."

"Minimum. We don't have a couple of days. The Russians have a big advantage over us—torture."

Vail turned left, and she realized he wasn't heading back to Wash-ington. "Please tell me you're not going to break into a Russian safe house."

"You're the one who demanded to be *inside the investigation* this time. Now come the liabilities that you were warned about. You can't have it both ways."

"Here's four words I'm going to assume you've heard before: *You can't do that.* It belongs to the Russians."

"First of all, the correct pronoun is 'we.' And I can foresee only one possible problem. I noticed in the photo you took that there's an alarm-company warning sticker in the front window."

"That's why we need our tech and lock people to get inside."

"Who do you suppose was the last person out of the house that night?"

"If he was doing the technical stuff, I suppose Calculus?"

"If he left evidence for us in there, do you think he would have set the alarm?"

Kate let her head fall to her chest as if surrendering all hope. "You know, it's being exposed to guys like you that makes online dating seem so promising. The only thing a girl has to worry about there is the occasional serial killer."

FIVE

K ATE LISTENED TO VAIL'S SHALLOW BREATHING AND FOUND IT REMARKABLE that he could sleep anywhere, and apparently under any circumstances. They had been watching the suspected safe house for a couple of hours, waiting for dark, and Vail, after giving her a nod that he was going to do so, had drifted off. She wondered how much sleep he'd actually had in the past two days. For the last half year, she had been back in Washington, away from him. Back to the daily dictates of organization and rules. Beyond all else, rules. So many, in fact, that following every one of them left not the slightest opportunity to get anything else done. But Vail was an outsider, someone who couldn't exist in such an inertial state. He was about to commit a burglary that carried with it the potential of international consequences. It scared the hell out of her. She looked over at him sleeping and wondered why she couldn't wait to be part of it.

As if sensing that the sun had finally set, Vail opened his eyes. He looked at the small house and said, "No lights. So far so good."

"What if someone from the embassy came back out here and reset the alarm? If it was turned off in the first place?"

"Then I would assume we'll hear some sort of loud noise or see flashing lights. There's only one way to find out."

"Did it ever occur to you that the Russians might have some sort of sensor that goes right into the embassy and isn't connected to this alarm system?"

"That's more than an hour away."

"They could call the local police."

"We're FBI agents. We saw someone breaking in and went in after them. They must have heard us and gone out the back."

"I don't know how I could ever question you. Apparently this is another foolproof plan. I'm psyched. Dibs on the crowbar."

"That's what I like to see, Kate, some genuine enthusiasm." Vail glanced at her feet. "I guess I should have told you to wear more sensible shoes." He manipulated the map on the dashboard GPS to search the surrounding areas.

"Sensible shoes? At this moment my footwear choice is what you think may not have been well thought out?"

He pointed to the GPS screen. "I want to go through the woods behind the place and get in through a rear window or door."

She reached over and removed the keys from the ignition. "Fortunately, I have my gym clothes in the trunk." She got out and retrieved her running shoes.

As she put them on, Vail drove past the house and, then a quarter of a mile farther, turned onto a dirt road. A hundred yards later, he found a place on the shoulder wide enough to pull over and park. After taking a last look at the map on the screen, he asked, "Ready?"

"Let's burgle."

Grabbing a flashlight from the glove compartment, Vail led the way through the woods, which although heavily treed had little underbrush to navigate through. Ten minutes later they stood at the edge of a tree line looking at the back of the house. It was completely dark. The rear of the structure had no doors, but there were three identical windows. "Go knock on the door."

"Of a Russian safe house. Shouldn't I have a stack of Girl Scout cookies or be wearing a Brownie uniform?"

"This is no time for sexual fantasies. Tell them your car broke down and you need to call the auto club."

"And why would someone as together as I am—discounting my shoes—not have a cell phone?" she asked. "Is that fantasy about me or Thin Mints?"

"Tell them it's dead. You know, act like a ditz."

"There are some subtle rewards to working with you, but I think my favorite part is the Taliban-level degradation."

"I told you, save the dirty talk for later."

Kate walked to the side door and knocked. When there was no answer, she pounded her fist on it loudly, glancing back at Vail. After a minute he stepped out of the cover of the trees and waved at her to come to the rear of the house. "Start trying all the windows. If he was going to leave the alarm off, maybe he left us a way in."

The second window Kate tried slid open. "Over here."

Vail came to her and lifted himself through the window. "Hold on while I look around." She watched anxiously as the beam of his flashlight swept the room and then disappeared. When he came back, he offered her his hand. "All clear."

Once inside, Kate asked, "What are we looking for?"

"Anything locked. Doors, cabinets, anything where Calculus could have secured whatever he left."

"If he left anything. If we're burglarizing the right place."

Vail walked over to a window shade that was pulled down. He put his hand behind it and then stepped to the side so Kate could see.

"One-way shades, just like at the observation post. We're in the right place."

"Then since we have only one flashlight, how about we pull all the shades down and turn on some lights?"

Vail flashed the beam around the room, trying to determine what kind of lighting the house was equipped with and if it could be seen from outside. He turned his flashlight up to the ceiling, examining the fixtures.

"What kind of bulbs are those?" Kate asked.

"Good question." He pulled over a table and got up on it. He unscrewed the bulb. It was heavy and appeared to be filled with something black. He turned it upside down and felt the granules inside shift. He screwed it back in carefully.

When he got down, Kate said, "What is it?"

"I can't be sure, but I think they were filled with gunpowder and then reassembled."

"Gunpowder?"

"If you turn on the light switch, the electricity going through the element will set them off."

"Why would they do that?"

"My guess is that Calculus did it."

"Why?"

"I'm not sure. For now just stay close to me."

Kate and Vail moved from room to room, and he scanned each section of the ceiling with his flashlight. "The Russians spent some money upgrading this house." He pointed with the beam of the flashlight. "See, they've got a sprinkler-system head in every room. Probably because their embassy is so far away. They didn't want someone to be able to come in here and burn it down."

"Like an 'accidental' fire started by a rival agency?"

"Pretty silly, huh? Can you imagine being that paranoid?" Vail walked along a short hallway into a room that looked like it was furnished and set up for meetings. He examined one wall closely, slowly sweeping his light across it. "There," he said. "Do you see it?"

Kate stepped closer. "A pinhole camera."

Vail patted the wall the camera was embedded in. "Did you notice how thick this wall is?"

"No."

He led the way back into the room on the other side, and Kate said, "Now I see what you mean. It's got to be four feet wide."

Vail started checking the narrow panels that covered it. He tapped along the wall, looking for an access point. Using both hands, he pushed against each panel. The third one clicked open an inch or so. Behind it was a four-by-six-foot room that had been soundproofed. On a shelf were a series of audio and video recorders.

He could now see the pinhole camera attached to the interior of the wall, a lead running to a video recorder and then to a small monitor, so that the asset being paid off could be carefully watched and recorded as the event was occurring.

On the sidewall was a circuit-breaker box for the entire house. Vail guessed that it had existed before they built the narrow room around it. He turned on the DVD recorder and pressed the Eject button, but the carousel was empty. On top of the monitor was a plastic kitchen bowl that seemed out of place. Inside it was a sealed paper packet. Directly above it was another sprinkler head, presumably to protect the equipment should anything happen. Instead of taking the packet out, Vail picked up the bowl and examined the paper envelope without touching it.

"What's that?" Kate asked.

Handwritten in the bottom right corner was the name "Ariadne." Vail bent closer to it and held the flashlight at an angle so he could see the paper around the writing. He looked up at the sprinkler head again. "It's good news and bad news. See if you can find a plastic bag somewhere, something big enough to carry this packet in."

Kate wanted to ask Vail what he thought was inside the envelope, but she also wanted to spend as little time as possible inside the house. She hurried to the back, and Vail could hear her opening and closing drawers. She returned and handed him a torn plastic grocery bag. "This is all I could find. What is that?"

He picked up the packet, using the bag to grip it. "Something I suspect I don't want touching my skin." He flexed the packet. "It feels like a disc packed in powder."

"Do you think Calculus left it?"

"I know he did."

"How?"

Just then they heard a car pull up next to the house. "Go see what that is," he told her while he carefully wrapped the envelope in the bag. Cautiously, Kate went to the window and peeked outside. "This can't be good," she said in a strained whisper.

"Who is it?"

"Best guess is the Russian embassy's SWAT team. Three guys in cheap suits and bad haircuts, pulling down ski masks and carrying large black automatics."

Vail reached over to the circuit-breaker box and threw all the switches to the "off" position. "Quick, go turn on all the light switches."

"What?" Kate asked in an incredulous whisper.

"I've cut the power. Go!"

Vail headed in the opposite direction, flipping up wall switches. Just as the house door opened, they both had made it back to the concealed room, and Vail closed the panel door quietly. Kate drew her weapon and eased back the slide far enough to confirm that a round was in the chamber.

Even though the small room was soundproofed, they could hear the three men moving roughly through the house, occasionally calling out to one another in a foreign language. Their footsteps eventually slowed, and they started talking in lower tones. It sounded like they were now just outside the hidden room. Kate knew that if they were from the embassy, they would be aware of the room and would check it before leaving. A set of footsteps started toward them, and Vail wrapped his arms around Kate, pulling her over to the wall where the circuit breakers were located. He held her a little tighter and then flipped all the circuit breakers as fast as he could.

Instantly there was a series of explosions, and fire flashed under the panel door briefly. The men screamed and ran for the front door. Still holding Kate, Vail punched open the panel entrance and said, "Out the back window." Suddenly the overhead sprinklers kicked on and soaked both of them as they ran to the rear of the house.

Kate reached the window, pulled it open, and climbed out. Vail followed her and closed it behind them. They hurried into the cover of the woods. The night air seemed twice as cold now that their hair and clothing were wet. As soon as they got into the car, Vail started it, revving the engine to boost the temperature. He went to the trunk and retrieved Kate's sweat suit and then waited outside while she changed. When he finally climbed back in, he was shaking. Kate said, "Tell me that part again about how nothing can go wrong."

"They got there fifteen minutes after us, so they didn't come from D.C. That leaves a distinct possibility that Calculus is talking. They must have come here to retrieve the disc." Vail turned the car around and headed back toward the highway.

"Then why would they come with ski masks and guns drawn?" she asked.

"If Calculus talked, he had to tell them that he'd left a clue for us. Maybe they were just being overly cautious in case we were there."

"Well, they'll know we were there now that we tried to blow up the place."

"Especially when they don't find the disc," Vail said. "That's why we have to get this package processed as quickly as possible. I assume you can have someone from the lab meet us as soon as we get back."

"What kind of examination are you talking about?"

"Chemical."

They pulled onto the highway, and Kate adjusted the heater. "Okay, now that we have time, what's with the packet? 'Good news and bad.' What did you mean? And how did you know that Calculus left it?"

"The first clue was the gunpowder in the lights. Since he's an engineer, Calculus would have known that as an antipersonnel mine it would inflict just minor wounds, because the only projectiles would have been the bulb's glass, which would have broken into very small fragments."

"Then why would he rig them?"

"Besides the explosion and the flying glass, what else happened?"

"The fireball from the explosion, which would probably have caught some things on fire if it hadn't been for the sprinklers."

"Exactly, the sprinklers. That was his purpose. When I saw the bowl directly under the heads in that hidden room, it didn't seem right. The ink on the outside of the packet had caused the paper to deteriorate slightly. I think it's made of water-soluble paper, so when it got wet, it would expose whatever powder is inside to more water. I think his intention was for us to destroy the disc."

"Why would he direct us to the disc and then want to destroy it?"

"If he was still here to work with us on the list, he would have told us about the booby-trapped lights and the powder. But he put them in place so if the Russians somehow got onto him, we would hopefully beat them to the disc and unwittingly destroy it so they would have no proof against him. And if the Russians got there first, and he didn't tell them about the lights, they would destroy it."

"How's a plastic disc going to be destroyed by water?"

"There's also the powder. Did you have high-school chemistry?"

"No."

"I think it's potassium, which when exposed to water has a violent chemical reaction. It would have turned the disc into liquid plastic. That was the bad news, but since we got it without any damage, that leaves the good news."

"Which is?" she asked.

"That he wrote the name 'Ariadne' on it."

"Who's that?"

"It's from Greek mythology. She was the lover of Theseus, who volunteered to kill the Minotaur, a creature that was part man and part bull. It was kept in this complex maze from which it would have been impossible for Theseus to escape after killing it. So Ariadne gave him a golden cord to find his way out. In Logic, there's a process referred to as Ariadne's thread. It's used to describe the solving of a problem that has a number of ways to proceed."

"So that means what?"

"I'm hoping Calculus's choice of 'Ariadne' means there's a subtle set of clues for us to follow from mole to mole."

"But he wanted to sell each name to us, one at a time. Why would he link them all together with the possibility of our being able to find them on our own?"

"Let's not forget he tried to get us to destroy the first clue and any others that might have evolved from it so the Russians couldn't retrieve them to use against him. We weren't supposed to come out of that house with the disc unless he was controlling the situation. Again, it's like the maze: Even if you killed the Minotaur, your punishment was that you'd never be able to find your way out. And as far as why he would provide a link from one to the others, he's a smart guy, probably smarter than his pay grade.

"Most spies have one thing in common," he continued. "They

believe they're underpromoted and underappreciated. They have contempt for everyone around them. Maybe he put the link in there to prove how much smarter he is than everyone else—the Russians because he's selling their secrets under their noses and the FBI because we had the answer and didn't realize it. Probably after he'd led us to the moles one by one, he would have exposed how they were all linked together, thereby proving how inept *we* are. It's like some serial killers. They're compelled to send solid but subtle clues to the newspaper and the authorities as to their real identity. And when they're caught by some other means, the media will look at the clues and say, 'How could the police not have figured it out?' Then, even after they're caught, they have eternal revenge against the legal system by letting everyone second-guess the cops' inability to decode the 'obvious.' It's all about control and ego."

"Maybe he was hoping that if something went wrong and we were able to follow the string on our own, we'd do the honorable thing and send the money off to Chicago?" Kate said.

"Actually, that's a more pragmatic analysis than mine. This is America—maybe he thought we would do the right thing."

"So if there is a cord, not only will we have evidence on that disc of Pollock's spying, there'll also be a lead to the next mole."

"Unless I'm wrong."

She adjusted the heat vent so the air blew directly on her soaking hair and started running her fingers through it, trying to dry it. "Don't be absurd. You, wrong? That hasn't happened, for . . . what? Almost fifteen minutes?"

SIX

IT WAS ALMOST 11 P.M. BY THE TIME VAIL CHANGED CLOTHES, AND HE AND KATE drove back to FBI headquarters. At the lab Nate Wilhelm introduced himself as being from the Chemical Unit. Vail took out the plastic-bag-wrapped packet and handed it to him. "We think there's a disc inside the envelope and that it's covered with some water-catalyst powder, possibly potassium, meant to destroy it," Kate said. "The envelope appears to be water-soluble, too."

Wilhelm pulled on a pair of thick latex gloves. "Do you need to preserve the package for prints or handwriting?"

Vail looked at Kate. She said, "Just to be on the safe side, you'd better try."

The examiner put on a pair of safety glasses and a dust mask. Then, with an X-Acto knife, he slit open the end of the envelope. Careful not to drag out any more powder than necessary, he used a pair of padded forceps to remove the disc from the paper container. He took the packet to another workstation and shook out all the powder he could. Then he put a small amount of it into a test tube. Using a pipette, he dripped a couple ounces of water into the tube. The powder bubbled furiously. "It looks like potassium, and it reacts to water like potassium."

He pulled off the gloves and put on a fresh pair, going back to the disc. He dusted it off with a large fingerprint brush, then held it up to the light. "No latents." Out of a box that dispensed them, he took a sterile cloth and wiped the disc off on both sides. He did it twice more with fresh cloths and then took off his mask, glasses, and gloves. "That should do it."

Vail took it by the edges and touched his fingertip to the non-play side of the disc, testing it for any reaction to the moisture from his hand. There was none. He asked Wilhelm for a plastic protective sleeve and dropped it into his side jacket pocket.

Kate said, "Nate, we don't want this to show up on any paperwork. Will that cause you any problems?"

"Less paperwork is never a problem, Kate."

"Thanks."

As Kate and Vail started toward the elevator, he said, "Should we wait until tomorrow to see what's on this?"

"Like you could wait."

He laughed. "I was just trying to see how tired you were."

When the elevator door opened, the only passenger, a black man, said, "Steve Vail?"

It was Luke Bursaw, an agent Vail had worked with in Detroit more than five years earlier. "Luke," Vail said, shaking hands with him. "What are *you* doing here?"

"I finally got my 'office of preference' transfer. I'm at the Washington Field Office now, working general criminal. Are you back with the Bureau?"

Vail looked at Kate. "I'm sorry. This is Kate Bannon. She's—"

"Sure, I remember Kate from Detroit. And now she's a deputy

assistant director. We get most of the memos over at WFO. How are you, Kate?" He extended his hand.

Kate took it. She remembered him because he was the only agent Vail had worked with in Detroit, usually when a difficult arrest needed to be made. The most memorable one was where Vail and Bursaw came barging into the office with four bank robbers handcuffed together early one morning. One of them, also wanted for murder, had been on Michigan's ten-most-wanted list. It happened shortly after she'd arrived in Detroit, and the thing that had always stuck with her was that no one seemed to think it was out of the ordinary, at least not for Vail.

Bursaw had gone to Penn on a wrestling scholarship and majored in philosophy. He'd gained a couple of pounds since she'd last seen him, but he still seemed to move with an athlete's ease. "And I remember you, Luke. What brings a WFO agent here at this time of night?"

"I caught a couple of shifts as night supervisor that nobody wanted—you know, holiday pay. And I had some evidence to drop off at the lab on the way home." Bursaw turned back to Vail. "One thing I do know about you, Steve, is how good you were at ducking questions. So what are you doing here?"

"Actually, I am back with the Bureau, sort of as an independent contractor, working with Kate."

Bursaw glanced at him carefully, letting Vail know that there were still holes in his story that would be queried later. "Small world. Where are you staying?"

"Over on Sixteenth Street."

"Any chance we could get together? Share some lies over a beer?"

"Sure. I'll give you a call."

"Actually, I've got a problem, and you're the perfect person to run it by."

"What kind of problem?"

"A woman from headquarters, an intelligence analyst, went missing a few months back, and I wound up with the case. So far I'm getting nowhere."

Vail took the DVD out of his jacket and handed it to Kate. "Any reason this can't wait until morning?" he asked her.

"It can wait. Besides, I am beat."

"We'll get a running start at it first thing tomorrow."

"Sure." The elevator opened onto the first floor, and the two men got out. "Nice seeing you, Luke."

"You too, Kate."

As they walked toward the street exit, Bursaw said, "Any idea how long you're going to be here?"

"To tell you the truth, it's starting to look like the minute I stepped off the plane, I'd already been here too long."

VAIL AND BURSAW found a bar that wasn't far from headquarters. Since it was relatively empty, they went to the far end and climbed onto a couple of stools. After the bartender had brought them beer, Bursaw asked, "So what could possibly have brought you back to the Bureau after the way they treated you?"

"You know you're one of the few people I ever trusted."

"I can't really remember you trusting anyone. Sounds like you're about to tell me that you can't tell me."

"If you knew what this was about, you'd thank me for not involving you, especially when they start hooking people up to the polygraph."

"That serious?"

"I think you know I wouldn't be keeping it from you if it weren't."

Bursaw nodded and then took a sip of beer. "You're right, I don't want to know. But how did *you* get involved in it?"

"I did some work for the director six months ago, in L.A."

"That Pentad thing, that was you?"

"More Kate than me. I was just looking for a change of pace."

"From the little I heard, you got it—and then some." Bursaw looked at him for some reaction, but Vail just shrugged. "You never did like a lot of noise." Bursaw chuckled salaciously. "But you and Kate, huh? That's got to be a major factor in you being dragged back in."

Vail snorted. "It was supposed to be, but unfortunately we don't seem to be a good fit."

"You know what Nietzsche said—'Woman was God's second blunder.'"

"Is that a shot at me or at Kate?"

Bursaw took a scholarly tone. "Philosophy is not a discipline of answers but one of contemplation."

"Great, things aren't surreal enough around here. Now I've got a black guy quoting Hitler's favorite philosopher."

"Whether it's working or not, that's still a good-looking woman," Bursaw said.

"She is that," Vail said. "But enough about my blundering celibacy. What's the story on the missing employee?"

"Her name is Sundra Boston. She's an intelligence analyst at headquarters, or at least she was. I didn't know her. She disappeared about three months before I was transferred back here. I've got this cousin, Eden. Nice gal, but she married a loser. Actually, 'drunk' would be a more accurate description. They got a couple of kids, and he's always going off on these drinking binges, leaving her with nothing to get by on. Anyway, she met Sundra at church, and they became friends. My cousin may have made a couple of bad choices in her life, but she's not a complainer. When her husband takes off, she sucks it up and doesn't say anything to anyone. I suppose it's as much out of embarrassment as anything else. She said that somehow Sundra always seemed to know when she was going through those times, and she would show up unannounced at Eden's with a carload of groceries. She'd been doing it for over a year. When I got back here, Eden pulled me aside at a family get-together and asked me if I could find out what happened to her. She thought Sundra had been transferred to some secret assignment or something.

"So I checked indices and found that we had a case on her disappearance, and that it was being handled on my squad. I'd been back in D.C. less than two weeks, knew nothing about the case, and I hadn't caught on to my supervisor yet. So I went in and asked him about it." Bursaw shook his head and took a long pull on his beer. "Steve, this guy is everything that is wrong with the new Bureau. He actually grew up in Beverly Hills—that's right, my brother, 90210—and couldn't get through an hour of the day without performing some affectation. He calls the bad guys 'thugs' and 'hoodlums.' When I asked him about Sundra, he gave me the rundown and told me that the investigation was at a standstill. Then he cocks his head to the side in thought and says, 'You know, she's an African-American, too. You could probably find her, because these people would talk to you.' And you think the leadership was bad when you were in. Then he reassigns the case to me as if he had just had some sort of movie-of-the-week life-altering epiphany."

"I take it you haven't had any luck getting those African-Americans to tell you where she is?"

Bursaw grinned. "Don't start," he said. "So I pull the file and find out that very little had been done after the first thirty days. I made up my mind right there to jump on it with both feet."

"Not to belittle your altruism, but what does she look like?"

"You're right, she is good-looking. Which doesn't hurt. But I figure with what she did for my cousin, she must be a good person and deserves to have someone searching for her for real."

"A Bureau employee disappears and no one is making it a priority?"

"At first they did have the full-court press on it, but when they found that she was in major debt . . . well, like you always said, they prefer the theory that requires the least amount of work. So they decided that she probably just took off for parts unknown and changed her name or got married or both so she could wipe the slate clean."

"Define 'major debt.'"

"Almost fifty K on credit cards alone."

"Isn't it hard to run up a bill that big without enjoying some of society's moral taboos?"

"You don't spend much money, do you, Steve? Even though you won't read it in the file, I think that's what they thought," Bursaw said. "It wasn't drugs. She'd just had a physical and been screened. And all her phone records and credit-card receipts have been checked, so it's unlikely that she had a gambling problem. But she did like nice things. She'd recently bought a house and had a nice car. From what I've been told, she always dressed much better than the rest of us government humps. With that kind of taste, fifty thousand isn't such a big leap."

"So they're trying to put it to sleep, and you're going to make them pay for it by embarrassing them with their ineptness."

"I would like nothing better, but I'm not sure anyone will notice."

"You haven't changed much, Luke."

Bursaw smiled slowly. "As if I have to explain the joys of belittling management to you. The good news is that I'm not getting any pressure to solve it. The bad news is, there's something wrong with it that I can't figure out."

"Wrong how?"

"Okay, let's assume she took off to get out from under that debt. The search-warrant inventory at her house showed that she left everything there, and I mean everything. She had a fairly new laptop computer. It was still there. Seven-hundred-dollar shoes that hadn't been worn. And for me, maybe the toughest thing to explain, her designer suitcases were still there. The price tags still on them."

"Have you called the locals to see if there've been any other incidents of women missing under similar circumstances?"

"Some sort of serial thing, yeah, I thought of that, but you know what a mess that can start. I do have some feelers out, though."

"When did you last check her credit cards?" Vail said.

"I look at them once a week. Nary a blip anywhere." Bursaw took another sip of his beer. "I'd like you to look at it."

"What is it that you think I can do? I didn't go to an Ivy League school."

"I don't know, maybe I'm on tilt with this. Maybe I'm trying too hard to show the world how smart I am or, more likely, what a moron my supervisor is. I don't know. You were always good at finding things no one else could. Maybe take a look at the file. See if I'm missing anything."

"Right now my days are pretty full."

Bursaw gave him an easy grin. "How are your nights?"

"With everything I've got going on, I would have to be a blithering idiot to say yes."

Bursaw drained his beer. "Then let's go take a look at the file."

IT WAS A LITTLE AFTER NINE when Kate got to the off-site the next morning. She was surprised when she heard the shower going. Evidently Vail had slept in. She made a pot of coffee and, when it was ready, poured herself a cup. In the observation room, she started reviewing the information Vail had pinned to the wall. A few minutes later, he walked out of the kitchen and held up his cup. "Thanks."

"You and Luke reminiscing over too many beers last night?"

"Actually we were at WFO until about four A.M. reviewing the case file on his missing analyst."

"I thought you didn't like this work."

"I like the work just fine. In fact, it's the reason I dislike the people who keep getting in the way of it."

"That sounds more like a rationalization than a defense, Vail."

"Of all the times Luke helped me in Detroit—and some of them were pretty touch and go—the guy never once asked me for a favor. Until last night."

"Sorry. It's just that I would have thought you had enough to do."

"I guess that's when you find out if someone is truly worth your friendship."

"Were you able to help him?"

"I gave him a few suggestions. I'm not sure he needed them. He's not the guy I'd want after me," Vail said. "You ready to watch that disc? Or did you peek last night, Katie?"

"No." She took it out of her briefcase. "But I was a little surprised you trusted me with it."

"It wasn't me trusting you that was the problem—it was me trusting me if I held on to it."

She laughed cynically. "Oh, honesty. Is that your latest tactic to deceive me?"

"I figured if anything would keep you off balance, it would be telling the truth. Apparently that's not going to work either."

She set the disc in the DVD player. On the monitor screen, they recognized the meeting room at the Denton safe house. It was followed by a couple of seconds of static and then by someone holding a hand-printed sign in front of the camera. On it were written the date, the time, and the name Charles Dennis Pollock. "That should eliminate any guesswork about who's starring in this little production."

Another few seconds of static were followed by two men sitting in the room. Pollock, recognizable from his security-background photo, was unknowingly facing the camera. He opened a briefcase that was on the floor next to him and handed a sheaf of papers to the other man. In turn, the man, who carefully never let any of his face be exposed, handed Pollock three bundles of bills and then in heavily accented English demanded, more than requested, that it be counted. While Pollock obliged, the handler deliberately held up the documents he had received and slowly paged through them so they could be captured on video. Several had CLASSIFIED stamped across them. Pollock then placed the money in his briefcase. A brief discussion ensued about what other material Pollock could provide. The screen again went to static. Vail fast-forwarded it until the end. There was nothing else on it.

"That's it? What about the golden thread or whatever you call it?"

"The golden cord," Vail said. "I don't know."

"Maybe Calculus was just screwing with us and wrote 'Ariadne' on the envelope to frustrate us so we'd be willing to pay more."

"That's a possibility. Spies do love mind games. Maybe Pollock somehow has the answer to whoever's next. There's only one way to find out."

"You want to arrest him?"

"That does seem to be the next logical step now that we have irrefutable evidence that he's a spy."

"Then I've got to let Bill Langston know."

"Come on, Kate. You know that finding the next name is going to be tough enough without going through the *system*."

"Even you can't arrest someone for espionage without somebody somewhere authorizing it. There's no other way but the *system*. Finding out who Pollock is and that he's a spy has brought us back into the aboveground world of rules and—God forbid—the law."

It was moments like this that reminded Vail he'd been correct in choosing a life in which he answered to no one. And since Kate had told him that a relationship with her was no longer possible—everything else being equal—he would have gone off on his own and done whatever he needed to do to resolve the situation with this man who had committed treason. But the only reason, or at least the deciding one, he'd taken this assignment was to help Kate regain her reputation. "How about if we just interview Pollock? If he doesn't cooperate, *I'll* call Langston for authorization. But first I want a chance to find out if he has the key to the next name before he disappears into a bureaucratic maze that in all likelihood will shut this down. With Calculus gone, it looks like he's our only shot."

"What are you going to do if he does cooperate, leave him out there?"

"If he's cooperative, we'll ask him to take a ride and hand-deliver him to Langston so he can take all the bows. That'll keep him happy, and hopefully we'll have the next clue."

"So either way, by the end of the day Langston will be notified."

"If that's what you want, absolutely."

"I really hate it when you start a promise with 'if.'" She studied his face briefly for signs of deception. As usual there were none. "Okay, but I'm driving. That way I can abandon you at the first sign of trouble."

Vail laughed. "That off-ramp was three or four exits ago."

SEVEN

KATE FOUND A PARKING SPACE NEAR THE MAIN ENTRANCE OF ALLIANT INDUS-
tries in Calverton, Virginia, Pollock's employer. Vail opened the
folder containing the information they'd printed from Pollock's security investigation and dialed the work number, holding the phone so
Kate could hear. "Charles Pollock, please."

"I'm sorry, he's not in today."

Vail looked at Kate apprehensively. "This is Hank Bass, I'm a friend
of his. Could you tell him I called?"

"Certainly, sir."

"Wait a minute, I've got his home number. Will I be able to reach
him there?"

"I'm sorry, Mr. Bass, I'm not sure."

"Don't bother with the message. I'll track him down." Vail thanked
her and hung up.

"That can't be good. It sounds like he didn't call in. Maybe we
should get some help and put on a full-court press."

"Normally I'd say that made sense, but don't forget, if we're right about Calculus giving everyone up, the Russians could be moving Pollock out of here right now. Proper channels would slow us down and ensure his getting away. Let's try his house. Maybe he's just taking a day off."

Kate stared past him for a few seconds. "God help me, I think I may need some sort of therapy, because that actually makes sense to me."

CHARLES POLLOCK'S HOUSE was surprisingly large but in a state of advanced disrepair. It was a half-timbered Tudor and in need of a fresh coat of paint. A front gutter hung by one end, angling across the first-floor windows. The second-floor stucco had some deep cracks in it and was chipping off. Weeds were over a foot high and frozen upright in the lawn. As the two agents pulled in to the driveway, there was a stillness that made Vail wary.

He got to the door first and unbuttoned his topcoat, hitting the thumb release on his holster. Gently he pushed Kate behind him. He knocked loudly. After a few seconds, he put his ear against the door and listened. "Can you check for his car?"

Kate went over to the attached garage and peered into the window. "Empty." Vail watched her as he continued to listen for movement inside. She cupped her hand over her eyes to cut the sun's glare and searched the garage's interior. "The inside house door is open. As cold as it is outside, that can't be intentional."

Vail walked over and pulled up the overhead door, drawing his Glock. Kate slipped hers out of the holster in response. They walked into the garage, and he pushed the door leading into the house completely open.

Once in the kitchen, they listened for anyone moving around. "Hello!" Vail yelled. When there was no response, he nodded toward the doorway leading to the rest of the house, and without another word he and Kate swept from room to room, covering each other. "Okay, do you want the upstairs or the basement?" he asked.

"Basement."

They split up, each heading for a different set of stairs. Five minutes later they were both back to the kitchen, their handguns reholstered. "Do you think he's onto us?" Kate asked.

"Could be, if Calculus is talking. The Russians would most likely warn him then. Or he could just be at the grocery store. We'd better pull back and sit on it until we figure out which."

Kate found a spot almost a block away and parked. She went to the trunk and came back with a pair of binoculars, handing them to Vail. "Pretty high-tech for us, isn't it?" he said.

"I figured it was time to move our little adventures forward into the seventeenth century."

Vail looked at Pollock's house through them. "Nice." Still holding them to his eyes, he turned and scanned Kate up and down. "Very nice." She hit the front of the binoculars, causing them to bang into Vail's eyes. "Ow!"

"I thought you bricklayers were a tough bunch."

"Not us blind bricklayers."

"What are we going to do if Pollock doesn't come home?"

Vail picked up the pages from the suspected spy's file and leafed through them. "There's a cell-phone number here."

"You want me to call it?"

"I'm not sure how much good that will do us, since we won't know where he's at."

Kate thought for a second. "You want me to have it pinged?"

"As a deputy assistant director, you should be able to get something like that done pretty easily. I mean, there's got to be some advantage to having you along."

"You'd be surprised how there's absolutely no advantage to working with certain highly rated people." She jerked the sheet of paper out of his hand and dialed her cell phone.

It was late in the afternoon before Kate got a callback. She made some notes and hung up. "He had the phone turned off until about an hour ago." She started the car and handed Vail her notes. "Just west of McLean. Those are the coordinates. If you've recovered your eyesight, please punch them into the GPS."

DAYLIGHT WAS FADING as Kate pulled over. "Do you think that's it?"

Vail glanced at the dashboard locator. "It's the only building within a half mile."

They were looking at an ancient ten-story brick building. Kate was on her phone again, calling the McLean police to find out what the structure was. After waiting for a while, she made some more notes and hung up. "It's some sort of historical building that housed World War One wounded soldiers who were brought back here to recuperate. After the war it was turned into a government warehouse. Because its heating and electrical were so out of date and rehabbing it would have been too expensive, they were going to tear it down. But then the historical people got involved. They started filing injunctions, and it's been going back and forth for longer than anyone can remember."

"Why would Pollock be in there? It doesn't make any sense," Vail said.

"Maybe he was just parked here when he made the call."

"Why don't you see if there've been any calls since the first one."

Kate called headquarters again and, after being on hold for a couple of minutes, hung up. "Nothing. They're going to check it every fifteen minutes and let us know if there's a change."

When they hadn't heard anything an hour later, Vail opened the car door and said, "I'll be right back."

"Where are you going?"

"To see if there's a way into that place."

"You think he could actually be in there?"

"If there's no way in, then we'll know he's not. At least we won't have to sit here the rest of the night."

Kate said, "I'm going to call his house and see if I get an answer."

Ten minutes later Vail got back into the car. "I take it he's not at home."

"No answer."

"I found a way in."

"What does that mean?"

"Could have been just kids breaking in. Hard to tell." He picked up the binoculars and used them to explore the building's windows. After a few minutes, he said, "There! On the fifth floor. Did you see it? A light, and then it disappeared."

"You're sure?"

"Yes. Let's go."

Taking a flashlight, Vail led the way around the back of the building to a door that had been carefully jimmied open and then closed, giving the appearance that it was still secure. He pushed his fingers into the narrow crack on one side of the door and pulled on the edge until he worked it free. They both stepped inside. Vail stopped and listened. He snapped on the flashlight. "I think the stairway is straight ahead."

Kate followed him in the semidarkness, occasionally stepping on something soft that she hoped were articles of abandoned clothing. Then they started climbing the stairs.

At each landing Vail stopped and listened, every so often turning to look at her. "You okay?" he whispered with uncharacteristic concern.

"Yeah, fine. You?"

He smiled. "I'm okay."

When they reached the landing between the third and fourth floors, he stood motionless for a good five minutes. Kate could see that Vail sensed there was going to be trouble—and it was going to be soon. Her suspicion was confirmed when he drew his automatic. She did the same. As cold as it was, she felt a bead of sweat work its way down her spine. Slowly, Vail stepped onto the next stair.

On the fifth floor, they could see as some light from the street seeped in through a hallway window. Vail swept the floor with his flashlight to make sure there was nothing underfoot that might announce their arrival. The creaking floor was bad enough. He walked forward to the door of the room he thought he'd seen the brief flash of light come from. The number 508, painted on it in gold-edged black paint, had all but peeled off. Standing to the side, he tried the knob. The door was unlocked. He looked at Kate to see if she was ready, and she gripped her weapon with both hands. Vail turned the knob and pushed the door open.

It was pitch-black inside, no ambient light anywhere. Still at the side of the door and without being able to see in, he flashed the light into the room to see if it would draw fire. It didn't. He motioned for Kate to stay where she was. He turned off the flashlight, took a deep breath, and stepped into the room. Quickly he moved to the side so he wasn't outlined by the light coming from the hallway. He looked back and could see Kate leaning into the room. When he didn't give her any instructions, she moved into the room and stepped from in front of the door as well. Vail held his light as far to the side as he could and turned it on. Other than some scattered debris on the floor, the room was empty. Ahead of him was another closed door to another room. They both moved to opposite sides of the door, and Vail opened it.

He flashed the light in and saw Charles Pollock slumped in the corner of the room. A syringe was stuck in his arm, and his throat had been cut.

Before entering, Vail scanned the light around the room, because he could see that Pollock had been dead for a while and couldn't have been responsible for the light Vail had seen from the street. There was another door. He and Kate entered the room and felt something sticky on the soles of their shoes. He moved the light to the floor and could see that it was blood in an inordinately large pool, starting to coagulate. Vail noted that there were no drag marks from there to the corner where Pollock's body was now propped up. They went over to him.

Vail pulled the syringe out of Pollock's arm and held it up to the flashlight. "The color of the residue looks too dark to be heroin."

Suddenly a burst of gunfire came through the unexplored door. Both agents dove to the floor. Vail opened fire, letting his Glock stitch the door as he emptied the magazine. He rolled back into a safe position, dropped the empty magazine, and jammed in a fresh one, letting the slide go home.

He nodded to Kate, and she knew what he wanted. She fired a half-dozen rounds slowly at the door while he crawled forward. He pulled himself up against the wall next to it and pointed his automatic at the doorway as Kate got to her feet, rushed forward, and pinned herself against the wall on the opposite side of the door. Vail pushed it open, again trying to draw fire. None came.

He rolled around the doorjamb, his automatic at eye level. A hole large enough for a person to escape had been cut through an adjoining wall. "Come on."

She followed him as he went back the way they'd come and into the hall, running to the stairwell. He opened the door and listened for whoever it was that had shot at them. Kate could hear faint footsteps. Vail's head cocked to the side in disbelief. "He's going to the roof."

Taking the stairs two at a time, Vail tried to close the gap. Kate was right behind him, pushing a fresh magazine into her automatic as she ran. Then they heard a door slam.

When they got to the roof entrance, the door was closed. The lock had been taken out, leaving a two-inch circular hole in the steel door. Vail pushed on it carefully, but it would not give. "He's blocked it with something." With measured force, he bounced his shoulder against it, testing its resistance. "There's some give." He stood back and kicked it hard, but it held. He took two more steps back and leaped forward, landing his foot where he thought the device was holding it closed. He did it again, and still the door remained blocked.

Kate said, "Do you smell smoke?"

Vail turned toward the stairs and inhaled. He holstered his gun and grabbed Kate's hand. "Let's get out of here." When they got down to the next floor, he could smell gasoline mixed in with the choking odor of the smoke. He looked over the railing and could see that the stairwell two floors below was engulfed in flames. "Back to the roof."

When they got to the door again, Kate said, "Can't we shoot it open?"

"I doubt it, it's steel, and whatever is jamming it is below the lock hole." Once more he took a couple of steps back and this time charged the door, ramming his shoulder into it, but it held. "I have to find some way to get a little more into it. It's close to going." He grabbed her by the arm and pulled her to his side. "We've got to ram into it as one body. When I say go, keep pasted against me so our weights combine into one. Ready?"

She drew her hips up so they were touching his and nodded.

"Go!" Vail said, and they lunged at the door. Their timing was a little off. Vail hit it first and a fraction of a second later she slammed into his ribs. Both of them stepped back a couple of strides, and he said, "Again . . . set . . . go!" This try their timing was in sync, and there was a loud wooden crack as the door flew open. They both fell over the threshold.

"I'll check for a fire escape. Call 911," he said.

Vail ran to the side of the building he hadn't seen before breaking in. When he came back, Kate was giving the address to the emergency operator. She looked at him anxiously. He said, "There are no fire escapes."

EIGHT

THE TALL, SLENDER MAN WITH THE SPLAYED NOSE SAT BEHIND THE WHEEL AND watched as one of his men lowered himself carefully down a rope that hung from the roof of the burning building. A second man came from around the back of the building and stood underneath until the first man was safely on the ground. Once he was, the two of them looked up before casually walking back to the waiting black SUV. They got into the backseat without saying a word. One of them smelled of gasoline and smoke. Sitting next to the driver was the big man with the eyes that barely moved. "Was either of them shot?" he asked in a heavy accent.

"I'm not sure. Possibly," answered the man who had come down the rope.

"Which means they weren't," the driver said, his voice both apologetic and angry.

The passenger shifted himself in the seat and watched the top of the building as smoke continued to pour out of it. "It will be more entertaining this way."

"THEN HOW DID THE GUY we chased get off the roof?" Kate asked.

Vail saw what looked like a cable hanging over the side of the building. They both went over and examined it. It was about thirty feet long but was tied to a much longer rope. Both together were long enough to reach to within ten feet of the ground. "That's how." The end of the cable was anchored in a nearby water drain. Vail pulled on it, testing his weight against it. "Think you can make it?"

She looked back at the smoke billowing out of the door they had forced open. "You mean there're other choices?"

Holding on to the cable, she was starting to climb over the low wall when he said, "Hang on a minute." He went back and closed the door. The smoke started streaming out of the cracks around it and from the lock hole. He picked up the now-broken board that had been snapped in half when he and Kate forced open the door. It was a length of two-by-two that had been jammed against a short section of two-by-four nailed to the roof. The two-by-four had a notch cut into it to hold one end of the two-by-two in place. The other end had been notched also and jammed up under the door handle. "If they'd used a two-by-four, we'd still be in there."

"Maybe they didn't have any."

"Two-by-fours are a lot easier to find than two-by-twos."

"At the risk of sounding like I'm giving you an order, can we discuss this on the ground?"

Vail walked back to the braided cable and examined it more closely. He took out his lockback knife and opened it. "Are you still carrying that thing?" she asked.

Carefully, he cut into one of the strands and sniffed it. He looked at her soberly. "It's det cord."

"Det cord as in detonation cord?"

"I've seen it on demolition jobs. When it's ignited at one end, it explodes so fast you can't tell which end was set off."

"Why would they use that?"

"That's something we have to figure out before we go any further." He got down on his knees next to the drain that the end of the cable disappeared into. "Let me have that flashlight." He tried to pull the drain cover off. When it wouldn't budge, he said, "It's been spot-welded." He got closer and used the light to peer down into the small crack surrounding the cable. After a few seconds, he stood up and snapped the light off with finality.

"What is it?"

Vail didn't answer right away but instead looked over the side of the building and tugged easily on the braided cord.

"What is it?"

"There's a device connected to the end. Det cord is set off with a blasting cap. There's one of those in there, too. There's also a battery and a large, heavy-duty spring. What happens is when there's enough weight on the cable and rope, the metal spring lengthens and makes contact, closing the circuit between the battery and the blasting cap, which in turn sets off the det cord. If we're both hanging on it ten stories up—*poof*. It's gone, and so are we."

"But whoever was shooting at us used it."

"We never got a look at him. We don't know how much he weighed. He could have been a hundred and thirty pounds for all we know."

"How much do you weigh?" she asked.

"One-ninety. What are you, about one-eighty?"

"One-thirty-five, Vail."

He got down on his knees again and turned on the flashlight. He took a few extra seconds looking into the thin opening before getting up. "You should be all right."

"What about you?"

"They had to build some tolerance into it. I'm guessing that to open that spring up fully and set it off, both of us would have to be on it together. You go first. Once you're down, I'll get on it."

In the distance Kate could hear the sirens now. "Maybe we should wait for the fire department."

"They haven't got anything that can reach ten floors." He squatted down and put his hand flat on the deck. "It's getting hot. We don't have that much time."

Kate went over to the side and grabbed the cable. Vail could see the uncertainty in her eyes. "I could be wrong about how much weight this can hold. Maybe you should take off your clothes just to be safe."

She got a new grip on the cable. "Vail, I'd rather do a two-and-a-half into the concrete." She slipped over the side and looped the cord around her foot as a brake to control the speed of her descent.

FROM THE BLACK VEHICLE, the four men watched Kate come over the side of the roof and wrap the cable over her foot. As she started down, all of them looked back anxiously at the roof to see where the second agent was.

Suddenly it seemed as if the sirens doubled in volume. The driver's eyes darted over to his passenger, but he was still watching the roofline intently. The sirens grew even louder.

The driver started the engine as a plea to leave. The passenger snorted in disappointment and then turned forward in his seat and closed his eyes. The SUV made a U-turn and drove away just below the speed limit.

AS SOON AS KATE let go of the rope and dropped the last few feet, Vail was over the side as fast as possible. Just as he reached the ground, a fire truck pulled up, and Vail told the crew about the explosive cord. "The fire shouldn't detonate it, but if it does, I don't think it'll hurt anyone inside the building. It's only the upper thirty feet or so."

Kate and Vail went to their car to get out of the way. He started to say something, and she held up her hand. "Not a word until I call Bill Langston."

"Okay, but I can tell you he's—"

She thrust her hand at him to demand his silence as she dialed. Without supplying any details, she told the assistant director that they had identified Pollock and how they tracked him down, finding him dead. She told him about escaping from the burning building and that the fire department was there now trying to extinguish it. At last she said, "I'll be here," and hung up. "If you were planning to say he's not going to be happy, congratulations on your extraordinary understanding of the human mind."

"Just for that, next burning building you can stay home."

"This isn't funny, Steve. I'm not letting you talk me into anything like this again."

"You act like it's the worst thing I've ever done to you. How about when I stole the three million dollars from your safe? And you didn't know what I was doing and, even worse, where I was so you could yell at me."

She finally smiled. "Okay, that was worse."

"And what happened? You were a hero, even got invited to the Irish ambassador's New Year's party. Of course, I got the best night of my life out of it."

She turned to him and searched his face for a moment. "I bet you say that to all the women you seduce with sculpture."

"Less than half, I swear."

Kate laughed. "You'd better let me handle Langston when he gets here."

"That's the best offer I've gotten all day."

"Enjoy it, because that's the *only* offer you're going to get all day. And by 'all day' I mean ever again."

"You say that now, but a few more dead bodies, another shoot-out or two, maybe an explosion, and you'll be putty in my hands."

Kate stared out the windshield for a moment. "I guess there's no doubt now that the Russians have Calculus talking. But why kill Pollock? And why try to kill us?"

"Think about what would have happened if their plan had succeeded. The det cord would have exploded, leaving us dead on the ground with a rope that would have appeared to have come untied. For lack of a better explanation, it would have looked like we ineptly started a fire to destroy evidence. Inside was a murdered spy whose blood was all over both our shoes. Not only do the Russians no longer have to worry about what Pollock might tell us, but the Bureau gets a huge black eye out of it."

Kate said, "That seems a little drastic, but maybe the Russians have decided to play hardball. Didn't Calculus say something about how they were under orders not to get caught spying?"

"There's only one reason they would have gone to all that trouble—it's the disc. The way we snuck into the safe house, they probably figured the two of us were freelancing. And then again tonight it was just the two of us. If we're sneaking around on the Bureau, they probably assumed—correctly—that no one else knows about the disc. If they got rid of us, they don't have to worry about it. Which means there's something else on it that leads to the next spy."

"That's a lot of supposition, Steve."

"There's one way to find out. We need to take another look at the DVD."

Thirty minutes later Bill Langston pulled up next to their car; his deputy, John Kalix, was driving. Vail said to Kate, "We can't let him know about the disc."

"That shouldn't be a problem, since I'm not sure *I* believe it contains anything. We've already looked at it, remember?"

As Kate started to get out, Vail nodded toward the assistant director and said to her, "Boy, am I glad I'm not in your shoes. He looks mad."

A few minutes later, Kate got back in the car. "He wants to talk to you."

"You told him I was here?"

"We'll see if you still have your sense of humor when you get back."

Vail slid into the rear seat of the assistant director's car. Langston turned around, and his look of displeasure was clear. "I thought you were instructed to keep me advised of any developments."

"You don't think this is a development?"

"I think this is at the end of a chain of developments."

Without mentioning the possible lead to the next mole, Vail answered Langston's questions. He laid out everything that had led them from Calculus's text message to tracking Pollock to how he died. "You broke into a Russian safe house?" Langston thundered.

"That's where the answer was," Vail said, with a calm that was intended to contrast the assistant director's anger.

"You can't do that," Langston said, his voice quieter now but still strained.

"Not the first time I've heard that this week," Vail said. "To keep this civil, I'm going to pretend that you are going to accept what I'm about to say, although I seriously doubt you will. You and I come with two different sets of instructions. Where your methods end, mine begin. I wasn't brought into this because I was likely to follow the agent handbook. And I'll continue to do what I think is necessary until the director tells me to turn around and go home. Don't take my tactics personally. What I do has only one purpose—to find the answer. It has nothing to do with you."

"I'm not asking you to do things differently. I'm just asking you to keep me informed."

Vail laughed. "Did you really want me to let you know I was going to break into property owned by the Russian embassy?"

It was at that moment Langston realized how foolish he was being. Of course Vail was right. He was taking all the chances, and although Langston wasn't exactly in charge, his division's major problem was being resolved. The time would come when Vail was no longer needed, a time when the assistant director could grab the reins of the investigation from him and claim its success. As though in response to Vail's question, Langston laughed. "I didn't say I wanted to be informed of *everything*."

Vail was surprised at Langston's apparent change of heart. "Good, because right now this is a race between us and the Russians, and they have Calculus, a distinct advantage."

"Your argument is not without merit. But if you do identify any more spies, please let me know. Preferably before you kill them."

Vail started to climb out of the car. "If not before, you're the first one I'll call from the lockup."

Langston watched him get back into his car. He said to Kalix, "What do you think about all this?"

"In the plus column, there's one less spy to deal with. However, he is dead, so there will be no intelligence to come out of it. And politically, because of the director, you have no choice but to give Vail his head. He may well find all these spies if you don't try to control him. But you have to protect yourself if this blows up—which, given the way he operates, it most likely will."

"From now on, John, your number-one priority is to make sure anything that Vail does is not traceable to me. That I had no knowledge of his activities beforehand. If we can manage that, he's got a deputy assistant director at his side, and she'll have to take the hit."

An unmarked police car pulled up, and two detectives got out. Vail went over to them and introduced himself, giving them a brief explanation of what had happened.

"We're going to be at the scene for a while. Can you come in and give us a statement tomorrow morning, say, nine o'clock?" one of them asked, handing Vail a card.

"I'll be there."

KATE AND VAIL had been driving for a few minutes before she said, "You know that when Langston reports to the director that you found the first name on the list, he's going to try to turn it around and blowtorch you."

"The next time you feel the need to ask me why I don't come back to the Bureau, please remember that."

"Believe me, I won't bring it up again," Kate said. "What do you want to do now?"

"Smelling all this smoke, I was thinking barbecue."

Once they got into Washington, it didn't take long to find a neighborhood barbecue restaurant. It was an old place, with sagging wooden floors and rickety Formica tables. The embossed-tin ceiling was stained brown from decades of cooking residue. When Kate and Vail walked in, the place was filled with regulars, who cautiously sized them up at a glance as cops. The house specialties were ribs and brisket. Kate watched the waitress deliver a plate full of meat and fries to an adjoining table and ordered a salad. Vail ordered the brisket.

"What makes you so sure that there's something else on the disc?" she said.

"I can't imagine Calculus leaving that Ariadne clue without there being anything to it. But if Pollock was supposed to supply the next step, we may be finished. Which, if nothing else, will make Langston happy. He'll be able to lay it all off on me, and I'm not sure he'd be wrong."

Kate laughed sarcastically. "Come on, Vail. Contrition? It doesn't come in your size. And surrender? You? What are you planning that you're not telling me about? You're going to break into Pollock's house, aren't you?"

"You're forgetting that I'm just passing through. And although I enjoy being shot at as much as the next guy, one of these fools might actually hit me."

"You were passing through Los Angeles, too."

"I was blinded by your charms."

The waitress brought the food and asked Vail if he needed anything else. He tilted his head playfully and said, "Would you tell my sister here that you can't live on salad?"

The waitress laughed agreeably, handed him the check, and went back to the kitchen.

"Cute," Kate said.

"Sorry. I went weak in the knees from having a woman smile warmly at me."

"It didn't look like your knees from here, bricklayer." She ate a forkful of salad, then said, "So that's it? You can't think of anything else to do?"

"How about we go back and take another look at everything, including the DVD."

She watched as Vail started working his way through the mounds of smoked meat and potatoes. He'd been right about the waitress; she had kept eye contact with him a moment longer than necessary. Kate had seen other women look at him the same way. Although he wasn't particularly handsome, women sensed something about him that was both primal and protective. She had noticed it as far back as Detroit. The night before, in that secret room with the gunmen closing in and Vail about to set off an explosion of unknown intensity, it had never occurred to her that he wouldn't get her out. And it hadn't been any different tonight on that rooftop. The tough times would never be the problem between them. It was the danger, she supposed, that kept them close. But without it, even the simplest date invariably turned contentious.

NINE

WHEN THEY WALKED INTO THE OBSERVATION ROOM AT THE SIXTEENTH STREET off-site, Vail dropped the DVD into the player and said, "We've got to be missing something."

"Why are you so sure there's something to miss? Maybe there are a bunch of clues hidden and Calculus didn't have time to tie them together."

Vail took a few seconds to consider what she'd said. "Good point. Maybe he was waiting to see if we would make the first payment before linking them up. Or maybe the relative at the Chicago bank has the key." Vail picked up the phone.

"What are you doing?"

"I'm calling Langston and having him forward the payment for Pollock to Chicago."

She took the phone from his hand. "I'm not sure he wants to hear from you just yet. I'll call."

Vail watched her as she argued with the assistant director.

"I know he's dead, I was there, remember?"

She glanced at Vail, and he noted an unusual disdain in her eyes.

"This is why Calculus set up the alternative, in case something happened to him," she continued. "We think there's a possibility that the relative in Chicago may have the key to identifying more of them." Her voice was gradually becoming insistent, its momentum unyielding. "I think we'll get the next name if the money is sent. That's what we were told."

She looked at Vail again, and her mouth relaxed into a smile the way it always did when she was about to prevail.

"It's not costing us any more than if Calculus were right here handing us the next name. . . . Then this investigation is over, Bill. We've got nothing else. . . ." After a few more seconds, she said, "Thank you," and hung up.

"It'll be wire-transferred first thing tomorrow," she said.

Vail was smiling.

"What's so funny?"

"How Langston never had a chance," he said, his voice softening, no longer ridiculing. "How so few of us do."

She tried not to blush, and then, to change the subject, she said, "So what now? You're not going to search Pollock's house?"

"If Pollock was in possession of the next name, there would have been no reason for Calculus to try to destroy the disc at the safe house."

"So if there is a string tying names together, there's only one place it can be—on the DVD," she said.

Vail turned on the monitor and pressed the Play button.

Again they watched carefully as Pollock traded documents for money. Then the screen went to static. Wondering if Calculus had hidden something beyond the end of the video, Vail let it run for half an hour before turning it off.

Finally Kate said, "I didn't see anything."

"Me either," Vail answered slowly, his voice containing that distracted hollowness that always meant that something beyond the obvious was being considered. He got up and retrieved the disc from the player. Holding it up to the light, he checked both sides, looking for anything that didn't belong there. He sat down and rolled the disc back and forth between his fingertips. Something along the edge felt irregular, as if it had been scuffed. He went over to the desk lamp and switched it on.

"What is it?"

Searching through the desk, Vail found a fingerprint magnifier, the kind used by Bureau examiners. He held it up to the disc's edge. "There are a bunch of tiny nicks on the edge."

She got up and watched over his shoulder. "'Nicks' as in a pattern?"

"They're very slight, but uniform. Evenly spaced. There are two kinds—cuts, like the edge was slashed, and then just points, like they'd been bored straight down to make a tiny round divot. A couple dozen of them." Vail ran his finger around the disc's edge again. "They're hardly noticeable." He picked up a pencil and put the magnifier up to the DVD again. "Write this down."

Kate grabbed a pad of paper and a pen and watched as he ran the pencil point into each one to ensure he didn't miss any.

"Line, line, line, line, dot, dot, dot, dot, line, line, line, line, line, dot, dot, line, line, line, dot, dot, line, line, line, line, dot, dot, dot, dot, dot, dot, dot, dot, dot, dot. Okay, let's see what we got."

Kate gave him the pad and he studied the configuration.

$$||||\bullet\bullet\bullet\;|||||\;\bullet\bullet\;|||\;\bullet\bullet\;||||\;\bullet\bullet\bullet\bullet\bullet\bullet\bullet\bullet\bullet\bullet\bullet$$

"Any idea what it is?" Kate asked.

"With just two characters, maybe it's a binary code, ones and zeros."

"We've got code people. Why don't we let them take a crack at it?"

"If we have to. Remember, the director's mandate: the fewer people the better. But with just two characters, it's got to be something fairly simple. Let's try to figure it out ourselves first."

Vail sat down at the desk and tore off the page. He copied it and counted the marks. "There are thirty-five characters." He took the examiner's loupe and, carefully rotating the disc, studied the edge again. "I see some spaces. It appears to be seven groups of five."

Vail rewrote the characters with the spacing:

$$||||\bullet\ \bullet\bullet\bullet||\ |||\bullet\bullet\ |||\bullet\bullet\ ||||\bullet\bullet\ \bullet\bullet\bullet\bullet\ \bullet\bullet\bullet\bullet\bullet$$

He showed it to Kate.

"If this is going to identify or locate an individual, each grouping has to be either a letter or number," she said.

"And since the first and fifth groups represent the same thing, as do the third and fourth and the last two, it's more likely they represent numbers, because there are only ten digits as opposed to twenty-six letters in the alphabet, which would show more variations and less repeating."

"Of course," she said, "seven digits. It's a telephone number. And since there apparently isn't an area code, we'll have to assume it's local—202."

"Very good, Kate. Now all we have to do is figure out the code."

Kate said, "Since the last two digits are the same, maybe they're zeros, like a business phone."

Vail stared at the patterns for a long time. Then he went to the couch and lay down, closing his eyes. Kate waited, and after a few minutes she wondered if he had fallen asleep.

"Maybe it's some sort of auditory clue," he said finally. "Could you read them to me?"

Kate sat down at the desk and read the groupings aloud. "Just keep reading them for a while," he said.

Kate read them again, and when he didn't react, she started over. Vail's eyes remained closed, his body motionless. On the fourth time through, she let her voice slip into a singsong rhythm.

Vail jerked up to a sitting position. "It's so simple. When I heard you repeating 'dot, dot, dot,' it came to me. It's not 'line, dot'—it's *'dash, dot.'* It was easier and more economical to cut a perpendicular line across the edge than a dash. It's Morse code."

He was at the computer now, looking for the symbols of the code. Once they were on the screen, he said, "Write this down. Four dashes and a dot is the number nine. The first and fifth number is nine. Three dots and two dashes is three. Three dashes and two dots is eight. And five dots is five, so the last two numbers are five."

Kate said, "It's 938-8955."

Kate picked up the phone and dialed. "This is Deputy Assistant Director Bannon. Extension 3318 Tango, please." She then enunciated the number clearly, as one does when responding to voice prompts. She repeated it. Then, after a few seconds, she smiled, wrote down the subscriber information, and hung up. "It comes back to the Russian embassy."

Vail walked over and took the number from her, pointing at the phone on the desk. "Which line has the recorder on it?"

"Line three." As he lifted the receiver to dial, she pushed the first button on the row along the bottom of the phone. He leaned toward her and turned the handset so she could listen. After four rings the voice of a middle-aged male with a noticeable Russian accent asked the caller to leave a message. Vail listened to the beep and waited until the line disconnected. "Anything?" he asked her.

"Think that was Calculus?" she asked.

"It could be. Did you hear anything out of the ordinary?"

"You mean like an anomaly?" she teased.

"Yes, Katherine, like an anomaly."

"Nope."

Vail looked back at the handwritten dots and dashes. "That's got to be it. But the message doesn't say anything."

"Maybe you need the access code to get into it—you know, to retrieve a message like on your home machine."

"Good idea," he said. "But those can be two, three, or four digits. I suspect that with Calculus it's four digits. That's ten thousand combinations. Then no one can accidentally access it."

"Maybe it's in the phone number, the first four digits or the last four."

"Give it a try."

Kate pressed the Speakerphone button and then hit Redial. The same message played, and after the beep Vail entered the first four digits of the telephone number: 9388. There was no response. Kate disconnected the line and hit Redial again. The message replayed, and Vail tapped in 8955. Still there was no response. She said, "How about first and last four backward?"

Vail went through the procedure twice more, entering 8839 and 5598. Neither gave them access.

"Just nine thousand nine hundred and ninety-six more to go," Kate said.

Vail studied the seven digits to see if there was another logical set of four to strip out and try. Finally he turned the sheet of paper over so he couldn't see it. "It has to be something else. Something we can figure out, something so simple it's invisible."

"Like Pollock being our first fish."

Vail smiled. "You're really getting good at this. This guy isn't our first fish, but . . . ?"

"Our second," Kate said. "Zero, zero, zero, two."

Vail stood up and waved his hand at the phone ceremoniously so she could sit down and dial. Once she hit 0002, a message started to play:

"Hello, it's me—you know, Preston. *I've got those infrared facial-recognition schematics you wanted, but the price has gone up. This time I want a hundred thousand dollars in cash, just for me. I've been getting the*

short end while taking all the chances. So this will keep it, you know, level and true." The voice chuckled briefly before he said, *"You've got my number."*

The caller hung up, and Kate started to say something, but Vail held up a finger for her to wait. After a few seconds, they heard the tones of a phone number being dialed. The line went dead. "Another phone number?" Kate said.

"Sounds like it."

"At least this time we got his first name. Preston."

"Did you notice that there was a slight emphasis on it? I would guess that's his code name. It's traditional cloak-and-dagger stuff to have one for identifying yourself to the other side."

"Then how are we supposed to figure out who this guy is? The phone number dialed at the end?"

"That was done after Preston hung up. I'm guessing Calculus punched in those numbers. Hopefully to help us identify this guy. This time he gave us the evidence first, and the puzzle is to find the name that goes with it."

"Let me get the number converted, and maybe we can go from there." She picked up the phone and called headquarters, asking for a different extension from before. "This is Deputy Assistant Director Kate Bannon. Need a readback on this touch-tone number." She pressed the phone recorder's button, and Vail listened to the number being played back. After a few seconds, Kate wrote down the number and hung up. "It reads out as 632-265-2974. Any idea where that is?"

"No."

She turned to the computer and entered the first three numbers. "There's no such area code. How can that be?"

"Maybe it's not a phone number. Maybe it's some other type of code. The first two clues were different." He stared at the ten numbers, trying various combinations. "Calculus apparently likes creating puzzles to show how smart he is."

"Or how dumb we are." Kate was also studying the numbers, looking for patterns. "Obviously we're missing something." She got a distant look in her eye, which then focused all of a sudden. "That's it! What's missing?"

Vail said, "What? What do you mean, what's missing?"

"There are no eights, ones, or zeros."

Vail looked at the line of numbers. "I still don't get it."

"Look at your cell phone."

At first he didn't understand but then examined the keys more closely. "There are no letters on the number one and zero keys. He's telling us to convert these numbers into letters from the phone." She picked up a pen, rewrote the numbers and then, underneath, the corresponding letters from the phone dial:

6	3	2	2	6	5	2	9	7	4
mno	def	abc	abc	mno	jkl	abc	wxyz	pqrs	ghi

She said, "It must be a ten-letter clue—one from each of the groups?"

"Very nice, Katie."

"Do you think it could it be a name?" she asked.

"With all the variations and spelling combinations, a name would be difficult to decode. And these clues are getting more difficult. A name seems a little too direct after all the work we had to do to get the embassy phone number and access code. Chances are it's something else."

"Like what?"

"I don't know, but let's listen to it again." He played the recorded message back. Vail struck slashes between the letters. "There are three hesitations between the groups of letters dialed. He showed her:

mno def / abc abc mno jkl / abc wxyz / pqrs ghi

"So it's a two-letter group, then four letters, a two-letter, and another two. Do you think it's four words?"

"Let's assume it is. Try the two-letter words first, since there are fewer possibilities."

Kate said, "Okay, with a letter from each group, the only possibilities for the first group are 'me' and 'of.'"

"And the third word could only be 'ax' or 'by.'"

"The last one has just one vowel, *i,* and that doesn't match up with *p, q, r,* or *s.*"

Vail, listening intently, played the recording again. "No, that's definitely the way they're spaced. Let's try the four-letter word."

They both took a sheet of paper and wrote at the top:

abc abc mno jkl

Then they started writing down letter combinations, one from each group. After a couple of minutes, Kate said, "Have I got this right? There's only one word that you can make out of it?"

"'Bank'?" Vail asked.

"That's what I got."

Vail rewrote all the letters with the second group decoded:

mno def / BANK / abc wxyz / pqrs ghi

"'Of bank' or 'Me bank'? Neither one makes any sense," he said.

Kate said, "He's directing us to a bank. The first two letters must be an abbreviation for the name of the bank." She was up and started pulling open desk drawers until she found a phone book. Once she located bank listings, she ran her finger down the page and then stopped, smiling. "OD—Old Dominion Bank."

"I might as well go for coffee while you finish this."

Kate flashed him a brief grin of appreciation. Vail rewrote the name on another blank sheet of paper:

OLD DOMINION BANK / abc wxyz / pqrs ghi

"And what were the two words—'by' and 'ax'?—for the third word? If the bank was by something, he wouldn't need the word 'by.' In a ten-letter message, he wouldn't waste two of them on an unnecessary preposition. So it's probably another abbreviation."

Kate wrote everything on her pad of paper again. After looking at the options for only a second, she said, "How about a combination of 'by' and 'ax'—'bx'? *Box.* It's a bank box."

Vail laughed. "How about giving us common laborers a chance?"

"And the last two are not letters—they're the original numbers from the message. The bank-box number."

"Old Dominion Bank, box 74. Very impressive, Bannon. For upper management—extraordinary."

She noticed him looking at her somehow differently, as if rediscovering something he had forgotten or never known.

"In the morning we'll have to figure out which branch has box 74," he said.

"I'll call Langston and let him know."

"How are you going to tell him we found this?"

Kate said, "He's going to have to get a court order, which means probable cause, which means we've got to tell him about the clues Calculus has left. It's urgent that we get into that box so we can identify any other spies."

"Which means he may want first crack at everything from now on."

"Yeah, Vail, like you'll let that happen."

TEN

VAIL WAS SITTING AT THE KITCHEN TABLE WITH HIS INJURED HAND UNWRAPPED, trying to cut away the stitches with a small pair of scissors when Kate came in. Without a word, she took them from him and turned his hand over so she could see the sutures better. With tiny, careful snips, she cut them loose and then pulled each one out slowly. "It looks pretty good."

He flexed his hand into a fist and then pressed the injured edge against the table. "It feels fine. What did Langston have to say last night?"

"In a very official monotone, he thanked me for the information and said he would have Kalix get to work on it. On the way over here, John called and said that after a discreet call to a contact at the Old Dominion Bank he was told that box 74 was at their Vienna, Virginia, branch. He is meeting with the prosecutor at eleven and will meet us at the bank at one o'clock unless we hear otherwise."

Vail flexed his hand again. "Did you tell him how we connected the identities?"

"No, but he's got to be starting to wonder."

"Don't forget, he's an administrator. He's used to figuring out what to do when answers are brought to him, not where they came from."

"Let's hope it stays that way."

Vail checked his watch. "We've got to talk to those homicide detectives about Pollock. We should be done in time to get to the bank."

"What are you going to tell them about why we were looking for him?"

"We'll tell them it's a terrorist investigation. Very hush-hush."

"You know there are laws about lying to the police, even here in Washington."

"With these guys' caseloads, do you think they're going to worry about whether it was terrorism or counterintelligence? They're probably trying to figure out how to get fifteen minutes' more sleep a day."

AFTER THE HOMICIDE INTERVIEWS, it was almost one o'clock by the time Vail and Kate arrived at the bank in Vienna. Bill Langston and John Kalix were already there, waiting for them in the parking lot. While she got out and went back to talk to Langston, Vail opened the trunk and loaded his briefcase with evidence gloves and envelopes. Kate came back and handed Vail the court order, which he also put in his briefcase. "Did Kalix have any trouble getting it?" he asked.

"Some. The whole thing is a little more complicated because of the secrecy angle. And you've got to admit that we are reading the tea leaves as far as what that message says. It could be an entirely different code. But I guess John finally wore them down."

"It's going to be embarrassing if we've come up with the wrong person," Vail said.

"Don't think that hasn't crossed my mind. They're going to wait in the car so it doesn't look like the FBI is overrunning the bank," she said.

Behind closed doors Kate and Vail explained to the manager about the need for confidentiality due to national security. He seemed to take the warning seriously. The bank computer revealed that an Alex Markov had rented safe-deposit box number 74 with a second name on the account of Yanko Petriv. The bank manager printed out all the account information and gave it to them.

For employment Markov had said that he was a correspondent for the Moscow newspaper *Izvestia*. For his phone number, he had given the same one Vail and Kate had called at the Russian embassy to receive the clue to Spy Number Two's identity. Vail thought it was a nice little touch by Calculus to tell them they were on the right track. Apparently there was an Ariadne thread after all.

Vail also suspected that the name Markov was another false identity that Calculus had used to open the account. The bank box was smart, a way to transfer money and documents without the risk of being seen together. At least that's how Calculus would have sold the idea to Petriv. But now it looked as if Calculus had done it to set him up. It was an easy way to plant and protect evidence that, because Petriv's name was the only true name on the box, provided irrefutable proof of treason.

Now Vail needed to determine if Yanko Petriv was the mole's real name. His employer was listed as the U.S. government. The phone number had a Virginia area code. "Can we get into the box without anyone else knowing?" Vail asked the manager.

"Sure. Just let me go tell my assistant that the boxes are closed for the next hour due to a lock malfunction. Then I'll take you down there. We're going to have to break into the box. If either of the box holders wants in, they won't be able to access it after we replace the lock. By law, the next time they try to access it, we'll have to tell them that the FBI was here and that a court order was served."

Vail wrote down his cell-phone number and handed it to the manager. "If either of them shows up, call me immediately."

"Sure."

"Okay, let's open it."

After the manager oversaw the drilling of the lock on box 74, he led Kate and Vail to a small room and left them, closing the door behind him. Kate said, "Think Markov is Calculus?"

"You recognized the phone number, too. If he is, that should mean that whatever is in this box has a lead to the next name." He lifted the lid, and they both put on evidence gloves. Inside were banded stacks of hundred-dollar bills. A quick count revealed almost forty thousand dollars. There were also a number of documents, most of which had CLASSIFIED stamped on them. Other pages included some handwritten lists, which were mostly names and phone numbers. Underneath them were two passports, one Czechoslovakian in the name of Lev Tesar and a Hungarian one with the name Oszkar Kalman. Kate opened them both and saw that although the hair color and length were different in the photos, it was the same individual. She said, "Looks like part of Mr. Petriv's compensation package included escape plans."

"Notice anything else about this?"

"What?"

"If they were using this box as a dead drop, there should be only money in here, or documents, not both."

"Which means what?"

Vail studied the account printout the manager had given him. "Two weeks ago there was activity four days in a row. Petriv came the first day to put documents in the box. Markov—or Calculus, if you prefer—came the next day to remove them and leave money. The third day Petriv comes back and verifies the payment and moves almost ten thousand to his checking. On the fourth day, Markov makes sure some of the money is still there and puts back the documents, or probably copies of them, for us to recover. He knew that Petriv wouldn't go back into the box until another exchange was set up. That left everything there for us to find."

"Which we hope means that Calculus hid a clue to the next name in this pile of documents," Kate said. She examined the papers more closely. "According to some of the stampings on the pages, I think these might be NSA reports. I've seen similar ones. If they are, maybe this is the intelligence agent that Calculus was referring to. Maybe there were only two spies he was going to give us."

"Maybe," Vail said. "Let's pack everything up. Keep your fingers crossed that Langston won't want to see any of it."

"I'll make sure he doesn't," Kate said.

"How are you going to do that?"

She said, "We'll give him Petriv's name and phone number and tell him we need him to find out who Petriv really is and where he works. A little distraction."

"It's obvious that somewhere in your life someone taught you some bad habits."

VAIL PUSHED THE CODE into the off-site's alarm. As he and Kate climbed the stairs, he asked, "Did Langston seem satisfied with the division of labor on Mr. Petriv?"

"He seemed suspicious. I know he can be a little pompous, but don't take him for a fool."

"Define 'suspicious.'"

"He asked me how we came up with the bank-box information. I told him we stumbled across it. He pressed me, and when I wouldn't be more specific, I think he assumed we had done something illegal. Of course he didn't want any of that to get on his shoes. But when I told him we'd look over everything from the box and let him know if there's anything of interest, I got the feeling this is the last time we're going to get away with disguising light lifting as heavy lifting."

"Let's worry about next time next time."

After putting on a fresh pair of gloves, Kate handed a set to Vail. He spread the documents out on the table, and she asked, "How do you want to do this?"

"Let's split them into two piles. You read one while I go through the other. If we don't find anything, we'll switch."

After a few minutes, he said, "I think this document is talking about a wiretap. It refers to a target phone. Can you call and see what the number is?"

She dialed headquarters and after a short conversation hung up. "It's an importer that specializes in items from Eastern Europe."

"What government agencies specialize in wiretaps of East Europeans?"

"Which ones don't?" She smiled. "I'd better call Personnel and make sure that Petriv isn't a Bureau employee."

Vail continued looking through the papers while she made the call. After hanging up, she said, "He's not one of ours, at least not under the name Yanko Petriv. That leaves the likely suspects CIA and NSA."

"Then your initial guess of NSA is probably a good one. Just make sure you act surprised when Langston calls."

They both went back to reading the documents. After twenty more minutes, Vail pushed his last item across the table and leaned back in his chair and waited for Kate to finish.

Finally she set down her last page. "Any anomalies?"

"None. You?" he asked.

"Other than two blank sheets of paper stapled together with a couple of dates written at the bottom of one, nothing."

"Let me see them?"

She searched through the stack of pages and pulled them out.

Vail held the two papers gently between his fingers. The bottom one was a common size, about eight and a half by eleven, but the one stapled on top of it was an eight-inch square. At the base of the full-size page were the dates 12/27 and 1/6. They were written with the same careful penmanship and medium-blue ink that had been used to inscribe "Ariadne" on the water-soluble envelope. "This is what we're looking for. And these sheets have one additional *anomalous* quality: They're glossy."

"Which means?"

He turned them over a few times, finally holding each page up to the light at different angles. He took them over to the window and raised the shade. Tilting the larger page up to the bright sunlight, he shifted it around for a few more seconds. He held up the smaller one. "This is the same size as what else?"

"I don't know, what?"

He went over to the desk, set down the pages, and put the finger-print magnifier on top of the square sheet.

"A fingerprint card," she said. "That's why he cut it to that size. So we'd recognize it."

Vail went back to the window and used the natural light to examine the smaller page with the loupe. Then he flipped it behind the full sheet and examined its surface. "I know that engineers have a reputation for not being creative, but I think Calculus is an exception. It's so simple. And so ingenious."

"What is it?"

Vail held up both his hands and spread the fingers apart. "What am I holding up?"

"Two hands," she said. "Ten fingers."

"Another name for fingers."

"I don't know . . . 'digits.' What?" Vail didn't answer but watched her face. All of a sudden, it dawned on her. She took the loupe from Vail's hand and locked her eye against it, running it over both sheets. When she straightened up, she smiled. "You're right, it is ingenious. He's using fingerprints as a code."

"Each finger has a number on the fingerprint card we use. The right thumb is number one, all the way to the left pinkie being number ten—or, for code purposes, zero."

After a few seconds, she again scanned the larger sheet. "The message is on this page, but we wouldn't be able to assign a number to each one without a control set of prints. The *fingerprint card,* so to speak"—she bent over the smaller page and ran the magnifier across it to confirm what she was about to say—"has a set of ten in the same order in which they'd be rolled during an arrest. From them we know what number to assign to the latents on the big page, which is the code to lead us to the next mole," Kate said. "But then what do the dates mean?"

"I don't know. First we've got to get both of these pages fumed so we can see exactly what Calculus is telling us."

Vail's cell phone rang. It was Luke Bursaw. "Steve, remember we talked about seeing if the police department had any similar patterns of missing females? Well, they do. I got copies of their reports and was wondering if you could give me a hand for a couple of hours."

"Hold on a second." Vail covered the phone. "It's Luke. He needs some help. An hour or two. It'll take that long to get those pages processed, won't it?"

"With the fuming process, yes. Go ahead, I'll get this done."

"Luke, why don't you come over here. . . . Okay, I'll see you then."

After he hung up, Kate asked, "You're going to let him see all this?" She waved a hand at all the documents and photos covering the wall.

"First of all, he is an agent. Second of all, he's Luke. I'll ask him to pretend that it isn't there, and he will."

"You're right." As though they were as fragile as archival material, Kate cautiously packed up the two sheets of paper, threading them into a clear plastic envelope before putting them into her briefcase. "I'll call you when I'm done. You and Luke aren't going to get lost, I hope. Remember, we're in a race here."

"He said a couple of hours. If it takes longer, you're going to have to yell at him."

"If there's one thing I've learned in the last six months it's who to yell at."

ELEVEN

LUKE, DO YOURSELF A FAVOR AND IGNORE THE STUFF ON THE WALL," VAIL SAID. Bursaw let his eyes briefly scan the documents and said, "You always did thrive on chaos." He took out a sheaf of papers. "These are homicide reports on three women who were killed in the last six months."

"Give me a few minutes to read them." The ability to ignore agency boilerplate was a necessary skill for anyone in law enforcement, and Vail had regained his in the few days of being back to reading Bureau reports. "I think there's some coffee."

"I could use a couple of cups." Bursaw got up and started toward the kitchen. "What is this place?"

"Across the street is the old Russian embassy. You know, before they built the new one up on Tunlaw Road."

"Then this was an observation post?"

"Tough duty, huh?"

"You want some coffee?" Bursaw called over his shoulder as he entered the kitchen.

"No!" Vail yelled after him. "All three of these women were prostitutes."

Bursaw came back in with a cup in his hand. "I know that Sundra doesn't exactly fit into the victimology pattern of these women, but she disappeared during the same six-month period as they did," Bursaw said. "Does that mean you don't think they're related to her disappearance?"

"Not necessarily. If it is the same guy, she could have known him or unwittingly presented him with an opportunity. His MO is to take women in very low-risk situations. Prostitutes have to go with him. It's unlikely that he would try something risky like grabbing Sundra anywhere she would have a chance to resist."

"If you're suggesting it might be someone who knew her, I've already interviewed everyone I could find, from names in her address book to people my cousin knew, including casual acquaintances like the UPS guy or anyone else she might know without really knowing. So far nothing."

"Then I'd say this is your best bet right now."

Bursaw took a sip of his coffee. "Come on, Steve." He waved at the wall. "I can see you've got a lot going on, but I need you to fire up that twisted brain of yours in Sundra's direction."

"Give me a few minutes to think about it." Vail walked into the kitchen and poured himself a cup of coffee. When he came back, he said, "You told me that Sundra had a new computer. Was it taken into evidence?"

"Yes. I've already gone through it. There really wasn't much on it."

"Take it to the lab and have them go through it. I read about a new forensics technique called Volume Shadow Copy. It allows them to reconstruct a computer's hard drive on any given day. Start with the day she disappeared and then each day before that to see if anything was purged. If it was, get a copy of it, and we'll take a look at it."

Bursaw made a note. "Volume Shadow Copy. Okay."

"What about her work computer?" Vail asked.

"I know they've downloaded everything off it from the server and then dry-cleaned it so no one else could get access to it. As far as I know, nothing was found."

"Again, get a printout, and we can take a look at it. Maybe the two of them together will tell us something that each alone wouldn't."

"Actually, that's not a bad lead. Although it was strictly against Bureau policy, she was known to copy files onto her personal computer and work on cases at home. I'll get on it."

"In the meantime we should look into the three dead prostitutes. I assume you're checking to see if there are any women out there who've gotten away from this guy."

"As we learned in Detroit, a surviving victim is still the best way to find out who's killing hookers. I'm having them put together a list of serious assaults on ladies of the evening in that general area right now."

"All you need is one."

Bursaw drained his cup. "Thanks, Steve. So, you staying here? I saw the cots in the room off the kitchen."

"Free room and board. Life is good."

"I thought maybe you were staying at Kate's."

"At the moment it's all business."

"Moments pass."

"Evidently you don't know Kate as well as you think you do."

VAIL WAS JUST DOZING OFF on the couch when Kate called. "I've got the pages fumed. Are we going to need someone to figure out which finger is which?"

"How clear are they?"

"As clean as if they'd been inked," Kate said.

"Then I can do it."

"I'm on my way."

"HI," KATE SAID as soon as she came through the door. "How'd it go with Luke?"

"More tilting at windmills than finding lost women, I'm afraid."

"So you're done with it now?"

He looked at her, and she knew his answer before he said anything. "Probably not. Sorry." He pulled on a fresh pair of gloves. "Let's see what we've got."

Amused, Kate said, "So you came here to go to a cocktail party, and now you're working a third case. Sounds like somebody needs to learn how to say no."

He gave her a sarcastic grin. "Should I decide to get some instruction, I know an expert who delivers the word with extreme malice."

"I'm willing to bet you know several." Carefully, she pulled out the sheets of paper, which now had a purple cast to them.

He took the fingerprint loupe and said, "On the code page, there are three prints on each line and three lines, nine impressions. So we're going to get nine numbers out of this. With any luck they won't represent something else. Start thinking about what has nine numbers and can identify a person."

"Actually, I was thinking about it on the way here. There's only one that comes to mind—a Social Security number."

"Sounds reasonable." Vail examined the top row of prints. He compared it to the prints from the "fingerprint card." "The first one is the left ring finger, so number nine." Kate wrote it down. He examined the second latent. "The left index finger—seven." He continued, line by line, until all nine latents had been decoded. "Okay, what have we got?"

She handed Vail the pad of paper with the nine numbers written on it. She had placed dashes after the third and fifth, making it read like a Social Security number. He handed it back. "How can we find out who it belongs to?"

She went over and sat down at the computer. "Let me see if they have an Accurint program on here." After logging on to the Internet and clicking the mouse a couple of times, she said, "Yes." She signed in to the program with her password and then typed in the nine digits. After a few seconds, a secondary screen popped up. "James Dellasanti. Currently residing just outside Wheaton, Maryland."

"Can it tell us where he works?"

"Sometimes, but it's a different query." She punched a few more keys, and the screen changed. "No, not this time. Let me check and see if we did a background investigation for his clearance." She switched into a Bureau program and queried the name. "Well, the good news is, he doesn't work for the FBI or any agency we do the backgrounds for." When Vail didn't say anything, she said, "We could give this to Langston, too. Let him do the cut-and-paste stuff."

"We can't. We don't have any evidence against this Dellasanti. With the others we have a DVD and then stolen documents with money in a bank box. Here we have nothing but a set of numbers that we're not even sure is a Social Security number. And where's the link to the next mole, if there is one? There's got to be more to this."

"Then it has to be the dates." She looked at the page. "December twenty-seventh and January sixth."

"Maybe, but what do they mean?"

"One date has passed, and the other's coming up in two days."

Thinking about what she'd said, Vail walked over to the wall covered with the maps and reports documenting Calculus's travels. "Can you get into the spy satellite again?"

Kate started tapping the keys and after a minute said, "We're up."

"Okay, let me read you his coordinates from December twenty-seven. Just the places he stopped for more than five minutes."

After she wrote the numbers down, he moved behind her and watched as she manipulated the mouse until the coordinates were in the small windows on the screen. She zoomed in. "The first one is the Russian embassy compound."

"That's to be expected. Try the next one."

She entered it and then zoomed down to ground level. "That's a fairly busy intersection with a McDonald's right there."

Vail went back to the wall. "He was there about twenty minutes and it was approximately eleven thirty. So it was probably a Big Mac lunch. Next one."

After locating the third coordinate and zooming down to it, she said, "It's a public park in Maryland."

"That's it!"

"That's what?"

"That's what January six is. A dead-drop date."

"How do you know that?"

"It's well documented that the Russians love parks for exchanging money and information. And it's also well known that they hate changing a procedure when they find one that works." Vail went back up to the wall and rechecked the entry. "He was there eighteen minutes. Calculus was picking up the information from Dellasanti, who evidently is supposed to go back there on the sixth and retrieve his payment."

"Don't you think that's a lot of supposition based on a couple of written dates?"

"You're right." He turned back to the wall and searched Calculus's movements again. "Here," he said, pointing at a document, "the following day he was at the same coordinates for twelve minutes."

"He was putting the documents back."

"Probably copies. He would have to turn in the originals because his bosses would have to see them to okay the payment."

Kate said, "So the day after, he put the copies there with the payment? For us to catch Dellasanti with?"

Vail was tracking Calculus's movements again. "He never went back there after that, so it has to be. And by writing down the second date, he's telling us exactly when he'll pick up the package."

"And then Calculus told him the money wouldn't be there until January sixth. This time the evidence is actually catching him in the act," she said. "What better proof?"

"Exactly," Vail said. "Can you walk the camera around a little?"

"Sure. What are you looking for?"

"Someplace for the drop. Someplace you could hide a package of documents or money and not have it bothered by people or weather. That's why parks are so popular for this kind of thing. Especially in the winter."

Kate's eyes were locked on the screen as she virtually strolled through the park. "Here's something close by, maybe twenty yards away—a footbridge."

Vail came around the computer and stared at the monitor. "Perfect," he said, then pointed. "See underneath the end there? You could easily hide a good-size package." Vail went back to the wall to check the coordinates of the bridge. "Okay, he was there for about three minutes, and then he walked around a little, stopping here and there for a minute or two. Probably to look less conspicuous."

"But the bridge, that's where you figure he left the package."

"That'd be my guess."

"Can I call Langston now?"

"Okay, but tell him not to send anyone to the dead drop. We have to assume if Calculus told the Russians everything, they could be watching it. If they spot our people, there's probably a good chance that Dellasanti will be killed."

Kate asked, "If the Russians do have the Calculus list, why aren't they just taking all of them out instead of waiting to see if we're going to arrest them?"

"They're probably still productive sources, and good ones are not easy to come by. Also, should it ever surface in the future that the Russians are killing their moles, recruiting new ones would be impossible."

"I'd better quit putting off calling Langston. Even though this should be good news, that we've found another one, I've got a feeling he isn't going to like it. We're figuring out who these people are faster than we can arrest them."

"Actually, it only seems a little complicated at this point. Spy Number One, Charles Pollock, is dead. Spy Number Two, Yanko Petriv, with a little luck is in the process of being fully identified for arrest, and Number Three, James Dellasanti, will be caught in the act in two days in Maryland. As you reminded me earlier today, speed is what's important here. It doesn't matter if everyone's happy about it, or if it's legal enough to put in their memoirs. The Russians already have the list and apparently are willing to kill these people to keep them out of our hands. And don't forget the 'big fish.' That's the real prize we're trying to beat them to."

"That all sounds nice, but in case you haven't noticed, very little of this has gone as planned. What if something happens, like Dellasanti deciding to pick up whatever's at the drop before the sixth?"

"He's probably been told that the money won't be there until January sixth. And spies hate going to the dead drop—it's when they're most exposed. If Calculus put the documents back like he did in the bank box—and according to that tracking phone, it looks as if he did—we'll have him along with the evidence and money all in one nice neat little package. We just have to make sure that you and I get our hands on whatever documents might be there before anyone else does. Especially if Dellasanti isn't the 'big fish.' I don't want to lose control until we figure out who that is. If Langston gets the idea in his head that he can take over, he'll have to play by the rules, and I think if this case has proved anything, it's that this isn't going to get solved that way."

"As uncomfortable as I am with deceiving him, I guess you're right." Kate looked at her watch. "I desperately need to catch up on my other job's paperwork. And I'd better let Langston know about this upcoming drop by no later than tomorrow morning. We'll need to get surveillance on it ahead of time."

"Just make sure he's going to let us handle that package."

"I'll do my best. In the meantime, if Langston has Petriv identified, we should be able to round him up tomorrow. And then, with a little luck, Dellasanti the next day," Kate said. "This whole thing wouldn't seem nearly as daunting if we knew how many names were left."

"I told you before, spies love mind games. Answers are better protected if they're surrounded by confusion."

Kate slipped her coat on. "What are you going to do with the night off?"

"I hadn't thought about it. Maybe have dinner with Luke."

"By 'dinner' you mean work on his missing analyst."

Vail smiled. "I wouldn't be surprised if it came up."

TWELVE

VAIL AND BURSAW SAT IN THE FRONT SEAT OF THE WFO AGENT'S CAR. BETWEEN them were take-out orders of hamburgers and fries. They were in southeast D.C. watching a street corner that was busy with prostitutes flagging down cars. "Is this what passes for dinner theater in Washington?" Vail asked.

"I thought it would be nostalgic for you. You probably haven't talked to a hooker since you were run out of Detroit."

"For the record, I wasn't run out—I walked. Let me see her picture again."

Bursaw handed him the mug shot of Denise Washington. Her hair was matted, and her skin was washed out and blemished by continual drug abuse. Vail handed it back. "I could be wrong, but didn't you bring her to the Christmas party one year in Detroit?"

"That's right. It was the year you brought that 'exotic dancer' with the Adam's apple."

"Fool me once . . ."

Bursaw laughed. "I wish she'd show up. It's getting to be the drive-by-shooting hour, and I'm already spending way too much time in court."

They continued eating for the next few minutes. "Maybe we should deputize one of these girls. Put her on the payroll, and she could give you a call when the fair Denise shows up."

"What are the chances of a hooker calling me?"

"A good-looking African-American like yourself, plus twenty dollars? Don't sell yourself short." Vail straightened up. "That's her there, isn't it?"

Bursaw took a closer look at the young woman getting out of a pickup truck. "Now, see, Vail, that's why I wanted you here. Not because you're any kind of agent, but because you are the world's luckiest white man." Pulling away from the curb, Bursaw drove for a half block before making a U-turn. He coasted back to where the young woman stood and stopped in front of her. He rolled down the window and leaned across Vail. "Denise!"

She looked at the two men who were obviously law enforcement and shook her head disgustedly. "I ain't doing nothing," she protested.

"We're not here for that. Get in the backseat."

"I didn't do nothing." He flipped open his credentials, and she said, "FBI? I sure as hell didn't do nothing *that* bad."

"I'm here about the man who attacked you."

The other girls were starting to move away from the corner. Denise smiled. "Well, what kept you boys?" She strutted comically for the other girls, as if she were getting into a limousine. Once the door was closed, she said, "I hope you're here to tell me that you caught that freak."

Bursaw turned around in his seat and said, "I just found out about it today. But I'm making it a priority. Did you know him?"

"Never saw him before."

"Ever date him?"

"Not me, but some of the other girls told me they did."

Bursaw handed her the photographs of the three prostitutes that had been murdered. "Any of these girls?"

She shuffled past the first two, but the third girl caused a reaction. "You think he's the one who killed Darlene?"

"That's what we'd like to ask him. Tell me about what happened with you."

"You sure we're cool?"

"This is what it is, Denise. Nothing else."

"Okay, but if it ain't, this is entrapment."

"I'll consider myself warned," Bursaw said.

"I guess it was two or three months ago. He pulls up, and I ask him what he wants. He agrees to the money, and I get in. He had this old van, the kind with no windows. He drives for a couple of blocks. I could tell he knew where he was going. Some dead-end street, just factories and stuff. I tell him I need the money up front. He gives me a twenty, and we start to get busy. All of a sudden, he's got this screwdriver pressed to my neck and tells me to get in the back. I hesitate, and he jabs it into my skin." She lifted her head. "I still got a scar." Both agents inspected the rectangular mark that the tip of a screwdriver would leave. "So I get in the back. Once I'm there, I see he's got ropes tied to the inside braces on the walls, four of them. I've been doing this long enough to know I was in trouble. He sets down the screwdriver so he can use both his hands to tie me. I waited until he was just about to tighten the first knot, and then I picked up the screwdriver and stabbed him with it. I must have hit him pretty good, because he fell back yelling in pain. Then I jumped out and ran as fast as I could."

"Have you seen him since?"

"I haven't."

"Did you talk to the other girls about him?"

"Sure. We're always warning each other. But if it's slow out here, you know, you're not as careful."

"According to the report you filed, it happened after Darlene was killed."

"That sounds about right. You think it was this freak?"

"She was tortured, and both ankles and wrists had rope burns on them."

"Jesus Almighty. It's got to be him, then."

"Tell me about the van—what color, make, model, whatever you can."

"All I remember is it was old, maybe white, with some big rust spots on it. I couldn't tell you what kind. There was fast-food wrappers and a bunch of other garbage in the back, like he never cleaned it."

"Describe him."

"Black, maybe in his thirties. Medium build. Had his head shaved. Never saw him standing up, so I don't know how tall he was, but probably average."

"Where did you stab him?" Vail asked.

"You know, I just lashed out. I think it was in the chest."

"Think you got any depth?"

"It felt like it. And the way he fell back, I'm pretty sure I did."

Bursaw took out a dozen business cards and handed them to her. "Give these to the other girls. Anybody sees him, call me twenty-four hours a day. Let them know there's a decent chance that one of them could be next. The best thing we can get is a license plate. It's worth some money."

"If this's the fool who did Darlene that way, it'd be an insult to her to take money."

She got out of the car and leaned back in the window. "You really FBI?" she asked Bursaw. Then she got a mischievous grin on her face. "Ain't this the part where you're supposed to give me the lecture about getting out of the life?"

"Since you didn't pay any attention to the guy with the screwdriver, why would I bother?"

She laughed a single syllable and backed away from the car. "I'm going to call you, Mr. FBI. One way or the other."

As Bursaw pulled away from the curb, Vail said, "Looks like somebody's got a date for this year's Christmas party."

AT A FEW MINUTES BEFORE NINE the next morning, Vail walked into the assistant director's office. He had received a call from John Kalix that a meeting had been scheduled to plan Yanko Petriv's arrest. Kate was sitting at a small conference table, along with Kalix and the three unit and section chiefs Vail had been introduced to at the off-site on New Year's Day. He sat down next to her. "Where's the boss man?" he asked.

Kalix, said, "He's at the Department of Justice, getting authorization for Petriv's arrest."

"Have you found out where he works?"

Kalix said, "NSA. He was born in Bulgaria, and currently he's a Bulgarian and Czech interpreter for them. Those lists of handwritten phone numbers you found in the safe-deposit box are some of the phones they're up on. Bill talked to his counterpart over there last night and let them know what we've found. They called back this morning and said they haven't gotten anything off those wires in over two months. Previously they'd been fairly productive."

The door opened, and Bill Langston walked in with another man, someone Vail hadn't seen before, but he had an idea who it was. "Everyone, this is Lance Wimert from OPR."

Vail leaned over to Kate. "I wonder who he could be here to see."

Langston continued, "We're green-lighted to detain Mr. Petriv."

"By 'detain' you mean arrest, right?" Kate asked.

"I mean *detain,* as in hold with extremely slow due process. Justice has consented to this approach because of the possibility of others on the list fleeing. Once we grab him, our ten-day clock will start ticking.

I've talked to NSA and explained the evidence to them. They're setting up Petriv at work for us. He'll be called away from his desk, and we will casually escort him out. I should be getting a call any minute to let us know that everything is set."

Vail said to Kate, "Did you tell him about Dellasanti?"

"Yes, she called me last night," the assistant director said. "So I called the director. Mark, you're handling that."

The unit chief, Mark Brogdon, straightened up. "I have an entire surveillance squad ready to go. They'll be in the park late tonight and look for some good spots to get an eyeball on the bridge. They don't know any of the specifics, except that they'll be covering a potential dead drop."

Kate looked at Vail and, as if anticipating what he was going to ask, said, "If Dellasanti does pick up the package, Bill wants us to take custody of it and see if we can find the next link."

Langston said, "I have to give it to you, Steve, the two of you figuring out that fingerprint code. Very slick. Apparently Calculus left clues each time so we could figure out the next name. Am I correct?"

Kate had been right about Langston's being nobody's fool. He had figured out the connection between the moles without the advantage of the Ariadne inscription. "He has so far."

"Knowing your disdain for management, it's not that hard to figure out why you didn't tell anyone about it." He looked at Kate. "At least not any of my people."

"If you check my old performance ratings," Vail said, "you'll see that 'doesn't work well with others' was one of my more consistent character flaws."

Langston chuckled. "I could see where you'd be a nightmare to manage, but you do get results. It's unfortunate you won't be able to go with us today to detain Mr. Petriv."

Vail looked at the agent from OPR and then at Kate. "Me and Lance going to spend a little time together?"

"There are some legitimate concerns about Pollock's death that need to be answered immediately," Langston said.

"Like what?"

"The syringe that was recovered from the crime scene had one set of prints on it—yours. Do you know what was in it? Temazepam. Do you know what that is?"

"A depressant."

"Yes, it is, but do you know what intelligence agencies have been rumored to use it for? Truth serum. Pollock looked like he'd been tortured and then given a truth drug. By us. The Russians don't use it. They have their own proprietary blend, something called SP-17, according to a defector. So that leaves us holding the temazepam bag. Do you see a pattern here? There can be no explanation that doesn't sound like we're covering something up. Especially with you being—no pun intended—a *contract* employee."

"There was a deputy assistant director with me. Do you think she was involved in torture?"

"I don't think either one of you was," Langston said. "This is a potentially catastrophic public-relations problem that has to be defused immediately. OPR spends a lot more time clearing our employees than having them prosecuted. And Kate will be interviewed, too, once your statement has been taken and analyzed. OPR has decided to interview you first because of your constant threat to just quit and jump on a plane to Chicago."

Vail laughed and then looked at Kate. She looked away. So she knew that this was coming, he thought. The only reason he'd accepted the director's offer was the hope of reinstating Kate's reputation, which had been momentarily tarnished by the ridiculous assumption that she'd attempted suicide. He got up and walked to the door. He turned and looked at Kate and the men around her. Evidently she had been returned to a full-share member of the team. For whatever that was worth. Would her career always come between them? He turned back to Langston. "Nicely done, Bill."

"I had nothing to do with this. You're the one who went sneaking off on your own and wound up in the middle of this mess."

"That fingerprint exam on the syringe and the blood chemistry that found the temazepam—you didn't have that expedited?"

Langston's usual stoic expression twisted into a knot of anger fueled by the embarrassment of being caught in a lie. Just then his phone rang. He took his time going to his desk to compose himself. "Bill Langston." As he listened, he sat down and pulled a pen out of a desk holder. "I see. . . . Yes, I do, but give it to me anyhow." He wrote something down and hung up. "Petriv didn't show up for work today, and he didn't call in," he announced to everyone, and then looked at Vail.

Vail glanced back at him and then at Kate. Still she didn't meet his eyes. Apparently he'd been in denial about her truly wanting to end their relationship. But was he reading this correctly, or was he just feeling contempt for everything because he was being so artfully removed from the case? Something this confusing usually just made him mad, but instead he was feeling defiant, defiance being his oldest and most reliable ally. "Good luck."

Kate knew what that meant. Everybody in the world was on his own. Especially Steve Vail. She had seen something deep in his eyes, something only she recognized—revenge. It was perhaps his only self-ish indulgence. He would find some way to involve himself in the case and succeed when everyone else failed. And then he would walk away, his final measure of contempt for the FBI and those who thought they ran it.

After Vail and the OPR agent left, Langston tore the page off the notepad. "I've got his home address. Let's go."

THIRTEEN

IT WAS IN THE MIDDLE OF THE AFTERNOON WHEN VAIL FINISHED WITH OPR. THE two agents who interviewed him had never been involved in a murder investigation before and peppered him with clumsy questions and half-thought-out accusations in an attempt to force inconsistencies in his story. He suspected that this was also part of Langston's delaying process. When they started asking the same questions for the third time, Vail said, "You do realize that you have no jurisdiction in a murder case? The only authority you have over me is as an employee, which in a couple of days you'll have to be a Chicago building inspector to maintain. But you can now tell Langston that you did your job and kept me from being involved in what he's doing. Congratulations, I'm sure it won't be long before you'll be promoted to assistant bosses in the field, where you'll be able to obstruct more than one agent at a time." He got up and walked out.

Vail checked his watch and, reluctantly, turned on his cell phone. He was hoping Kate had called, but she hadn't. He took a moment to scold himself for not being able to let go of her apparent siding with

Langston. There was one message, though. It was from the manager at the Old Dominion Bank where they had broken into Yanko Petriv's safe-deposit box.

Vail called him back. "Yes, Agent Vail, Mr. Petriv called this morning and spoke with one of the assistant managers. I had flagged his file, so when she saw it, she came to me."

"I appreciate it."

"He told her that he wanted his accounts transferred to a bank in New York and was in the process of doing the paperwork with them. In the meantime he wanted his ATM limit upped. She told him he was already at the max, four hundred dollars, and bank policy wouldn't allow it to be increased. She said he was not happy."

"Did she tell him about his safe-deposit box being opened?"

"I'm the only one here who knows about that, so she couldn't have."

"Can you take a look at his account right now?" Vail asked.

"Give me two seconds." Vail's thoughts again drifted to Kate while he waited. "Yes, I've got it up now."

"Did he make any ATM withdrawals yesterday or today?"

"Ah, let's see. Yes, this morning. Looks like just before he called us. Four hundred dollars."

"Where at?"

"At one of our branches in Arlington. In fact, I don't live far from there. It's right next to the old Adams Hotel."

"Thanks for your help," Vail said, and hung up.

He drove back to the off-site and ran upstairs to the workroom. He leafed through some of his notes until he found what he was looking for. Back in the car, he headed to the Adams Hotel.

THE TWO MEN SAT PARKED in the SUV, which was positioned anonymously among the rows of cars at the strip mall, watching the entrance to the

Adams Hotel. Vail pulled up and turned his car over to the valet. The SUV's driver dialed his cell phone, calling the man who had set the fire at the historic building, trying to kill Vail and Kate. "He just arrived."

"He's alone?"

"Get things ready there," the driver said.

"I thought the woman was our target."

Instead of answering, the driver hung up.

The big passenger with the Russian accent said, "We'll wait until he leaves to make sure he's heading in the right direction."

THE ADAMS HOTEL was one of those grand old wooden structures that looked as though Civil War generals had stayed there. It almost seemed out of place with the modern Old Dominion Bank on one side and the tall, gleaming gold-glass office building on the other. The desk clerk was an older man with a thin, waxy mustache who looked like some-one out of a 1940s black-and-white movie. "May I help you?"

Vail flashed his credentials and leaned closer in confidence. "I'm looking for a fugitive. His name is Yanko Petriv. I'd like to know if he's staying here. P-E-T-R-I-V."

The clerk studied Vail's face briefly and then, apparently satisfied, tapped a couple of keys on his desktop computer. "I'm sorry, no."

Vail took a slip of paper out of his jacket pocket. "How about Lev Tesar?" Vail spelled the last name. When the bank manager told him during the call about the hotel's being next door, Vail thought it was a possibility that Petriv might be staying there. Since Petriv had false passports, Vail reasoned that the Russians would have provided him with other corroborating identification that, since it wasn't in the safe-deposit box, might have been kept in a more immediately accessible place.

"No, sir, he's not one of our guests either."

"Last one, how about Oszkar Kalman? With a *K*."

The clerk tapped in the name. "Yes. He was."

"Was?"

"Yes, he checked out around noon today."

"Did he make any phone calls?"

"Ahhhh, yes, one." The clerk read the number, and Vail recognized it as the call to the Old Dominion Bank that morning.

"What address did he give you?"

The clerk looked around and then said, "I don't know if I'm allowed to provide that information without a subpoena or some other legal order." He then half turned the monitor toward Vail and gave him a tacit glance. "I have to go do something. I'll return in a couple of minutes."

"Thanks for your help," Vail called after him as he disappeared through a doorway behind the desk. He swung the monitor enough so he could read it and copied down the address Oszkar Kalman had used. It was in Oakton, Virginia.

The drive took longer than Vail had predicted, and it was almost five o'clock by the time he got to Oakton. The traffic was heavy, and two separate accidents hadn't helped. The address turned out to be an old, weathered, two-story home with a large attached garage that looked like it could have been a separate barn at one time. In an attempt to update the structure, a breezeway had been built connecting the house and garage. The nearest neighbors were a half mile in either direction. Due to some intermittent stands of pine trees, Vail was able to find a place to park seventy-five yards away that was ideal for watching the house. The thick wooden sliding doors to the garage were open a few inches, and he tried to see if he could spot any vehicles inside. He took the binoculars from under the seat and peered through them, but dusk had started to take over and the winter light was fading.

Vail thought he saw some movement in a second-floor window, but by the time he swung the binoculars toward it, there was nothing he could see. He lowered the glasses but continued to watch the second floor. A few seconds later, in the same window, he saw definite movement. As dark as it was getting, that there were no lights on meant that someone was trying not to be detected.

Vail put the car in gear and started toward the house. As it got closer, he let it glide to a stop fifty yards in front of the garage.

Suddenly a three-round volley was fired from the second floor, at least two of the slugs slamming into the front of his car. He dove out of it and took cover behind the vehicle. After a minute or so, he peeked over the trunk, looking for any further movement inside the house.

"I thought the bumper sticker said that Virginia was for lovers," he muttered to himself.

Two more rounds were fired at him, this time from the first floor. "Evidently it's gun lovers."

He stood up and fired a burst into the first-floor window. Almost immediately he was fired at again, this time from the breezeway. He suspected that whoever was shooting at him was working his way to the garage, probably trying to get to his car. Vail shifted his angle behind the car to the garage and put his point of aim at the six-inch opening between the two heavy doors, then waited.

Almost too predictably, a three-round fusillade came from the narrow black opening between the garage doors. Vail opened fire, letting his Glock come back down level before pulling the trigger each time, as though he sensed that his rounds were finding their mark. Maybe it was the tiny after-echo that couldn't have been anything but lead slamming into tissue. He rolled back into a safe position on the car's trunk, dropped an empty magazine, and shoved in a fresh one.

Raising his head for a few seconds, he tried to draw more fire. When none came, he assumed a two-handed grip on his gun and started cautiously toward the garage. Every few feet he took a step to the right or the left so he wouldn't be a constant target. When he got to within ten feet of the garage, another eruption of gunfire came from the opening.

Vail went into a deep defensive crouch and fired at least ten rounds in the direction of the garage while he maneuvered quickly to his left and ran to the door on that side, flattening himself against it. Now the gunman would have to actually stick his weapon outside the opening to get a shot at him. He was about to take hold of the left edge of the door and slide it completely open, all the time ready to shoot anyone who stepped out, when the sound of an engine roared inside the garage. He leaped to the opening and pulled the door open.

Tied to the front of a car, spread-eagled and gagged, was Yanko Petriv, the NSA translator. At least a half dozen of Vail's rounds having found his chest and stomach.

Out of the rear of the garage, which had identical sliding doors, a blue sedan screamed away and down a back road.

Vail ran around to the other side of the garage, trying to get a shot at the car, but with its lights off it disappeared behind a stand of ever-greens and into the winter night.

Vail holstered his weapon and returned to the body. Placing an index finger on Petriv's carotid artery out of habit, he withdrew it almost immediately.

He realized now that they'd had Petriv use this address so Vail would be led here. And then started the running gun battle so he'd fire blindly into the garage. Of course it wasn't his fault, and yet he couldn't help but wonder if they'd staked Petriv out like that because they knew the way Vail went after things.

FOURTEEN

VAIL HAD GOTTEN IN ABOUT FOUR HOURS EARLIER, AFTER A LONG SESSION WITH the Oakton police. He'd called them to the scene and, as soon as they arrived, had explained that he was the one who'd shot Petriv. As he walked them through the shoot-out, they found cartridges at every location where Vail said he'd received fire. The bullet holes in his car matched the caliber of the casings recovered. When asked who the victim was, Vail said that Petriv had been a person of interest in a Bureau investigation, a man he was trying to locate, and that he had finally found him at this house.

The detective asked him more than once to clarify "person of interest," to which he answered that it was a classified matter. Finally Vail had them call Kate at home and have her verify that it was a sensitive investigation. She asked to speak to the chief and eventually convinced him that it was a matter of national security and that as soon as it was resolved, he would receive full details. After a few more hours of interviews by different combinations of officers, detectives, and even the chief, Vail was allowed to leave.

Vail woke up abruptly, thinking he'd heard Kate calling his name. "Steve, we're coming up." It was her. He jumped out of bed and pulled on a robe.

Vail went to the top of the stairs and was surprised to see Langston and Kalix with her. "I wonder what this could be about," Vail said to himself quietly. And then, "Great, now I'm being sarcastic to myself."

They all went into the workroom, and Langston immediately noticed the wall where all the photos and documents were displayed. For a moment he tried to comprehend how they had translated into the identification of three spies, but he didn't want Vail to think he was there to admire his work.

Vail said, "Anyone want coffee?" and started for the kitchen.

Langston finally sat down on the sofa and called in to Vail, "I've briefed the director about last night, and of course he knew about the murder of Charles Pollock. Needless to say, he's not happy. Two suspected spies, both dead. Both, it appears, were tortured and killed. Both times you're right in the middle of it."

Vail came out of the kitchen. "That shows you how misguided I am. I would think it was a good thing for the Bureau to be right in the middle of things."

"And you had to go out there by yourself to do this. Was that to embarrass me?"

"I went by myself so your rules wouldn't get in the way. Embarrassing you was just a bonus."

"Apparently you don't understand what a potential nightmare this could be if the media gets hold of it."

"That's exactly why the Russians did it," Kate offered.

Langston said, "I'm well aware of that, but who's going to believe us?"

Vail sat down in a chair. Kalix, in an attempt to reduce the tension, said, "I think the big question here is why would the Russians kill Pollock and Petriv? That's never been their style."

Kate said, "Maybe this is a small group of loose Russian cannons inside the SVR who are trying too hard to please their superiors— or, more likely, not wind up in gulags. When you have an asset exposed, it makes you look incompetent. You've got to hand it to them. They've found a way to turn their losing a spy into a black eye for the Bureau."

"That's a reasonable explanation, Kate," Langston said. "Do you or Steve have any idea how they knew we were onto Petriv?"

Vail said, "The only thing I can think of is Calculus giving up his list. If he did, the Russians would be watching those individuals. Maybe even asking them that if anything unusual happens to contact the embassy immediately. In Pollock's case they probably knew we were coming because of the break-in at the safe house and the missing DVD. With Petriv, he knew we were onto the bank because he tried to get more money through the ATM when he had much more in his safe-deposit box. Somehow he knew we had been to the bank and probably assumed we were staking it out. Or maybe someone let the cat out of the bag at NSA after you contacted them the day before. You know how there are no secrets inside the Bureau. You have to assume NSA has the same rumor mill. And since we found the false passports, the Russians had probably told him that they would get him out of the country should anything happen. If so, his next step would be to call his handler."

"That also makes sense. All the more reason to bring Dellasanti in as soon as possible," Langston said. "So let's get focused on today. Surveillance is already on the drop at the park. There's no activity yet. We've also got two crews on Dellasanti—who, by the way, works for the State Department."

"I assume we're going to arrest him as soon as he makes the pickup," Kate said.

"Uh . . ." Langston glanced at Vail.

She, too, looked over at Vail, who had a small, cynical grin on his face.

"What the assistant director doesn't want to tell you," he said, "is that I will not be making the trip to Maryland."

"Since you figured that out, Steve, I assume you understand why," Langston said.

"I'm oh for two bringing in spies alive, and because I'm a very temporary employee, someone might interpret those deaths as the reason I was brought into this case."

"Is that true?" Kate asked Langston.

"Obviously it makes enough sense that he figured it out."

"You do realize that we've gotten this far only because of Steve," she said.

"It's okay, Kate," Vail told her. "They're right. The Russians are playing this beautifully." He turned to Langston. "Maybe it's time for me to bow out permanently."

Langston said, "Absolutely not. The director was vehement about that. No, we just want some space between you and Dellasanti. And I think you understand that ultimately, by using this tack, you'll be protecting yourself."

"Yes, that's always been my favorite thing about the Bureau, how they look out for me," Vail said.

Langston's cell phone rang. "Assistant Director Langston." He listened for a moment and then hung up. "Dellasanti has just left his home. It looks like he's heading to work."

"Is the drop on his way?" Kate asked.

"No. Not in the direction he's heading. We've got time."

Vail stood up. After his call to Kate in the middle of the night and her efforts to get him cleared of the Petriv shooting, he felt that maybe he had judged her too quickly after he was excluded from the Petriv case. There was one way to find out where she really stood. "It appears

I've got the day off. Since Kate hasn't knifed or shot anyone, I assume she's going with you."

"Yes."

Vail stared at her for a second too long, hoping it would remind her of their deal that he was supposed to get a first look at the documents from the impending dead drop. "Don't forget you promised to call that guy Ariadne," he said to her.

VAIL SAT ALONGSIDE LUKE Bursaw's desk, scanning the mountain of information printed out from the missing analyst's work computer. "I'm never using a computer again. There isn't a keystroke that isn't permanently recorded."

"It would take a year to analyze all this," Bursaw said.

"What about her personal laptop?" Vail asked.

"That—what did you call it?—Shadow Copy stuff? They're working on it now."

"Good. Have you heard anything from your girlfriend Denise?"

"Nothing. You know the attention span of a hooker. It's only about as long as their tricks."

"All this wheel spinning is making me hungry. How about I let you buy me some lunch."

"The way you eat, it'd be cheaper for me to get you a hooker."

"Sounds like somebody's been getting the law-enforcement discount."

BURSAW AND VAIL sat in a booth eating corned beef sandwiches at a deli two blocks from the Washington Field Office. "Does your supervisor know you're putting all this time in looking for Sundra?"

"We're all a little surprised when he actually finds his way to the office every day. The word is he's got much greater ambitions. All indications are that he's saving himself so when he gets back to headquarters he can screw up cases Bureau-wide."

"So what do you want to do with Sundra next?"

"Me? You're the idea guy. Why do you think I'm buying lunch?"

"You feed me salted meat and expect my A stuff? There better be a promise of pie attached to your next request."

"I wish I could get up off of this, but I can't. It's waking me in the middle of the night. No matter what I'm doing, I start drifting away thinking about it. I mean, Christ, I didn't even know her. Not really. I guess it's become personal because of my cousin."

Vail took the last bite of his sandwich and pushed the plate away. "You know she was a good person. If we don't give them a little extra, who do we do it for?" Vail took a drink. "I'd never say dump it. Nobody else is looking for her, so you have to. It's part of the idiot agent's code. Running in the wrong direction is our life. When we're done here, let's go back to the office and go through the file again."

"That's your great insight? Go through the file again? I could have done that."

"You're mixing up cause and effect. The insight comes when I find something in the file. If that isn't good enough, next time ask a psychic to lunch."

"Okay, okay. You ready to go?"

"What's the magic word?"

Bursaw signaled the waitress over to their booth. "Pie, please."

FIFTEEN

SITTING IN THE BACKSEAT, KATE LISTENED TO KALIX AND LANGSTON. THEIR CONversation had a controlled excitement to it. The car was positioned a good half mile from the entrance to the park where it was believed that James Dellasanti was going to pick up the package left by Calculus. He thought it was going to contain only money, while the agents hoped for money and documents. The surveillance crew that had gotten there first thing in the morning had found a package wrapped in black plastic and sealed with tape. It had been found where Vail had predicted it would be, under the end of a small footbridge, a five-minute walk from the parking lot.

The staccato radio transmissions between the surveillance teams at the drop site and those following Dellasanti's car cut back and forth through the air rhythmically like a slow, efficient tennis match. Both Langston and Kalix shifted in their seats anxiously. Kate should have been more excited about what was getting ready to happen, but Vail's not being there was dulling this once-in-a-career experience for her. She thought about the Russians trying to kill him the night before and how if she had been there he might not have been at as great a risk. After he called her from the Oakton station, she felt sick, not because of what he'd gone through but because she hadn't taken a stronger stand against Langston's excluding him. She drew in a sobering breath and tried to not think about Vail.

She leaned her head back and started drifting off between transmissions. Every third one or so, Langston had Kalix send some unnecessary instruction. She could picture the men at the other end rolling their eyes.

"We're approaching the park," the team leader following Dellasanti said.

Langston sat up a little straighter and took the mike out of Kalix's hand. "Make sure you give him enough room. We've got people inside the park. We'll have nothing if you spook him off the pickup."

The assistant director waited a few seconds for his transmission to be rogered. The radio remained silent. Kate smiled. She knew that it was a tacit protest. This is what these agents did all day, week in and week out. The disdain that street agents developed for upper management certainly couldn't be called a mystery. "Did you copy?" Langston asked, his tone becoming more imperious. Again there was no answer, and just as Langston was about to retransmit his demand, two slow, static-punctuated pushes came from the surveillance leader's mike button, confirming that the instruction had been received.

Less than a minute later, Kate watched Dellasanti's car pass by, recognizing it from the surveillance description. Neither Langston nor Kalix seemed to notice. *"We're pulling into the parking lot,"* the team leader said.

"Let's go, John," Langston said. Kalix eased the car into gear and drove at a controlled pace through the entrance to the park. The terrain surrounding the parking lot was slightly rolling and heavily treed with hardwoods that now stood stark in the winter sunlight. In the distance ahead, winding footpaths disappeared into long stretches of evergreens.

A large sign gave the park hours and listed the different trails, all coded by color.

There was about a half hour of daylight left, and a few hundred feet away, Kate could see their target exiting his car. She said, "That's him getting out of the green station wagon just ahead, John."

There were a handful of commuter cars scattered throughout the lot, and Kalix pulled into the first space he saw, turning off the engine. They watched as Dellasanti looked back once and then took off at a pace that indicated he knew where he was going, entering the trail marked "Green." The leader of the unit that had followed him handed off the "eye" to the surveillance people hidden in the park. *"Okay, Twenty-seven Three, he's all yours. We'll set up outside the entrance in case you need us to get back on him."*

"We'll keep you posted, Twelve Two."

"Come on," Langston said, opening the car door. "Did you see the way he was looking around? You could convict him on body language alone."

"A suggestion, Bill," Kate said. "I'd let the surveillance people handle this. Nobody is around. If he sees us, especially the way we're dressed, he'll make us in a heartbeat."

Langston looked down at his suit and then at Kalix. "You're probably right. We'll wait here."

The three of them listened in silence as the agents hidden in the woods described every move Dellasanti made. *"Subject has crossed the bridge and then stopped. He's looking around . . . coming around the end of the bridge . . . squatting down . . . reaching under. . . . All units, be advised the subject has the package. He's put it inside his coat and is starting back across the bridge."*

Langston held up the mike to his mouth. "All units, this is Assistant Director Langston. We'll take him when he gets to the parking lot."

"Ten-four."

Langston opened the door and grabbed a handheld radio. "Let's go." Kalix and Kate got out. Langston and Kalix started walking quickly toward the path that Dellasanti had used to enter the park. More agents were pulling into the lot, getting out of their cars, and feeling the excitement of catching a spy red-handed; they hurried to intercept him. Kate leaned back against the car and let her mind drift off, wondering what Vail would do if he were there.

"THE GIRL ISN'T GOING with them!" The two men sat up straight in the same black SUV a hundred yards outside the parking lot, watching the activity through a small spotting scope.

"Patience," the passenger said, and took the scope. "As the Americans say, 'There are numerous ways to skin a cat.'" He flipped a toggle switch on the radio-transmission box sitting on the seat next to him, and a small red light lit up, indicating that it was armed.

AS SOON AS Dellasanti stepped into the clearing, Langston barked into his portable radio, "Take him!"

THE LARGE MAN SITTING in the passenger seat watched carefully through the scope as the agents started to rush at Dellasanti. Calmly he pressed the button.

KATE WAS STILL leaning on the car when the package under James Dellasanti's coat exploded, cartwheeling his body through the air. All the agents charging at him dove to the ground as if expecting more detonations.

Kate ran to Dellasanti with her gun drawn, searching the perimeter for any further attack. She reached him first. He was facedown and motionless. She holstered her weapon and carefully rolled him over. A huge hole had been ripped through his overcoat. The blast had gone in the opposite direction as well. The left side of Dellasanti's rib cage was gone, and Kate could see into his body cavity. There were bits of currency around the periphery of the wound, plus some kind of cloth that had been in the package. She checked his carotid artery for a pulse and then pushed up his eyelid. He was dead.

Suddenly realizing the extent of the brutal execution she had just witnessed, Kate collapsed into a sitting position on the ground. Her adrenaline subsided as quickly as it had risen, and her mind fell into a stupor. It took all her strength not to vomit.

ALTHOUGH VAIL was at the off-site reading some of the missing-analyst reports that Bursaw had discreetly copied for him, his mind kept straying to the Calculus case. He tried to shrug the thoughts off, but still something in his subconscious was sending up a small flare of protest. He stepped over to the wall covered with the details of the case and started tracing the intricate web of clues that the Russian had left.

The phone rang. It was Bursaw. "Denise just called. Our guy came back."

"Is he there now?"

"Have we ever been that lucky?"

"Your voice sounds like there's good news in there somewhere."

"She got his plate."

"I hope you're calling from your car."

"I'll be there in fifteen minutes."

WHEN VAIL GOT into Bursaw's Bureau car, he took a moment to read his friend's face. There were tiny creases of excitement at the corners of his eyes. "I guess you think this is your guy."

He pulled away from the curb. "My guy, I don't know. But the guy who killed these prostitutes, yeah, I think this is him. As far as him being responsible for Sundra, it's a leap from hookers to middle-class FBI analysts, even if they are all black. But I've got nothing else going right now." He looked over at Vail. "Besides, this is like a time machine, you and me on the street, at night, freezing cold, trying to find some animal that has a million places to hide."

"I think you're remembering only the good parts."

Bursaw laughed in disbelief. "Tell me you don't miss it."

"Not enough to reenlist."

"So you'd rather be a bricklayer?"

"You sound like Kate. She thinks I should do something more meaningful, but I have no complaints. I've tried to figure out why. The way my old man shoved it down my throat when I was a kid, hating it would make more sense."

"'Having no complaints' is a long way from being passionate about something," Bursaw said.

As Bursaw slowed the car and started looking for the address from the plate Denise Washington had supplied, Vail said, "There's our van," pointing to the vehicle the prostitute had described.

Bursaw drove a block farther and turned around. "That's a nasty-looking apartment building it's parked in front of."

"Are we going in?" Vail asked.

"We'd have to get real lucky to find him in there. The apartments won't be marked and the bells never work. And no one in there is going to help the *po*-lice." Bursaw checked his watch. "It's after midnight, too late for him to go cruising. And I'm not going to sit on it all night." He put the car in park, got out, and went to the trunk. Vail watched as he walked toward the van, a pair of pliers in one hand and a wire in the other. He started stripping the ends.

When he reached the van, Bursaw looked around casually before lifting the engine cover. In less than a minute, the van's horn started blaring. He lowered the hood and walked back to the car. "Let's just hope his apartment is close enough to the street for him to hear that."

The two men watched the windows at the front of the apartment building as a couple of lights came on. Five minutes later a black man in his early thirties with a shaved head came out and unlocked the van's door. They could see him pushing angrily on the horn, trying to get it to release.

Bursaw put the Bureau car in gear. "Get a big mouthful of this warm air, because if this moron runs, he's all yours, Steve."

They pulled up to the van, and Vail rolled down his window. "Can we give you a hand, sir?"

The man turned and started to say something. But then he saw that the two men were law enforcement. "No, that's all right, I got it." He disappeared around the front of his van and raised the hood.

As quietly as possible, Vail opened the car door. Bursaw said, "Hey, Steve, remember that time in Detroit when you left me outside to cover the back of that house for an hour in below-zero weather? Remember how sick I got?"

Vail looked back inside the car and saw Bursaw's hand move to the siren switch with the impending ceremony of a symphony conductor. Vail started to laugh. "Come on, Luke, don't. I'm begging you."

"I know what a proponent of revenge you are, so this is for you." Bursaw flicked the switch on and off rapidly. It gave a brief yelp. Vail hurried around the front of the van. The man turned quickly and slashed at Vail's face with a screwdriver. Vail fell back out of the way, and it was all the delay the man needed to take off running.

Vail looked at Bursaw, who was laughing. "Keep laughing and I'll let this guy get away."

"It's impossible for you to let anyone get away with anything," Bursaw said. "The idiot agent's code, remember?"

Vail took off at a dead run. Bursaw pulled the car up next to him and drove at the same speed. "A white man chasing a black man. Sounds like we're about to have a violation of civil rights."

Vail glanced over at him and tried to look angry.

"Appears like you've lost a step since Detroit. Get those knees up, Vail. I think you're losing him. Knees up."

Vail struggled not to laugh. It was hard enough running in the cold air. He watched as Bursaw pulled ahead and turned right.

Vail could still see the man almost a block ahead of him now, also turning right. Somehow Bursaw had guessed correctly. Vail pushed himself harder. When he got to the corner and turned, the man was gone. And there was no place to hide. Vail sprinted to the next corner and looked both ways. To the left, half a block up, Bursaw had the man pinned against the car and was applying some sort of jujitsu arm bar, causing the man to rise to his tiptoes and whimper in pain.

Vail ran up and handcuffed him. Bursaw pulled out the man's wallet. "Mr. Jonathan Wilkins. Congratulations, you have just received a demonstration of the old hammer-and-anvil tactic, which goes all the way back to Alexander the Great." When Wilkins didn't say anything, Bursaw said, "Not a history buff, huh, Jonathan?"

"I didn't do nothing," Wilkins said.

"You know, Jonathan, I'm really starting to hate my job. In the fifteen years I've been with the FBI, not once have I arrested the right man." Bursaw pushed him into the backseat, and Vail got in next to him. As they drove to the Washington Field Office, Vail advised him of his rights.

VAIL WATCHED the monitor as Bursaw started interviewing Wilkins. There was no table or desk between them, and the black agent was in the prisoner's body space, their knees almost touching. Bursaw handed Wilkins the photographs of the three dead prostitutes. "Ever see these girls?"

Wilkins looked at the photos, trying to appear disinterested. "No."

"They're prostitutes. Ever go out with a prostitute?"

"Never paid for it in my life."

Bursaw noted his overall slovenliness. "A real ladies' man, huh, Jonathan?"

"I do all right."

Bursaw held up the photos fanned out. "You're sure you don't know any of these women." Wilkins kept his eyes down, refusing to look at the photos again. "Jonathan, look at me." Without looking at the photos, Wilkins's eyes found Bursaw's. "This is very important. You've never seen any of these women before?"

"No."

"Then I'm assuming it would not be possible for your semen to be found inside them."

Vail could see the statement hit home. Wilkins's posture pulled back defensively. It was unusual for a psychopathic killer to have such poor lying skills, but his reaction left little doubt that he had killed the three women.

"Unless somebody planted it there."

Bursaw smiled crookedly. "Are you in the habit of giving your sperm to people who would want to frame you?"

"You said they're prostitutes. Maybe I, you know, had a date with them or something."

"So you have paid for it."

"Sometimes. You know a man's got to be a man. Don't like to admit it, though."

"I understand, Jonathan." Bursaw leaned closer and lowered his voice. "Since we're both telling the truth here, I'm going to tell you something you've got to promise not to tell anyone."

"What?"

Bursaw leaned in another inch. "I don't care about these three whores. I only care about this woman." He showed Wilkins a photo of Sundra Boston.

This time Wilkins studied the photo before answering. "Man, *her* I don't know."

Bursaw looked up at the hidden camera and gave an almost imperceptible shake of his head, letting Vail know that it was apparent that Wilkins had nothing to do with Sundra Boston's disappearance. "Take off your shirt, man."

"I don't have to," Wilkins said.

"Did you want another jujitsu lesson?" Reluctantly, Wilkins pulled his shirt over his head while he glared at Bursaw. There was a three-inch scar on his chest that looked like it could have been caused by the screwdriver attack Denise Washington had described. "See, Jonathan, that scar was caused by a screwdriver, and we have the witness who did it to you. She'll testify about you trying to tie her up in the van, like the other three were. And we'll find their DNA in your van and on those ropes, which I'm sure you didn't bother to change each time. I'm sorry, man, it's over." Bursaw let it all sink in for a few seconds and then said, "But like I told you, I don't care about those three, just this one." Again he held up Sundra's photo. "Tell you what I'll do. We have her killer's DNA, so if you'll give me a sample of yours to prove that you weren't involved in her death, you and I will be done."

"I'll give you DNA, hair, blood whatever you want," Wilkins said, pointing at Sundra's photo. "But you can't use it for the others."

"Agreed." Bursaw opened his briefcase and took out a cheek-swab kit, extracting a long Q-tip. "Open up."

Wilkins opened his mouth, and Bursaw got the swab to within an inch of Wilkins's cheek before breaking it in half and throwing it on the table. "You've convinced me, Jonathan. You had nothing to do with Sundra's disappearance."

"Then I can go?"

"Not just yet." Bursaw stood him up and handcuffed him. "I think the Metro police are going to want to talk to you."

IT WAS A LITTLE AFTER 4 A.M. when Vail and Bursaw dropped Wilkins at the Washington Metropolitan Police homicide unit. Forty-five minutes later, Luke Bursaw pulled up in front of the off-site. "Any idea what you're going to do now?" Vail asked.

"Sleep and not think about it for a while. Do you have any idea how much longer you're going to be around?"

"I think this other thing is getting close to being resolved." Vail handed him a key. "In case something comes up, take this. The alarm code is 9111."

"Does that mean it's going well or it's going badly?"

"We're making progress. Unfortunately, it's in the form of one disaster after another."

"Just remember, when it comes to the government, disasters aren't necessarily bad. If nothing else, it means somebody is doing something."

Vail got out and started toward the door when Bursaw hit the siren with another brief yelp.

VAIL HAD STARTED TO UNDRESS when the phone rang. It was almost six in the morning. Chances that this call was good news were not high.

It was Kate. "Dellasanti's dead."

"How?"

"There was a bomb in the package. As we were closing in on him, it exploded."

"Did he set it off?"

"We don't know. It didn't go off until he saw us coming. So either he committed suicide to keep from going to prison or Calculus put it in the package. Which doesn't make any sense."

"Or maybe the Russians did it to make sure the thread between the pieces of evidence would be broken once and for all. Then we couldn't go any further."

Kate said, "I hadn't thought of that. It's definitely a possibility, the way they've been killing their sources."

"Where are you now?"

"I'm still at the park. Langston's got three forensics teams here processing the scene, and we're just about done. He's ordered all the autopsy and lab work be done by noon so we can get a couple of hours' sleep. There's a meeting in his office, at noon, to analyze everything. He wants you there."

"Okay."

"Really? I thought you'd take the opportunity to ride off into the sunset, yelling 'I told you so' over your shoulder."

"Dellasanti would be just as dead if I had been there. Did any of the evidence survive?"

"I don't think any of the money did. We're not sure about the documents. Something was blown into Dellasanti's body cavity. We decided to let the medical examiner extract it."

"Are you doing all right?"

"I'm seeing a few more bodies than I'd like, but I'm fine."

"I'll see you at noon."

SIXTEEN

THE THREE UNIT AND SECTION CHIEFS WERE ALREADY SEATED IN THE DIRECTOR'S conference room when Vail walked in. Kate was getting coffee from a side table. Vail went over and poured himself a cup.

"You look like you didn't get much sleep," she said.

"I was out celebrating not killing Dellasanti."

"With any luck there are a couple spies left so you can get your batting average back up."

Langston hurried into the room followed by John Kalix, who was carrying a stack of files. "We're in the director's conference room because he wanted to attend this meeting, but at the last moment he was called before a congressional oversight committee."

Vail leaned close to Kate. "Hopefully that isn't about us."

"The good thing is, you'll probably be fired and back in Chicago by the time Congress gets the final body count."

"You really are a silver-lining kind of girl, aren't you?"

Langston sat down at the head of the table. "As if our latest spy getting killed wasn't bad enough, the lab was unable to find anything to give us a clue as to the identity of the next one."

The section chief, Tony Battly, said, "Maybe there are no more. Calculus said the last one would be an intelligence agent. I suppose someone in the State Department could be considered in intelligence."

Somebody said, "Apparently you haven't spent much time around the State Department."

"Or maybe he instructed his relative at the Chicago bank to get us the name after the payments for the first three are deposited," Mark Brogdon said. "Bill, you've had me pay the first two—should I wire another quarter of a million for this one and see what happens?"

Langston said, "We've already sent them half a million dollars. That seems like we'd be throwing more money away."

"I know, but on the off chance that the relative can help us, I think we should consider it. The money's already been earmarked for this."

Vail said, "If you send them a quarter of a million and Dellasanti was the intelligence agent, maybe they would somehow let us know we owe them another quarter of a million. Then we'd be sure he was the big fish and be through with this."

Langston said, "You're right. Besides, it's not like the money's coming out of my pocket. Make the payment, Mark." Nervously, the assistant director straightened his tie. "Anything else, Steve?"

"Mind if *I* see the reports?"

"Sure, you may." Langston pushed them down to him. "What exactly are you looking for?"

"Kate, tell them," he said as he started scanning the reports.

"Anomalies," she answered in an amused tone.

As Vail continued to read, flipping past boilerplate pages, everyone sat quietly and wondered if he would find something that they'd all missed. The lab had recovered a small piece of a circuit used in remote-control devices. That meant that Dellasanti had not killed himself, and neither had Calculus. It had to be the Russians waiting until the last possible second before disposing of a potentially embarrassing double agent, something they had now done twice before. "I'm not going to find anything in the lab reports," Vail said. "Those guys are too thorough. Was there anything left from the package?"

Kate thought Vail's tone was a little too civil. He had to be hiding something.

"The one with the dark blue cover has photographs of everything," Kalix said.

Vail started through the pictures. "What's this one?" He held it up to Kalix.

"It's some sort of sleeve. A packet of money was inside it and intact. The lab is doing more testing on it. It's some kind of material that is virtually indestructible. The best guess is that it might be from the days of the diplomatic pouch, to protect documents."

"Our diplomats or theirs?"

"At this point we have no idea."

Vail went back to the photos. "Let me have a couple of minutes."

A clerk came in with a tray of fresh coffee. The others got up and poured themselves a cup. Kate brought one to Vail and set it next to him. Focused on the photographs, he didn't seem to notice. The men stood around saying little, occasionally glancing over at Vail, trying to see which photographs he was looking at.

Inside the protective sleeve had been two bundles of banded fifty-dollar bills. Finally Vail closed the file. Without a word, everyone sat down. "Bill, can I see the money?"

Langston nodded to Kalix, who went to the nearest phone. "Did you find something?"

"Not really. That's why I'd like to see the actual items." He picked up his coffee and took a swallow. "Thanks, Kate."

Ten minutes later a woman in a gray lab smock walked in with a cardboard box, and Langston told her to give it to Vail. Each bundle of fifties was in a clear plastic envelope. They all had the same purple tinge to them after being fumed for fingerprints. Vail lifted each stack out carefully, examining both sides before setting it down. Finally he picked up one of the bundles and riffled through it. He opened the file and checked the photos of the bills, trying to make out the serial numbers. "Here's a question I hope someone can answer: Are these bills in their original order? You know, before they were fumed." He looked from face to face, but no one replied. "That's what I was afraid of."

Finally Kalix said, "Wait. There were lists made of the bills." He picked up another folder and flipped through it. "Yes, here they are. I assume they're listed in order."

Vail examined the list. "Very good. If you're right."

"What is it, Vail?" Langston asked.

He was still examining the money. "The bills are nonsequential, which is the way spies are supposed to be paid. Did anyone consider the way they're arranged in the stacks? Like taking the first digit from the top ten bills? If this is what Calculus intended, I don't know which stack would be the coded stack. Maybe it's the last ten bills in one of the stacks. Get ahold of whoever made the list and ask him if any of the bills were upside down or backward. If that is the code Calculus used, it's going to take more work to untangle, which isn't surprising, since his clues seem to get more complicated as they go along. That's the only thing I can see. But if there was a clue, maybe it was on the documents." He looked around the table and was surprised that no one seemed to realize that the Russians had put the package together and that as a result there would be no clues. But Vail wanted them to be kept busy. He had seen something in the photographs.

Langston said to Kalix, "Get somebody up here from Cryptanalysis." Then he turned to the group. "We're starting to get calls from the media regarding the bombing at the park yesterday. Once again, refer them to Public Affairs. It's only a matter of time until they start putting together the other deaths with this one. Let's hope we'll be done by then and we can let them know what we've accomplished. If no one has anything else, that's it."

Kate said to Vail, "Speaking of the media, I heard an interesting item on the radio this morning. Seems two FBI agents caught a serial murderer last night and dropped him off at the locals. Know anything about that?"

He smiled. "I don't know, I don't have a radio."

"It *was* you."

"Actually, it was Luke. But unfortunately it had nothing to do with his missing analyst."

"And where are you off to now?"

"I don't know. I'll find something to do. There are a lot of computer records I need to look through for Luke."

"That's twice in the last ten seconds you've said 'I don't know,' which isn't a commonly used Steve Vail line. You've figured out some-thing, haven't you?"

"You think I'm keeping something from Luke?"

Kate lowered her voice to a whisper. "I'm talking about this." She pointed to the material on the table.

"I just gave you and the rest of the brain trust the only lead I could think of. As a tactic, your accusing me of not being forthcoming is get-ting a little old."

"That's because it's usually true."

"Listen, I've given you people everything in this case, and what did I get for my trouble? I got cut out."

" *'You people'?* Cutting you out wasn't my doing."

"I didn't hear you objecting. I know we're not happening, but you were supposed to protect our interests and get me first crack at the evi-dence. So when do I see it? When the guys who the director supposedly can't trust with the investigation are done pawing over it. Do you think if they do find anything in those bills, I'm going to get a call? It's a different year, but these are the same people who ran me out of the Bureau five years ago. They'll always be the people who cripple this organization." Vail stared at her as if making some judgment. "You want to know where I'm going—I'm going to pack."

Kate wanted to say something, but she knew he was right, not only about who ran the FBI but also about her not standing up for him. Vail was the reason they'd accomplished what they had. He was the one who had survived two attempts to kill him. Against his wishes, he had agreed to work on the case. And in return he only wanted to conduct the investigation his own way. Which was exactly why he had been brought in. Until completed, he believed the challenge belonged only to him.

Suddenly she was overwhelmed with the perverse hope that with Vail gone they wouldn't find the last spy, if there was one. Without Vail they might never identify him. She wanted them to fail, all of them, herself included.

VAIL TOLD HIMSELF to slow down as he drove back to the off-site. He had not been as upset with Kate as he had pretended. Although he was disappointed that he wasn't allowed to be involved in Dellasanti's arrest or get first look at what had been recovered, he knew that inevitably men like Langston couldn't live with someone else being perceived as the point man. Vail had warned everyone that it would happen, even though they assured him that this time it wouldn't.

He knew that what had happened to Dellasanti wasn't Langston's fault, but right now the investigation had been brought to a halt. Vail had no choice but to proceed by himself. He'd given Langston and the others the serial-number possibility because he knew that the combinations would be infinite and would keep them busy while he checked out what he'd seen in the photos.

He parked outside the off-site and went upstairs. He needed to recheck Calculus's movements the day he'd originally planted Dellasanti's package in the park. After putting it under the bridge, he had walked around the area for a couple of minutes, not something spies do. The longer you're there, the greater your chances of being connected to whatever you left behind. Get in fast, get out faster.

He turned on the computer and went to the wall with a pencil and paper. All the coordinates and times at the park varied little as Calculus moved around those few minutes after being at the bridge. Then Vail went back to the computer and linked onto the Bureau satellite. After zooming down into the park, he carefully manipulated the mouse until he could see Calculus's exact path that day. Did it indicate that he'd hidden something else? Something, even under torture, he hadn't told the Russians about? It would be a way for a dying man to get even with them. Retracing the movements once more on the computer, Vail memorized the terrain Calculus had moved through.

It was a little over an hour's drive to the park in Maryland in the early-afternoon traffic. He parked in the same lot where James Dellasanti had been killed the day before. At the entrance to a footpath, he saw small traces of blood where the body had lain on the ground. He looked around and decided there were a number of different locations from which the bomb could have been detonated.

The footbridge where the package of evidence had been secreted was about a quarter of a mile in, about a five-minute walk along the winding path. Included in the pictures he had seen that morning was a shot of the exact spot where the plastic-wrapped material had been picked up. It was an all-metal bridge, cleverly constructed almost entirely of two-inch-square steel tubes. About twenty feet long, it sat less than two feet above a small brook, which was dry this time of year.

He stepped down into the streambed and tried to re-create the angle at which the photographer had taken the picture. What had caught his attention was a small mark on one of the five steel tubes that ran under the bridge's flooring pieces as supports. At least he thought it was a mark. It was hard to tell in the photograph; it looked like an elongated checkmark or a single-barb arrow, pointing down. He had seen similar ink markings in engineering drawings, and since Calculus was a trained engineer, it could have been made by him. With each clue left for the FBI, subtlety had become the Russian agent's signature. And the mark had been the same medium blue as Vail had encountered twice before on items left by Calculus.

There it was. He moved closer. It was an abbreviated arrow drawn in blue marker, its line thin and barely noticeable. But pointing to what? There was only about a foot between the sloping stream bank underneath it and the supporting steel tube. Reaching under it, he probed it with his fingers but couldn't feel anything. He checked the arrow again and wondered if it meant that something was buried in the streambed directly below.

The ground was mostly sand and stone, now stiffened by winter temperatures. Any attempt to dig it up would have been difficult to disguise, and to his eye the streambed appeared undisturbed. He looked more closely at the arrow. The square tubing had rounded corners, and the arrow was drawn completely on the side except for the point, which wrapped slightly underneath the tube. Vail got down on his back and shimmied under the bridge. Drawn in the same blue ink on the underside of the tube were two concentric circles inside an oval, a simple rendering of an eyeball.

Vail stood up and took off his topcoat, brushing the back of it while he thought. After a few moments, he decided he had no idea what Calculus had intended. Maybe it was one of those instances of being too close to something to accurately assess it.

Walking back fifty feet along the bank of the small stream, he examined the structure. The steel tubes supporting the walkway were completely hollow, and from that distance he could actually see light coming through the one with the arrow drawn on it.

That was it.

He hurried back to the bridge and squatted down so he could look through the marked tube. The only thing directly in his line of sight, thirty yards on the other side, was a sign marking the path in case of snowfall. Because its purpose was seasonal, it was set in a concrete-filled rubber tire that allowed it to be taken away and stored during warmer weather. Apparently Calculus had moved it so it could be sighted through the steel tube.

Walking over to the sign, Vail tipped it over. The base was hollow. He reached up under it and could feel a small plastic-wrapped object taped to the inside. He pulled it out and opened it. It was a computer flash drive, a device about the size of a thumb that was capable of storing a large amount of digital information. Its shell was plastic and on the back side, handwritten in Cyrillic, was the word *конец*. If Vail remembered his college Russian correctly, it meant "the end." Apparently this was the last spy that Calculus was going to lead them to.

конец

Vail put the device in his pocket, along with the plastic it had been wrapped in, and headed for his car.

As he came off the footpath into the parking lot, he was stunned to see Langston and Kalix standing next to their car. There were four other cars in the lot, each with a lone driver—FBI surveillance.

Vail couldn't believe that he'd been followed and hadn't noticed. He scanned the sky looking for a Bureau airplane. There didn't appear to be any, at least not any longer. After his three years as an agent in

Detroit, he had always been surveillance-conscious. Even when he returned to the everyday existence of a bricklayer, he couldn't help being vigilant. But, more important, he wondered what had made them follow him. He'd given them a plausible distraction, which apparently they hadn't bitten on. Had he underestimated them? Then he thought of Kate. She was probably the only one capable of figuring out what he was up to. She had even accused him of it after the meeting. But it was hard for him to believe that she would have given him up.

Without a word, Vail walked over to Langston and handed him the flash drive. "And whatever it was wrapped in," the assistant director demanded.

Vail pulled the section of plastic out of his coat pocket and gave it to him. "I guess I underestimated you," Vail said. It was a statement of apparent surrender carefully designed to judge Langston's reaction, to see if following him had been his idea or someone else's.

"One of arrogance's consequences," Langston said, his response giving no clues.

Vail smiled and shrugged his shoulders. "Then it would appear that my work here is done." He took off his Glock and handed it to Kalix, along with his credentials. "As always, working with management has been a delight."

"The real question is not whether you underestimated us but whether you overrated yourself," Langston said. "Please be out of the off-site by noon tomorrow."

Vail watched the two men get into their car and speed out of the lot. The four surveillance vehicles fell into line behind them and within seconds were gone.

SEVENTEEN

ONCE VAIL REACHED THE HIGHWAY, HE STAYED IN THE RIGHT LANE AND DROVE AT the posted speed limit, forcing cars to stream around him so he could lose himself in thought. He still couldn't believe that he'd missed the surveillance. But being followed wasn't the issue. He was using it to avoid thinking about the possibility that Kate had told Langston of his deception. Someone had figured out what he was doing, and the others in the room didn't seem to possess the aptitude to get a read on him that easily. Kate knew how, given the slightest opportunity, he gladly sent bosses in the wrong direction. If it had been anyone but her, he would just have confronted the person, but he realized now that he was afraid what he might find out.

As soon as he arrived at the off-site, Vail called the airline and made a reservation to Miami early the next morning. He still had his wreck-diving trip to look forward to. Not that he'd enjoy it now. But at least it would be warm and provide enough of a distraction that he wouldn't dwell on how this had ended. He made himself a sandwich and ate only half of it. Fatigue burned his eyes, and his thoughts kept wandering off into meaningless directions when he tried to avoid thinking about her. Maybe if he slept for a while, the confusion would disappear.

He lay down on the cot and forced his eyes closed. After a few minutes, he knew he wouldn't be able to sleep. He got up and, to busy himself with mindless work, started packing. He should call Luke Bursaw and let him know that he was leaving, but he had no desire to talk to anyone. Once he got back to Chicago, he would call him and apologize for the abrupt departure. He felt bad about leaving the analyst case unresolved, but Bursaw was a tenacious investigator and in time would find the answer on his own. Vail pulled on his topcoat, picked up the car keys, and headed out the door. There was a bar less than four blocks away.

IT WAS A LITTLE AFTER 2 A.M. when Vail woke up to someone pounding on the front door. He could still taste the Irish whiskey in his mouth, reminding him why the thumping was so irritating. When he finally opened the door, he was surprised to see John Kalix standing there.

"What's the matter?" Vail asked.

"It's Kate. She's been arrested."

"What?"

"I'm sorry, Steve, it's true. That flash drive you recovered, it named the intelligence agent who Calculus promised. It was Kate."

Vail laughed without humor. "That's absurd."

"That was my first reaction, too, but the evidence is overwhelming. There was a typed list of eight FBI-CIA joint investigations, along with their named targets. It had her thumbprint on it."

"Her actual thumbprint?"

"Yes."

"Wait a minute. You mean it was on a *copy* of the list."

"Well, yes. Actually, it was a digital copy of a photograph of the document."

"Then how can you have latents on something that is twice removed from an actual piece of evidence?"

"You're right, you can't. But you could see that each of the pages had been fumed before being photographed. On one of them, you can see the smudge of a print on the lower-right-hand corner. The next page is a blowup of the print. It's a ten-point match with Kate's left thumb."

"I'd hardly consider that *overwhelming*."

"Steve, she spent two years as liaison with the CIA. There's less than a handful of people who could have put that list together, and she's one of them."

"Wait a minute. Could the examiner see the ridge detail in the latent on the copied document?" Vail asked.

"No, the lab tried to enlarge and enhance it, but the digital quality wasn't good enough. That's probably why Calculus included the page with the blowup."

"If it really is Kate's print, why didn't he provide the actual documents?"

"That was brought up. They thought that he probably wasn't able to remove the documents, so he just photographed them."

"If he couldn't remove them, then how did the page get fumed for prints?"

"Before the Russians started recording the exchanges, they would sometimes fume documents so that if they could produce the mole's latents on them, they'd have leverage if it ever became necessary."

"But there's no way of knowing for sure that the latent was actually lifted off *that* document."

"I guess not. But there is other evidence."

"Like what?"

"There are a couple of photos of her with a man named Nikolai Gulin, who is a known SVR intelligence officer."

"Any kid with a computer could do that. I suppose the quality of the photos, like the documents, precludes any definitive laboratory examinations."

"Yes, but—"

"You can't believe any of this."

"I don't know Kate that well, but it is hard to imagine. There is one more piece of evidence, though—one that's impossible to ignore. Do you know what spy dust is?"

"The ultraviolet powder that the Russians developed in the sixties or seventies."

"Nobody's supposed to know, but we use it, too. Three months ago one of our sources told us that we had a mole at Bureau headquarters, and the SVR officer who was handling him was this guy Gulin. We put him under intense surveillance for a couple of months, but he was very cagey. Almost every time he went out of the compound, he lost the teams following him. We did manage to get video and photos of him all over Virginia and Maryland, but nothing to prove he was spying. However, he liked this one restaurant, so we put an agent in there as a parking valet. Eventually he showed up and left his car with our man, who planted the dust on the passenger seat and on the carpeting. As you probably know, the purpose of the dust is to track who's meeting with whom by identifying the minute particles being transferred from person to person, which in this case was from car to clothing. Every night for the next month, we swept the Counterintelligence section offices with a UV light, looking for traces of the dust to identify the double agent in our unit. Nothing. It never occurred to us that it was someone from a different division. Once we saw the pictures of Kate with Gulin, Langston got a search warrant. While all her clothes appeared to be dry-cleaned regularly, one pair of her shoes had the dust on them."

"She could have picked that up anywhere."

"The Bureau has taken the technology to the next level. We can now color-code it. For each operation we use a slightly different color. Hers matched up with the Gulin dusting."

"You know this is wrong. Let me talk to her, I'll get to the bottom of it."

"Think about it a minute. If she is being set up, that would mean the Russians gave up three assets to frame a woman who has nothing to do with counterintelligence. Why would they do that?"

"This is so stupid it's laughable."

"Steve, don't get it in your mind that this is some comedy of errors that will eventually right itself. The Department of Justice is charging her with treason. They think they've got enough evidence right now to put her in prison for the rest of her life. And they're going to do their damnedest to make sure they do."

Vail could feel Kalix's words tightening around his heart like an iron fist. This wasn't something he could just run out and fix. For the first time since he'd pinned on the FBI badge eight years ago, he felt the real fear of impending failure.

He took a few seconds so the emotion of the moment could leave him. "Why are you here? You're Langston's man, and I would imagine his making this arrest has made him quite the hero, no matter who it hurts."

Kalix stared at Vail as he contemplated what he was about to reveal. After a few more moments, he said, "Your reputation is that of a man who can keep his mouth shut, and obviously you have no career aspirations. What I'm going to tell you would wreck my career if it went beyond you and me." Kalix looked at Vail for agreement, and the expression on his face said that none was needed.

"Will I do whatever I have to to become an assistant director someday? Yes," Kalix said. "If it means kissing up to Langston or anyone else, so be it. That's the only way it gets done anymore, but I figure once I'm an assistant director, I can do a lot of things right that are now being done wrong. However, my compromises do not mean that I don't know right from wrong, and despite the evidence I just offered, I suspect that Kate is innocent. This is no small wrong. If you hear me agreeing with Langston that Kate is a spy, it's just a means to an end. I have too much time invested, and I've accepted too much abuse, to give it all up now. But between you and me, I'll do whatever I can behind the scenes to help you as long as you promise never to out me."

Vail wasn't convinced that Kalix had been completely forthcoming about why he was there. "Does the director know about Kate?"

"Yes."

The single syllable was delivered abruptly, as some sort of implied message. "Did he send you here?"

"If I had to guess," Kalix said, "I'd say he didn't believe any of the charges either. Of course I'd just be guessing, because the director couldn't get personally involved in a case with the ramifications that this one promises to carry. Especially with how much he likes Kate. You have to remember, however, that the Justice Department has got their teeth into this, so his hands are tied. They won't even let us interview her, because she's so high up in the Bureau." Kalix opened the briefcase he was carrying and took out Vail's gun and credentials, handing them to him. "I would also guess that if he had his way, Director Lasker would want you more than anyone to do something about this."

It was apparent that the director had sent Kalix unofficially to enlist Vail's help.

"John, I'm starting to think that Langston's not the only one I've underestimated. It looks like you have more than one backup plan."

Kalix smiled. "I've built a career on letting people underestimate me. I am what I am." He started to leave. "Let me know if you need anything."

As soon as the door locked shut, Vail sank down on the marble stair where he'd been standing. Thoughts were rushing through his head at blurred, indecipherable angles. He sat paralyzed, a prisoner of what he'd just been told. After a moment he leaned back, setting his head on the black stone tread above him, looking for the comfort of its hard, cold reality. He closed his eyes and searched his memory, trying to find the image of Kate's face. At least her smile. Then he realized that more than anything he wanted to recall her laugh. Its slightly husky tone, its honest depth. But it wouldn't come to him.

He thought about how confused she must be, how she certainly wasn't laughing at the moment. Was that why he couldn't hear her? Because she couldn't laugh?

Vail bolted upright in anger. Someone had to pay for this. No, *everybody* was going to pay for this.

He turned and ran up the stairs two at a time. In the workroom he let his eyes run along the wall covered with photos and reports. He started pacing back and forth. Since her innocence was not a consideration, only one conclusion could be drawn: Kate had been framed. To clear her he would first have to answer two questions: Who? And, more important, why?

The who had to be the Russians. Calculus, whoever he was, was not a double agent but a front man for the plot to take out Kate. With his mission completed, he probably had disappeared into the maze of his country's bureaucracy. He was probably in Moscow, not being tortured but being decorated. And Vail had fallen for it, all of it.

They had known how to appeal to his ego. He had figured out each of their codes because he was supposed to. If he was really that smart, he would have seen through the plot from the start. There were all those little inconsistencies that he'd explained away so that his answers were the only ones that were acceptable. Ariadne's thread—he had to admit that was the one thing that drew him in. Although its presence didn't make any sense—and Kate had questioned why Calculus would leave a trail of clues if he wanted money for each of the individuals being exposed—Vail had invented a reason so he could feed his own ego.

And now Kate was paying for it.

If he was going to figure this out, the first thing he had to do was disconnect himself from all the emotion of the situation, and that included self-recrimination. He went to the desk and found the file with Calculus's grainy photograph. He pinned it to the wall to remind himself that, although extremely elusive, his enemy was not invisible. He started searching the face for clues of his deception, but of course there were none. Finally he saw the Russian as just another face, his true identity meaningless. The only thing that mattered now was finding a way to destroy his plan.

He got up and went into the kitchen to make some coffee. After filling the pot with water, he started measuring the coffee. As he was about to put in the third scoop, it hit him. He dropped everything and headed for the shower.

EIGHTEEN

THE FLIGHT ATTENDANT ASKED VAIL IF HE WANTED ANYTHING TO DRINK. HE smiled absentmindedly and said no. Checking his watch, he looked out the window. They were crossing Lake Michigan, and he could finally see Chicago's ice-covered beaches. The white-and-gray bleakness swept under them, and his thoughts returned to Kate. The one good thing about something as catastrophic as Kate's arrest for treason was that it reduced everything around it to a level of insignificance. Whatever problems there were between them, real or imagined, they would have to wait. Right now her freedom was the only priority.

The thing Vail admired most about money was its way of leading to the truth. Stories could be faked and lies told, but when money was introduced into the equation, honest answers had little choice but to rise to the surface.

While the three-quarters of a million dollars the Bureau had already wire-transferred to Calculus's designated account in Chicago was a drop in the bucket for the Russians, it was still seven hundred fifty thousand dollars American, and chances were that some enterprising soul wasn't going to just let it sit there unclaimed. Even dishonestly gained money had a way of tracing itself back to the truth.

Since he no longer had to worry about Calculus's Chicago "relative" warning him that the FBI was trying to discover anything about the account, Vail could now go to the bank and ask direct questions. Once the plane landed and he collected his luggage, he took a cab to his apartment. He dropped his bags inside and, after spending a half hour clearing the snow off his truck, drove to the Lakeside Bank and Trust in downtown Chicago. It was an eight-story building on LaSalle Street.

Vail flashed his credentials and asked to see the head of security. A few minutes later, a gray-haired man in his late fifties walked toward Vail. Although Vail had never seen him before, his smile was one of familiarity, causing Vail to check the man's hands. He was wearing an FBI ring made from a twenty-five-year service key. Vail stood up and smiled back. "Steve Vail," he said, extending his hand.

"Les Carson." He shook Vail's hand. "I know a lot of the guys from the Chicago office. Are you new here?" There was the slightest edge of suspicion in Carson's voice.

"Can we go somewhere a little more private?"

"Sure, my office." Carson led him to an elevator and then to an office on the third floor.

As soon as Carson closed the door, Vail said, "Actually, I'm out of headquarters, working a special for the director. And it's extremely confidential."

"I'm sorry, Steve, can I see your creds?"

Vail took them out and handed them to Carson. He looked at them for a moment, running his thumb over the embossed seal at the edge of the photo to verify their legitimacy before handing them back. "Why is there something familiar about your name? What other offices have you been assigned to?"

"I was in Detroit for three years, but that was a long time ago."

"That's it. You're the one who was fired during that cop-killer investigation the year before I retired."

Vail smiled. "Sounds like me."

"And now you're back, and at headquarters?"

"The director asked me to come aboard to handle this one case."

"Why would he do that?"

"I did it once before, and it worked out. No one was supposed to know about it."

"What do you do when you're not on the Bureau clock?" Carson asked.

"I'm a bricklayer. I actually live here, on the Northwest Side."

Vail could see that Carson was questioning the plausibility of his background. "And what exactly is it that you need, Steve?"

Vail took out a slip of paper and handed it to Carson. "In the last week, there have been three deposits wired into that account, each for a quarter of a million dollars. I need all the information available about whoever it belongs to."

Carson fell back in his chair. "Come on, Steve, you know that banking information is impossible without a court order. I could lose my job."

"I can get the director on the phone if that would help. It's a matter of national security."

"If you got Jesus Christ himself on the phone, I couldn't help you, and I'm Catholic. I like it here, and I really doubt I'd like being sued. And as far as it being a matter of *national security,* do you know how many times I used that line in twenty-five years?"

"Les, this is extremely important. And I don't have time for a court order. Besides, I can't let the local U.S. Attorney's office know about the specifics of the case." Vail could see that the real problem was Carson's suspicions about him and his story. It was understandable—a stranger was asking him to risk his job on his word alone. He would have been crazy to agree to chance everything for someone he didn't know he could trust. "There's got to be some way you can help me."

The appeal didn't seem to register with Carson. He was studying Vail's face. After a few seconds, he pulled open a file drawer behind him and took out a thick folder. He started flipping through the pages inside. He found the one he was looking for and held it up as though placing it side by side with Vail's features. After studying it for a few more seconds, he looked back at Vail and his mouth curved upward into a smile of discovery. "This is a flyer another bank distributed state-wide. It seems last year they had a robbery that went bad, and more than two dozen customers and employees were taken hostage. Then a lone male customer overpowered the two robbers and threw them through the bank's windows. When everything quieted down, the man had disappeared into the crowd. They said he was dressed like a construction worker, and the bank was on the Northwest Side. He was never identified. That's why they sent this out, trying to find out who he is. They wanted to reward him. Why do you think someone would vanish like that?"

"Maybe he didn't want to pay for the windows," Vail said. "Or answer a lot of useless questions."

Carson turned the flyer around to show Vail the surveillance photo of the man who had disrupted the robbery. "You wouldn't know anything about it, would you? What with both of you being from the Northwest Side and in the construction business."

Vail didn't look at the flyer. "Retired or not, Les, you've still got a pretty good eye."

"We heard that when you were fired, it was for doing the right thing, but nobody ever got any particulars. And that bank robbery . . . well, that tells me a hell of a lot more about you than a set of credentials. I assume that any good faith I might show you will be reciprocated."

"Just give me someone to throw through the window."

Carson typed the account number into the computer on his desk. "The balance on that account is zero."

"That's good. What's the holder's name?"

"Donald Brown. With an address in Evanston." Carson started writing down the information.

"Is there a phone number?"

"Yes," Carson said.

"Let's find out if any of this *isn't* phony. Can I use your phone?" Carson pushed it toward Vail and wrote down the number for him.

"Can I ask what kind of case this is?"

"This has to stay right here. The only thing I can tell you is that it is a counterintelligence matter, at an extremely high level." Vail dialed the number. He listened for a few seconds and hung up. "It's a restaurant. Did this Brown withdraw the money himself?"

Carson queried the computer again. "No, all three deposits were wire-transferred out of here the day they were received."

"To where?"

Carson hit another key. "That's odd, it doesn't show. That information has to be listed."

"Does someone have to authorize those transfers?"

"Yes," Carson said. "But the data can't just disappear. Let me get ahold of our IT guy." While Carson made the call, Vail wondered if he hadn't run into another dead end.

He felt something he wasn't used to—panic. What if he couldn't figure this out? What if Kate went to prison? How could this be happening? He thought about what she must be going through, the confusion of being one of the top law-enforcement officials in the country and then, the next moment, a prisoner. And even if they were able to clear her, was her career over? Her competence was already being questioned because of that ridiculous suicide rumor. How could she recover from this? She must be going crazy right now. At least he was able to do something about it to keep his sanity.

He hoped she would realize that he was working on it. If only there were some way for him to get word to her that he was, but that might prove just as difficult as tracing the three-quarters of a million dollars that had seemed to vanish from the bank.

Carson said, "He's going to trace everything through the computers. I told him to make it a priority, but it'll be at least an hour. Come on, I'll buy you lunch."

WHEN THEY RETURNED, Carson called the computer analyst back. Almost immediately he started writing on a pad of paper. "Okay . . . Okay . . . Really? That's odd. Can you trace that? . . . Okay, thanks, Tommy." He hung up. "All three transfers out of the bank were authorized by employee code '13walker13.' And it looks as if the same person wiped the transfer information from our computer."

"What's his name?" Vail asked.

"It doesn't matter."

"Why?"

"That was the user ID for one of our vice presidents who retired six months ago and moved to Arizona. His access to the system was never canceled. Someone got ahold of it and used it."

"So the Bureau sent three-quarters of a million dollars to this bank and there's no way to track where it went."

"The IT analyst says he doesn't think so, but he's going to keep at it. I have to apologize, Steve. Security at this bank is my responsibility, and obviously I've got some work to do."

"Don't disembowel yourself just yet. The people involved in this investigation are very smart and have gone to a great deal of trouble and possess unlimited resources. If it's any consolation, I've been made a bigger fool than anyone. We'll just have to get creative."

"How?"

"Whether you're after the lowliest of thieves or the president of the United States, what's the one tactic that rarely fails?" Vail said.

"I don't know, what?"

"Follow the money. Is there a phone somewhere I can use in private?"

"Use mine. I'm going to go find out how this happened."

"Actually, if you could, leave that access in place. I think I know a way to use it."

After Carson left the office, Vail picked up the phone and dialed John Kalix's number.

NINETEEN

AT A FEW MINUTES BEFORE EIGHT THE NEXT MORNING, VAIL WALKED INTO LES Carson's office and asked, "Your people ready?"

"I just talked to Tommy. They're locked onto that account. In fact, the deposit won't move out of here until he personally releases it."

"And if 13walker13 accesses it, we'll be able to trace it to whoever is using the password?"

"To whatever computer is being used in this building, yes," Carson said. "This *must* be a big case. One phone call and you get them to send half a million dollars that's just going to disappear into . . . who-knows-where."

When Vail had called Kalix, he told the deputy assistant director he wanted the half million dollars they had promised Calculus for the final double agent to be wired to the same Chicago bank first thing in the morning. Kalix had argued that was in effect tantamount to giving the Russians half a million dollars more for framing Kate. He feared that when it got out, which the Russians would make sure happened eventually, it would be highly embarrassing for the FBI's Counterintelligence Division.

Vail said, "It's the only way to track whoever set up Kate."

"As much as I want to help Kate, I simply cannot authorize the release of that much money, knowing that it's probably going to wind up in the hands of the Russians. We've already given them three-quarters of a million dollars."

"Actually, we're not going to give them anything. When you send the money, we're hoping that their man here will transfer it to wherever he sent the other payments. I'll have the bank put a twenty-four-hour hold on whatever bank it's transferred to. Once it's transferred out of here, we'll immediately be able to determine the bank and the account number it's being sent to. Then we'll invalidate the transfer from here, and the money will be sent back to the account you forwarded it from. Zero loss."

"Steve, it sounds like there are too many things that could go wrong, and then we're out five hundred K."

"John, take a few minutes to meditate over this. Even consult your 'higher authority.'"

"Uh . . . oh, yes, yes, I could do that." Kalix realized that Vail was hinting at contacting the director for approval.

"Good. Call me back when you're done mulling it over." An hour later Kalix called and told him the payment would be ready to be sent first thing in the morning.

Vail said to Carson, "Let me call Washington, Les, and then we're on."

While Vail made his call, Carson stayed on the line with the bank's IT manager. After a few minutes, Carson hung up and said, "Okay, the half a million just arrived."

Vail asked, "Right now, who can check on the account's balance?"

"There are dozens of employees who have general access to account information, depending on their jobs."

"And how many people can actually order transactions involving that account?"

"It takes a completely different level of clearance to move money out of it, generally vice presidents and above. You said these people are smart. Aren't you afraid they won't fall for this?"

"That's always a possibility, but we have one thing going for us: *five hundred thousand dollars*. That's halfway to seven figures. The best thing about greed is how quickly it melts even the smartest person's IQ."

"As many employee embezzlements as I handle in a year, I should get that little bon mot framed." Carson checked his watch. "I don't suppose there's any way to tell how long this'll take."

"No, I'm not even sure this person is still working here." Vail considered the possibility that with Kate in custody the Russians might have pulled their man out of the bank. But if he was still checking the account, no matter what he'd been told to do, the amount of money just transferred into it might be too great a temptation. "If he is, I would think he wouldn't check that account any more than once a day—otherwise someone might notice. So if you've got work to do, Les, don't let me keep you from it."

Carson took a stack of papers from his in-basket and started initialing them. Vail picked up the newspaper from the small table next to him and began reading it.

A little before noon, Carson had lunch brought in, and the two men, evidently believing that a watched pot would never boil, found other things to talk about. When they were done eating, Carson went back to work, placing a call to Tommy to make sure everything was still being monitored. Vail started on the crossword puzzle.

At a few minutes to five, Carson noticed that Vail had fallen asleep. As quietly as possible, the security chief started clearing his desk. Suddenly the phone rang, and Vail's eyes snapped open. The two men looked at each other. Carson straightened a little and picked it up.

"Yes." He listened for only a moment before disconnecting the line. "The money's being transferred right now." He dialed a four-digit extension. "I want everybody to the basement immediately. Someone's on the computer terminal there. Whoever it is, I want held until I get there." Carson pushed the phone back into the cradle. "He used the same password as before." Both men were moving toward the door. "We have one computer terminal in the basement, mostly for storage inventories."

Once they were in the hall, Vail said, "Will the stairs be quicker?"

"No, the only access is by elevator. You need an override key." They ran to the elevator, and Carson pounded the button repeatedly. Finally the car arrived.

Just as the doors opened to the basement, the two men heard three quick gunshots.

Vail drew his automatic and ran toward someone yelling for help. In a large room stacked with boxes, one man in a suit was on his knees tearing open the shirt of another man who'd been shot in the stomach. Carson, directly behind Vail, said, "Those are both my men."

Vail raised the muzzle of his weapon upright. "Who was it?"

"That guy Sakis from accounting, Jonas Sakis. He went out that way." He pointed to a corridor beyond the computer station.

The security man's wound was now exposed, and Vail looked at it. He checked the man's face for signs of shock. Carson was already calling 911. Vail took out a handkerchief and placed it over the wound, then pulled the kneeling man's hand onto it. "There, use that much pressure. Watch him for shock. Les, where does that lead?" Vail nodded at the corridor the shooter had disappeared into.

"It's a dead end. There's no way out."

The man on his knees said, "Except the old railroad tunnel."

Vail remembered the news story from the early nineties, when an engineering miscalculation had caused the Chicago River to seep into the sixty miles of tunnels, forty feet below the downtown area. They had been built to move freight under the downtown area in the early 1900s. With typical Chicago buoyancy, a city that had been rebuilt after the Great Fire, the incident was referred to as the Great Chicago Leak. "The old freight tunnels?" Vail asked. "I thought those were sealed."

"Our door is, but that's the only thing back there."

As Vail started in that direction, Carson said, "Steve, you'd better wait for the cops."

"Either of you have a flashlight?" Vail asked.

The kneeling man pulled one out of its carrier on his belt and handed it to him.

"I've got a feeling that door is no longer sealed," Vail said.

Without turning on the light, he followed the corridor until it turned right. As soon as he looked around the corner, he could see the door. It was made of steel and was three times the width of a room door. And it was open.

Before entering, he stood and listened. He couldn't hear anything, so he leaned his head in. It was dark except for the ambient light from the bank's storage space. The tunnel itself was concrete—floor, walls, and ceiling—six feet wide and maybe seven feet high. He snapped the flashlight on and then quickly off so he wouldn't provide a lasting target. Thirty yards in was a concrete bulkhead with a gate, a lock and chain lying on the deck next to it. Without turning the light back on, Vail started toward it, his Glock raised to eye level. *What is it with me and tunnels?* He flashed back to the electric train tunnel in which he'd been buried alive during the Los Angeles case. *Maybe I should wait for the cops.*

Then he thought about Kate. When he'd been an agent, after a while there was a gamelike quality to working cases. They rarely took on any real urgency, any real consequence. If he failed on one, there were dozens more to take its place, and he still got to go home and watch the game that night. But he was getting just one shot at this, and it was ahead of him in the tunnel. He couldn't risk losing the only lead that could free Kate. Whatever might happen to him was no longer a consideration.

When he reached the gate, he turned his light back on. Once he determined that the shooter wasn't on the other side, he picked up the lock. It appeared to have been cut with a bolt cutter—and, from the surface rust, not recently. That meant the tunnel was a planned escape route, so Vail didn't have to worry about being ambushed, because the shooter wanted to put as much distance as possible between himself and anyone foolish enough to pursue him. At least it sounded like a good enough theory to let him rationalize throwing caution to the wind. He turned on the light and broke into a trot.

Another hundred yards ahead, he found a second bulkhead with the padlock cut away. Vail noticed that the odor in the tunnel was becoming more pungent, and he thought he could detect the slightest trace of methane. The air was stale and felt heavy in his lungs. He tried to measure his rate of breathing to see if his lungs were requiring more oxygen, but he wasn't feeling light-headed, so it probably wasn't going to be a problem. Besides, the shooter had apparently been through here before without a problem.

After a few more minutes, Vail found himself at a three-way fork in the tunnel. Stopping at its intersection, he turned off his light and listened. There wasn't a sound. After turning the light back on, he could see he was standing in a couple inches of water that had accumulated because the floor at the intersection was an inch or two lower where the old switching tracks had been removed. In the left-hand passage, the floor was dry. The same in the center. The floor of the right branch revealed some partial footprints left by the shooter's wet shoes. Vail took the right branch and after ten feet turned around and compared his tracks against those of Sakis. The rate of drying was difficult to judge, but the early tracks weren't that much different. He was still close enough for Vail to catch.

Seventy-five yards later, Vail came to a right turn. It was impossible to tell what direction he had traveled in, but he thought it was initially south and now possibly west. As he was about to make the turn, he heard the sound of metal on metal. He peeked around the corner and saw another bulkhead with a steel gate. The man he'd been chasing, illuminated by his own small flashlight, was busy working on something attached to the ceiling of the tunnel. Vail drew his weapon and carefully inched forward.

When he got to the gate, he saw that it was chained and locked shut from the other side, separating the two men. Carefully, Vail pushed his Glock through the bars, aiming it at Sakis. He couldn't be sure, but it looked as if three linear-shaped charges had been attached to the ceiling in a triangular pattern. Each one had wires coming down from it to an electrical detonator. Vail snapped on his flashlight and said, "I guess I'm a little early."

Sakis looked up, unruffled, keeping his hand on the detonation box. "You are. I thought maybe I lost you at the fork. If not lost, at least delayed."

Vail could hear a slight accent in the man's speech but couldn't tell its origin. "Why don't you carefully set the box down and come over here and unlock the gate?"

"You are evidently not a student of game theory. What you are proposing is a zero-sum game—all the advantage goes to you while I lose."

"I'm fairly certain that zero-sum games are exactly what gun manufacturers have in mind. I believe their collective motto is 'If you have the gun, you win.'"

"But this detonation box makes it a non-zero-sum situation."

"Actually, this is more like a game of brinkmanship. We're each promising to cause the death of the other to gain an advantage. I could kill you with one shot, and if I did, you would flip that switch and set off the charges on the ceiling."

"True," Sakis said, smiling. He raised the box in front of his face so that Vail wouldn't have a clear head shot and end Sakis's life before he could throw the switch. "Do you know where we are standing right now?" When Vail didn't answer, he said, "Directly under the Chicago River. If the blast doesn't kill you, the tunnel will flood instantly and you'll drown. It's too far back to the bank to outrun it. Too bad the gate between you and me is locked, because the way out for me is about twenty yards ahead. Of course, you can't get to it. Unless you think you can shoot that lock off, but that's a heavy-duty lock I put on it. I guarantee a handgun won't dent it."

"It'll dent you. If you even twitch, I'll empty this magazine into you."

Sakis smiled calmly. "There is one solution. We could each go our own way, you back to the bank and me out through the exit. A draw."

"And what's to prevent you from coming back and setting off those charges once I'm around the corner?" Vail asked.

He laughed. "Nothing at all. But I suspect you know that if we both stay here in this stalemate, the police will eventually find us, and I'll lose. Or maybe we all will. So I guess I'll just have to take a chance your marksmanship isn't that good."

Vail said, "You're ten feet away, and I have a couple of full magazines. Do you really think anyone's that bad a shot? Maybe I'm the one who should take a chance that those charges won't go off."

Sakis smiled. "They're triple-primed. They'll go off."

Vail laughed and then in a theatrical voice said, "What we have here is a failure to compromise." The man looked at him uncomprehendingly. *"Cool Hand Lukesky?"* Still there was no indication of understanding from Sakis. "I guess they don't allow American prison movies in Moscow. Even the southern road gang is better than the gulags."

Finally Sakis smiled as if he knew something Vail didn't. "Exactly what compromise did you have in mind?"

"I'll back up five feet from the gate. Then you come up to it and set down the detonator at one side. With me that far back, it would be too difficult a shot to risk hitting you through the bars. You stand at the other side as far as possible from the detonator, take the key to the gate, and throw it as far down my part of the tunnel as you can. By the time I retrieve it and come back to the bulkhead, you'll have enough time to make it to the next turn and out of range. Once I get the key and can open that lock, you'll be gone and I'll be five minutes behind you. Then there'll be no reason to set off the explosives."

Sakis considered the proposal. Evidently this FBI agent had forgotten the gun he had shot the guard with. It was now tucked behind his back. "You have to lower your gun."

"Okay," Vail said, dropping his arm to his side. Then he stepped back the agreed-upon distance, never taking his eyes from Sakis's.

Sakis figured that once he threw the key behind Vail, the agent would have to turn his flashlight away from the gate and in the other direction down the tunnel. If he did glance back momentarily, he would be watching the box, making sure Sakis was not moving toward it. As soon as he fully turned to search for the key, his own light would silhouette him, and Sakis would shoot him in the back. Then he could trip the detonation timer before making his escape.

Sakis took the detonator and set it down along the wall about a foot from the gate, so Vail couldn't reach through and disarm it. He then moved to the opposite wall, dug a key out of his pocket, and held it up so Vail could see that it was a padlock key. "Okay?"

"Toss it."

Sakis threw the key as far as he could, at least ten feet past the agent, who was now casually leaning against the wall. Vail gave him one last careful glance. Then he swung his flashlight around, and its beam glinted off the key on the concrete floor ahead. Vail turned the light back onto Sakis and the detonation box. "I've got a feeling it won't be too long before we meet again." He turned and started toward the key.

Sakis reached behind his back and carefully drew his gun. As he raised it, Vail dropped into a crouch, pivoted, and fired. The bullet tore into Sakis's throat.

Vail hadn't forgotten about the gun. He knew that Sakis would use it if Vail created a scenario in which Sakis could shoot him in the back. The ploy was the only way he could separate him from the detonation box. Vail had hoped to shoot up through his throat and sever his brain stem, not only instantly killing him but also paralyzing him so the switch could not be thrown. The odds of making the shot were astronomical, but he had no other choice. The bullet had missed by almost two inches.

Although fatally wounded, Sakis was not paralyzed. He sank to his knees and fell forward, reaching for the box. Vail started to squeeze off another round but realized that it was too late when he saw Sakis's index finger trip the switch.

He ran up to the gate as Sakis rolled off the box, his eyes vacant with death. In the darkness Vail could see the red LED display. It read 2:58 . . . 2:57 . . .

Vail ran back and retrieved the key. At the gate again, the lock was on Sakis's side and the chain was thick and difficult to maneuver. The bars on the sides of the gate were narrower than the gate itself. Vail's hand barely fit through. With his right he grabbed the chain on his side and manipulated it to bring the lock closer to his left hand. 2:43 . . . 2:42 . . .

Carefully, he tried to place the key in the keyhole, but the lock was large and had a spring-loaded metal cover to protect it from debris and weather. He pushed the cover back with the key and just about had it seated when it slipped from his hand and fell to the floor. 2:07 . . . 2:06 . . .

Dropping down to his knees, he shoved his hand through the bottom of the bars, but it was well out of reach. 1:59 . . . 1:58 . . .

Vail stripped off his belt, then his shirt and T-shirt. There was a small puddle of water under the gate; he soaked his T-shirt and then tightened his belt around it. 1:42 . . . 1:41 . . .

Threading them through the bars, Vail threw his shirt at the key, holding on to the end of the belt. His first cast landed on the key. Slowly, he drew it back to him, the weight of the water keeping the key under the shirt as it was pulled toward him. 1:30 . . . 1:29 . . . 1:28 . . .

Finally he was able to grab it with his fingertips. He delicately inserted it in the lock—this time it seated fully. He tried to turn it, but it wouldn't move. Vail then realized that Sakis had thrown him the wrong key, maybe one for a gate ahead.

Vail's laughter bellowed down the tunnel. "If I had a hat, I'd tip it to you for making that switch." He glanced at the timer: 1:14 . . . 1:13 . . .

The closest part of Sakis's body was his foot. Vail reached through the bars and could get just two fingers on his trouser cuff. He pulled it to the bulkhead. Working his way up Sakis's leg, he eventually had the entire body against the gate. He pulled part of the other man's suit coat through the bars and patted the pockets, hoping there was another key. He couldn't feel anything through the cloth. 1:01 . . . 1:00 . . . 0:59 . . .

He grabbed at Sakis's left trouser pockets, front and back, pulling them close enough to pat them. Still nothing. 0:47 . . . 0:46 . . .

Using only his fingertips, Vail grabbed Sakis's belt and pulled it toward him to roll the body partially over. Finally he was able to feel the right front trouser pocket. There was a set of keys in it. But he couldn't roll the body over any further, because it was against the bars, and the pocket, although he could grasp its opening edge, was facing away from him. He took out his lockback knife and slit the material open, exposing a key ring.

From behind him Vail could hear voices and footsteps. The cops. And it sounded like there were a half dozen or more of them. He looked at the timer: 0:31 . . .

Vail took the ring and was relieved to see a key similar to the one Sakis had decoyed him with. He stood up and, holding on to it with both hands, worked it into the lock. It turned. He pushed the gate open. 0:24 . . . Vail ordered himself to stop looking at the timer.

The device appeared to be basic. Timer, power supply, electrical blasting caps wired to the three shaped charges attached to the concrete ceiling. Vail wondered if the timer had been booby-trapped, but then he reasoned that he was never supposed to get to it. So he took the first blasting-cap wire, doubled it over, and stuck his knife's blade into the loop and pulled. The wire severed cleanly. Quickly, he did the same to the other two. The first cop's flashlight finally came into view. Vail looked at the timer and watched as it counted down from 0:11. "Plenty of time," he said out loud. He watched as the readout continued, which it would even if the bomb was defused. When it was about to go to 0:00, he closed one eye, squinting at it. The display went black.

"Let me see your hands," the first police officer said.

Vail raised them and then heard Les Carson say, "That's all right, he's the agent."

Vail stepped back through the gate, partially closing it. "Sorry, guys, there's explosives in there. I think they're defused, but you'd better get someone down here who knows what he's doing."

A sergeant walked forward and peered through the gate. "That the shooter?"

"It was."

"Why was he trying to blow a hole in the ceiling? To escape?"

"We're under the Chicago River. Actually, he was trying to kill the rest of us," Vail said.

Les Carson came forward and looked at the body. "Yeah, that's Sakis. At least that's the name he gave us."

Vail straddled the body. Remembering the fake passports and escape plans that Petriv had been supplied with, he started going through Sakis's pockets. There was no wallet, but in the suit coat Vail found a grainy photograph. Recognizing the background, he realized that it had been taken in Washington. But it still surprised him.

It was a photo of himself.

TWENTY

JOHN KALIX WATCHED VAIL COME THROUGH THE GATE AFTER THE FLIGHT BACK from Chicago. He searched his face for any indication that he had just killed another man, but he couldn't see any. "How you doing, Steve?"

"Good. Any word from Ident on Sakis's prints?"

"There's no record. And that security director at the bank, Carson, forwarded his résumé. He started checking it and said so far the work history appears completely phony."

"He was a lot more educated than a bookkeeper should be," Vail said. "When we were nose to nose, he started discussing game theory with me. It's scary to think the Russians plant one of their people in a Chicago bank for that length of time just to handle wire-transferred funds. Makes you wonder how many more there are out there."

"Maybe the Russians didn't plant him there only for the Calculus scam. Maybe they were washing money through the bank, or something else. I'll open a case on it and have Chicago check it out. Some

Russian operations have been around for twenty years. There's probably some that have been in place since the thirties, and we just haven't uncovered them yet. They're not like us—they're got that long-haul mentality."

"Maybe you should let them know the Cold War is over."

"It's all about technology now. They want to steal as much of it as possible. It converts directly into their country's economy."

"Did you get the court order for the bank here? What's the name of it?"

Kalix tapped the breast pocket of his suit coat. "Right here. Northern Virginia Trust in Annandale. When do you want to go out there?"

"Kate's still in custody—what do you think?" Vail increased his stride, and Kalix hurried to keep up.

Once they were in the car, Kalix said, "After your not-so-low-profile shooting, I had no choice but to tell the assistant director that you'd been reinstated."

Vail laughed. "Sorry I missed that."

"I wish I had. If I hadn't implied that it was the director's idea, I'd be working the Migratory Bird Act in the Bronx right now."

"Why don't you just give me the court order? I can take it from here if you want to go repair some bridges."

"I think I'll hang in there a little longer."

"I'd almost admire your courage if the director weren't your ace in the hole."

Kalix smiled. "Actually, he's more like a royal flush in the hole, so I'm with you—unless, of course, he becomes disenchanted with you. Then I'll be calling for your head," he said. "I assume this bank account will also turn out to be a phony?"

"I'd be surprised if it were legit, but it's our best shot right now."

AS THEY WALKED THROUGH the bank lobby, Vail started scanning the faces of the employees, wondering if one of them was another plant by the Russians, put there to move money. Kalix led the way to the manager's office and flashed his credentials, introducing himself and Vail. Once he did, he handed the bank officer the court order and pointed out that it instructed him to provide the mentioned records and that any disclosure regarding the FBI's visit would be a violation of federal law.

"Sure, I understand." After reading the document, the manager started typing at his desktop computer. He took a pen and wrote down a woman's name, her phone number, and an address in Alexandria. "This is all the info we have on the account holder. There was a transfer of five hundred thousand dollars to it yesterday, but that was canceled first thing this morning. The balance is zero." He slid it across to Kalix, who glanced at it and handed it to Vail. The manager went back to the court order. "What are these three other dates you're requesting?"

Vail said, "They are additional transfers made from the same Chicago account. We're not sure whether they came to your bank, but if you could check, we'd appreciate it. They were each a quarter of a million dollars."

After a few more minutes on the computer, the manager said, "They weren't sent here."

Vail said, "Again, if someone asks, it's best that we were never here."

"I understand," the banker said.

As they left, Vail said, "I'll drive," and got behind the wheel.

"I assume we're going to Alexandria."

Vail glanced over at him, indicating that an answer wasn't necessary. "Can you get that name checked?" Kalix pulled the radio mike from its mounting, and Vail put his hand on top of it. "I don't think you want that name going across the air, even if the channel is scrambled."

"You're right. I wasn't thinking." Kalix dialed his cell phone and after giving some instructions waited a couple of minutes before saying "Thank you" and hanging up. "Nothing on the name, but according to the utility check the address is good."

"Let's go take a look at it." Vail glanced at him as if trying to decide something about him. "Are you carrying a gun?"

Kalix blushed a little. "For the first time in years."

"Really? Why now?"

"I guess for the same reason I'm helping you instead of fully protecting my flank."

"Which is?"

"Do you remember when you got your appointment to new agents' training, what an adventure this all was going to be? How daily life was going to go from ordinary to fantastic? That's what I thought. Then I got to the field. The first two years in WFO were spent working wiretaps. I had no choice but to go into management to get out from under the earmuffs. In seventeen years with the Bureau, I haven't had one of the days I signed up for." He looked at Vail to see if what he was saying was registering. "This may be my only chance to be something other than the man in the gray paper suit."

Vail laughed. "It sounds like you're ready to do something stupid."

"Is that a bad thing?"

"Do you really think I'm the person to ask?"

For the next twenty minutes, neither of them said anything. Finally Vail pulled over and motioned to a house in the distance. "That's it there."

Kalix sat up. "It doesn't look like much."

"One of the little lessons I've learned during my stay in Washington is that the Russians prefer their ambushes to be isolated."

"You think this is a trap?"

"A trap or a dead end. Unfortunately, a dead end isn't going to help us." Vail opened his cell phone and dialed the number that the bank manager had given them. He held it away from his ear so Kalix could hear. After three rings a woman with a heavy Eastern European accent answered. "'Allo."

"Is Clarence there?" Vail asked.

"No one that name here," she said, and hung up.

Vail put the car in gear. "So far so good."

"What's good? You're not going to the house, are you?"

"I thought you wanted to do something stupid."

"Shouldn't you get some help?"

Vail smiled at him. "I've got some. When I go to the front door, you take the back." Kalix had his hand on his automatic, unsure whether he should draw it or not. "It's okay, John. Haul 'er out."

Kalix gave him an embarrassed smile and eased the automatic from its holster.

They pulled up in the driveway, and as both men got out, Kalix hurried to the back of the house. Vail walked up the three stairs onto the front porch and knocked hard on the door's window. He didn't wait for an answer, knocking again even more loudly. After a third time, there still was no answer. He yelled back to Kalix, "I'm going in!"

The house was a small one-story structure, and Vail could tell by the exterior construction that there was no basement. The door wasn't locked, so he pushed it open, drawing his own automatic.

Someone had tried to rehab the drab interior cheaply. The floors were unfinished plywood, and the walls were mostly unmatched paneling. Like most houses that old, it was a basic rectangle with low, seven-foot ceilings, which were clogged with spiderwebs. To the right, through a doorway, Vail could see into the kitchen. There were two partially eaten carry-out meals on the table, which was a card table flanked by two folding chairs. Two beer bottles sat next to two empty glasses. At the bottom of one of the glasses, Vail could see small bubbles hugging the inside, indicating that whoever had been drinking beer had been gone no more than a few minutes. Since Vail and Kalix had been sitting outside that long, it meant that at least one person was still in the house. Not able to remember how to say "good afternoon" in Russian, Vail yelled *"Dobroie utro!"* and then, in English, an even louder "Good morning!" There was no answer.

Vail backed out of the kitchen and into the entryway. Straight ahead was what looked like a living room, although it was difficult to say without any furniture. Carefully, he walked into the room, his face brushing against more cobwebs. He caught a glimpse of Kalix out the back window, peeking in. Vail tried the door on the right side of the room, but it was locked. He moved from in front of it and knocked. *"Dobroie utro."*

Again there was no response. The dead-bolt lock on the door looked brand new and out of place on an interior door. Across the room, directly opposite, was another door, leading to the left rear of the house. It was ajar and without any sort of visible lock on it. Cautiously Vail moved to it and pushed it open. At the top of the door, he noticed that some of the cobwebs that hung from the ceiling were matted against it, indicating that it had been closed recently. As he peeked around the jamb, he could see that the room had probably been a bedroom, with a surprisingly large closet crudely constructed in one corner.

Vail pulled his head back and leaned against the wall. Someone was in the house, and as far as he could tell, there were only two places to hide: in the locked room across from him or the closet in this bedroom. The fact that the one room had a locked door made it the more logical. The door, a hollow-core laminate, would not present any problem to kick in, but he wanted to eliminate the closet first. Once he determined that it was empty, then he could call Kalix in and they wouldn't need to watch their backs as they went after the more likely target. With the two of them working in tandem, they could safely make entry into the locked room.

Raising his handgun to eye level, Vail went into the bedroom and moved quietly to the closet. Standing at the side, he grabbed the wooden knob on its door and pulled it open. When nothing happened, he looked in. It was empty, except for a full-length mirror that ran from the top to the bottom. What a bizarre place for a mirror, he thought.

He turned to go but then realized something that hadn't immediately registered when he looked inside. At the top of the mirror, as on the door of the room, the ceiling cobwebs were matted against it. At the same moment, he heard a tiny metallic click that he'd heard a thousand times before. He spun around 180 degrees and fired four shots into the mirror. It exploded as the body of a man fell through it, a silver automatic dropping from his hand.

The cobwebs that were caught against the top of the mirror were in a triangular pattern, indicating that it opened on a hinge, catching them in a pattern similar to the one above the room's door. Vail could now see the secret compartment behind it. The click he'd heard was the gun's safety being released. As he stooped to pick up a piece of the mirror, there were a half-dozen shots fired from behind him. He dove to the side and rolled over, looking for a target.

In the doorway was a second man, slumping to the floor. Vail could see Kalix looking in through the window he'd just shot through. "Steve, you okay?" he shouted, his adrenaline apparently still pulsing.

"Yeah, come around to the front." Vail went to the man whom Kalix had shot and verified that he was dead. Holstering his gun, he walked back to the closet and picked up a piece of the mirror, examining it.

Kalix came in at a trot. "You really are okay, right?"

"Are *you* okay?"

"I heard some shots, and when I looked in the window, I saw this guy coming up behind you ready to fire, so I opened up. He is a bad guy, isn't he?"

Vail smiled. "Not anymore." He held up the mirror fragment. "Two-way glass. I should have realized that the closet was deeper, but the mirror was meant to distort its depth."

"Any idea who they are?"

"I would imagine they're guys who get their paychecks in rubles." Vail looked up at Kalix, who continued to stare at the man he'd just killed. "You want to go wait in the car? I'll take care of searching these two."

"No, no, I'm all right," Kalix said. "Should I have yelled for him to surrender or something first?"

"This isn't exactly a surrendering bunch. If you had yelled, I'd be dead." Vail rolled over the body of the man he'd shot and started going through his pockets.

"They were here to ambush us?" Kalix said.

"They were probably here to ambush me. But now that you've killed one of them, maybe they'll give you equal consideration next time. With Kate in custody, they probably figured I'd be alone."

"Why you?"

"Apparently they're finding me to be a bit of a nuisance. Sakis had a photo of me in Chicago."

Kalix studied Vail's face, looking for fear. "Doesn't that bother you?"

"Never look a gift horse in the mouth."

"A gift horse?"

"I must be moving in the right direction, otherwise why try to kill me? I just have to figure out exactly what I've been doing to upset them."

Kalix chuckled. "Better you than me."

"You're about to have your own problems."

"I am?"

"Somebody needs to call your boss and bring him up to date."

The smile disappeared from Kalix's face. "Who would have thought that keeping you from getting killed would be a bad thing?"

Vail laughed. "Is that a rhetorical question, or do you want an alphabetical list?"

Kalix squatted down next to the second man and started searching him. He pulled a cell phone out of the man's pocket and turned it on. Staring at the screen, Kalix said, "Whoa."

"What?"

Kalix turned the phone so Vail could see it. On the screen was the same photo of Vail that had been found in Sakis's pocket. Vail took it from him and scrolled through the phone's options. "It was sent last night around eleven thirty."

"They must have figured that this would be your next stop. And where one man failed yesterday, they felt two would succeed today."

Vail pushed a couple more of the phone's buttons and handed it back to Kalix. "There's the number the photo was sent from. Think you can get someone to break it down?"

Kalix started dialing his own phone. "What do you think it is?"

"I'm hoping it's a link to whoever is behind all this. But I'm not betting anything over a dollar. Someone's trying awfully hard to make sure Kate stays in prison."

TWENTY-ONE

AFTER MORE THAN THREE HOURS OF INTERROGATION BY THE ANNANDALE POLICE and Bureau agents, Vail and Kalix headed back to Washington and the off-site. "Come on in. I'll buy you a beer," Vail said.

They walked into the workroom, and Kalix motioned toward the wall. "You and Kate sure covered a lot of ground on this."

Vail came back from the kitchen and handed him a beer, cracking open his own. "A lot of it is the tracking information from the phone you guys gave Calculus."

"It looks like a lot more than that." Kalix opened his beer and took a small sip as his phone rang. "John Kalix."

He went over to the desk and got ready to write. Then he dropped the pen and straightened up. "There's no way to trace it at all. . . . You're sure? . . . Okay, then your best guess. . . . Okay, thanks." He disconnected the line. "That was one of the techs. The phone company has no record for that number."

"How can that be?"

"After being told it didn't exist, he called the number and got a busy signal. So, since the number was active, he called a contact who handles covert government 'contingencies,' as he calls it. Best guess is that it's CIA. It's a clearing number. If a source needs to leave a message, he leaves his code name so it'll get routed to his handler. But it's mostly used for dry-cleaning traces, a dead end in the trail. Say you wanted to make a pretext call, like you did today before we went into that house, but you didn't want anyone to be able to trace it. You dial the covert number plus a code and then the number you want to call. It's then put through like a regular call. You can send photos, or text, or anything else you can do with a regular line. And if anyone tries to track it, you get the answer we just did. It doesn't exist. If you call it, it rings busy unless you enter the code."

"How do Russians get access to a CIA tool like that?" Vail asked.

"Maybe one of their moles sold it to them. Once you pay a source for something, you generally feel it belongs to you. But the problem is, we can't even determine if it was the CIA who gave it up. Other agencies know about things like this. We figured it out. Even if we did find out it was CIA, there are hundreds of employees who probably have access, authorized or unauthorized, to that number."

Vail said, "Instead of this getting clearer, it seems like we're getting further and further from any answers."

Kalix didn't answer. He was back at the wall, studying the charts. Vail could see that something had caught his attention, so he sat down on the couch and sipped his beer, waiting.

Finally Kalix turned around. "I haven't told anyone this, but ever since I was up here with Langston and saw these charts and realized that's how you found the three spies, I had a duplicate set made for me from the file. I've been spending a lot of time studying them, especially while you were in Chicago. I really wasn't making too many connections until we came up with this CIA number. See if this makes sense: We know that someone has framed Kate. Most likely the Russians. But why Kate? She's not in counterintelligence, at least not now. And she was only exposed to that work twice. Once in Detroit when you were there and she was supervising a squad covering the Middle East, right?"

"Right."

"And her only other CI assignment was when she had liaison here at headquarters with the CIA. So now with this phone number probably being the agency's, that's twice we've had the CIA come up. The big question is, how do the Russians and the CIA fit into a frame of Kate?"

Vail said, "I don't know."

"I can think of one possibility. Let's say the Russians have a highly placed source in the CIA. But there's a problem. Somewhere in his travels, he ran into Kate Bannon at the wrong time. Maybe he was doing something he shouldn't have been, something that might compromise him, something that, coupled with an upcoming event, might click together for her. So this CIA agent and his Russian handlers now have a problem. Maybe they decide to kill her, but they can't just assassinate her, because the investigation would never cease, and once solved the Russians would be considered more evil than they were during the Cold War. So they decide to make it look like an accident. I assume you know about her 'suicide attempt.'"

"The director told me. He thought it was as ridiculous as I did. If your theory is right, maybe the Russians were trying to make it look like she took her own life. She did think she was slipped something. And once that didn't work, maybe an accidental death would work just as well. Like when we had to rappel off that building and the rope was rigged to look like we'd died trying to escape the fire. We're sure the Russians orchestrated all that. But then they tried to kill just me when I went after Petriv."

"Maybe they thought she'd be with you," Kalix said. "Up to that point, you two had been into everything together."

"So then the Russians went to Plan C, to provide proof that she is guilty of treason and get rid of her permanently. Which was their final, fail-safe plan all along. It's hard to believe that the entire Calculus ruse was set up to protect somebody in the CIA who's spying for the Russians," Vail said. "But it's the only thing that makes sense out of all this." He went to the wall and started examining the charts.

Kalix asked, "Do you think Calculus's movements have something to do with it?"

"I don't know. But Calculus is the key to this, and thanks to these we know everywhere he went until he disappeared. Maybe they are the answer."

Kalix stepped up next to him and glanced at the maze of photos, charts, and notes covering the wall. "Do you want me to stay and help?"

"No, why don't you go get some sleep, and we'll start fresh tomorrow. I'm going to go to bed myself. Call me first thing in the morning." Vail smiled crookedly. "If you dare."

After Kalix left, Vail lay down on the couch and stared at the wall. It was too far away for him to read, but that was good, because he was starting to wonder if there were any larger patterns he was missing. He started to retrace Kalix's theory through the different sections of the information on the wall, but then his burning eyelids slid shut.

VAIL FELT SOMEONE tap him on the leg. "Steve." He opened his eyes and was surprised to see Lucas Bursaw standing over him. "I know it's late, but I saw your car outside and the lights on."

Vail checked his watch. "Late? It's almost five A.M."

"The computer geeks finally finished that Volume Shadow Copy query you suggested. They found fourteen files on Sundra's laptop that had been deleted in the thirty days before she disappeared." Vail sat up, and Bursaw handed him a thick stack of pages with the contents of the files printed out.

Vail let his thumb riffle through them. "That's still a big haystack."

"I was up most of the night with it. There are five of them that look like she was working pretty hard."

"And the other nine?"

"She found nothing illegal and closed them, giving her a reason to delete them."

Vail thought for a second. "So if she was still working on the other five, why delete them?"

"That's why I'm here. They were all wiped from the computer the day she disappeared."

"Sounds promising. Have you taken a look at them?"

"Yeah, but there's nothing that I can see. What do you say we check them out and see if we can get someone to flinch?"

"Luke, I've got something to tell you. Kate's been arrested."

"What!"

Vail then proceeded to tell him everything, from being picked up at the hospital New Year's Eve to his trip to Chicago to the shoot-out the day before.

"Kate? A spy? Even the Bureau can't be that stupid."

"You're right, it's the Justice Department. And they're low-keying everything about it. She hasn't been formally charged. I guess they're hoping if she spends enough time locked up, she'll tell all."

"Don't they have to arraign her?"

"Special provisions have been made. They can hold her for up to ten days before letting her see a judge."

"Whatever misguided thing you're about to do, I'm in," Bursaw said.

"I appreciate it, Luke, but—"

Abruptly Vail got up and walked away as though Bursaw wasn't there. He went to the workroom wall and picked up a blue highlighter. He drew a streak through one of the entries, and then, after searching a few more seconds, he drew the blue slash through a second, then a third. He picked up the phone and dialed Kalix's home number. "Get over here."

Vail hung up and said to no one in particular, "Why didn't I see this before?"

KALIX KNOCKED on the front door, and Vail went down to let him in. "What is it?" he asked Vail.

"I think I found something. Come on."

Once they were upstairs, Kalix noticed Bursaw. "Who's this?"

Vail introduced them. "Luke is at WFO, and he and I go back to Detroit. He's been deputized and given the appropriate death threats."

Kalix shook Bursaw's hand. "That's good enough for me. . . ." The deputy assistant director's voice trailed off with a trace of apprehension.

Vail pointed at the newly highlighted entries on the wall. "On three different occasions, Calculus went to the exact same coordinates. A place that it doesn't make sense for him to go even once."

Kalix studied them for a moment. "What is it?"

Vail went over to the computer and moved the mouse, lighting up the monitor screen. The Bureau satellite was online. "Bryn Mawr Park. About a five-minute drive from . . ." Vail moved the cursor as it traced the map along Route 123 and then Chain Bridge Road.

Kalix took a step closer to the screen. " . . . CIA headquarters at Langley."

"And that means what?" Bursaw asked.

Vail looked at Kalix and then at Bursaw. "I have no idea."

Kalix said, "It means we're one step closer to . . . What time of the day were these three contacts?"

Vail picked up a file and started making notes. When he finished, he handed Kalix a slip of paper. "At 10:03 A.M., 1:42 P.M., and 10:48 A.M."

Kalix turned around and smiled at them.

"What?" Vail asked.

"All three are during working hours. Have you ever been to Langley?"

"No."

"You can't get in or out without swiping your ID."

"So the CIA will have a record of people leaving headquarters on those dates, around those times. That's great, but I doubt they'll be willing to share that with us."

"I have a good friend over there. We went to law school together. And he's in Personnel."

Vail pushed the phone toward Kalix. He picked it up and dialed.

After Kalix hung up, he said, "Maybe by this afternoon. He has to sneak around a little to do it. He's going to call me at the office. As you probably heard, I had to promise him first notification if something comes up on one of theirs." Kalix got up to leave.

Vail asked, "Where are you going?"

"Back to the office. I have a meeting I can't miss. I'll call you as soon as I hear anything."

After he left, Vail went back to the wall and started scanning it. Finally he turned to Bursaw and said, "Let's get out of here for a while. What do you say we go cover some of those leads on Sundra?"

"You sure you want to bother with that now?"

"I need something to do. Let's go make some people nervous."

FOR THE NEXT THREE HOURS, the two men fell into an old rhythm developed during three years of friendship and working together in Detroit. They complemented each other well, picking up on the familiar nuances of criminal behavior, which weren't much different whether they were in D.C. or Michigan.

The first stop was a Middle Eastern travel agency. Sundra's file did not document why she was investigating them, but once Vail and Bursaw started interviewing the owner, they discovered that he had a large marijuana-growing operation in the building's basement. They decided that someone had flagged the premises based on the inexplicable electrical consumption caused by the massive lighting system used.

The next one turned out to be an identification mill operated out of a residence. The individual in charge of the operation provided forged driver's licenses and car titles for a hundred dollars apiece. He had been arrested years before and received probation. When he told the two agents that his lawyer said he would probably be continued on probation if caught, Vail and Bursaw felt satisfied that he had nothing to gain from Sundra Boston's disappearance.

"Two down, three to go," Vail said as they got back into the car. "Lucas Bursaw, tell us who our next contestant is?" Before Bursaw could answer, Vail's cell phone rang. It was Kalix. Vail listened for a few seconds. "Okay, we'll meet you there."

Bursaw said, "What's up?"

"We're going to have to put this on hold. John has that list of CIA employees."

TWENTY-TWO

WHEN THEY GOT TO THE OFF-SITE, JOHN KALIX WAS PARKED OUTSIDE WAITING for them. They went upstairs, and Kalix handed Vail the list of names, along with their photos.

"Names and photos—you must have something on this guy."

"Actually, I do. Like I said, he and I went all the way back to law school. We were pretty close. We were out one night having a few cocktails, and he spotted a source of his in the bar. I guess he thought I'd be impressed, so he introduced me to the guy. The source was horrified that someone would see us, and he tried to leave. My friend caught him outside and started slapping him around. The asset made a stink, and I wound up lying about it to a couple of their internal grunts. He was absolved, and now he's paying the bill."

Vail made a quick count. "Nine. That's not bad. Have you run the names through indices?"

"Personally searched them myself. Nothing."

"We have one advantage right now—surprise. If we confronted them, we'd lose that. Besides, from the moment these people decide to start spying, they're constantly rehearsing their answers to any questions about their loyalty. Anybody have any ideas?"

Kalix and Bursaw both shook their heads.

"Sorry, boys, there appears only one thing we can do," Vail said. "We've got to show the photos to Kate."

"How are you going to do that?" Kalix asked. "They won't let anyone from the Bureau near her."

"John, this is where we separate the temporary help from the truly self-destructive."

Kalix laughed. "Talk about making something sound irresistible."

"Come on, how many FBI agents can say they helped a federal prisoner escape?"

"If you mean without becoming a federal prisoner themselves, I'm going to guess zero."

ALFRED BEVSON, the United States Attorney for the District of Columbia, sat at his desk rereading a newspaper article regarding a shooting in Annandale the day before. The facts seemed deliberately vague, and that, coupled with the participants' being two unnamed FBI agents and two suspected East European illegal immigrants, made him wonder if it had something to do with the Kate Bannon case. His secretary buzzed him. "Yes."

"There's an attorney by the name of Karl Brickman on the line. He insists on talking to you."

"Just tell him I'm in a meeting and I'll call him back."

"He said he was representing Kate Bannon."

"What?" Bevson swore under his breath. The FBI must have leaked her detention. "Okay, Claire, put him through."

Bevson knew that the Bureau was upset with him for cutting off their access to her, but by his own admission their director was too close to her to let the FBI stay actively involved. The last thing Bevson needed right now was more bad press. They'd been all over him recently on the issue of the escalating crime rate in the District, and there were rumors that the present administration was about to replace him because of it. The Bannon case was supposed to sweep all that into obscurity, and it probably would once its depth was reported to the world.

If they fired him anyway, the important thing was having a soft place to land. If he could publicly manipulate his role in this treason case against an FBI higher-up, the big firms would be calling. Washington loved a good spy story, and there were firms that would hire him for no other reason than to hear the insider gossip. But all that would be diluted if the FBI was going to leak every detail of the case, as they usually did when it was to their advantage. For once he was going to beat them to the punch. But first he would have to put out another one of their well-placed brush fires. "This is Al Bevson, can I help you?"

"Karl Brickman. I see from your online bio that you went to Georgetown Law, so I know you were taught the concept of due process. Apparently you think there's some exception to the rule when it's an FBI agent who's been charged."

"I'm sorry, who is your client again?"

"You want to know who my client is? Put on the six o'clock news tonight and you'll find out. It won't matter which network—they'll all be carrying it."

"You told my secretary it's a Kate Bannon."

"And you've had her in custody for three days without taking her before a judge or a magistrate. In civilized countries that's called an abduction."

"Mr. Brickman, if we were holding someone as you have suggested and you went to the media, be advised you could be violating national security."

"If you consider what you've done to Kate Bannon as being in the best interests of national security, then it needs to be violated."

"There's a lot you don't know about the case."

"Apparently there's a lot you don't know about prosecutorial malfeasance. I've already contacted the assistant director at the FBI who has jurisdiction over this case, William Langston, and given him the same option I'm about to give you. If I don't meet with my client within three hours, in three hours and one minute I start making calls to the media."

The door opened, and Bevson's secretary came in and handed him a note.

Assistant Director Langston, line 3. Urgent!

"Mr. Brickman, can I call you back?"

"No, you can't. In exactly three hours, I'll be at the FBI building. If I'm not immediately taken to see my client, you know where I'll be going next." The line went dead.

Bevson punched the line-three button. "Al Bevson."

"Bill Langston. I'm the Counterterrorism AD. Did you get a call from a lawyer named Brickman?"

"That's who I was on the phone with. Who is he?"

"I made a couple of calls after he threatened me. His practice is primarily criminal. A one-man firm, and he is not a media hound. I guess that's why I've never heard of him, but the word is he's the last guy you want to have coming at you."

"How the hell did he find out about Bannon?"

"I was going to ask you. You're the one who won't let us near her, remember?"

Bevson said, "Someone might think a call to a lawyer would be a good way to get even with us for that."

"It's just as likely that someone from your side did it. You're the one with all the lawyers. Maybe you should ask around and find out if any of your people know him personally."

Bevson knew that was true. These days, "leaking" was an act of self-indulgence. "It's out there now, so it doesn't matter. What do you think we should do about it?"

"This cannot get to the media. Until we can secure some cooperation from Bannon or we can be sure no one else is involved, we've got to keep this buttoned up. Every time there's the least hint of someone's being identified, that person is murdered, and each time it's arranged so it looks like the Bureau had a hand in it. How about this: Have a couple of marshals bring her over with one of your assistant prosecutors, and we'll give her the full-court press one more time before Brickman shows up. He told me he was coming over at three o'clock. In fact, how soon can you get her here?"

"I'm guessing an hour or so."

"Good, I'll line up our best available interviewers, and they can take a shot at her."

"Can my man sit in?"

"The best interviews are done one-on-one, but if she breaks, your man can draft up the formal statement, and then you'll be able to spin it any way you want."

"I don't care who gets credit, I'm just—"

"Please, Al, save it for the press conference. Just have them call my extension when they bring her in—2117."

KATE SAT IN HER CELL at the Correction Treatment Facility in southeast Washington. It was where all female prisoners arrested in the District of Columbia were housed. The cell had a window, but it had been covered over with sheet metal, which made the cement-block cubicle seem that much smaller. She had never experienced claustrophobia, but the moment they shut the door, she felt a sense of mild suffocation, as if the air were being secretly drawn out of the space, or at least the oxygen level was being manipulated to a level that would not allow logical thought.

A concrete bed with a thin mattress, a seatless toilet, and four pale green walls were all she'd seen for the last three days, except for the matronly guard with a lifeless face who brought her meals twice a day.

Kate was well aware that this sensory and social isolation had a purpose. It was to soften her up. But it wasn't the austere surroundings that were having an effect. It was the three days. Three days without someone rushing to her cell, throwing open the door and telling her that a terrible mistake had been made, something she was waiting for even now.

When arrested, she was confronted with the evidence: the photos, the prints, and the dust on her shoes. She had to admit that if she'd been on the other side of the table, she wouldn't have been interested in listening to the unprovable denials that she presented in her defense.

All of a sudden, she realized she was crying. Not full sobbing, but she could feel the weight of her tears working their way down her cheeks. She couldn't remember the last time she cried, probably when her mother had died. She suddenly realized just how scared she was.

Even if she were somehow miraculously cleared of the charges, her career would be destroyed. It had been hanging by a thread ever since her "attempted suicide." Legally, people could be found not guilty, but within the pedantic confines of the Bureau she would never be judged innocent.

Isolated like this, with no apparent end in sight, she couldn't help but worry that somehow this case would be proved at trial. The evidence wasn't airtight, but conversely she had absolutely nothing to refute it. The only thing that was keeping her sane was knowing that Vail was out there somewhere. If anyone could unravel this, it would be him. But there was a very good chance he didn't even know she'd been arrested. She let out a short, hysterical laugh. It had been part of their plan to keep these arrests out of the public eye. And the last time she saw Vail, she'd sided with the Bureau against him. Then she was told that he had again been stripped of his credentials. Because she'd told him there was no possibility of a personal relationship between them, he'd undoubtedly left Washington by now, on his way to Florida, where no one knew how to contact him. Luke might have been able to track him down, but of course Luke wouldn't know about her arrest either.

Her thoughts were broken by the sound of the cell door opening. She stood up in anticipation of rescue, but it was the same female guard, her face stony as usual, who set down a metal tray and left.

ASSISTANT UNITED STATES ATTORNEY Fred Bisset had been put in charge of Kate Bannon's prosecution the day she was arrested. The case against her had been damning, with one exception: She'd helped gather the evidence against the other spies that had led to her unmasking. But in all probability, Bisset theorized, she was trying to find any evidence against her and destroy it before it came to anyone's attention. Despite everyone's best efforts, she had steadfastly maintained her innocence. Then, an hour ago, he'd received a call from the United States Attorney himself, ordering him to get her over to FBI headquarters ASAP.

That was why he was now walking into the J. Edgar Hoover Building with Kate, who was flanked by two U.S. Marshals, one male and one female. Bisset had made the decision that if she were handcuffed and brought into her place of employment, any remaining secrecy about her status would be destroyed. And that would certainly preclude any admissions she might be about to make.

Bisset went to the receptionist, showed his identification, and told the woman that they were expecting him at extension 2117. She dialed the number and said, "Someone will be right down."

Within a minute Lucas Bursaw got off the freight elevator that was away from the mainstream traffic and held the door open. He was careful not to show any recognition of Kate, hoping to send her the message to do the same. "Mr. Bisset!" he yelled over to the group. "We can take this one!"

They walked to the elevator, and as they got on, Bursaw moved to the back of the car. "We're going to room 349." He leaned forward slightly and pointed at the buttons. "Can you press the third floor, please?" As the female marshal hit the button, Bursaw slipped a small, folded piece of paper into the back of Kate's waistband.

When the door opened on the third floor, Bursaw said, "It's to the right. Number 349."

Once the four of them were in the room and seated, Bursaw said, "Can I get anyone anything?" When they declined, he said, "I'll be standing by in the director's suite if you need anything. The extension there is 1207." He wrote down the number and handed it to the AUSA. Then Bursaw closed the door behind him.

Immediately Kate said, "I'd like to use the ladies' room before we get started."

Bisset looked at the marshals and pointed at the female. "Okay, but she'll be going inside with you."

"Fine." Kate led the way, and when they got there, the female marshal went inside and checked it for avenues of escape while the male stayed with the prisoner. When she came out, she said, "No other doors or windows." The male nodded. Once the two women were inside,

Kate went into the stall and shut the door. She took out the note and read it: *Tell them you'll talk, but only after you apologize to the director in person.* It was in Vail's handwriting. "About time, bricklayer," she whispered.

"What?" the female marshal called in to her.

"Sorry, nothing." She flushed the note down the toilet and came out.

Once they were back in the interview room with Bisset, Kate, for the first time, took a good look at him. He was in his early thirties, and even though he was severely balding, he kept the remaining patches of his hair closely cropped. Without paying much attention to his attempted banter on the way over, she remembered his using the line "I'm no fool—I graduated from Stanford Law School."

"What time is it, Fred?" she asked.

Though he hadn't noticed it before, he now detected some warmth in her attractive face. He quickly checked his watch and said, "It's almost two."

Kate examined him more closely and decided that anyone who would cut his hair that short, drawing attention to the uncomeliness of male pattern baldness, was someone who probably had an inability to interpret common social cues, especially those of rejection. Book-smart with absolutely no people skills, something she suspected was going to be to her advantage. "I'm sorry, where did you say you went to law school?" She was careful to ask the question with just a hint of sarcasm.

"Stanford. I thought I mentioned that."

"I guess you did. I'm just a little tired. Bet you were the top of your class." This time the sarcasm was as obvious as she could make it. She glanced at the two marshals and could see that they were experienced enough in handling prisoners that all conversations around them were no more than white noise.

"I made law review," he answered, trying, but failing, to sound humble.

"It's pretty obvious how smart you are. Me, I just *thought* I was smart. I'm tired of all this. I'd like to make a statement."

Bisset straightened up, appearing as though he hadn't been paying attention and wasn't sure what she'd said. "You want to make a statement?"

"Can't get anything past you law-review boys. Yes, I'd like to make a statement."

"Now you're being smart." Quickly he dug into his briefcase and pulled out a pad of legal paper. "Where would you like to start?"

"I'd like to start with an apology to my director, Mr. Lasker."

"As soon as we get your statement."

"I see him first or there is no statement."

"You're the prisoner, Miss Bannon."

"This offer expires in five seconds . . . four . . . three . . ."

Bisset grabbed the phone on the desk. "Okay, I'll get him on the line."

"No. This has to be in person. Face-to-face. He's been very good to me, and I owe him that much."

Bisset stiffened, and it took a moment for him to realize what had to be done next. He dialed the number that the black agent had left him. Bursaw answered, "Director's office."

"Yes, this is Assistant United States Attorney Bisset. Miss Bannon has had a change of heart and is willing to make a statement, but first she says she needs to talk to the director."

"About what?" Bursaw asked, as skeptically as possible.

"She wants to apologize to him."

"I don't know if he wants to talk to her."

"She says she won't make a statement until she can."

"Hang on." Bisset heard the line go on hold, and then, within a minute, Bursaw came back on. "He said he'll see her. Let me get another agent, and we'll come down to get her."

Ten minutes later there was a knock at the door, and when the marshal opened it, Luke Bursaw was standing there, and behind him was Steve Vail. Bisset said, "You'll bring her right back here after she's done with the director." It wasn't a question but an order.

"The director says she's got five minutes and that's all," Bursaw said. "So you'll have her back in no more than twenty minutes."

The elevator car that Kate, Vail, and Bursaw got into had a half-dozen other employees in it, so they didn't speak until they were out the front door of FBI headquarters. Kate said, "It took you long enough. I almost forgot what you looked like, Stan."

As they walked toward their car, Vail watched her profile in the clear winter sunlight, her breath clouding the cold air in rhythmic streams. She took a deeper, stuttering breath, her freedom evidently registering. "Actually, it's Steve."

"I assume that since you've turned me into an escaped federal prisoner, you still haven't figured out who's responsible for setting me up."

"After looking at the evidence, I'd say your innocence is questionable."

"Then why did you break me out, Stan?"

"I thought by now you'd be ready for a conjugal visit."

"Suddenly prison isn't looking so bad."

They got to the car, and Bursaw climbed in. Kate grabbed Vail and turned him around, kissing him fully. "Thanks, bricklayer." She got in.

"Let's see if you're thanking me when this all goes south."

Suddenly her smile was gone, and her eyes started to well up. "Sorry, Steve, but all this is scaring me."

"You'd be a fool not to be scared." He put his arm around her. Then he took out his credentials and showed them to her.

"I thought you had to give those up to Langston."

"And who's the one person in the Bureau who can rescind my being fired?"

"The director?"

"So you've got friends in high places. Plus, you're innocent. Or so I'm told. I promise you you're not spending another minute in jail." Then Vail filled her in on his trip to Chicago and the shoot-out he and Kalix had been involved in. He told her about his phone call to the United States Attorney, with him posing as her attorney and Kalix playing the telephone role of his boss, William Langston.

"Kalix did all that for me?" she said.

"What about me?"

"How many times do I have to thank you? You've really gotten needy while I've been in the big house."

"But unlike John I'm not trying to suck up to the director," Vail said.

"That's a great way to talk about a guy who saved your life."

"Yeah, well, I'm sure you'll find some way to get even with him for that."

AUSA FRED BISSET checked his wristwatch again. It was now exactly twenty minutes since the two agents had left with Kate Bannon, and it was starting to seem a little too long. He again called the extension the black agent had given him for the director's office. It rang six or seven times before a female answered it. "Hello."

"*Hello?* This is Assistant United States Attorney Fred Bisset. Let me speak to the director, please."

"The director? This is the employees' break room. Let me get you back to the switchboard."

When the operator came on the line, Bisset again identified himself and asked to be put through to the director's office. He waited a moment, then heard, "Director Lasker's office."

"This is AUSA Bisset. Could I speak to the director, please?"

"I'm sorry, he's in New York for a regional conference."

"Then can you transfer me to Assistant Director Langston?"

"I'm sorry, he's with the director."

TWENTY-THREE

AS BURSAW DROVE CAUTIOUSLY THROUGH THE CITY'S STREETS, VAIL ASKED Kate, "Do you have any idea what this is about?"

"It's all I've been thinking about since they came for me. I have no idea."

"Could it be something to do with the CIA?"

"The CIA? Why them?"

"It's better if you answer my questions first."

"Okay. Let's see, the CIA. The only real contact I've had with them was when I had Bureau liaison with them. I was over there almost every day. More there than at headquarters, actually. But I think I already told you about that."

"Ever have problems with anyone there? Any suspicions about anything?"

"No, not that I can remember."

Vail took out the nine photographs of the CIA employees that Kalix had given him and handed them to her. "Do you know any of these people?"

Kate went through them slowly, carefully studying their features, knowing that work ID photos, due to the regimented posing and general lack of quality, can be more difficult to identify. When she finished, she shuffled back and picked out one. "He's the only one I know. Myles Rellick. He was one of my contacts there."

"Anything about him that didn't sit right with you?"

"Not really. Do you think he's involved in this?"

Vail explained about finding the CIA safe phone number, Calculus's three Bryn Mawr Park visits, and how Kalix had narrowed the times down to the nine men in the photos. "You must have seen something, or at least they think you did."

"I don't know, the guy was beige wallpaper. Nothing sticks out about him."

"You don't need to dwell on it. Just let it roll around in the back of your head for a while. Maybe something will surface."

"Where are we heading?"

"Thanks to Luke, we have a safe place to stay."

"Didn't Bonnie and Clyde say that once?" Kate said.

Bursaw said, "My sister is a history professor at Georgetown, and right now she's on a sabbatical, in Portugal. That's her area of expertise. She has an apartment near the school. There's a car. I'm kind of in charge of maintaining both. She won't be back until May for a summer course she's teaching. It's just a one-bedroom, but it's well stocked with food. And she's about your size if you need clothes."

"What about all the files and information we have at the off-site?" she asked Vail. "Won't we need that?"

"It's all in the trunk. And we took photos of everything on the walls. I don't know if they're going to go public looking for you—and me, I suppose, since it won't take long to figure out who helped you. But I don't think they can announce to the world that you escaped, seeing as how they refuse to acknowledge that you'd been arrested. Lasker's got Langston out of town for a couple of days, leaving Kalix in charge of counterintelligence operations, so the Bureau won't be burning a lot of manpower hunting for us. And Luke should be cool for a while, because if they do try to identify Unknown Black Agent Number One, they'll start at headquarters. No one knows about us being friends. We should have a couple of days before there's any type of full-court press."

Bursaw turned off Rock Creek Parkway onto Pennsylvania Avenue and then turned up Twenty-eighth Street. Three blocks later he pulled up to a small apartment building. "This is it," he said, getting out and opening the trunk.

Inside his sister's residence, Bursaw put the box containing the files on a desk in the living room and handed Vail the keys. "You're now officially in charge of them." He pointed at a large fish tank with a couple dozen disinterested tropical fish swimming around. "The car is a powder blue VW Bug. It's parked in the garage. The key card to get in and out is over the visor."

"Are you going somewhere?" Vail asked.

"I've got to go home, change, and go to the office. I hope you're right and they won't be looking for me. As soon as I put in an appearance and see if there's any general alarm for you two, I'll be back to give you a hand."

"Thanks, Luke," Kate said, and kissed him on the cheek.

Vail walked him out. "Is there an access code for your sister's answering machine?"

"Good idea. We can leave each other messages on it if you go out. It's 777."

"I'll call Kalix and let him know what Kate said about the photos. It looks like Myles Rellick is our best bet, but I have no idea where to start. We can't do surveillance, or a wiretap, or even search his financial background. This fugitive stuff isn't as easy as it looks."

"I'm sure you'll figure something out. Especially since it's for Kate, her being such a good *friend* and all."

"I told you, it's complicated."

"The best things always are."

When Vail came back in, he found Kate looking through the bedroom closet. "Sorry we didn't have time to get some of your clothes."

"I'd rather wear three-day-old clothes than a nice crisp prison uniform."

"Anything there?"

"I'll find something," she said. "I'm sorry I got emotional in the car."

"Any CIA epiphanies yet?"

"Not yet, but I'm too tired to summon up any real memory. I'm going to take a shower and get some sleep. You could probably use a couple of hours yourself. You look beat."

He smiled at her mischievously. "I could use a shower, too. This place looks like it would have a limited supply of hot water."

"That's good," she said in a playful tone, "because it sounds like you could use a cold shower."

After a couple of seconds, Vail said, "Kate, I'm sorry. This is all my fault. The whole thing was a setup, and you're paying the price. I was so smug figuring out those puzzles. 'Ariadne's thread.' I should have picked up on something."

"Like what? Everything was falling into place."

"Like their killing the moles, and just as we got to them. They knew just when to kill them—because they were sending us to them. That should have registered with me."

Gently she took his hand in hers. "I should be terrified right now, but— No, that's not right. I am terrified. But with you here I know this is going to end well. So *please,* don't stop being you."

"Probably the smartest thing you could do right now is be worried."

"Well, bricklayer, I'm so worried that I'm going to sleep. You probably should, too."

Vail picked up one of the pillows from the bed. "Maybe you're right. I'll stretch out on the couch and see if I can't nod off as soon as I call John."

A FEW HOURS LATER, Kate walked into the living room, her face still full of sleep. "Tell me it's New Year's morning and I just had a bad dream."

Vail sat up on the couch. "I don't suppose you dreamed about who would do this to you."

"Nothing. As far as the CIA people at Langley, I was kind of a ghost. Float in, do a little paperwork, say hello to a few people, and float out."

"You've got the Russians on you. You're a threat to somebody. I know you supervised security work in Detroit, but that was the Middle East, right?"

"Right."

"When was the last time you worked the Russians?"

"Never. When I rotated out of Detroit, I went to OPR for a year, and then I was a unit chief in the Counterintelligence Division, but it was an administrative position, the liaison with the CIA. I had a desk at Langley, but it wasn't like I was there sixty hours a week."

"Where else were you assigned?"

"After my CIA stint, which was about a year and a half, I got tapped to go to New York as an ASAC. But just before I was to leave, the director called me in and told me he wanted me to be the deputy AD in the general criminal division. So I haven't been in counterintelligence for almost two years. And then it had nothing to do with the Russians."

Vail was silent, staring back at her without seeing her. He was quiet longer than usual. "Did you handle any assets when you were there?"

"No, I haven't seen an informant since I was a street agent," she said. Vail just shook his head.

There was a knock at the door, and then they heard a key in the lock. Bursaw walked in, carrying a large pizza box.

"How's the manhunt going?" Vail asked.

"Not a word about it at WFO and nothing on the news. I went by the off-site, and there are a couple of guys sitting on it. They look like marshals."

Vail said to Kate, "Then they're on your apartment, too."

Bursaw opened the box and pulled off a piece of pizza. "So what's the plan?"

Vail pulled off a slice and handed it with a napkin to Kate. "I wish I knew."

A few minutes later, there was another knock at the door, which caused everyone to stop talking. Vail peered out the peephole. It was John Kalix. He came in carrying an oversize briefcase. "I think I found something," he said.

Kate stood up and hugged him. "Thanks for everything, John, except for maybe keeping the big galoot here alive."

"I'm kind of new at all this, but I'll bear that in mind next time."

"What's going on at headquarters?" Vail asked.

"I wish you could have seen that AUSA when he came storming into my office. He was making all kinds of threats until I asked him, with as incredulous a tone as possible, why his boss would accept a lawyer's identity over the telephone. He said the entire hoax was perpetrated by FBI agents in the FBI building and that he was going to get to the bottom of it. Needless to say, he didn't ask for any Bureau manpower to hunt down the wily Katherine Bannon. My sources tell me he has two two-man teams of marshals looking for you, and that's all."

"As long as Luke isn't identified as part of this, we should be safe here," Vail said. "You said you found something."

Kalix took a portable DVD player out of his case. "While I was sitting around trying to look nonchalant after you and Kate disappeared, I got an idea. I started thinking about the spy dust that's part of the evidence against Kate. Since we know she's innocent, it means that the Russians must have collected it when we used it on that SVR intelligence officer, Nikolai Gulin. And maybe it isn't a coincidence that he's also the one in the photo with Kate. So I ran him through everything we have. Remember I told you that he was very elusive, but that we did have photos and videos of him taken during surveillances a couple of years ago? When I reviewed everything, I found this. It was taken at the Fredricksburg Antique Mall, which is far away enough from Washington that it was a good spot for a meeting or a drop. Anyone ever been there?"

Kate said, "I was there once . . . I don't know . . . a couple of years ago, visiting a girlfriend of mine who had just moved to Fredricksburg from Colorado. It's kind of a fun place. They had some interesting stuff."

"Then you know people don't go there without some interest in antiques, even if it's casual. According to the surveillance log, Gulin never went into one shop or even looked in a window. It is, however, a place where it's not easy to follow someone, which is probably why he chose it. As I said before, we had information that he was working an FBI agent. In this video it looks like he could be meeting with someone, but we couldn't be sure because we lost him within minutes of this being shot. There was never any real effort to identify the second individual."

"Why not?" Kate asked.

"This doesn't leave the room." He looked at each of them to make sure they understood. "Langston reviewed the matter, watched the video, and made the decision, almost arbitrarily, that the second individual had nothing to do with Gulin." Kalix set the player down in front of Kate and pushed the Play button.

Everyone crowded in behind her and watched. The secreted camera bounced as it followed the Russian. Finally the target stopped and turned around. Kalix hit Pause. "That's Gulin," he said. "Ever seen him before, Kate?"

She studied the image for a moment. "Not that I remember."

"Now watch when he stops in front of that bench." Kalix hit Play once more. Gulin's back was again to the camera, and a man walked up next to him, his back also to the camera. Then the man turned around, and they could see his profile. Kalix reached over Kate's shoulder and hit Pause. "What do you think, Kate? Do you recognize him?"

She leaned forward. "It does look like Rellick. Maybe if I saw him move around a little more."

Kalix hit Play again. The individual turned his back to the camera and appeared to be discreetly talking to Gulin. Then he casually looked to his right and abruptly turned to his left. He lowered his head and said something brief. For an instant the camera jerkily panned over to the right, trying to film whatever it was that had caught his attention. "I think it is him," she said. Both men on the screen then separated and walked off in different directions.

Kalix hit the Stop button. "I spent an hour looking at his photo and then the at video. It's hard to tell if you don't know the person, but it looked like a match to me."

Kate replayed the video a couple more times. "I'm almost positive that's him," she said. "Does this mean I'll be cleared?"

"It would be better if we could be positive it's him. What do you think, Steve?"

Vail didn't answer but instead reached over and backed up the DVD. Then he pressed the Slow Motion button. When the camera panned over to what had distracted the individual believed to be Rellick, Vail hit Pause. Kate gasped. "That's Jennifer. And me." The woman she had identified as the friend she'd been at the mall with was near the edge of the frame, and half of Kate was next to her. They'd been all but invisible when the video was run at normal speed. "He must have seen me, and that's what spooked him."

"Then all this was to protect Rellick," Kalix said. "He thought you could put him with his Russian handler." He laughed. "All this to get rid of you, and you never even saw him. He must be a very good source for them to go through all this to protect him."

"But why now?" Kate asked. "That was a couple of years ago."

Vail said, "Maybe it was your momentary appointment to Counter-intelligence AD. Even though you turned it down, they probably figured it could happen again at any time."

Bursaw said, "I hate to be the bearer of grim reality, but we've still got to prove that Kate is innocent. We can't go to the prosecutor, because Kate is in escaped status, Steve is wanted, and if I show my face, they'll know who the colored guy was. Even if you took this back to the Bureau and got everybody on board, John, wouldn't surveillance and wiretaps take months or longer?"

Vail said, "Luke's right. You're the only one with any mobility, John. Can you go back to your CIA contact and give him what we've found so far and let them run with it?"

"I can, but they're going to do the same surveillance and wiretaps that the Bureau would do. And don't forget it's their agency, so they're not going to be in any hurry to prove that one of their own has gone over. Eventually, because there's no hard evidence, it could get swept under the rug. In the meantime Kate is still wanted."

Vail said, "We have one weapon we're ignoring—the petty jealousies between the Bureau and the CIA. When is Langston due back?"

Kalix said, "He and the director should be returning tomorrow afternoon."

"Go tell your contact that you're repaying him for his information and the photos. Give him everything. But tell him that the director and your boss are due back the day *after* tomorrow, and then you've got to give it to them. Tell him he's got two days to make a move against Rellick if he doesn't want the FBI to make the arrest."

"That just might work. They would do anything to prevent that embarrassment," Kalix said. He unplugged the DVD player and put it in his case. "I'll give you a call as soon as I talk to him."

Bursaw said, "I'll walk you out, John. I want to take a quick stroll around the neighborhood and make sure our friends from the Marshals Service aren't watching us."

After they left, Kate asked Vail, "How'd you see Jennifer and me on that DVD?"

"As good-looking as she is, how do you not see her? To tell the truth, I didn't even notice you."

Kate laughed. "Then how did you know it was Jennifer? You've never met her."

"Like I said, I just saw a pretty girl and wanted to see more of her."

"She's a very good friend, but I've got to tell you, she's very particular about who she dates. White-collar only, so reel it in, bricklayer."

"I'll bet you used to say the same thing."

"Okay, we'll go with 'used to.'"

TWENTY-FOUR

THE PHONE RANG. BURSAW PICKED IT UP AND PUSHED THE SPEAKER BUTTON. "Go ahead, John. We're all here."

"My guy went for it. In two months Rellick is being posted to a foreign assignment. He wouldn't say exactly where, but it sounded like someplace critical. They're about to start a reinvestigation of him, including a polygraph, which is routine with any sensitive assignment. It may be another reason he's still worried about Kate. Anyway, they're going to ambush him with the polygraph first thing tomorrow morning, making some excuse about an upcoming shortage of polygraphers that necessitates it being done now. Once they get him strapped in, it'll be all ahead full on the video and Gulin. That, along with the usual questions about contacts with foreign nationals, accepting money, et cetera, should blow the needles off the box."

"Are you going to be there?"

"Yes. I told him I'd like to watch, just out of curiosity, but I think my pal suspects it's because I want to make sure that they're pushing it. Otherwise we'd have to take over."

"We'll wait to hear from you."

Vail disconnected the line. "Let's hope he breaks."

"And if he doesn't?" Kate asked.

"I'm turning you in for the reward."

"In that case you should take me to dinner tonight. You know, the condemned, a hearty meal and all."

Bursaw said, "There's a couple of decent restaurants within walking distance." They both looked at him as if they'd forgotten he was there. "No, no, I'm not inviting myself."

"Please come, Luke," Vail said with mock insincerity.

He laughed. "Just for that, I should go along. But I have a life of my own to screw up." He got up and slipped on his topcoat. "I'll be by first thing in the morning—unless there's a tie on the doorknob or U.S. Marshals crime-scene tape across the jamb."

DUSK ADDED TO THEIR ANONYMITY as Kate and Vail strolled down M Street, ignoring the falling temperature. She had ahold of his arm and pulled herself closer with each sharp gust of wind. "Sure it's not too cold to walk?" he asked.

"After three days in a cell, it feels good." They were early for their dinner reservation and turned into a brick courtyard that housed several small shops and art galleries to window-gaze. One of them displayed several sculptures and ceramic works. "Anything you like?" she asked idly.

She was wearing Luke's sister's navy camel-hair coat. There was something about the color that made her hair and skin luminous. Her long, dark lashes contrasted her flashing blue eyes perfectly. He took a half step back to look her over. "As a matter of fact . . . there is."

He continued to stare at her until she bumped her hip into his in amused protest. "I was referring to the items on the other side of the glass."

A series of sculptures were displayed, some metal, some bronze and clay. There was even one in wax of a heavy-bodied figure lying on its side in a catatonic curl. A series of semicollapsed ceramic containers caught his attention. They leaned at different angles and, although the same general shape, were different in size. Vail appraised all of them. "These people are legitimate artists."

"I don't get it. Why do you think this stuff is good and yours isn't? I know I've only seen two of your sculptures, but they were at least as good as these."

He waved his hand across the window respectfully. "This isn't about technical ability. There's an instinct involved in creating something like this, an instinct that even they don't understand. They are real artists because they have to let loose on the world what they create. The belief in themselves to say, 'This is my art, and if you don't like it, I don't really care. Here it is anyway. I'd almost rather that you didn't buy it. It's what separates me from people like you.'"

" 'People like you'? You actually mean *you*."

"That's right, people like me, because I can't put it out there for anyone to judge."

"Because they might not like it?"

"Everything I do is carefully orchestrated so people aren't allowed to examine me. That's why I sneaked out of that bank robbery, and that's why no one except you has ever seen my sculptures."

"So what you're really saying is that it's not just your art, but you're not willing to put any part of your life out there to examine."

"That's my choice, yes."

"Why would you sculpt if you didn't want anyone to see it?"

"It's something I want to be good at."

"And how will you decide when you're good enough?"

"I guess I'll know."

Kate stared back through the window, carefully measuring what she was about to say. "Now I know why you like being a bricklayer."

"This should be good."

"All brick walls look the same. As long as they're level and straight, they look like every other wall in the world. No creativity, no individuality, and—apparently most important—no judgment."

Vail stared at the objects in the window for a while longer, ignoring the icy wind. Kate stood huddled against him. The expression on his face told her she'd stirred something that had been deeply buried. She waited for one of their arguments to begin.

"On my fourteenth birthday, my father announced to me that he was going to start teaching me to lay brick. I had worked the summers and weekends for years as his laborer, probably since I was ten or eleven. Naturally I was excited to finally learn. I'd watched him for years, envious of his skill. Something a boy does no matter what kind of father he has. That day we were building a chimney, and he let me lay the last three feet of it. When I was done, I thought it looked pretty good, at least for a first try. He sent me down to start cleaning up. Fifteen minutes later he came down without saying a word. The next day I was surprised when we went back to the same job. He put up the ladder and told me to go up on the roof. When I got there, the entire top of the chimney I'd built had been torn down, the bricks scattered all around it. He told me that I'd done a lousy job and that this was the only way I'd learn. He then had me go down and mix the mortar, bring it up, and watch him rebuild it."

"That's awful. But at least you learned how to do it, right?"

Vail laughed with a tinge of anger, not at her but at what he was about to recall. "This wasn't some apprenticeship hazing or poor parenting technique, this was him getting even."

"Even for what?"

"Who knows? For having to raise me by himself. I don't know. It seemed as if his whole life was about getting even with everyone. That's who he was."

"That happened a long time ago."

Vail laughed again, and this time it had an edge to it that told her she was being naïve. "If that had happened once, it would probably be the kind of story you'd laugh at during a Thanksgiving meal, but every time I finished something after that, he would send me to clean up while he stayed behind. I never knew until the next morning whether he'd torn it down or not. Sometimes I wouldn't sleep, wondering if I had pleased my father, which is very important to a fourteen-year-old, especially if there was no one else around. He did it the rest of the summer. If we stopped somewhere for lunch and he started drinking whiskey, I didn't have to wonder—tearing it down would be automatic."

Kate understood now why Vail's approach to work was so intense, why it crowded out everything else. She thought about when she'd recruited him on that Chicago rooftop to help with the Pentad case six months earlier. After she made her appeal, he worked almost in a rage. She thought it was because of what she'd said, but now she wondered if it wasn't because she was invading his privacy, at a time when he held at bay the demons his father had left behind. A feat that became impossible when someone else might be able to detect the tiniest flaw. It had to be why he never stopped working on a case, even after it was *solved*. "Have you ever thought about confronting him and showing him what you've accomplished?"

"Accomplished? I'm a bricklayer."

"Actually, you choose to be a bricklayer. Maybe you continue to do it because it's the only way to show your father how wrong he was. You need to go see him and tell him what you've done, your education, your work with the FBI."

"I can't."

"Why not?"

"I just can't."

"Why not?"

"All right, I won't."

"That's your father. You can't put the rest of your life on hold because of one bad summer."

"You're right, it was only one summer, because by the time I turned fifteen, I could lay brick as well as he could. And, more important, I was much faster, which translated into more money. Not that I ever saw any of it. But when I was sixteen, he found a new way to 'parent.' That entire summer we worked building a hospital, a huge job. There were other contractors on the site—roofers, Sheetrockers, carpenters, everything. I was always big for my age, so he started lining up fights for me. On Fridays he would have me fight grown men for their paychecks. The first time I lost. Three of my ribs were broken. But he was very reassuring. He told me it was all right, because he'd get better odds the next time. Maybe that's why I've never looked forward to paydays. When I turned seventeen, I refused to do it anymore. The next year was—to put it mildly—contentious."

"When's the last time you saw him?"

"My eighteenth birthday. I got up in the morning and packed. He was eating breakfast. I stopped and looked at him. I suppose I wanted him to have some remorse, maybe even try to stop me, but I think he actually looked relieved."

She pulled on Vail's arm to get him to start walking. He took one last look at the pieces in the window. After a few blocks of silence, she said, "Am I really the only one who's seen your sculptures?"

"Even though I told you I didn't want you to look at them, yes."

"Then I'm glad I didn't follow orders. That one of me is—"

"I destroyed it."

"What?"

"A few nights after you left, I sat in front of it, drinking. Finally I got drunk enough to see the truth, so I broke it down."

"What truth? It looked exactly like me."

He stopped and faced her, putting his palm on her cheek. "One of the things I like best about you is that you really don't understand your own beauty. I understand it better than you do, and I don't understand it at all. I had to do that bust of you, to try to understand exactly what it is about you that haunts me. When I destroyed it, I destroyed my obsession with perfection. You're right, me being a bricklayer is about not being judged. But destroying that bust of you was the healthiest thing I've ever done."

Tears started down Kate's face. She buried herself against his chest. "Who are you?"

"Haven't you been listening? For better or worse, I'm a bricklayer." Vail took out a handkerchief and handed it to her. "If it's any consolation, since then—for the first time ever—I've kept the things I've made, all of them. I think I'm actually starting to like what I make."

Kate gave him his handkerchief back and took his arm again. "And will *I* get to see them?"

"You'll have to come to Chicago."

"Uh-oh."

"That's right, Katie, there is an admission price."

They started walking again. "I'm hungry."

"I hope you're speaking biblically."

"I'm talking seafood, Vail, and as much of it as you can afford."

"Well, aren't you the demanding little fugitive?"

"If I were, I wouldn't be dating a bricklayer pretending to be an FBI agent pretending to be a sculptor."

"If I remember my time in the Bureau correctly, everybody was pretending to be an agent."

"That's the problem, no one pretends anymore."

KATE PUT THE KEY in the lock and turned around to face him, flattening her back against the door. "I had a very nice time tonight, Steven," she said, her voice feigning a this-is-our-first-and-last-date rejection.

She had been relatively quiet during dinner. His flirting usually elicited playful banter from her, but tonight she'd been largely unresponsive, seemingly lost in her own thoughts. He even threw her a couple of lines she could have used to unload on him, but they didn't seem to register. Vail guessed that it was the arrest and the charges pending against her. He knew she was grounded enough to understand that with the evidence they'd uncovered so far, she would never be formally charged and that complete freedom was not far away. But maybe being put in such a precarious position and having to be so dependent on him was causing her to finally understand why he had such disdain for the Bureau. The organization she'd given so much to had been unwilling to risk anything to help her.

But now maybe she was trying to tell him that she'd made some sort of decision. He hoped so.

"I'd like to see you again," he said.

"The truth is, Steven, the last few days I've been spending all my time with women. If you know what I mean."

"If that's supposed to turn me off, you may want to take it in a different direction."

"Let me put it another way—no, we can't see each other again."

"I think I should at least get a good-night handshake."

"Yeah, like that's going to happen."

"Come on, Katherine. How about I come in for a cup of coffee?"

"I don't know, my roommate is a bit of a psychopath." She whispered, "He's in the building trades."

Vail put his hands against the door on either side of her. "Have you two got something going on?" He leaned in and put his cheek against hers.

She nuzzled against the heat of his neck. "It's complicated."

"That sounds like a yes. Is he here now?"

"He's very close by."

He kissed her gently on the mouth. "How close?"

"Very, *very* close."

"I say we chance it."

"Well, that was an expensive dinner," she said.

"I won't stay any more than four or five hours."

"You promise?"

"Certainly no later than spring."

She turned around and opened the door. "Just coffee, right?"

They were inside and quickly dropped their coats where they stood. She threw herself against him and kissed him almost angrily.

He said, "For some reason I have a sudden taste for Girl Scout cookies, too." He unzipped her dress, and she stepped out of it, then unbuttoned his shirt. "You're sure there's no chance of a handshake."

She pulled at the end of his belt. "Absolutely not."

TWENTY-FIVE

THE FIRST GRAY LIGHT OF MORNING SEEPED INTO THE BEDROOM, BUT VAIL HAD been awake for almost a half hour, sitting up, watching Kate sleep. Even the darkness couldn't mask the remarkable balance of her features, which seemed to pulse in the low light. Her hair, though messed by Vail and sleep, had a provocative quality to it. A few strands streaked past her ear, a sheaf above it against the part, rising up and then tracing the contour of her head. More of it fell across her pillow, haloing her perfectly round cheekbones. In a flash he saw his next sculpture: a prone figure, vague, its sex barely discernible until the eye found the hair, displayed exactly like Kate's was now.

As quietly as possible, he got up, taking his pillow. As he reached the bedroom door, he heard her pick up the telephone and, after pretending to dial, say, "Is this 911? Yes, I'd like to report a hit-and-run."

"Luke could be here anytime." He smiled.

She got up and pulled him back into bed. "I don't care if he knows. I don't care if anyone knows."

He threw his pillow next to her. "Actually, I was worried about my reputation."

VAIL HEARD THE DOOR opening quietly and sat up on the couch. He had moved there just minutes before. The sound of keys jingling against one another on a ring told him it was Bursaw.

Bursaw walked into the living room and looked at Vail's pillow and blanket on the sofa. He shook his head, smiling. "Don't blame me. That restaurant has always worked for me. It'll probably take Kate a while to adjust, what with being locked up with all those good-looking women and you not exactly leading-man material."

"If you think the women in jail are good-looking, it's no wonder that restaurant always works for you."

Bursaw held up a paper bag. "See, that's why I brought you fresh bagels, I know how cranky you get when you haven't eaten in thirty or forty minutes."

Kate came out of the bedroom tying her robe. "Hey, Luke."

"Mmm, mmm, mmm. Now I see why you're the most wanted woman in D.C.—even before you went over the wall."

Kate laughed musically. "Somebody needs coffee awfully bad." She held out her hand for the bag.

"Have you heard anything?" Vail asked him.

"Not a word. I drove by the off-site, and the marshals are still sitting on it."

"Hopefully Kalix is making some progress—otherwise your sister'll have to find a new place to live," Vail said. "I'm going to get cleaned up."

When Vail stepped out of the shower, he could smell the coffee. And he could hear Kate and Bursaw talking. Occasionally a short burst of her laughter reached him in the bedroom. Unable to make out what they were saying, he sat down on the bed for a while to listen to her laugh.

When he walked into the kitchen, he poured himself a cup of coffee. "You want me to toast a bagel for you, Steve?" she asked.

He tore one in half and said, "Thanks, this is fine."

"So what do you think John's chances are today?"

"I think they're good, but you can't go by me. I'm frequently wrong because of my overly optimistic attitude."

"Actually, you're rarely wrong, precisely because of your cynicism," Bursaw said. "But I got a feeling this *is* turning around."

Kate said, "Is there something else we should be doing? You know, in case John strikes out?"

"I guess I can start going through everything again," Vail said.

She studied his face for a minute. "I don't need you sitting around here reassuring me that everything is all right. If you want something reviewed, I'll do it. You and Luke can make better use of your time looking for Sundra. Besides, watching you sit around here all day will drive me crazy."

"You up for that, Luke?" Vail asked.

"Thanks, Kate. Now I'll have to put up with him all day."

Vail took a last swallow of coffee and said to Kate, "Don't answer the door for anyone. If the phone rings, don't answer it. If you need anything, call Luke's cell."

"Anything specific you want me to look for in the files?"

"Why don't you take a look at all the moles they gave up that lead to you. There's something rattling around in one of the subbasements of my brain telling me we've missed something. There's got to be at least one mistake they made. Maybe something else that'll expose Rellick."

She walked them to the door. "Boys, don't forget to say please and thank you, and absolutely no gunfighting." She pushed them both out the door and locked it.

Once they were in Bursaw's car, Vail said, "Okay, who's next on the deleted-file list?"

"Kate seemed a lot less tense this morning. You wouldn't know anything about that, would you?"

"If you're going to use your Vulcan mind meld, this could turn out to be a very long day."

"Okay, I'll let it drop, but be advised I have made a mental note that there was no denial." Bursaw reached over the seat and grabbed his briefcase. "Let's see." He flipped through some pages. "How about the El Mejor Car Service?"

"Is that Spanish?"

"In this town it could just be misspelled."

The address was in a commercial neighborhood. The building was two stories and ran a long way back into the property. There was parking all around the rear, and several of the cars were older limousines. Vail said, "Let's take a ride through the lot and see if we can figure out what we're looking at here."

Bursaw coasted around the building, which was, judging by the high overhead doors, mostly garage in the back half. Vail looked at the cars that were not part of El Mejor's fleet but more likely belonged to the employees. He pointed out Colombian-flag bumper stickers on two of them. Bursaw said, "You want to pass, maybe come back with some help when you're off the marshals' Top Ten list? I think there's a rule right in the handbook which states that wanted FBI agents should not get into shoot-outs with drug dealers."

"No, I'm feeling very docile today."

Bursaw snorted a single syllable of laughter. "Docile? You? I guess you should 'sleep on the couch' more often." He parked against a back wall near a walk-in door.

As they entered, they counted seven men scattered around five vehicles. The hot smell of oil and grinding metal hung in the warm air. Every one of the workers stopped what he was doing and scrutinized the two agents. No one said anything, and as Vail started to slowly unbutton his topcoat, he and Bursaw casually stepped away from one another, minimizing themselves as targets.

"Who's the boss?" Vail asked. No one answered. "Who's the boss?" he asked again, a little more impatiently.

Still nobody spoke up. He took a couple of steps toward the closest man, who had the dashboard from a Cadillac next to him on a bench and was working on one end of it.

Suddenly, from behind Vail, a man spoke with a slight Hispanic accent. "I am the owner."

Vail turned around as Bursaw continued to watch the men. He flashed his credentials. "We'd like to talk to you."

"Do we have something to talk about?"

"It's not about what you think it is. It's about a missing person. But if you send us on our way, others will come back, and it won't be to talk."

The owner weighed his options. "I guess I have a couple of minutes."

The three men walked into an overly ornate office. "What's your name?" Vail asked.

"Alberto Clark."

"Americanized?"

"My parents did it when we came here. I was three. I didn't know the FBI was so interested in genealogy."

"Actually, we're more interested in true names."

Bursaw handed Clark a photo and said, "Her true name is Sundra Boston."

"And?" Clark asked.

"Know her, seen her, heard of her?"

He handed back the picture. "I don't know her. Why would you think I did?"

"She's an FBI employee, and now she's missing. She was investigating your business."

"This is a legitimate business. I pay taxes. I am a citizen."

"This has been a paid public service announcement," Bursaw said in a sarcastic monotone. "And your employees?"

"I'm not a fool. They are all here legally on work visas."

Vail said, "And those cars out there, the ones they're working on. That's part of your business?"

"Those are their cars. When it's slow, I let them work on them."

Bursaw threw his head back and laughed. "I'd like an employment application because you must have the best wages in America. Those guys don't know three words of English, and they're all driving luxury cars? The one working on the dashboard was swapping VINs. I expected you to lie to me, but try to keep it at a level that's not completely insulting. You're from Colombia. You're supposed to be dealing cocaine, not stolen cars. Have you no ethnic pride?"

"Alberto, we're with the FBI, where lies will get you five years apiece," Vail said. "Now, have you had any contact with the FBI regarding your *business*?"

"No, I swear," Clark answered, the concern growing in his voice.

"Convince us."

Clark thought for a moment. "We've been operating here freely for three years. We have little concern about the police interrupting our operation. Do you think that if we had done something to a federal agent we would be doing business as usual with the door open so any FBI man could walk in?"

Bursaw and Vail looked at each other and shrugged in agreement that it was a strong argument. "We're going to push you—temporarily—to the bottom of our very short list. If we don't come up with something better, we'll be back," Vail said.

"I don't know what else I could do, but if I can help in any way, just call me," Clark said.

As Vail started toward the door, Bursaw said, "I'll be right there."

Five minutes later Bursaw came out of the building and slid in behind the wheel. "What were you doing?" Vail asked. "I'm not going to see you driving a new Cadillac, am I?"

"Actually, I was deputizing my newest informant. We don't really have anybody working stolen cars, so I thought someone with Alberto's talent and range of friends was worth a ninety-day audition. I'm sure he knows other Colombians who still believe in the sanctity of their country's leading export. We do have people working drugs."

Bursaw's cell rang. When he saw that it was Kalix, he handed it to Vail. "No one knows where Rellick is," the deputy assistant director blurted out.

"What happened?" Vail asked.

"Apparently the CIA can be just as inept as the Bureau. One of their polygraphers. They wanted to make sure he'd be available to test Rellick this morning, so they scheduled him yesterday but didn't say anything about this guy possibly being a double agent. Well, you know how examiners are. They have a whole checklist they give the subject the day before. No excessive drinking, no mood-altering drugs, make sure the wind is out of the southeast at no more than eight knots. The people here are theorizing that Rellick might have gotten spooked and took off."

"Are they doing anything to find him?" Vail asked.

"They've called his home, and there's no answer. They're getting a search warrant for his house and bank records. They still don't want us involved in it officially, so they're moving at warp speed before the director and Langston come back."

"Okay, I'm going to let Kate know."

"I'll stay with them until we get an answer one way or the other. Keep your fingers crossed."

TWENTY-SIX

BURSAW PARKED THE BUREAU CAR IN HIS SISTER'S GUEST PARKING SPACE, AND they went up to the apartment. Vail used a key to open the door and yelled inside, "Kate, it's us!"

She came around the corner wearing an apron, a curious expression on her face. "I thought you'd be longer." Then she read something positive in Vail's expression. "You found Sundra?"

"No, not yet." He told her about Rellick's vanishing act. "When John called to tell me, he said the CIA was getting search warrants for his bank and house. There's a good chance that he wouldn't have confessed to the polygrapher, so this might turn out even better."

"Except he had time to clear out anything incriminating."

"You weren't supposed to figure that out, at least not so quickly. Stay positive—this is moving in our favor."

"You're absolutely right," she said. "Lunch is not going to be ready for a while. You guys want something to drink?" she asked with surprising nonchalance.

"No thanks," Bursaw said.

"I'm all set," Vail said. "You're taking this well."

In a faked whisper, she said, "Don't tell anyone, but I've got a couple of really good guys looking out for me."

Bursaw said, "You went and got somebody else?"

After lunch Vail picked up one of the Calculus folders and started rereading it. Ten minutes later he tossed it onto the table in front of him. "That's it, I can't read anymore. I've been over this stuff so much that I wouldn't recognize the answer if it were highlighted."

Bursaw's phone rang; it was Kalix again. He put it on speaker. "I'm with the group going to Rellick's house with a search warrant. They pinged his cell phone, and it shows he's home. I'll call you—we're just about to make entry."

Everyone tried to appear unexcited, as though too much optimism might jinx the outcome. Kate went back to the kitchen, and Bursaw turned on the news. For the next half hour, he listened to the local broadcast. Vail became lost in his thoughts, reexamining everything, looking for another way to prove Kate's innocence in case Rellick proved to be uncooperative. When nothing came to him, he got up and went into the kitchen. He stepped up behind her and slowly pulled on one of the apron strings. "I think I know what we need."

She let him get it completely untied before she turned around. Reaching behind her, she retied it. "Yes, Steve, that's exactly what we don't need right now."

"I never even got a real New Year's kiss." He put an arm around her waist.

"I kissed you. Which, by the way, triggered my one New Year's resolution—to only kiss men in tuxedos."

"I've been thinking about canceling my diving trip and going to maître d' school."

"You greeting people for tips. That sounds like a shorter career than you had with the FBI."

Bursaw's phone rang again. He called in to Vail that it was Kalix. Vail put Kate at arm's length—"It's so easy to mock someone else's dreams"—then walked into the living room and took the phone. "Yes, John."

"Is everyone there?" Kalix asked.

Vail called Kate in from the kitchen and pushed the Speaker button. "We're all here."

"Rellick's gone. He left his phone here and turned it on as a decoy. That's the bad news. But up in his attic, there have to be fifty of those banker's boxes—you know, for storing records. Not only his own, but all kinds of family stuff his parents must have accumulated for decades. Everything—his divorce records, stocks sold twenty years ago. So far they've found five or six of them with classified documents in them, all copies he evidently made. So now the CIA will be able to reconstruct exactly what information he turned over to the Russians. They're most appreciative."

"Will that be enough to clear Kate?"

"It will be with what they found in one of them. Remember on that thumb drive, the typed list of eight FBI-CIA joint investigations along with their named targets? The one that Kate's latent was supposed to have been on?"

Vail looked at Kate. "It was in there?"

"They're going to examine it for prints to see if Rellick's are on it. It hasn't been processed before, so the Russians must have copied it and fumed the copy for the flash-drive setup."

"You'd think Rellick would have destroyed everything, especially that."

"He probably panicked, and maybe he intends to defect. If so, why bother? Considering where this box was, under all the rest, he may have just forgotten it, and even if he didn't, it would have taken him some time to find it in all that mess. From the other documents in the box, it looks like it's a couple of years old, so if he did think about getting rid of it, he probably knew that it would take too long to find."

Vail said, "That sounds like all good news to me."

"For us, yes, but for them there's a new problem. As soon as they discovered he was gone, they unleashed the techs on his work computer. They found a deleted file that he'd cobbled together from a bunch of different files that he shouldn't have been able to gain access to. They're thinking maybe the Russians helped him 'jailbreak' some of the CIA security measures."

"What was on it?" Vail asked.

"Dozens of the agency's European sources. If he's taking it to the Russians, the likelihood of their being killed is quite high. It would set the Agency back ten years."

"You said 'if he's taking it to the Russians.'"

"The last entry in the file was just two days ago. And it was deleted last night after the polygrapher told him about the impending test. So they don't think he had completed the list yet. But somehow they were able to tell that it was downloaded before it was deleted."

"Did they check his e-mail?" Vail asked.

"Both at the office and here. He didn't send it through either of them. I don't know, maybe he put it onto another thumb drive. As you can imagine, there's a fairly large amount of panic around here. Right now they're trying all their super-secret spy stuff to find him. The problem is that he knows how to avoid it," Kalix said. "Steve, they found one more thing on his computer here. That photo that was sent to the two guys at the house who tried to kill you, through that untraceable CIA phone line—it was on there. The Russians must have had him send it so it wouldn't come back to anyone."

"Well, that answers who," Vail said.

"Anyway, before Kate's innocence gets lost in all the impending catastrophe, I'm going to go see the United States Attorney. He says he'll see me as soon as I get there. In the meantime, maybe we can find something else here that will eliminate any doubt that Kate wasn't part of this."

"I don't know how to thank you, John," she said.

"You're not clear yet, Kate. As long as Rellick's on the loose, they are going to need somebody to blame. They've got evidence against you, and even though it's all manufactured, the United States Attorney probably isn't going to be a fan of yours the way you made a fool out of him when you escaped. But I'll let you know once I talk to him."

After Kalix hung up, Vail said, more to himself than the others, "He's right."

"Think so?" Bursaw said.

Realizing he'd said it out loud, Vail looked at Kate. "Sorry. It would be better for you if they found Rellick. Much better."

She thought for a second and then said, "See if this sounds right: Rellick left his cell phone behind at his house, mostly as a decoy. Would he have another one? You know, just for spy business?"

"That makes a lot of sense," Vail said.

"You have that CIA dead-end number, right?"

"Yes."

"Since you were last in the Bureau, we've developed fairly sophisticated reverse-toll record traces, especially for cell phones, because every call is noted for billing. So we can take a call if we know the date and time and, with a fairly simple computer run, determine the phone it was made from."

Vail said, "So if Rellick does have another cell and we can identify it through the reverse records, if he's got it on, we can ping it."

"And find out where he is," Bursaw added.

Vail had his pocket notebook out, turning pages. "Here it is." He started to write it down, then stopped. "But how do we get it done? Technically, you're still wanted."

"If you think about it, there aren't many people at headquarters who know my situation. The worst thing that could happen is that someone could find out I'm here. We really have no choice." Both men nodded. "Why don't you guys get out of here, and I'll make the call. That way if something happens to me, you'll still be able to look for Rellick."

"Just remember, if you get locked up again, you're on your own."

"Talk about your one-night stands."

Vail looked over at Bursaw, who had a huge, self-congratulatory smile on his face. "Thanks, Kate. Now I can spend the rest of the day fending off questions from the Special Agent Lust here."

AFTER EATING BURGERS in the car again, Vail and Bursaw sat parked a half mile from the apartment, where Kate was making calls. "Steve, do you think we'll actually find out what happened to Sundra?"

"Huh? Oh, I don't know. We could. Right now I'd guess fifty-fifty."

"You're worried about Kate, aren't you?"

Vail looked at him carefully to make sure this wasn't a lead-in to a salacious line of questioning. "The way everything's gone today, I shouldn't be, but every once in a while I get worried that things won't work out. That usually happens when I can't do anything except sit and wait." He took Bursaw's phone and dialed Kate. After a number of rings, he hung up. "Does your sister have call-waiting?"

"I think so."

"I didn't get the machine, so hopefully Kate was busy on the line."

Then almost immediately the phone rang, and Vail could see that it was Kate. "Everything okay?" he asked.

"Put me on speaker. . . . It looks like we got Rellick's second cell. They queried that CIA dead-end number on the date and time you gave me and came up with a phone whose subscriber is William Jackson, with a billing address at that Russian safe house in Denton you tried to burn down. There were a number of calls on it from another cell that comes back to a Vladimir Demeter, same billing address. I'm sure they're both aliases, one for Rellick and the other is probably Calculus's, since the two of them were meeting regularly around that time."

"And you're having them ping Rellick's number?" Vail asked.

"They've already started, but it's not on right now. They'll ping it every ten minutes. Our people at headquarters are going to track it with the Bureau satellite. Where are you?"

"About a half mile from you."

They heard her other line click in. "Okay, hold on."

Bursaw said, "You ever think about moving here?"

"You mean because of Kate?"

"We've got brick buildings, too."

"I'm thinking Kate's a little too well adjusted to handle me full-time."

"Hey, contrarians need love, too."

"That's true, they do, but never each other."

"In philosophy that would constitute a paradox. Just remember, a paradox, while seemingly illogical, is in fact true."

"Go ahead, caller, you're on the line with the love doctor."

"Deflection is a sure sign of hitting a nerve."

"Yeah, the auditory nerve."

They heard Kate click back. "They've got him. He's not far away. The GW Memorial, heading north just below the Arlington Memorial Bridge."

Bursaw put the car in gear. "We're on our way."

It was starting to grow dark, and the evening traffic was getting heavier. Just as Bursaw's car reached the on-ramp for the GW Memorial Parkway, his phone rang again. Kate said, "He's pulled off the GW just after the Roosevelt Bridge. The only thing there is the parking area for Roosevelt Park."

Vail said, "I told you the Russians love parks. He may be meeting his handler there. If so, they're probably going to try to get him out."

"I'll have them keep tracking him in case he starts moving. I'll call you back in five."

Bursaw pulled into the lot. There was only one car, a midsize Chevrolet. It was freshly washed, and there was a car-rental sticker on its bumper. Both men drew their guns and, leaving their doors open should they need cover to retreat to, approached the car from opposite sides. It was empty.

Bursaw said, "He must have crossed the footbridge into the park. There's nowhere else to go."

"Is there another way out of there?"

"It's an island. The footbridge is the only way on or off, unless you want to swim across a freezing Potomac."

"How many flashlights do you have?"

"Just one."

"Okay, you lock up the car and I'll make sure he can't drive out of here."

As Bursaw went to the trunk to get the light, he watched Vail pull out his lockback knife and slash all four tires of the rental. Then he took out his phone and turned it on. "Put yours on vibrate," he told Bursaw. "We're going to have to split up. When we get across the bridge, you go north and I'll take south. If you spot him, call me and we can pin him in."

Vail then called Kate. "I've turned my phone on. It looks like Rellick's in the park. Luke and I are going to split up. Just keep on Rellick's phone." He hung up. "Ready?" he asked Bursaw.

"I don't think we should cross the bridge together. If he's waiting for us, all he'll have to do to take both of us out is fire straight along the bridge. There's no place to get cover unless we're willing to go into the water."

"Sounds right. You go first."

"Hey, it's your girlfriend we're trying to get off."

Vail stepped onto the footbridge. "Okay, but next New Year's I'm definitely getting a hooker. In Chicago."

TWENTY-SEVEN

AS SOON AS VAIL REACHED THE OTHER SIDE, HE TOOK UP A DEFENSIVE POSITION to cover Bursaw while he crossed the bridge. He checked his watch—almost eight o'clock. It was dark, but there was enough light from the roadways crisscrossing the island to follow the footpaths. Without a word the two men glanced at each other, Vail heading south and Bursaw north.

Vail walked a hundred feet and then stopped to listen. Since the only car in the lot besides Bursaw's was the rental, Vail felt that Rellick had to be there waiting for someone to arrive. Possibly one of the Russians, so he could exchange the list he'd downloaded from the CIA files for a way out of the country and probably one last, very large payment. Rellick still had his phone on, so there was a good chance he was making calls or waiting for one. A gust of frigid wind came off the Potomac, and Vail waited for it to subside before he continued.

He was surprised at how rustic the park was. Except for the footpaths, some of which were endless three-foot-wide wooden planks, the ground was heavy with trees and undergrowth, creating more of a wooded setting than an urban park. There were very few evergreens, and the hardwoods were bare. The path he was on was dirt, and there were still leaves cluttering it. The lights from the surrounding cities allowed him to find his way south.

Off to his left, Vail could see a frozen pond. He took out his phone and made sure it was on. As he neared the southern end of the island, he could see the tall buildings of Arlington across the Potomac. There was another path off to the right, and it seemed to head toward the great dark shadow of the Theodore Roosevelt Memorial Bridge as it passed overhead connecting D.C. to Arlington.

He thought he heard something and stopped. After thirty seconds the wind blew from the same direction where the suspected sound originated, and this time he recognized an indistinguishable voice. Vail thumbed the safety off his Glock and lightened his step, moving toward its source.

It seemed to be coming from the bridge's underpass, a corridor of fifteen-foot-high off-white concrete walls that curved overhead. At the other end, Vail could see the lights of downtown Arlington reflected off the Potomac. He stopped again and listened. Now, because of the hum of the tires driving over the bridge, he seemed to be in some acoustical dead space, because the voice suddenly vanished. It was the perfect place for spies to meet on a winter night. Especially for Russians, who loved parks, the cold, and vodka.

At the midpoint of each of the walls were walk-in doors, probably leading to maintenance storage. Vail wondered if Rellick had somehow gotten into one of them to wait. He started toward the closest one with his weapon pointed at the other. When he reached the door, he tried the knob. It was locked.

All of a sudden, ahead of him, around the end of the concrete wall, he heard a man's voice. "Call me back in five minutes, Tanner. . . . I'm not going to wait much longer. . . . Where else would I be?" Rellick walked around the corner and into view as he ended the call. Vail pointed the automatic at him. "That's it, Rellick, FBI. Right there."

The CIA agent raised his hands, still holding the phone. Glancing up at the lighted screen, Rellick pushed a couple of buttons and placed his finger on another, ready to press it. "Unless you want that list of European informants to be e-mailed to the Russian embassy, you'd better drop the gun." He lowered his hands slowly but confidently.

"How do I know you've actually got it on your phone?" Vail asked.

"By now you know I've downloaded the list. And I would need a quick way to send it from anywhere, even here, if I got in a tight spot. So I put it on speed dial. I thought it would be better than a gun. Was I wrong?"

Vail knew by Rellick's confidence that the list had to be on the phone. He dropped his gun on the ground. As soon as he did, Rellick drew a small revolver. "Now walk over here."

Suddenly Vail felt his cell phone vibrate. It was probably Kate, ready to tell him that Rellick and his cell phone were under the bridge. Vail kept walking slowly, hoping to get close enough to make some kind of move. But when he was five feet away, Rellick said, "That's close enough, on your knees. And put your hands in your pockets." Vail did as he was told and wrapped his hand around his knife. But he knew that even if he could get it out in time and open it, Rellick would still be too far away. Rellick carefully cleared the screen on his phone and put it in his overcoat pocket.

"Meeting your handler here?" Vail asked.

"My handler?" Rellick burst out laughing. "My handler offered to get me to Moscow, where I'd be a hero. I'd rather live in a federal prison than in Russia. So I told him I wanted a million dollars for the list. With that much money, I can live fairly comfortably in South America."

"So he says he's bringing you a million dollars here? Tonight?"

"You sound skeptical."

"The banks are closed, and I seriously doubt they keep that kind of cash at the embassy. I hope you didn't tell him where the list was." Rellick didn't answer. "You did. Myles, I think Moscow and federal prison aren't your only options. I'd consider the possibility of death. And not in that order."

"Shut up," Rellick said. "I've got to get out of here. That leaves only one option for you, and it isn't Moscow or federal prison. Unless you can come up with a fourth option." He raised his revolver. "No. Then death it is." Vail took his hands halfway out of his pockets and got ready to charge him; he had nothing to lose.

A gun exploded, and it took an instant for Vail to realize that the shot had come from behind him. The CIA agent looked surprised, even indignant, that a bullet had wound up piercing his chest instead of Vail's. Suddenly the hand holding his gun went limp, and the weapon dropped to the ground. He looked past Vail and tilted his head in confusion at the black man moving quickly toward him, ready to fire a second shot. Then he looked around as if wondering where he was and fell forward heavily, landing on his face. Bursaw snapped on his flashlight and moved past Vail, keeping his gun trained on Rellick in case another shot was needed.

It was then that Vail realized that his vibrating phone call with Rellick's location had gone to Bursaw first.

"Do you think you waited long enough, Luke?"

Bursaw's smile verged on laughter. "Remember that time you left me out in the cold and I got really sick?" He rolled over the body and holstered his weapon.

"Again with that. You know, at a certain point the need for revenge can become very unflattering."

"Not when it's you on your knees."

"I hope we're finally even." Vail took Rellick's cell phone out and made sure it was still on. Then he slipped it into his pocket. "No one needs to know that I've got this."

"Because . . . ?"

"If we give it back to the CIA today, it'll be worth a very nice thank-you. Give it back in a week and it will be . . ."

"Priceless," Bursaw finished.

"Maybe that Ivy League education wasn't wasted." Vail called Kate on his phone. "Rellick's dead."

"Both you guys okay?"

"We're fine."

"Should I ask?"

"Actually, it was Luke who shot him. Can you call Metro Homicide or the Park Police, whoever's jurisdiction this is?"

"Sure. Then I'm coming there."

"I appreciate it, but we're probably not going to be here very long. And you're not out of the woods yet, so let's not push it. When I find out where we're going, I'll let you know."

"You're sure?"

"Call Kalix and fill him in about what's going on." Vail hung up.

Bursaw was searching the body. He pulled out a stack of hundred-dollar bills, held them up for Vail to see, and then stuffed them back in the dead agent's pocket. "He doesn't have ID on him."

Rellick's phone rang. Vail took it out. "Excuse me a minute, I've got to talk to this Russian," Vail said. He pushed the Talk button. "Yeah."

The voice on the other end immediately became suspicious. "What is your name?" Vail knew the caller was asking for Rellick's code name.

"Rumpelstiltskin." The line went dead. Vail put the phone back in his pocket.

"You didn't really think you were going to fool him, did you?"

"I wanted two things: to see if he had a Russian accent, which he did, and for his call to go through, so his number would be in the phone company's computer." Vail checked his watch and noted the time of the call.

VAIL AND BURSAW explained to the responding Park Police what had taken place on Roosevelt Island so that the crime-scene examination could be conducted. Then they followed a couple of their detectives to their investigative offices in southeast D.C. Once there, the two agents were taken to separate interview rooms. When Vail finished, it was a little after four in the morning. He found Kate waiting in the reception area. "Everything all right?" she asked after hugging him.

"I don't think they handle as many homicides as Metro does, so their process was a little slower."

"What did you tell them?"

"The truth—the other guy did it." And then, without mentioning Rellick's cell phone, Vail explained about how the rogue CIA agent had gotten the drop on him and Bursaw had shot him to save Vail's life.

Just then Bursaw walked out. Kate gave him a hug, too. "They're not keeping you?" she said, an impish grin pulling at the corners of her mouth.

He laughed. "Careful, I could tell them who you really are." They left the building and started walking to the car. Bursaw said, "How about you, what's your status? I see you're out in public without a disguise."

"As soon as I got hold of the Park Police, I called John. He had just met with the United States Attorney. He picked me up at your sister's place and brought me here."

"I hope you're going to tell me we're all off the hook," Bursaw said.

"As far as I know, they never figured out who you were."

"Thank God."

Vail said, "How come you black guys are always complaining about how we all think you look alike until there's a lineup?"

"Kate, did I ever tell you about the dead guy we found wearing a negligee in the doghouse and what Vail had to do to get a confession from his wife?"

Vail waved his hand back and forth. "I don't think that's pre-breakfast conversation."

"I'm begging you, Luke, tell me," Kate said. "What—"

Vail interrupted. "I believe you were about to tell us how we're no longer in fugitive status."

"Okay—for now. To answer your question, Luke, everyone is off the hook. John said he was a little worried when he went to see the United States Attorney. Remember, he played Assistant Director William A. Langston on the phone when he called him to spring me. But I guess he disguised his voice enough that the USA didn't catch on. Anyway, John explained everything we found out about Rellick and his subsequent flight and how he tried to kill an agent. John said he huffed and puffed for a while but then decided that the evidence the CIA had gathered was convincing enough to drop the charges against me."

"And Luke and I?"

"Like I said, they never pulled Luke up on the radar, but you were identified and kind of marked as the ringleader. He said the USA was reluctant to give a pass to a jailbreaker. But then John reminded him that the press would probably view my detention as a serious violation of my rights. And although he might try to mitigate that through some convenient interpretation of national-security protocol, it wouldn't play well because that whole secrecy thing was created to catch the big fish, and since that was supposed to be me, it was no longer an excusable tactic. Finally he told him that I would seek no punitive action against his office if everything were dropped, against everyone. After weighing his liabilities for a few seconds, he agreed. On his way to get me, John called the director and brought him up to speed. He wants all of us in his office at nine A.M."

Kate glanced at Vail, expecting him to offer an excuse as to why he wouldn't be there. "You do know he's probably going to thank you?" she said.

Vail just shrugged his shoulders, making her wonder what he was up to now.

AFTER A PREDAWN BREAKFAST, Bursaw dropped Kate and Vail at his sister's apartment. "Sure I can't give you a ride?"

Kate said, "I want to clean up around here a little. We'll get a cab."

While Kate vacuumed, Vail packed up the files that had been taken from the Sixteenth Street off-site. Then he called a cab and fed the fish while they waited for it to arrive.

Once they were in the taxi, Kate asked, "Why are you going to the director's meeting? You hate things like that."

"Is that your real question, or do you want to know when I'm leaving?"

"Both, I guess."

"I told Luke I'd help him with his case. That means I'm going to need credentials a little longer. Hopefully the director won't mind giving me a couple of extra days."

"Then off to Florida."

"So far. Would you consider coming along?"

"I might be talked into it."

"Sun, warm water, gallons of rum, and me. The good, the bad, and the ugly. You can claim an alcohol-induced state to excuse the inevitable regrets you'll have afterward."

She smiled absentmindedly. "You know the director is going to offer you the job again."

"I suppose."

"And?"

"I'll listen."

"And then turn him down."

"Kate, we've been through this."

Her eyes softened as she looked away from him. "Do you know what our problem is? Two people cannot get involved with each other, truly involved, without becoming vulnerable, and that is something you and I have guarded against our entire lives." She smiled sadly. "Sorry, I was just hoping—you know. But no one understands better than Steve Vail how frivolous hope is."

"Hope isn't necessarily frivolous, but by inference it is a long shot," he said. "Right now you're still unsettled with all of this. Anybody would be. You may think you want things to be a little more permanent, but give it a couple of days. You go back to work, put up with me hanging around for a while, and then we'll figure out where everything is going."

She looked directly at him again and steadied her eyes against his gaze. "Right now I am feeling vulnerable, and for the first time in my life I'm not afraid of it. Maybe because I know that no matter what happens, you'll be there. That's a nice feeling."

"I'm happy for you, Kate. I genuinely am. I don't know if that's a possibility for me." He turned and watched out the window. She realized he was struggling to understand that kind of commitment.

"So, Vail," she said, her voice now lightheartedly official in an effort to change the mood, "I'm curious. Are you satisfied that we got everybody? You seem distracted since John gave us the news."

Vail turned back and gave her a small, courteous smile. "You know I'm never satisfied. I'm afraid that tomorrow I'll find that chimney torn down again."

"I know when you start thinking that way, there usually is someone else involved."

"Does anything bother you about this case?"

"Do you mean other than me being thrown in prison?"

Vail laughed. "Yes, other than that."

"We've talked about this before. Why did they kill all the double agents?"

"And our best guess was that they didn't want to embarrass Moscow with revelations of Russia spying against the U.S. But then why didn't they kill Rellick? He said they wanted to take him to Moscow because he had been exposed."

"Did they?" she asked. "Maybe they were setting him up to kill him, too. They just didn't know where he was."

Vail thought about the list of CIA informants Rellick was trying to sell and conceded that maybe Kate was right, that they would have killed him once they had the information. "You're probably right."

"What difference does it make? All those who should go to hell are on their way. And you and I are talking about scuba diving."

"We'll see."

"I really hope you're talking about the scuba diving."

WHEN THE CAB PULLED UP to Kate's apartment, she said, "Do you want to come in?" She knew he wouldn't, because she could see he was still distracted. And she suspected that her talk about vulnerability was making him cautious.

"Thanks, Kate, but I've got some things I need to do."

"Well, that's certainly vague enough," she said. "Tell me the truth, what are the chances of my seeing you at the director's office tomorrow morning?"

"I don't think I really belong there. You guys will be celebrating, and after Florida I'll be back in Chicago scratching for work."

"Did it ever occur to you that maybe the director would feel better about your turning him down if he could thank you in person?"

"He asked me to work on a case, not his feelings."

"I hope you're not planning on sneaking out of town tonight."

"I told you, I'm going to help Luke for a couple of days—or at least until we run out the rest of those leads," Vail said. "Why would you think I would do that? I came here to see you."

"And you've seen me. All of me."

"Let me just say in my defense, dating a jailbird isn't all that easy."

She leaned over and kissed him lightly on the lips. "We prefer 'ex-con.'"

TWENTY-EIGHT

KATE WAS THE LAST TO ARRIVE AT THE DIRECTOR'S OFFICE. "GOOD MORNING," Bob Lasker said. "It looks like everyone is still standing. Nice work, people." Nodding at Kate, he said, "I thought Steve might be coming with you."

"I think he didn't want to turn down another of your job offers. And you know how he likes to be thanked."

"He hasn't gone back to Chicago already, has he?"

"He promised me he wouldn't, but . . ." She shrugged her shoulders.

"I can't figure out what drives him."

"I'm sure hearing that would make him very happy, sir."

The director laughed. "Okay, let's get down to business." He turned to Bursaw. "Luke, let's start with you. Do you have any aspirations to come to headquarters?"

"Me? Coming to this building every day? I'm sorry, sir, but I enjoy bad-mouthing management far too much to give it up."

"I guess that answers the question of why Steve trusts you. Just remember you have a Get Out of Jail Free card should you need one."

"I'm sure you won't have to hold on to it for very long."

"And, Kate, you'll go back to your old job as deputy AD simply because of the amount of paperwork that has piled up in your absence. I wouldn't give that to my worst enemy."

"Nothing would make me happier."

"So do we have any loose ends we need to tend to?" No one said anything. "No. Then I've got one more item of interest. Bill Langston has been reassigned as AD in charge of training at Quantico. Effective immediately, I am appointing John Kalix to the position of assistant director of counterintelligence. I'm concerned about how the Russians manipulated the Bureau and almost destroyed the reputation of a deputy assistant director. John was involved, sometimes to the point of great personal danger, in the entire investigation and because of that is more equipped, I feel, to prevent it from happening again. "

Kalix's face was expressionless. Apparently the director had told him of the promotion previously. Kate recalled Kalix's comment that Langston had ordered an end to the investigation into whom the Russian handler Gulin had met with at the antique mall. If it had been pursued more thoroughly, Rellick probably would not have been able to do so much intelligence damage, and there would have been no need to frame Kate. She smiled. "Congratulations, John." But she couldn't help wondering if Kalix had been the one to tell the director about Langston's misstep. She decided it didn't really matter. He had helped her escape custody, cleared her through his contacts, and actually saved Vail's life in the process. Even if he had dimed out his boss, she had to give him a pass.

"Okay," the director said, "everybody get out of here and go back to work."

KATE OPENED THE DOOR to her office. The piles of mail and reports completely covered her desk. She stepped around behind it and started prioritizing the stacks. After an hour she could see that it was going to take at least a week of twelve- to fourteen-hour days to catch up. But suddenly there seemed to be a greater priority—to find out what Vail was doing. She locked the door and headed for the garage.

She let herself into the Sixteenth Street off-site and found Vail lying on the couch staring up at the wall. There seemed to be even more paper covering it than she remembered. Vail looked over at her absentmindedly and then back at the wall without saying anything. He hadn't shaved and appeared to not have slept. "I thought you might be sleeping," she said.

"I found a spy we missed."

"What?"

Vail got up. "I'm starving. Do you want something?" He went into the kitchen and took some cold cuts out of the refrigerator for a sandwich.

"No." She followed him. "Who did we miss?"

Without answering her, he started to make the sandwich, and although he wouldn't look at her, she could see a small smirk on his face. She slapped his arm. "Come on, Vail."

He put the sandwich on a paper plate and walked into the workroom. On the table was a digital recorder. He pushed the Play button and took a bite of his sandwich.

"Hello, it's me—you know, Preston. I've got those infrared facial-recognition schematics you wanted, but the price has gone up. This time I want a hundred thousand dollars in cash, just for me. I've been getting the short end while taking all the chances. So this will keep it, you know, level and true. You've got my number."

"Notice anything about that?" Vail asked. There was a knock

downstairs. Kate didn't answer, so he pressed Play again. "I'll get the door."

It was Bursaw. "Next time you're going to skip a meeting, how about letting me know? I don't enjoy being that close to the director."

"He's an honorable man."

"He's still *the* boss. My personnel file has many unanswered questions in it that I don't need someone at that level looking at."

"Come on, Kate's upstairs."

When they walked into the workroom, Kate was a little animated and said, "I think I know what you're talking about, Steve. Hi, Luke."

Vail said to her, "Okay, fire away."

Vail looked at Bursaw to see if he was curious. "Do I need to know?" he asked.

"It's part of the Russian business. It's something I'm going to have to take care of before we get back to Sundra."

"I thought everyone was dead."

"Apparently we missed one," Vail said.

"And I assume, because I'm going to be given the SS blood oath again, that no one else is to know about whatever the new plot calls for."

Kate said, "Don't you think we owe it to John Kalix to cut him in on this? He's an AD now." Kate told Vail about the promotion that morning.

"Then we owe it to him to keep him out of it. He's back to the rules. Let's allow him to enjoy his promotion for a day or two before we make him sorry he accepted it. Luke, can you give us a hand?"

Bursaw shook his head. "Okay, but this time I want first shot at the insanity plea."

Although Vail had given Bursaw the broad strokes of the Calculus investigation when he'd agreed to help with Kate, he hadn't told him the specifics about how the double agents had been uncovered through the Ariadne thread left by the Russians. "The first clue was a series of dots and dashes etched into the side of the DVD that Calculus left for us. That led us to a phone in the Russian embassy and an access code. Here's the message." He played it again for Bursaw.

Then Vail said, "And now, since the deputy assistant director has apparently figured out where we went wrong, she'll explain."

She said, "Let me give you a brief rundown on how we found these moles. The first one, Charles Pollock, we were given his initials and, to simplify it, where he worked. From that we recovered a DVD that recorded him trading classified documents for cash. In each case that's what we were supplied with, a way to identify the mole and physical evidence of his spying. And in each case there was a hidden or coded clue about how to find the next one. These are what we followed that led to recovering the phony evidence against me. Are you with me so far?"

"Yes."

"So on the Pollock DVD, besides the payoff, the edge had, in Morse code, a telephone number. When we called the number, we got that message you just heard played. And, as you heard at the end of it, there was a touch-tone number being dialed. We assumed that it was another code to identify the caller named Preston who was talking about the infrared technology at the beginning of the recording. We broke down that code, and it led up to a bank box that belonged to Yanko Petriv, the NSA translator. Things were moving pretty fast right then, so we went after Petriv, thinking he was the one selling the facial-recognition schematics. But what we didn't take the time to consider was that Petriv was born in Bulgaria and would probably have an accent, since he spoke Eastern European languages well enough to be a translator. The voice on the recording is definitely American, maybe upper Wisconsin or Minnesota. And he's talking about some very classified technology. Not something a translator would have access to."

Bursaw said, "Let me see if I got this right. The Preston recording is not this guy Petriv, but someone working in technology, selling it to the Russians."

"Right."

"That means that the recording is the evidence?"

"It's not as prominent as the others, but that's what it looks like. That's part of the reason we skimmed over it and missed him."

"So how are you supposed to identify him?"

"I don't know. The whole thing was a sham so I'd wind up in prison and out of Rellick's way. It didn't have to be flawless. It just had to move us along the chain of spies until it got to me."

Vail said, "For it to be convincing, there had to be enough information contained in the phone message for us to identify him. That's the only possibility."

"Play it again, Steve," Bursaw said.

Vail started the recorder and set it down on the table between them. When it finished, Bursaw smiled. "Did you hear it?"

"Hear what?" Vail asked.

"'Level and true.' Did you notice how it's emphasized slightly? Just like 'Preston.'"

Vail played it again, and he and Kate listened more closely. "You're right," he said.

Bursaw went over to the desktop computer and queried "level and true."

"'The Air Force Song,'" he said. "Fourth verse, second line: 'Keep the wings level and true.'"

"Our guy is in the air force," Vail said. "That makes a lot more sense with the 'infrared facial-recognition schematics.' And who knows what else he has access to and is selling to the Russians right now? Someone with this kind of access could do a ton of damage."

Kate said, "There's a lot of air force personnel within a hundred miles."

"Not with access to classified documents about cutting-edge technology," Vail added.

"The Pentagon," Bursaw said.

"That's where I'd start."

"But why did they make it so hard to recognize the clue?" Kate asked.

"They were all hard to recognize. Remember how long the code on the edge of the DVD took, how we thought it was a dead end. This one was just a little too hard, a little too easy to step over. We were looking for codes. This one was audio. They probably figured better too hard than too easy. Too easy might have tipped us off. And if we did miss one, the next clue was provided. Which is what happened."

"Okay," Bursaw said, "what do we do now? There's got to be twenty thousand people working at the Pentagon. It's not like we can just walk in and start demanding answers."

"You're right, Luke, but there is someone who can," Kate said.

"Who?" the two men asked at the same time.

"Tim Mallon."

"The Reston PD chief?" Vail asked.

"I told you he worked nothing but applicant and security clearance cases for twenty-five years. He knows more people at the Pentagon than anyone in the Bureau. And I believe he owes you a favor or two."

"Can you call him?"

Kate picked up the phone and dialed information.

While she was talking to Mallon, Vail said to Bursaw, "Have you had a chance to do any checking on the last two of Sundra's files?"

"Actually, I've been going over her phone records again. Seeing if they matched anything we've run into yet." Bursaw glanced over at Kate, who was still on the phone. "Not to change the subject, but I don't suppose there's any chance of you accepting the director's offer."

"Why?"

"Purely selfish reasons. Maybe it's the philosopher in me, but I too like chaos."

"I'm afraid it would create more problems than it would solve."

"The worst thing that could happen is you'd get fired or quit. That's hardly virgin territory for you."

"Walking away doesn't end all problems."

"Is it Kate?"

"She is certainly part of the geometry."

"Maybe if you were around here permanently, your problems would solve themselves."

Vail laughed. "A man so understanding of the complexities of the fairer sex, how come you never got married?"

"Steve, you've just asked a question that contains its own answer."

Kate finished her call. "Your luck's holding, bricklayer. Tim's downtown at a lunch meeting. He's going to stop by in a half hour."

"I'll get cleaned up."

When Vail reappeared freshly shaved and showered, Kate was introducing Tim Mallon to Bursaw. The two men shook hands, and then Mallon made his way over to Vail, offering his hand. "Steve, how are you?"

"I'm good. I haven't been shot since New Year's. How are those two boys?"

"The Walton boy is fine. Hardly broke stride. And Eddie Stanton is getting along with his parents. He's seeing a therapist, too. They're very optimistic."

"I'm glad. Has Kate briefed you about what we need?"

"Just what she told me on the phone. That you needed to make a few, very discreet contacts at the Pentagon, specifically with the air force."

"Tim, I'm going to tell you only the minimum you need to know. Not because you're no longer with the Bureau, but because we're not telling anyone else in the FBI about this, not even the director. I hope you won't feel slighted."

"I'm a little embarrassed to say I'm still eating free lunches off what you did. I don't think it's possible for me to feel anything but gratitude."

Vail told him that they were working a counterintelligence matter and then played the Preston tape for him. "We believe that this man is a member of the air force working at the Pentagon. We need to identify him without him getting wind of it. We're hoping you'll be able to narrow it down by the information he mentioned on the tape. That technology has to be singular in nature. Of course, the fewer people at the Pentagon that you have to tell, the better."

"Will I be able to play them the tape?"

"Yes, but again, the more people who hear it, the harder it'll be to keep this under wraps."

"Steve, I'll do whatever you and Kate want, but I don't know if I have a feel for all these nuances—who to tell, who to let listen. I can get to the right people, but who's told what is a tough call."

"I guess you're right. Will it be a problem if Kate goes with you?"

"More of an asset, if you know what I mean."

"Kate, do you see any problem going with him?"

"You don't want to go?"

"People might not notice two FBI agents, but three could start speculation. Besides, I've got some things I have to get done with Luke."

She took the digital recorder and put it in her purse. "I guess Tim and I can handle it. But before I go, I wanted to show you something in the kitchen."

Vail followed her from the room, and when they were out of sight, she pushed him back against the refrigerator, pinning him with her body. "Allowing little Kate to run a lap all by herself. You'd better be careful, someone might think you're letting your guard down."

He put his arms around her and said, "We've been too busy to get you drunk, so I had to try something."

She gave him a quick kiss on the lips. "Well, Silky, it just might be working." She pushed off him and headed toward the living room.

He called after her. "Said the good-looking blonde as she headed for the safety of witnesses."

TWENTY-NINE

I T WAS DARK WHEN KATE GOT BACK FROM THE PENTAGON. BURSAW HAD TAKEN off to WFO to put in an "end of the day" appearance for his supervisor. Vail could hear Kate's footsteps coming up the marble staircase. She rushed into the room. "I think we found him," she called out as soon as she saw him.

"Where's Tim?"

"He said he had a meeting with the town council that he couldn't miss. Actually, I think he was trying to impress you with his modesty by not bringing the news himself."

Vail looked at her patiently, tipping his head to one side, telling her not to draw it out herself.

"Okay, okay," she said, "the air force guy. I'm getting to that. Who knew that working applicants for decades would have an upside? Tim seemed to know everybody. The first stop was this air force colonel. He was in charge of personnel there. Tim explained about the sensitivity of the inquiry, and this guy was great. He explained that whatever he gave us would have to go through his commanding officer, who is an air force general. So I made the decision—let's go see him right now. He told the colonel to let us have carte blanche. The only thing he wanted was to be given the heads-up should we have to arrest one of his people. I told him I'd personally call him. The colonel found the infrared facial-recognition drone project almost immediately. We played the tape for him, and he didn't recognize the voice. He determined there were eight individuals assigned to it who could have had access to the actual plans. One is a woman, so she's out. Of the remaining seven, four are still there. The others either have finished their hitch or were transferred. Now it gets interesting. One of them disappeared over a year ago. They're still carrying him as AWOL, an E-5 staff sergeant named Richard David Gallagher. I got a copy of his service record. The colonel also gave me copies of the other six."

She handed Gallagher's file to Vail, and he flipped through its pages until he found what he was looking for. "Did you read this?"

"I haven't had a chance."

He handed it back to her. "Let me see the rest of them while you take a look."

She read a few pages and closed the file. Vail looked at her, and she said, "He was born and raised in Texas. Whatever accent Preston has, it's not Texan. I thought with him taking off, I was onto something, because we don't know how old that recording is."

"Actually, I think you are. The percentage of air force E-5s going AWOL has to be about zero. He may not be Preston, but that he's missing may not be a coincidence." Vail went back to reading the other files. When he looked at the fourth one, he read the first page and then handed it to Kate. He went over to the computer and started typing.

"Master Sergeant Chester Alvin Longmeadow, E-7, grew up in Patzau, Wisconsin."

Vail punched one last key on the computer and, watching the screen, said, "Which is in northern Wisconsin on the Minnesota border."

"He's had several Article Fifteens, whatever that is, for drinking-related incidents," Kate said, continuing to read the file.

"They're administrative actions taken by his commanding officers when something isn't court-martial serious. And it's not unusual for a double agent to have a drinking problem, or a gambling problem, or women problems. Actually, I believe it's a requirement."

"So do you think this is him?" Kate asked.

When Vail didn't answer, she looked over at him. He got up and started exploring the information on the wall. "Longmeadow—that's an unusual name. I've seen it before." He looked at the reports and files scattered around the room. To himself he said, "Please tell me I don't have to go through all this again."

He went to the window and pulled up the shade. Sitting down, he let his stare reach the old Russian embassy across the street. He picked up a pencil and tapped its eraser on the tabletop like a drumstick. Finally Vail snapped to his feet and walked over to a smaller table, where Bursaw had piled up the printouts from Sundra's laptop. He took them and sat down on the couch. "Can you call Luke and run Longmeadow's name by him?"

"You think he's involved in the analyst's disappearance? That doesn't make any sense."

"I know. For some reason I've got it in the back of my mind it's connected. Maybe Luke can eliminate it."

Kate dialed Bursaw's cell. "Luke, it's Kate. We got some names at the Pentagon that could be Preston. Steve wants me to run one by you—Chester Alvin Longmeadow. He thinks it might have come up in Sundra's case." She listened a moment and then said to Vail, "He's not sure."

"Tell him it might be something from the deleted files."

Kate relayed the message and then said to Vail, "He's still not sure, but there is something familiar about it."

"Then tell him I need him back here."

She told him and hung up. "Twenty minutes."

Vail patted the couch next to him, and Kate sat down. He handed her half the Sundra Boston pile. "If it's anywhere, I think it's in here. Somewhere."

Kate started looking through the pages, carefully piling the ones she finished next to her. "Are you sure you saw Longmeadow's name in this case? It just doesn't seem possible that the Russians could be connected to Sundra's disappearance."

"I know, but with that other air force sergeant, Gallagher, also disappearing without a trace, it's something we have to consider."

"But he wasn't the mole. Why would they make him disappear?"

"You weren't a spy, and they tried a different kind of vanishing act on you. Keep looking. If I'm wrong about that name being in here, then there's no connection."

Fifteen minutes later they heard Bursaw come in. He walked into the room and said, "What's going on?"

Vail told him what Kate and Mallon had found at the Pentagon, and that Longmeadow was currently their leading suspect to be Preston. Vail gave him half his remaining stack, and Bursaw started going through it, not even taking the time to pull off his topcoat.

Suddenly Kate said, "Here it is. Toll records for a Chester Longmeadow."

Vail and Bursaw moved closer and read over her shoulder.

Bursaw said, "Then her disappearance has to be connected to the Russians."

"Apparently so. We just have to figure out how." Vail told him about the missing air force sergeant.

"Why are they making these people disappear?"

Vail leaned back and closed his eyes for a few seconds. "There's a hidden level of this that we're not seeing."

"Like what?" Kate asked.

"I don't have the slightest idea, but our neat little explanation for everything so far being caused by old-school Russia versus old-school U.S. isn't going to work anymore. There's a well-camouflaged hand in this."

"Do you mean like an agent provocateur," she asked, "someone trying to use us against our own interests?"

"Something like that. But since we don't know whether it's a person, a group, or another country, and we don't know what their real purpose is, it's more like an agent X."

"This is getting too big. We're going to need some help," Kate said.

Vail just looked at her in response.

"Shouldn't we at least tell the director?"

"You don't tell *just* the director. There are people he has to inform, and so do they." Vail looked at his watch. "It's too late to get anything done tonight, but first thing in the morning, Luke, we've got to find out if there are more missing people who could be related to this whole thing. You made some contacts when you came up with those missing prostitutes. You're going to have to search Virginia, D.C., and Maryland and look for people with clearances who are missing. If you run into a possible, just check the name in indices, since we should have background-investigation files on them. If they're not in there, move on. Also, it would be nice to know why Sundra was looking at Longmeadow—where that lead came from."

"I'll make some calls."

"Kate and I will get Longmeadow's phone calls broken down and see who he's been calling."

"I assume we're not going to talk to him," Kate said.

"We're not going anywhere near him, his residence, his bank, or his dry cleaner. We need him alive. Luke, let's run this one backward for a while and see what you come up with. In the meantime Kate and I will figure out who's on Longmeadow's speed dial."

Bursaw said, "I should be able to get this done by sometime tomorrow." He got up and left.

Kate was studying Longmeadow's phone records. "We're going to need a subpoena to get information on this many phone numbers. We can sneak one or two by our contact at the phone company, but this is too much."

"Think Tim Mallon can help us out?" Vail asked.

"With the phone company?"

"That guy Hillstrand who took the two kids, didn't I read that he was coming up for trial?"

"Tim did say a hearing had been set for next month and that if Hillstrand didn't plead out, he'd need you and me to testify."

"Then I'm sure the prosecutor is in a frenzy, throwing subpoenas around like confetti. We'll get Tim to piggyback our numbers on one of them. I'm sure there's enough useless information being accumulated right now in the name of justice that you could probably sneak in a request for the invasion plans of North Korea and no one would notice. That's one good thing about a child's kidnapping: People become so emotional that they don't mind bending a few rules. Can you call Tim again?"

"Right now?"

"You said he owed us *two* favors, didn't you?"

"I was thinking more of the misdemeanor variety."

"There is a time for misdemeanors, and there is a time for magnificence."

"You sound like Fagin instructing the Artful Dodger."

"Actually, I think that's from Foghorn Leghorn."

"It doesn't really matter whether it's Dickens or Warner Brothers, the important thing is that it's an irrefutable source."

She found the number on her cell phone and dialed. Vail watched as she walked up and down the length of the room, slightly uncomfortable with what she was about to ask an old friend to do. She had slipped her shoes off and glided as if on skates across the hardwood floors, trying to make the call less rigorous. She laughed at something Mallon said. Her laugh was almost too husky to be feminine, but that's what made it seem genuine to Vail. Finally she made her request of the Reston chief and gave Vail a playful glare as she asked Mallon to falsify the subpoena.

After telling him she'd e-mail the phone numbers they were interested in, she snapped her phone shut at Vail in mild protest. "First thing tomorrow morning, Stan."

"Thank you."

"What else?"

"I think we're both off duty," Vail said.

"I should go get some sleep. There might be other friendships I have to violate, and I don't want to be dozing off during that."

" 'Should' makes it sound like you want to be talked out of it."

"Sorry, I'm saving myself."

"For?"

"I think it was Foghorn Leghorn who said it best—'a time for magnificence.' "

He moved close to her and put his arms around her. With a lopsided grin, he said, "I'll be quick, I promise."

Kate had to be careful not to show how painful it was to maintain her nonchalance. There was nothing she wanted more right now than to accept his offer. "See, there's the problem, bricklayer. Only men equate quickness with magnificence."

THIRTY

WHEN KATE CAME IN THE NEXT MORNING, SHE FOUND VAIL IN THE KITCHEN cooking. "Did you eat?" he asked her. He was piling French toast and bacon on a plate.

"It looks like there's only enough for six people, so I won't deprive you. Have you heard from Luke?"

"He's not big on checking in until he's got the answers."

"Too bad you two don't have more in common."

"Did Tim say he'd call?"

"Yes. And he has the fax number here."

Vail sat down and picked up a fork. "You sure?" he asked, pointing at the plate.

"I know that Chicago is 'hog butcher for the world,' but they have heard the rumors about cholesterol there, right?"

"'Stormy, husky, brawling / City of the Big Shoulders.' Does that sound like it was built by men who eat bran muffins?" He stood up and put his arm around her waist. Taking her right hand in his left, he started dancing with her and singing:

I saw a man, he danced with his wife
In Chicago, Chicago, my hometown

After a couple more turns, she stepped back, laughing. "Sit down and eat, you maniac." She watched him for a few seconds. "You're in an awfully good mood."

"Good food, a new mystery, and"—he leaned in close and lowered his voice—"an extremely lusty wench who I suspect I'm about to close the deal with. Life is bountiful."

"Apparently Carl Sandburg forgot to mention dementia in his list of Chicago's attributes." She went over to the counter and poured herself and Vail a cup of coffee. "Anything I can do until we hear from Tim?"

"Maybe you'd better make an appearance at headquarters. We don't need people getting curious."

"I do have a ton of mail that I need to get through, as boring as that suddenly seems."

"Hey, I offered you an alternative. You could be in there right now trying to keep me from falling off one of those army cots, but apparently I'm demented."

"Ah, yes, nothing says romance quite like 'army cot.'"

ABOUT 11:30 A.M. the off-site's phone rang. It was Kate. "Tim just called me. He's faxing the phone information to you."

"I still haven't heard from Luke. Can you get out of there?"

"I'm through about half this mess. If I set fire to the other half, I don't think anything would be lost or I'd be missed."

Vail looked over at the fax machine as it came to life and started printing pages. "We've got incoming facsimiles."

"I'm on my way."

By the time Kate got there, Vail had pinned sheets of paper to a new section of the wall. She went and stood next to him as he studied them. "Anything?"

"Fortunately, Master Sergeant Longmeadow doesn't appear to have many friends. And family, if they do exist, don't appear to be a priority. But he does have a small, inexplicable pattern of calling a car wash."

"A car wash? Who calls a car wash?"

"The phone is listed to the Sunshine Car Wash Company, but according to the utility companies the address comes back to the Lithuanian Chess Society."

"A chess club?"

"They probably figured if the mob could have hunting and fishing clubs, why not chess for them?"

"Do you think they're actually Lithuanian or a front for the Russians?"

"There's only so many things you can find out staring at a wall."

"We're going there, aren't we?" Kate asked.

"I seriously doubt that you dropped everything and ran over here to stay *out* of trouble."

AS KATE NAVIGATED through the crowded traffic of northwest D.C., she said, "This is the Adams Morgan area. Lot of Latinos and West Africans. And a mix of everything else—and now, I guess, even Lithuanians. Or maybe Russians pretending to be Lithuanians. This is it up on the right."

She parked in front of the address. It was a brick storefront with a long, thin slotted window too high up to see into. There was a small, hand-painted sign affixed to the paneled-steel front door, which read THE LITHUANIAN CHESS SOCIETY. The background was a black-and-white checkerboard pattern. Above it was a peephole and, to the left, a doorbell. "Apparently they're not looking for any walk-in members,"

Vail said. He rang the bell and held his credentials up to the peephole. Almost immediately he sensed that someone had come to the door and was watching them.

A man in his early fifties opened the door. He was dressed in a suit, and his hair was thick and carefully cut. "FBI?" he said, and stepped back. "Please come in out of the cold." Although his diction was flawless, it didn't take a trained ear to detect he was from somewhere in Eastern Europe. "Are you also with the FBI, miss?"

The question, trying to mitigate its condescension with the courtesy of "miss," was meant to inform this woman, no matter how attractive, of her second-class citizenship inside the walls of the Lithuanian Chess Society. Kate smiled perfectly to relay her understanding of the tactic, and its ineffectiveness. She opened her credentials with an experienced flick of the wrist. Intentionally, she gave no verbal response, enhancing her authority even more.

"I'm Steve Vail, and this is Kate Bannon," Vail said. "Actually, she's my boss." The man stared at him for a moment and then said, "Alex Zogas." He seemed to be speaking to Vail only, as though still trying not to acknowledge Kate's presence.

Although he knew the answer, Vail asked, "What exactly is this place?"

"This is a social club, but our main interest is chess. Everyone who belongs is a master."

"And Lithuanian?"

"Some of us are, but members come and go. You know how it is."

"And that's all you do here, play chess?"

"We have dinner a few times a week. We come here to get away."

"From?"

"In American homes there are pressures that men from our backgrounds are not accustomed to." Zogas smiled and glanced at Kate. "We come here to commiserate."

"Any chance I can get an application?"

Zogas laughed. "I don't know. If you are Lithuanian, it would help."

"Unfortunately, I have no idea what my heritage is. My father was always wanted by the law, so we were continuously changing names. The only thing I know for sure is that I'm a citizen of the United States."

"As are all of us, if that's what you are trying to find out with your little 'antibiography,' shall we say."

Vail grinned. "That was one of my curiosities."

"And the others are . . . ?" Zogas asked.

"I was wondering if there was any business purpose to your group."

"Other than members networking, no, none. This is strictly social."

"Are you the only one here now?"

"No, there are others in the back if you'd like to talk to them," Zogas offered. "Mind if I ask why you're here?"

Vail held out a photo of Sundra Boston. "She's why. Ever seen her?"

Zogas looked at it and said, "Around here? We discourage having members bring women in. Who is she?"

"Her name is Sundra Boston, and she works for the FBI. She's missing."

"Why would you look for her here?"

"Apparently she was looking into your club's activities."

"Chess?"

"She's a financial analyst," Vail lied.

"We collect dues from which our monthly expenses are paid. That's the only thing financial about our club. You're welcome to look at our accounts. It's all on the computer in the office, if it'll help clear this up."

"It would be nice if things were that simple. But we'll have a look."

Zogas gave Vail an inadvertent smirk. "Back this way." He led them through a large room that had a half-dozen tables with chessboards embedded in their tops, two of which were being used. None of the four men looked up at the agents as they walked through.

In the very back of the club were two smaller rooms, one a bathroom, the other an office, which Zogas led them into. Then he turned on the computer. Vail noticed a chessboard on a small table next to the desk. A game appeared to be in progress, but there was no room for a chair on the opposite side. "A game by mail?" Vail asked.

"Yes. Do you play?"

"I played for a couple of months in college. Very intently, but I just didn't have the patience for it."

"That's too bad. For someone in your line of work, it could be an asset." After opening up a file marked "Club Expenses," Zogas got up and offered Vail the chair. Kate moved behind him.

He scrolled through the last two years' entries, which showed a balance that was usually in the black, occasionally crossing into the red at the end of the month. He looked up at Zogas. "Pretty boring stuff."

"We are men who find chess fascinating. Did you expect our lives to be secretly interesting?"

"I must have missed something when I tried it. What is it about chess that you find so intriguing?"

"Are you familiar with the term 'zero sum'? It is from game theory. It means that someone has to win and someone has to lose. We find it a welcome relief from the constant compromising of present-day America and its obsession with equality."

"That has been this country's downfall," Vail said. "As far as you know, none of your members have had any contact with the FBI, for any reason?"

"Not that I'm aware of," Zogas said. "How would our name come up in one of your investigations?"

"I guess that's the real question, isn't it?" Vail wasn't going to tell Zogas that it was Longmeadow's phone records, in case someone knew him and might warn him. It was a long shot, but he didn't like the Lithuanian's calculated responses to his questions, so he decided that a couple of lies would give Zogas something to think about. "The woman I showed you a picture of did all kinds of investigations. Sometimes institutional irregularities came to her attention, sometimes people called in tips, and sometimes something was a spin-off of another investigation. The notes she left behind indicated that she was just getting started on the LCS—sorry, that was her shorthand for your club, or society if you prefer—so there wasn't much detailed information. Do you have any enemies who might have called the FBI about your club?"

"No."

"How about any bad business deals away from the club? What kind of businesses are your members involved in?"

"Nothing very exotic. We are all successful, with varying interests. It's kind of an unwritten requirement for membership here, to be financially established. I, for example, own eight coin-operated car washes in the D.C. area. They're all self-serve, so my time to run them is minimal. Others have dry-cleaning stores, car rentals, and hair-cutting shops. One of our members even does some translating for the government in immigration cases. Certainly nothing that would be cause for retribution against a group of men whose passion is chess."

"Well, this just may be one of those times that a mystery has to remain a mystery. Do you mind if I show the others the woman's photo?"

"Please do."

They walked back into the game room. Zogas spoke with the vague authority of a leader. "These people are from the FBI. They have a photograph of a missing woman who also worked for the FBI and was apparently looking into our club's activities." There was no reaction from any of the four men, none of them even looking up. Vail glanced at Kate to confirm the oddity of their lack of response.

Vail went over to the first table and showed the photograph. "Her name is Sundra Boston. Have you ever seen or heard of her?" Both men shook their heads in silence.

At the second table, Vail showed the photograph again, and after the two men glanced at it, he continued to study their faces. They both appeared to have dark circles around their eyes and mouths. "I'm sorry, you seem familiar," Vail said to the one who hardly looked at the photo. "Have we met before?"

Slowly the man raised his eyes to Vail. In a controlled tone, he answered, "No." Even though a single syllable, Vail could hear its heavy accent.

"I'm sorry, what is your name?"

The man glanced at Zogas, who gave an almost undetectable nod. "Algis Barkus."

Vail smiled. "No, I guess not. I would have remembered that name. Everyone, thank you for your time."

Zogas walked them to the front door. "If there is anything else we can do for you, please do not hesitate to ask."

"There is one thing that would help put this to rest. Do you think we could get a list of your membership?"

For the first time since their entering the club, Zogas appeared to be caught flat-footed. "That might be a problem."

"Why?" Vail asked, almost before Zogas finished.

"We have worked extremely hard since coming to this country and taking citizenship. We enjoy having this sanctuary and, in relative anonymity, being allowed to socialize with men of similar interests. This is a small but, we feel, elite group. I doubt that the membership would approve of the U.S. government knowing exactly who we are. We fear that it wouldn't be long before someone from some governmental agency would be demanding we admit two Hispanics, four females, and someone in a wheelchair."

"We're only looking for a quick way to cross you off our list of people who might know something about one of our employees disappearing. We're not going to turn your membership roster over to Health and Human Services."

"I'll tell you what, Agent Vail. I will present your argument to the members, and they'll put it to a vote."

"How long will that take?"

"A day, two at the most."

"I'll call you. Is there a number here?"

Zogas took out a business card and wrote it on the back. "Give me two days. By then I should have a definitive answer."

For the first time since entering the club, Vail heard the men in the back speak. He listened for a moment and then asked, "Is that Lithuanian?"

"Yes, it is."

"Interesting. People, probably myself included, have a tendency to lump all the Eastern European languages together. But it is definitely different from, say, Russian." Vail watched him closely to see if "Russian" hit any nerves.

"You have a good ear. They are definitely different languages."

Once they were outside, Kate said, "I guess we've solved one mystery today. Now we know the whereabouts of Himmler's, Goebbels's and Göring's sons." When Vail didn't laugh, she thought that his mind had once again raced ahead, trying to find the next turn. She glanced at him and saw something in his face she'd never seen before. He actually looked shaken. "Steve, what is it?"

He turned and searched her face as if he didn't know who she was. Then he said, "I know who framed you."

THIRTY-ONE

WHAT!" When Vail didn't answer, Kate asked again. "What did you say?"

"Not here." He grabbed her by the arm and glanced back at the club, pushing her toward their car.

He started the engine, and she asked again. "What is it?"

Still he wouldn't answer but pulled away from the curb and drove off, once more checking to see if anyone from the club was watching. When he got a block away and was certain that none of the Lithuanians could see them, he pulled over. "That night you and I broke into the Russian safe house in Denton, remember?"

"Guys in ski masks, large handguns, you setting off explosives, fire—something about it rings a bell."

"Did you notice anything funny about that guy Barkus or the other one playing chess with him?"

"Other than their warmth toward FBI agents, especially the female subspecies, not really," she said. "Oh, Barkus had dark circles under his eyes. Probably something to do with his not getting back to the coffin until after sunrise."

"You weren't as close to him as I was. Or the other one. They both had them, dark circles all the way around their eyes—and around their mouths, too."

"What were they?"

"Dozens of tiny cuts scabbed over."

"The areas left exposed by ski masks. From the shattered light-bulbs," Kate said.

"And that night they were speaking in some foreign language that wasn't Russian. It sounded Eastern European. It could have been Lith-uanian. It all makes sense now. That guy in the tunnel in Chicago, Jonas Sakis, he made a reference to game theory and zero-sum games. And when I said something about him being Russian, he gave me this strange smirk. It was because he was Lithuanian."

"That means—oh, my God!" Kate said. "That means these guys are tied directly to the Russians. They're working with them, and they have ears and eyes in the NSA, the CIA, the Pentagon, the State Department, and who knows where else."

"That's why we've got to be very careful. You, me, and Luke, no one else."

"*No one else?* The three of us against all of them?"

Vail ignored Kate's plea. "The real question is, what's the connec-tion between the Lithuanians and Sundra—and you?"

She shook her head in disbelief at his self-control, gaining her own calm from it. "Connected how?" she asked.

"I don't know, but I got the feeling that the Lithuanian Chess Soci-ety is going to vote nay to our getting a membership list. So let's drive around here while you write down as many tags as possible. Maybe we can identify some of them." Vail put the car in gear, and said, "There was also something Zogas said that bothers me."

"What?"

"You're familiar with statement analysis?"

"A little bit. It's been years since I used it at OPR."

"Do you remember what he said in his announcement to the others about Sundra?"

"No."

"I told him that she *works* for the FBI. He told them that we had a photograph of a missing woman who had *worked* for the FBI. Past tense."

"Couldn't that just be a translation problem for him?"

"It could be. He had an accent, but his grammar was almost flawless. Anyone who uses words like 'commiserate' or can explain game theory in a few words or think of something like 'antibiography' has a better command of English than I do."

"Then that's not a good omen for Sundra, is it?" Kate asked rhetorically.

WHEN THEY PULLED UP at the off-site, they saw Bursaw's car parked in front. "Good, Luke's here. Maybe he can help figure this out."

In the workroom they filled Bursaw in on everything that had happened and their conclusion that the LCS was somehow connected to both Sundra Boston's disappearance and Kate's being framed. Vail explained about Zogas's possible slip in verb tense concerning the well-being of the missing analyst.

Bursaw considered it for a moment. "More often than not, that stuff is accurate. I hope it *was* just a translation problem. I'd like to think we haven't been looking for a dead body."

Vail handed him the list of license plates Kate had taken down at the chess club. "Can you get these run, but not through WFO? Have the locals run them and keep it quiet."

"That detective from Metro Homicide we turned Jonathan Wilkins over to said if I ever needed anything. I've known him for a while, so it won't be a problem to keep it quiet."

"Until we figure it out, we don't need to be distracted by who might know what. You, Kate, and me—that's it. If something leaks out, we won't have to waste time wondering if someone from the Bureau innocently mentioned it to someone that they shouldn't have. We'll know it's something the opposition somehow came up with on their own and we can trace it back that way," Vail said. "How'd you do with the missing persons?"

"I found only one. Maurice Lyle Gaston, late of Matrix-Linx International, Springfield, Virginia. We did a security clearance on him. Matrix-Linx has a defense contract. The only fly in the ointment was that he disappeared in Las Vegas. A sister who lives here reported him missing to Fairfax County when he failed to come back from a weekend getaway there."

"Las Vegas. Interesting." Vail wrote down the information in a small notebook. "Good. Kate and I will look into it."

"On a more definitive note, I did find out how Longmeadow came up in her files."

"How?"

Bursaw smiled as if he were about to unveil an important piece of the puzzle. "In a counterintelligence case. Surveillance was following a Russian by the name of Dimitri Polakov. He was later expelled from the U.S. for suspected spying activities. It was Labor Day, last year, and a surveillance team was looking for a target to follow around. They had no reason to believe he was doing anything—they just wanted to log enough hours to qualify for holiday pay. You know, before they *lost* him and had no choice but to break off the surveillance and go home. All of a sudden, this guy coasts up to a mailbox and then takes off. The team leader sees there's a signal chalked on the box, so now they realize that they've stumbled onto something. There was going to be a drop. Polakov drives all over for the next two hours and lands at an apple orchard that's open to the public—you know, to pick your own apples. The target gets out of his car and wanders off down one of the paths. The crew goes into the parking lot, and they start copping tags, hoping that whoever he's meeting has a car there. They write down fourteen of them. Meanwhile two agents follow Polakov on foot, but he never makes a drop or picks any apples, so the team thinks that they may have gotten burned. But still they had the plates. Maybe one of the tags belongs to whomever Polakov was supposed to meet. They give all of them to Sundra to look into. Subsequently she was just running out the leads by the numbers when she requested tolls on the owners of the cars in the lot. One of them was Chester Alvin Longmeadow."

"So he was there for a drop but probably made the surveillance, and the exchange never took place. That's nice work, Luke," Vail said. "It ties Sundra to Longmeadow, who we now know is connected to the LCS through the sergeant's phone records. And we know that the Lithuanians are connected to the Russians because of their coming to the safe house in Denton."

Bursaw held up the list of license plates collected at the chess club. "I'll head over to Metro and get these run."

After he left, Kate said, "Well, it looks like we've got all the players. Now we just have to figure out how they fit together."

"That's why I thought the three of us should sit down and brainstorm this."

"You're going to wait until Luke comes back?"

"Actually, I thought we'd enlist the help of Sakichi Toyoda."

"Who's that?"

"He was considered the king of Japanese inventors, at least in the early twentieth century. He started a little company called Toyota,"

Vail said. "But more important, at least for us, he developed the concept of the Five Whys. Ever heard of it?"

"I don't think so."

"Toyoda figured out that when a problem occurs, if you ask why five times, give or take, you'll trace any problem back to its root cause and then can prevent it from recurring."

"I'm not sure I understand."

"Let me give you an example. You have a business manufacturing and selling porcelain dog figurines. One day your customers start calling to complain that the items they received all have the same damage. Let's say the left ear has a crack in it. So you ask *why* are they arriving in that condition? That's one. You find that every one was shipped that way. So, through a series of whys, you discover—number two—that they're coming out of the mold like that because the mold tears during the injection process. And—number three—that's happening because the person who's operating the machine isn't calibrating it properly. Why hasn't he been calibrating it? Number four—because he's new and he didn't know he was supposed to. And—number five—why didn't he know? Because it wasn't part of his training. So you make it a requirement that anyone performing that task has to receive *x* number of hours of training. Problem solved and, in all likelihood, permanently."

"So if we can answer enough whys, we can figure all this out?"

"I suppose if a person can answer enough questions, he can figure out anything. This is not easy to do. It takes a lot of discipline, a lot of looking at the big picture and the small picture at the same time. However, it does have a way of cutting through the layers of distraction, which in this case are everywhere. If we can do it, we might find a starting point."

"Okay, what's the first why?"

Vail moved to a wall adjoining the one with the documents pinned to it. "I think you've already asked that." With a black marker, he wrote:

1. *Why would the LCS be connected to Sundra, the safe house, & the Calculus list?*

Kate said, "Shouldn't that be 'How'?"

"The important thing is to pursue answers to the questions. Toyoda probably wasn't an English major, but he was a genius. Out of respect, let's just use his whys."

"Sorry." Kate thought for a second. "The LCS has to be working with the Russians."

"That's the only possible explanation, with them coming after us in that safe house. And now we can trace Sundra back to Longmeadow, who we know is spying for the Russians. But Lithuanians, historically, have never been fond of the Russians. In fact, Lithuania was the first of the Soviet states to declare its independence after the fall of the Berlin Wall. So . . ." Vail wrote:

2. *Why would the LCS and the Russians be working together?*

"I don't know, why?"

"What's always the best guess for motive? Someone wrote a song about it making the world go round?"

"I'm guessing it's not love, so you think this is about money?"

"Very few things aren't. Zogas described himself as a businessman. He said they all own small businesses. They're entrepreneurs. When the Russians need somebody taken out, they call the LCS and are able to keep their own hands clean. If that is true, it brings us to 'why' number three. If the Russians are paying the LCS . . ." He wrote:

3. Why do the Russians want their moles dead?

Kate thought about it for a second. "Like we've been saying all along, it doesn't make any sense, because historically the Russians have always done everything to help their double agents escape to Russia or some other communist country."

"That's a good point. And it brings us to the next why." Turning to the wall, he wrote:

4. Why didn't they kill Rellick immediately?

Studying the wall, Kate said, "We haven't really answered number three yet, have we?"

"No, we haven't. I think we need to consider both questions together. That Rellick was the exception might answer why the others weren't given the option to escape."

Kate said, "The whole point of framing me was to protect Rellick. Maybe he was that valuable to them. Maybe they thought that once he was safely in Russia, he would have been some sort of monument to Russian ingenuity and American decadence."

"Let's assume you're right, or at least partially right. That leaves one last unanswered question." He wrote:

5. Why are other people with security clearances, who are not spies, disappearing?

"First the air force sergeant and now—for the sake of argument— let's assume that Maurice Gaston with Matrix-Linx International is also part of this," Vail said.

"At this point that doesn't seem like much of a stretch."

"No, it doesn't," he said mechanically, his voice already slipping away. Vail took a chair from the desk and rolled it over in front of the wall. He sat down, and his face dissolved into a reflective blank. Kate lowered herself onto the couch to wait, occasionally glancing at the questions and trying to guess where Vail's mind was at the moment.

Almost fifteen minutes later, Vail stood up out of his chair. "There's only one possibility—at least that I can think of. The LCS isn't killing these people for the Russians, they're doing it to protect themselves."

"From what?"

"This is the age of outsourcing. They saw the need for a new service industry and offered it to the Russians. This is also the age of incompetence in government. Maybe the SVR wasn't recruiting sources like the old KGB had, and Moscow was pressuring them to find a solution. The LCS is a full-service intelligence enterprise. Not only will they kill someone for you, but they also recruit informants for the Russians."

"What makes you think that?"

"Two things. First, that's why they've been killing their own moles when we get close. They're afraid they may talk if we get them in custody, and once it's exposed, that would be the end of what I'm guessing is a very lucrative business venture for the Lithuanians. It's the only way to explain the two missing people. If you're going to go out and recruit people to betray their country, chances are you're not going to be one hundred percent successful. So if the LCS approaches someone and they're turned down, what would they be most afraid of?"

"Their recruit going to the FBI."

"And the LCS can't have that. So if you refuse, you lose—your life."

"They can't be approaching these people cold and expecting them to turn," Kate said.

"You're right, they're probably not. The key is Gaston disappearing in Las Vegas. Where better to compromise someone than a place with unlimited liquor, gambling, women, and desperation?"

"So they're blackmailing them into giving up classified secrets."

"That's the only way everything makes sense. I suppose they may occasionally get a lead on someone who's heavily in debt or overleveraged with the bookies, but I think their tool of choice is most likely extortion. It's as old as spying itself. Another advantage to it is that if you're just an everyday double agent for the Russians, you can quit anytime you want to, but if our Lithuanian chess players have got something on you, you're in forever."

"So these people they recruit aren't being paid?"

"Once they're compromised, and probably recorded, the LCS owns them. I'd guess they're given a small percentage of what the Russians pay. At this point I think we can safely assume that Longmeadow is Preston. Remember what he said on the tape: 'This time I want a hundred thousand dollars in cash, just for me.' In other words, he's tired of sharing. He wasn't talking to his Russian handler, he was negotiating with an LCS extortionist."

Now it was Kate who stared at the five questions on the wall. She filtered them all through Vail's conclusions. Finally she said, "You're making some leaps, but I can't think of anything to disprove it. It does all fit."

"For the moment."

"Meaning?"

"This *is* all supposition. They know that the only way we can prove any of this is by turning the people they've recruited. That's why they've been killing them as soon as we get close."

"So they've destroyed all the potential witnesses against them."

"Not all of them. We have Longmeadow, who evidently they think we've missed so they're leaving him be."

"Then why don't we go get him and see if he'll come clean? If he is being blackmailed, he'd probably be glad to get them off his back."

"Two things. First, we have no evidence other than that brief recorded conversation, and I'm not sure we could prove it's his voice or that there's any real spying involved. Second, every time we've gone anywhere near one of these people, they wound up dead. The LCS has some early-warning system in place. Until we can figure out what it is and how to get around it, I think we should let him be. With Rellick dead, they probably think we're satisfied that everything has been put to rest. A couple of days isn't going to make any difference. This is another advantage to our not telling anyone else; we don't have to worry about it leaking out while we wait."

"And in the meantime . . . ?"

"The routine stuff. We'll try to find out if they recruited someone else from Matrix-Linx after Gaston disappeared, like they did with the air force. We've got the advantage now. They don't know we're coming."

"You don't think our little trip to their clubhouse will force them to tie up loose ends like Longmeadow?"

"With Rellick dead, I'm hoping not. They've killed all the evidence, remember? But if they do get nervous, they'll have no option but to play defense, and that might mean eliminating all loose ends."

Kate asked, "Aren't we loose ends?"

"These people aren't fools. The easiest way to prevent Rellick from being exposed would have been to kill you. . . ."

Again Vail's thoughts were drifting in another direction. This time she couldn't wait. "What?"

"Your suicide attempt."

"My what? You knew about that?"

Absentmindedly, Vail said, "The director told me about it. That's how he got me to change my mind downstairs that day."

"You believed I would try to commit suicide?"

"Over you dumping me, yeah, that makes sense. He told me that your reputation was being questioned. I know how small-minded these people can be. He thought that if you and I could resolve the Calculus list, the rumors would be put to rest."

"And you never told me? Why? And why would you go through all this if you didn't believe it? You were almost killed—more than once."

He grabbed her roughly by her arm and pulled her against him. His lips were almost touching hers. His breathing quickened. "Aren't you ever going to get this?"

THIRTY-TWO

UNSURE WHERE IT WOULD TAKE THEM—AND NOT SURE SHE CARED—KATE touched her lips lightly to Vail's.

Suddenly the door downstairs opened. She drew her head back and, with her voice unintentionally throaty, said, "That's Luke."

"Luke who?"

She put her head on his chest. "I wish I could remember."

She started to move away, and Vail pulled her hand to his mouth, nipping the skin at the back of it. "What idiot gave him a key?"

As soon as Bursaw walked in, he sensed he'd interrupted something. "I . . . uh, forgot something in the car," he offered diplomatically. "I'll be right back."

"That's all right, Luke. We were just finishing an argument," Kate said playfully.

Bursaw noticed the new handwriting on the wall and went over to it. "Is there one answer to all five questions?"

"We think the LCS is doing contract recruitment of sources for the Russians. Using blackmail when they can."

Bursaw reread the questions and Vail's terse, cryptic answers. After a minute he said, "Impressive. Logically, it does answer all the questions."

Vail turned to Kate. "We must be right. Philosophers take a death oath to never agree with any definitive conclusion."

Bursaw said, "I guess the challenge is proving it?"

"That's what we were trying to figure out."

"Do you think Sundra was approached?" Bursaw asked.

"Hard to say, but my guess would be that they found out she was making inquiries about Longmeadow. Somewhere it leaked out. Maybe, like us, she picked up on all the calls to car washes and started making inquires into Zogas's businesses and he got wind of it. We may never know now. If they approached her, maybe she was offered money to shut her up. It wouldn't have been hard for them to find out how much debt she was in. If they offered her something and she refused, their only option left would be to make her disappear, along with her computer files."

Bursaw turned around, and the anger he was trying to suppress was obvious. "So she *was* just doing her job."

"Her problem was that she was doing more than her job. Don't worry, Luke, we're going to settle this, I promise. But right now we all need to be cool."

Bursaw took a few seconds and then nodded. "I'm okay." He opened his briefcase and removed a stack of papers. "I had those plates run and got only a couple of hits." He smiled more calmly now. "But I had an idea. The few plates that came back to them all listed the club's address, so I had this gal I know at DMV security run an offline search for all vehicles registered at that address for the last three years." He handed Vail a sheet of paper. "Everyone from Alex Zogas on down. Eight altogether."

Vail scanned the list. There was Algis Barkus, who'd had the cuts around his eyes at the club, and one other that Vail found very interesting. "Jonas Sakis." Vail turned the list so Kate could see it. "The guy who tried to kill me in Chicago."

She said, "Then two of them are probably the guys you and John shot in Annandale."

"Which would mean we're down to five."

"So what do we do now? Sit on the club?" Bursaw asked. "We don't have a home address for any of them."

"They'll be looking for us there. No, I was thinking that my car needed washing." Bursaw looked at him questioningly. "Zogas owns car washes. His machines have money in them. You don't think a good businessman would leave them full overnight, do you?"

"I'll go with you."

"Let me change into some surveillance clothes," Vail said. "Kate, you want to come along?"

"Surveillance? You mean me watching you sleep? As enjoyable as that would be, it'll be slightly less boring if I get back to the office and put another dent in that paperwork. You'll call me if you get anything?"

"Only if there's going to be shooting involved."

ALEX ZOGAS HAD BEEN BROODING since the FBI left, and he hadn't said a dozen words. The other four men knew not to say anything when he was like that. At the moment he was playing chess against Algis Barkus, and Barkus could tell by his distracted play that Zogas was planning something. Although he'd told the agents that all the men of the Lithuanian Chess Society were chess masters, only Zogas was, and right now Barkus was playing him even. It was part of Zogas's planning process. There was something about the discipline of the game that he used to unravel and reassemble the most complicated problems. Finally he shifted in his seat, redirecting his concentration to the board, and almost immediately made a brazen move, straightening up and smiling confidently. Whatever the problem was, it had been solved, and Zogas was now less than a handful of moves from checkmate.

It was Zogas's fourth move that caused Barkus to tip his king over in surrender. Zogas got up and went to the office. The men could hear him typing on the computer. A couple minutes later, he came back and gave Barkus a slip of paper with an address on it. "Nine o'clock. Meet me there." Zogas nodded at a second man playing chess, Bernard Mindera, to go with him. Short and powerfully built, Mindera seemed pleased to be chosen and started picking up his chess pieces from the board.

IT WAS AFTER 8 P.M., and the temperature had fallen well below freezing. Vail and Bursaw sat parked at a discreet distance from one of Alex Zogas's Sunshine car washes. "Man, I can't believe that in the dead of winter so many people stand out in the cold to wash their cars," Bursaw said.

"It does seem like a license to steal."

A silver Lincoln pulled in and parked in an out-of-the-way spot that precluded the possibility of its being there for a wash. The two agents watched the well-dressed man get out and tug up the collar on his topcoat. "That's Zogas," Vail said.

There were three washing bays, and they watched as Zogas emptied each of the machines of the day's receipts and put them into a canvas bag. "I had my doubts," Bursaw said, "but you were right about him not wanting to leave the money overnight."

Zogas got back into his car and waited for a break in the traffic. Vail said, "I assume you can follow him without getting made."

"Although I should never bet against you when food is at stake, dinner says I can."

"Why do I get the feeling that my supper tonight is going to be at some drive-through?"

The Lincoln pulled into traffic heading north.

"Any idea where he might be going, Steve?"

"I'm just hoping he leads us to where he lives. We have no background on this guy at all. With a residence we can get a phone number and all kinds of other information."

They followed him to a second Sunshine Car Wash, and Bursaw, once again, set up down the street.

After a third car wash, Zogas drove to a bank and parked in the lot. He sat in the car for a while before Bursaw said, "Looks like he's counting money and filling out a deposit slip."

"I do believe we have found where he does his banking. Those records should be interesting."

Finally Zogas got out of his car and walked over to the night depository, using a key to open it. On the way back, he checked his wristwatch. "Looks like he's got something scheduled. It's after eight thirty, kind of late. Maybe it's spy stuff," Bursaw said.

"Wouldn't that be nice?"

The Lincoln pulled back into traffic, and Bursaw waited for a couple of cars to get between them before easing into the same lane. "He's driving too slow. Think he's early for an appointment?"

They had been traveling southeast for almost twenty minutes when they reached Temple Hills. Zogas parked outside a large apartment complex. The two agents watched as he turned off the ignition and dialed his cell phone. "What do you think, Steve?"

"I have no idea. We've just got to stay with him." They could see him dialing a second number now. After a minute he hung up, started his car, and made a U-turn. Vail and Bursaw looked at each other questioningly. Bursaw turned the Bureau car around and maintained his distance behind the Lincoln again. They followed him for almost a half hour to an upscale neighborhood in Capitol Heights, where he pulled into a three-car garage and then closed the door. Vail made a note of the address.

"So now we know his bank and home address. Not a bad night's work," Bursaw said.

But Vail didn't answer. Bursaw glanced at him. He was sitting with his head back and his eyes closed. Finally Vail said, "Why did he go to Temple Hills to make a couple of phone calls?"

"Maybe he didn't want to call from his home because he's worried about us getting a fix on what cell tower he was running off of. You know these people always think we have more capabilities than we do."

"Maybe," Vail said. He took out a map book of the greater D.C. area. After studying it for a few seconds, he said, "Do you know what's less than two miles from where he stopped in Temple Springs? Andrews Air Force Base. Where does Longmeadow live?"

Bursaw reached into the backseat and retrieved his briefcase. He shuffled through the papers and pulled out Longmeadow's information. "His current address is in Camp Springs, Virginia."

Vail looked back at the map. "It's adjacent to the base, less than two miles from where Zogas made the calls. They're going to kill Longmeadow."

THIRTY-THREE

AS THEY NEARED THE ADDRESS FOR MASTER SERGEANT LONGMEADOW'S APART-ment, Vail spotted one of the cars he'd seen at the chess club. There were two men in the front seat. "Luke, there! The guy driving is the one who calls himself Barkus."

Bursaw waited until there was a little more distance between them before making a U-turn. "Think they saw us?"

"A black guy with a white guy, in this car? I wouldn't be optimistic."

"Do you want to try to stop them?"

"Not yet. If they did kill Longmeadow, he's either in his apartment or in that car. If it's the car, then we want to see where they're going with the body."

Bursaw knew what Vail wasn't saying. Wherever they were heading, if Longmeadow's body was in the car, they were taking it to someplace they considered safe to dump bodies. Maybe that was where Sundra was.

Vail picked up the mike and radioed the Washington Field Office.

"We are following a car with two men who may have just committed a homicide. We need you to call the Camp Springs PD and have them immediately check the following location for a victim." Vail gave them Longmeadow's address and apartment number.

Bursaw continued to follow the car at a discreet distance, keeping at least two other vehicles between them. "Looks like they're heading for 495."

Vail didn't say anything but continued to watch the car closely. It exited onto 495 and then 95 South. "Notice anything funny about the way they're driving?"

"It's by the book. Signaling lane changes, right at the speed limit."

"Who drives like that?" Vail said.

"Someone who doesn't want to get stopped. I'm guessing the late Chester Longmeadow is aboard."

For the next fifteen minutes, they followed the car driven by Algis Barkus. As the traffic thinned out, Bursaw was able to lengthen the distance between it and his Bureau vehicle. Suddenly the WFO radio operator's voice cut through the air. *"The Camp Springs PD just called back. They had the manager let them into the apartment, and it was empty. There were no signs of a struggle or that anything unusual had taken place."*

"Copy, Central," Vail said, and leaned back. "I guess we're on the way to a burial."

The area was more rural now and the road darker. Bursaw was able to drop back even farther. "Think we should call for some help? We're getting close to the Richmond office's turf."

"The whole point is to follow these two until we find where they're going to dump the body. The chances of someone jumping into the middle of a surveillance in progress and not getting burned are about zero."

Barkus signaled that he was exiting off the highway and onto Route

30. "Too late now," Bursaw said. He turned onto the ramp for 30 East. "Here we go."

Once they were on Route 30, Bursaw closed the gap between them. They had gone less than ten miles when Barkus turned right onto a dirt road. Bursaw slowed to let the distance increase, since it would be harder to go unnoticed in such an isolated spot. The road was little more than a trail, narrow and barely passable. Bursaw slowed the Bureau car to a crawl and switched his headlights to parking lights.

There was no illumination from the main road, but the moon had risen and was providing some light through the partially cloudy sky. The road wound around, and with their headlights off, the two agents didn't notice an overgrown path off to the right, which Barkus had turned his vehicle into. The Lithuanian had then made a left-hand turn and switched off his lights and engine, leaving him invisible as Bursaw went by with his parking lights now off. Barkus rolled down his window and listened. Once he heard the FBI car go by, he started the engine, backed up onto the dirt road, then shut the car off again, blocking the road so the agents couldn't drive out of the woods.

Without a word both men got out and went to the trunk. They shoved the heavy canvas bag containing Longmeadow's body to the side and took out night goggles, putting them on quickly. Ironically, Longmeadow had given Zogas the thermal-imaging devices when trying to demonstrate to him the utility of the larger system he was about to sell him the secrets to. Then they took out Russian-made Bison submachine guns, chambering the first round. Positioning themselves behind the car, they waited for Vail and Bursaw to drive back.

A hundred yards farther down the curving road, Bursaw hit the brakes. They were at the beach of a small lake. At one end of the sand was a dock with a ladder leading down into the water, presumably for getting on and off small boats. "Where did they go?" Bursaw asked.

"We must have missed some turnoff, but I didn't see anything other than an overgrown path."

"Think this is where the bodies wound up?"

"If it is, then why aren't they down here?" Vail said. "You'd better go back."

It took Bursaw a couple of passes before he could completely turn the car around. He still hadn't switched his headlights back on, but he drove a little faster in case the two men from the LCS had used the maneuver to lose them. He came around the curve and almost hit Barkus's car before slamming to a stop. "What the—"

Bursaw's unfinished question was answered by automatic fire that ricocheted off the front of the Bureau car. In the muzzle flashes, Vail could see that the men were wearing night-vision goggles. After the first burst, the two gunmen ran from behind the car and into the woods to get some flanking fire into the vehicle from a vantage point where they wouldn't have to fire through the engine block. Both agents saw where they were going and scrambled out of the passenger-side door. "Do you think they made the surveillance?" Vail asked.

"I'd go ask them if I spoke Lithuanian." Another burst of fire raked the car, taking out the driver's-side windows.

"I don't suppose you have anything useful in the trunk, like a SWAT team."

"Just a shotgun."

"Did you see the goggles? They're thermal-imaging."

Bursaw waited a moment for some explanation as to how that was going to help them and then said, "What a fun fact, Mr. Science."

"As soon as they figure out that we only have handguns, they're going to fire and maneuver until they can get around our car, and we'll be sharing a three-body condo with Longmeadow. Go back by the trunk. As soon as you hear them firing at me, look and see where it's coming from. Then start firing in that direction. Take your time, empty a clip—but slowly. As soon as you finish, I'll take off. Those goggles have a very narrow field of vision. I'll fire at them, and they'll see only me, but they'll think we're still together. Then get under the car toward the front. With the engine still running, there'll be a billowing heat signature down there, and they won't be able to distinguish you from the car. They'll chase after me, thinking we're together. Once they do, take the shotgun out and get down to the water as fast as possible."

Vail took off his jacket and pulled off his black sweatshirt, putting the coat back on against the freezing cold. He took out his pocketknife and cut two slits into the shirt.

"You're going down to the water?"

"Something like that. Once you hear gunfire down there, or me yelling . . . well, you can figure it out from there. Just remember, I'll be the guy *without* the goggles."

"There's no place to hide down there."

"Sure there is," Vail said. "You ready?"

Bursaw moved to the back of the car. "Ready."

Vail stood up, and almost immediately automatic-weapons fire raked the opposite side of the car as he ducked down again. Bursaw leaned across the trunk and fired in a slow rhythm.

As soon as he finished, Vail took off, firing a couple of shots to attract the two gunmen's attention. Bursaw scrambled under the car and waited, his handgun reloaded and ready.

When Vail reached the beach, he ran out onto the pier. At the end, by the ladder, he carefully placed his Glock at the edge. Then, without hesitation, he jumped down, breaking through the thin layer of ice covering the lake. Using the ladder to keep himself under, he held his breath in the freezing water that bit into his skin like hot needles. He held a finger to his carotid artery and timed his heart rate. If he and Bursaw were going to get out of there alive, he was going to have to induce the initial stages of hypothermia to lower his body's heat signature. After the run, his heart rate was at fifty-two. After a minute and a half, it had dropped to forty.

He raised his head out of the water and listened. He could hear the two men yelling to each other, working their way through the woods toward the beach. He lowered his head back into the water and waited.

When his heart rate hit thirty-six, he began to shiver uncontrollably, another sure sign of hypothermia. He started feeling light-headed and knew he was on his way to losing consciousness.

Slowly, so the dripping water couldn't be heard, he climbed the ladder, picked up his automatic, and shoved it in the back of his waistband. Then he crawled onto the dock, placing the black shirt over his head and positioning it so he could see through the slits he had cut. He lay still with his hands underneath him and waited for his clothing to freeze. He was shivering violently.

Less than a minute later, Barkus and Mindera stepped onto the beach searching for the agents, looking as much at the woods behind them as in the direction of the water.

The two men were speaking Lithuanian and sounded as though they were both now on the sand. Vail closed his eyes and put his head down so they wouldn't be able to detect the heat coming through the eye slits in his shirt.

Hopefully Bursaw had survived, but Vail couldn't depend on that. Then he heard one of their voices coming closer, almost as if it were aimed at him. Vail knew that besides the narrow field of vision of the thermal goggles, they had one other disadvantage: everything that didn't give off heat appeared green and lumped together, almost completely indistinguishable. Vail was depending on that one shortcoming, but he quickly became less confident when he felt one of his pursuer's step onto the rickety pier and heard him yell something to the other man in Lithuanian that had the unmistakable tone of discovery in it.

Suddenly there was an explosion from the edge of the woods. A single booming shotgun blast was fired in the direction of the voices. And another. Both the Lithuanians wheeled and fired at the large tree where Bursaw was taking cover. Vail got to his feet and, still almost paralyzed with the cold, squeezed his handgun tighter than he ever had before. He fired three rounds at the man closest to him, some fifteen feet away. The body thudded lifelessly onto the pier.

Vail hurried to him, ripped off the goggles, and put them on. He could see that the second man, thinking Vail's shots were his partner's, was moving quickly toward the tree that protected Bursaw. As he moved to within a few feet of the tree, Vail dropped to one knee, held his breath, and emptied his magazine, aiming as best he could with his hands and body shaking furiously. The Lithuanian went down, and Vail stood up, ramming another magazine from his belt into the pistol, not knowing if the time in the water would prevent the rounds from firing. He started running at the fallen gunman, ready to fire again.

As Vail got to him, he called to Bursaw. "Luke, you okay?"

"Yeah."

"They're both down." The second man was dead and on his back. Vail rolled him over. Of the ten rounds Vail had fired at him, only one had hit him, in the middle of the back, apparently finding a vital organ.

Bursaw walked up, and Vail handed him the other set of goggles. He put them on and looked at the body. "You hit him only once? I imagine that's about average for a bricklayer."

For the first time, Bursaw noticed that Vail was wet and that his clothes were frozen. "You went in the water? Come on, we've got to get you to the car."

The Bureau car was still running, and Bursaw turned up the heater as high as it would go. "Take those clothes off."

"Don't get me wrong. I do find you attractive, but . . ." Bursaw helped him pull his jacket off in the confined space. While Vail finished undressing, Bursaw called WFO and told them to get some agents out there.

When he was finished, he got out of the car and took a flashlight from the trunk. He headed back to the beach and five minutes later returned with a set of clothes. "One of the dead guys?" Vail asked.

"Quit complaining, you dress like a communist anyway."

Vail pulled on the clothes and could feel a wet spot on the back of the shirt where the blood of the second man he'd shot was now ice cold.

IT WAS ALMOST AN HOUR and a half before agents from the Richmond office arrived. Fifteen minutes later Kate drove up. She smiled at Vail, a mixture of sarcasm and relief. "I thought you were going to call me if there was shooting. And now I find out there was shooting *and* swimming."

Vail looked over at Bursaw. "Snitch. And you still owe me dinner."

Kate said, "I assume that's Longmeadow's remains in the trunk of their car."

"We're not sure," Bursaw said. "They're still processing the trunk. No ID, and with whatever they wrapped around his head, we can't even see what he looks like."

"Okay, let's go take a peek," Vail said.

"You're going to a hospital," Kate said.

Vail gave her a look that said there wasn't even going to be a discussion about it. He got out of the warm car, shivering slightly, and went back to Barkus's trunk. The heavy canvas bag containing the body had been opened up, revealing that the victim's head had been wrapped in some sort of plastic material. Vail felt a corner of it between his fingers. He smiled in appreciation. "It's bitchathane. Roofing material. They put it at the edge of roofs, six feet or so up, to prevent ice-dam leaks. You can put nails through it and it seals right up. When you get it off the master sergeant here, you'll probably find gunshot wounds to the head. They wrapped it around him and then shot him. That way there was no blood, skull, or brains leaking out at the scene. Pretty ingenious."

Kate said, "Do you think this is their dumping ground?"

"Thanks to Lucas Bumperlock here, they knew we were on them, so I don't know if they were about to lead us to proof of past misdeeds or not. They've been very careful about getting rid of evidence. Sometimes even before it becomes evidence, like Longmeadow here."

"It's still worth searching the lake. You never know," Kate said.

"I suppose so, but even if there are bodies here, it'll only take us back to these two. Maybe we've gotten as even with them as we're going to get."

Kate said, "Luke said it looked like Zogas was supervising the whole thing back at Longmeadow's apartment."

"We'd have to get his phone records and find out who he actually called. Maybe something could be made out of it."

"It's certainly not airtight," she said. "And with all the moles gone, there's no corroboration, so is that it?"

"Let me thaw my brain out and see if there isn't something else we can do."

"I still think you should get checked out at the hospital."

Vail leaned in close and whispered, "I just need something warm and exciting to get my heart rate up."

"I think I could arrange that." She smiled back seductively. "NASCAR is running in Florida this weekend."

THIRTY-FOUR

THE NEXT MORNING KATE PICKED UP AN ORDER OF STEAK AND EGGS FROM A nearby restaurant and let herself into the former observation post on Sixteenth Street. The night before, she had driven Vail back there and couldn't help noticing that his skin was gray from a lack of circulation, and every once in a while, out of the corner of her eye, she would notice his hands shaking. Again he refused medical treatment when she dropped him off. She offered to stay the night in case he needed anything, and when he didn't use the opportunity to suggest the ultimate act of warming, she knew that the cold had taken more out of him than he was admitting. At that point she thought about insisting they go to the hospital but caught herself at the last moment, remembering who she was dealing with. So this morning, instead of going to the office, she thought she should check in on him.

She found him still sleeping and went into the kitchen to make a pot of coffee. After pouring herself a cup, she went back into the workroom. Methodically, she scanned the walls to see if Vail had added anything. It didn't appear so.

She pulled over the desk chair and sat down to look at the graffiti-like displays that documented what they had done. As she sipped her coffee, she realized for the first time that the maze of documents, maps, and handwritten notes seemed to be almost an art form. Most of the writing was Vail's, and, like him, it was enigmatic yet somehow aesthetic. With all its charted paths and irregular branches, it was more of a two-dimensional sculpture than the record of an investigation. She took another swallow of coffee.

"Hi."

She spun around. Vail was in a T-shirt and pants. His color had returned. "I brought you"—she looked at her watch—"brunch. In the kitchen. It should still be warm."

"What is it?"

"Something very Chicago. Pure, slow death to go."

She got up and followed him into the kitchen. He got a fork and opened the Styrofoam container. "Steak and eggs. Whatever you're feeling guilty about, I accept your apology."

"Please, no more thank-yous. You're making me blush," she said. "And on the way here, I got a call from the director of the FBI."

"How is he?"

"Unhappy. He wanted to know why we haven't been keeping him or anyone else up on the investigative minutiae, like dead double agents and the shooting of suspects."

"You didn't mention my name, did you?"

"Believe it or not, of the million or so names that have worn a Bureau badge, yours was the only one that came up. He said he wanted to see you as soon as you had time."

Vail laughed. "I've been fired twice—or is it three times?—from this job, but this will be the first time by the director."

"I wouldn't start working on your exit speech just yet. He doesn't like being blindsided, but he probably figures he's not getting his money's worth out of you unless he is."

"You can't bawl me out and bring me steak. It's very confusing. And as you know, I've been sick lately."

Kate watched as Vail ate ravenously. "Then I'll wait until you get your appetite back." She got up and poured him a cup of coffee. "I don't suppose you've had any *more* epiphanies."

"Actually, I did receive a call from the two A.M. messenger."

He had explained his "messenger" allusion to her once before. Sometimes if he went to sleep with some unresolved problem on his mind, around 2 A.M., probably when his body was about to shift into one of its REM cycles, it woke him up with some sort of answer, probably trying to jettison the psychological baggage of the unresolved mystery to ensure a more recuperative sleep cycle. "And what was the message?"

Vail cut off a large chunk of steak. "As you know, the messenger frequently screws with me, so see how this sounds. It starts with the two air force sergeants. One disappeared and one turned spy. Why did one disappear?"

"If we're right about everything, it was because he didn't want to commit treason," she said.

"Correct. So the Lithuanians recruited someone else from the same project. They must have heard about the technology and decided they needed a piece of it to sell to the Russians, no matter how hard it was to get. Do you know where I'm going with this?"

"The missing guy in Las Vegas, Gaston. You think he disappeared because he refused the Lithuanians. And if you're right, they may have recruited someone in his place. There could still be an active mole at— where did he work?—Matrix-Linx International?"

"Yes. And if there is, and we can figure out who it is, maybe we can use him to get to Zogas," Vail said.

"So how do we find him?"

Vail pushed away the food container. "Unfortunately, the messenger is very lazy. He only leaves me one item at a time."

They got up and took their coffee into the workroom. As though they expected the answer to have been visibly written in their absence, they both searched the wall in silence. Finally Vail said, "I'm going to shower. You figure it out."

A HALF HOUR LATER, Vail reappeared dressed in a suit and tie. "Any luck?"

Her only response was to hand him a printout of a Bureau background investigation.

He read the subject's name. "Raymond Ellis Radkay. Why him?"

"I checked Matrix-Linx International. Maurice Gaston had a top-secret clearance. So I figured the LCS would recruit only someone with an equal level of authorization. There were just four. One was the missing Maurice Gaston, leaving three. Another left the company before Gaston disappeared, and one was a female. Who, because of the chess club's complete disregard for women, I would assume they would not lower themselves to recruit."

"And that leaves Radkay," Vail said. "Well, aren't you the little overachiever so early in the day?"

"It makes you wonder if there aren't more out there. Ones who were once useful but are no longer supplying information."

"It's possible, but we have no way of identifying them. Something occurred to me in the shower—other than you," Vail said. "Maybe the LCS has found another use for their no-longer-productive spies. Do you remember those Disney stores that used to carry the old cartoon cels? I think it was the eighties when they started springing up."

"Sure."

"They were created because one of the bosses at Disney was checking out some storage space somewhere and found tens of thousands of them lying around deteriorating. Because he knew that Americans would collect anything, he instantly saw their potential. Each one was hand-drawn, a legitimate piece of original art. He opened the stores and literally turned debris into millions and millions of dollars."

"What's that have to do with the LCS?"

"I'm sure our little band of entrepreneurs were sitting around their chessboards trying to figure out how to protect the Russians' favorite CIA agent from Kate Bannon when it occurred to them, 'Hey, we've got all these inactive and low-production double agents just lying around collecting dust. Let's figure out a way to turn them into money.'"

"So the LCS was getting paid by the Russians to frame me and getting us to pay them two hundred and fifty thousand dollars apiece for no-longer-useful spies."

"Literally turning debris into a million dollars. At a quarter of a million dollars apiece, I think the LCS would have given up every one of their lesser moles. All they would have to do was make Ariadne's thread a little longer. So there may not be as many as you would think," Vail said.

"That makes sense."

"What's Matrix-Linx's contract for?"

Kate took the report back and flipped through a couple of pages. "Ground weapon systems."

"Our chess players would know that ground weapons systems would be attractive to the Russians. Maybe they heard about the technology and asked the LCS to go find someone to supply it. And let's not forget that the LCS wanted someone at Matrix-Linx bad enough to travel out of state, where they're not nearly as comfortable, and go after a guy who apparently wasn't interested in spying."

"In other words, when Gaston said no and was presumably killed, they knew they had to find someone else at the same company, and as soon as possible."

"Okay, Radkay it is. But now we've got to prove it. Let's start with his financials."

Kate said, "But if, like you said, the LCS was actually paying these guys peanuts, what's going to show up in his bank statements?"

"Assuming he is the mole, they didn't have the same time and means to set him up with blackmail as they had with Gaston. Therefore the inducement was probably more money. At least initially. If so, maybe it'll show in either his bank account or his lifestyle. You don't commit treason out of the clear blue and say, 'I'm just going to save the money for a rainy day.' You start living for today."

"And what if we don't find anything?"

"One problem at a time. Can you strip the financial release forms out of Radkay's report and 'update' them?"

Five minutes later Kate held up the altered informational release for Vail to see.

"An impressive forgery," he said. "I think we're ready to go."

"Do you want to take your car?"

He looked at her as if the question had triggered something. He went to the wall and ran his fingers along the documents, stopping occasionally to read something in detail. "I'm an idiot."

"What?"

"Every time we take my car, we run into the Lithuanians."

"You think there's a bug in your car?"

"Some sort of tracking device, yes. It would answer how they were beating us to the moles."

"But how would they get it on the car?"

"It was probably easy. They knew we were going to trace Calculus's movements, because that's what they set us up to do. They could have done it any time we were out of the car. The ones they have now take seconds to attach."

"I'll get someone from Technical Services to sweep it." She dialed a number and then asked for a technician. After a short conversation, she hung up. "He's going to meet us at one of the surveillance off-sites." Vail was still studying the wall. His eyes were narrowed in an unusual way. "What are you thinking about?"

"My father."

"Your father?"

"Like him or not, he did teach me how to get even."

THIRTY-FIVE

THE SURVEILLANCE SQUAD'S OFF-SITE HAD BEEN CAREFULLY SELECTED. THE neighborhood was a mix of residential and commercial properties. The building was tucked away, down a side street. The front entrance to the building bore no sign to identify it. A driveway skirted the property, and in the back there was a parking lot containing a half-dozen cars.

The technical agent who met Kate and Vail there was a good fifty pounds overweight, but he slid under the back end of Vail's car without difficulty. Almost immediately he pulled himself back out holding a small black box about the size of a pack of cigarettes. He handed it to Kate and spoke with a quick, professional authority. "Held in place with magnets. You can buy these anywhere. Companies use them to keep an eye on their vehicles, parents to discreetly watch their teenagers, suspicious wives to check on husbands, just about anything."

"How is it monitored?" Kate asked.

"If you have a cell phone with a screen, you can load the software into it and you're ready to go. If not, a laptop works even better." He climbed under Kate's car and spent almost ten minutes inspecting it before reemerging. "You're clean," he told her.

"Can you set up my phone so I can monitor it?" Vail asked.

"I don't have the software for this brand. When Kate called, she just said it involved GPS trackers, so I brought a couple." He opened his case and took out a rectangular box that was half the size of the one he had removed. "This was made to our specifications. No connections, no antennas. You can put it in a glove compartment or anywhere else. It's extremely sensitive and tracks in real time. It works on a special network the government uses, so it can't be intercepted." The tech agent then took two cell phones out of his case. "With these you can follow the transmitter." He turned on the phones and walked them through the device's operation.

After he left, Kate held up the cell phone he'd given her and said, "Did you have something in mind with these?"

"Not at the moment, but you know how boys need their toys. We find them reassuring. If I'd had this on the enemy's car last night, I probably wouldn't have had to go swimming."

Vail handed the LCS's device back to the tech agent. "Put it back under my car." Kate looked at him questioningly. "I'll leave it at the off-site and we'll drive yours. If we turn it off, they'll know we found it."

After dropping off Vail's car, they drove to Radkay's bank in northwest D.C. When they arrived, Kate went in with the altered release forms while Vail called the radio room and had them query what kind of cars Raymond Radkay drove. There was only one—a Jaguar XKR. Vail didn't know much about luxury cars, but he had always coveted the Jaguar XKE, first manufactured in the sixties, an exquisite piece of sculpture that also happened to be an automobile. He occasionally checked on the Jaguar's new models to see if the manufacturer had come to its senses and started building the sleek torpedo again.

According to the rest of Radkay's FBI background investigation, he was a computer engineer with Matrix-Linx International and made sixty-eight thousand dollars a year. Give or take a few options, that was about the cost of the XKR. Vail asked the radio-room operator to determine when it was first registered. A few seconds later, he was told that the vehicle was first registered, apparently new, last June, two months after Radkay's co-worker, Maurice Gaston, had disappeared into the Nevada sunset.

Kate came out and got in. "Since last June he's had a couple of eight- to nine-thousand-dollar deposits in his checking account. He also started renting a safe-deposit box six months ago."

"The LCS must have handouts telling these guys what to do with their money. He also bought a sixty-thousand-dollar car last June."

"I guess we should get a court order for the box," Kate said.

"Actually, with you so blatantly altering that release form, it all becomes fruit of the poisonous tree."

"You did this on purpose so we'd have no choice but to go and confront him, didn't you?"

"You give me too much credit. It doesn't really matter if we get into that box. The most he's going to have in there is unexplained cash. That hardly makes him a spy. Don't forget that when we found incriminating evidence in a box before, Calculus had left it for us. We've got to get our hands on this guy and turn him."

"And how are you going to do that?"

"I'll let him know that all I have to do is get that GPS the Lithuanians are tracking me with to within a hundred yards of him and he's dead. The choice is relatively simple: a little time in prison for spying or forever in the great darkness beyond. We'll get Luke and go out to his house tonight."

"So that's your master plan? You're going to threaten his life."

"I'm a man of limited imagination."

IT WAS DARK before the three agents got to Raymond Radkay's home in Coral Hills, Maryland. Bursaw drove his car, and Kate and Vail rode together in hers.

Radkay's house was at the end of a cul-de-sac in a new housing development. Although there were several others under construction, his was the only one that had been completed. Vail pulled over in front of one of the partially built residences. "The lights are on, so it looks like he's home," Vail said on the radio.

Bursaw asked, *"So how do you want to do this?"*

"You and Kate wait in your car. I think this will go better if I talk to him alone. I don't want him to get the feeling we have to gang up on him to get his cooperation. See if you can find a discreet place to watch from. Let me know if you see anyone coming our way."

"This house behind me has the garage roughed in. I'll pull in there." Kate got out of Vail's car and into Bursaw's.

Vail pulled into Radkay's driveway and got out, watching the windows. He walked up the stairs and rang the bell. After a few seconds, a man in his late thirties opened the door. "Can I help you?"

"Raymond Radkay?"

"Yes."

Vail opened his credentials with a certain amount of authority, indicating that everything Radkay was about to be asked was merely a formality—the FBI already knew the answers.

"Come in." The engineer stepped back uneasily, and Vail could see that he suspected the reason for the visit.

They went into the living room, and Vail took a seat on the couch while Radkay sat down on a recliner opposite him. "Does this have anything to do with my security clearance?"

Vail laughed condescendingly. "Come on, Ray. The weapons information passed along. The only question I have is how much you knew about Maurice Gaston's murder."

"What are you talking about?"

"The Jag, the safe-deposit box, this house. We know about you and the Russians. And the Lithuanians," Vail bluffed. "Your reaction right now—it's obvious you realize why I'm here. I'm not going to waste my time. I'm giving you a chance to talk to me before we come back for you, and then it'll be too late." Radkay remained silent, and Vail could see the cold logic of an engineer taking over, analyzing his options. "If you tell us about the Lithuanians, we can make your life a whole lot simpler. There's a big difference between passing along a little technology for a few bucks and being an accessory to murder."

Radkay said, "Would it do any good for me to ask for a lawyer?"

"I don't think you were involved in the murder, but do what you want. If you call a lawyer, he's going to instruct me to leave." Vail stood up. "And when I do, so does this offer. Then we'll lump you in with the Lithuanians and you can defend yourself on the murder charges."

"Okay, okay. What do you want to know?"

Vail sat back down. "First, tell me how you were recruited."

"I was approached at my apartment one night. They offered me a hundred thousand dollars if I accepted. It was paid the next day, and I was told there would be plenty more. Two days later I gave them a dozen documents, mostly technical data and schematics. As soon as I did, they demanded to know when I could get more. I knew then that I had made the mistake of my life. They told me that they had video recordings of our exchanges, and if that wasn't convincing enough, they asked me if I wanted to end up like Maury Gaston. I had never associated his disappearance with what I was doing. I knew right then he was dead. It scared the hell out of me. After that their demands were relentless. Believe it or not, I'm relieved. When you introduced yourself, I knew that one way or the other the nightmare was over."

"It may not be as bad as you think. You have one very large bargaining chip at your disposal—we're going to need your testimony."

"Testify? Against them? I told you, they're crazy."

"The only other option is prison."

Radkay stood up. "I need to think. And a drink." The engineer went over to a hutch and opened the upper cabinet. "There is a third option you know," he said, his voice suddenly cold, mechanical. "I could just run." When Vail saw that there were no liquor bottles in the compartment that Radkay was reaching into, he jumped to his feet. As soon as the revolver came out, Vail dove behind the couch and drew his automatic.

Radkay turned and fired, hitting the cushion that Vail had been sitting against. He started to run toward the back door. Vail poked his head above the couch, and Radkay fired again. This time the bullet penetrated the padding and barely missed Vail. "I've got people in back," he lied. "And I parked my car so you couldn't get out."

Radkay glanced through the window he was standing next to and saw it was true about the car. "Then I guess I'll have to take yours." He started toward Vail and fired another round.

Vail realized he had no other choice now. He stood straight up and fired once, hitting Radkay in the chest. The engineer went down, and Vail hurried over to him. Radkay gurgled briefly, and then his head fell to the side, his eyes still open and blank in death.

The front door flew open, and Kate and Bursaw rushed in with their guns drawn. "You okay?" Bursaw asked.

"Yes, but it looks like I just did the Lithuanians a favor."

Kate looked at the body and let her weapon drop to her side. "He was our last chance."

"He may be dead, but that doesn't mean he can't still help us." Vail went into the kitchen and picked up Radkay's phone on the desk, dialing Kate's cell phone. When it began to ring, he said, "What does the caller ID say?"

"R. Radkay," she said. "With the phone number."

"I'll be right back." Vail went out to his car and brought back his briefcase. Shuffling through its contents, he found the business card Alex Zogas had given him for the Lithuanian Chess Society. He also took out the two GPS tracker phones the technical agent had given him and handed them to Kate and Bursaw.

After holding a finger to his lips, he dialed the LCS number into Radkay's phone. "Is Alex there? This is his guy from Matrix-Linx." Then, in a whiny voice, Vail said, "Well, tell him that the FBI was at my bank today. Tell him I'm freaking out and need him to call me right away." Vail hung up.

"What are you doing?" Kate asked.

Vail grabbed Radkay's body under the arms and dragged him inside the room that was farthest from the front door. "Making lemonade."

THIRTY-SIX

AN HOUR AND A HALF LATER, THE TWO MEN THAT ALEX ZOGAS HAD DISPATCHED from the Lithuanian Chess Society turned onto Raymond Radkay's street. Slowing down, they allowed their car to run at idle speed while they checked the other partially built homes in the development for vehicles. There were none. They switched off the car's headlights and dialed Radkay's number. "Hello."

They hung up, increasing their speed toward the house. There was a light on in a first-floor window. They pulled into the driveway, got out, and walked to the front door. It was locked. The bigger of the two men took a short crowbar from under his coat and placed it in the jamb. Following a short, quick pull, a loud metallic crack echoed through the empty neighborhood and the door was pushed open.

Inside, it was completely dark. Both men drew their guns and stepped into the foyer. As they approached the stairs, a shot rang out. The muzzle flash had been to their left. Instinctively, they moved away from each other, firing in the direction of the blast. They leapfrogged toward the shooter, continuing to fire. Then, during one of the pauses, they heard a body hit the hardwood floor. One of them snapped on a flashlight and saw that Radkay had been hit once in the chest. "Okay, let's get him out of here."

After carrying the body out to their car and putting it in the trunk, they tossed their handguns in, too.

Five minutes later Kate and Bursaw pulled up to Radkay's house in the two Bureau cars, and Vail came out. He jumped in with Kate, who had one of the GPS cell phones open in her hand. "Looks like they're heading for 95 South. Where did you put the tracker?"

"I taped it to the small of Radkay's back. They'll have to strip him to find it. Just make sure you keep enough distance between us so you can't see them. Then they won't be able to see us."

She handed Vail the phone. He picked up the radio mike. "Luke, have you got them?"

"I've got them five-by."

"Just stay behind us, I'll watch the screen."

"Any trouble inside?"

"Just picking Radkay up and dropping him while they were shooting at us."

"I know Radkay didn't mind, but for you I would strongly recommend therapy."

The two men from the LCS got in the right lane of 95 South and maintained the speed limit. It took them over an hour to reach Route 30, exiting onto the eastbound ramp.

"The two last night must have been going to the same spot," Bursaw said over the radio. *"Think they're going to that lake again?"*

"If they're not, that means last night was a contingency plan, which would be impressive."

"It would be if they weren't dead. Besides, these people are chess masters—supposedly. Chess is contingency planning at its purest."

Vail watched the cell phone as the car drove past the turnoff where the shoot-out had taken place the night before. "They just passed the lake turnoff," he told Bursaw.

"So far so good."

After another fifteen minutes, Vail said, "Okay, they're turning off."

When Kate reached the point where they had turned, she pulled onto the shoulder of the road, and Bursaw parked behind her. He got out and climbed into their backseat. "Up there by the mailbox is where they turned in," Vail said. "It looks like private property." Glancing at the cell phone, he said, "They stopped about a quarter of a mile in."

"How about getting the Richmond office out here?" Kate asked.

Vail said, "The king of Sparta once said, 'The Spartans do not inquire how many the enemy are but where they are.'"

"And I believe none of them survived," Bursaw said.

Kate said, "I'm calling Richmond."

"Go ahead and get them started this way, but last night it took them a long time. Right now we've got to find out where they're putting that body and catch them doing it. We'll finally have some hard evidence."

After identifying herself, Kate told the Richmond duty agent that they needed all available agents to their location immediately. She hung up. "I assume we're going to surprise these two." she said.

"We'll have to walk in to do it. Luke, have you still got that shotgun in your trunk?"

"After last night I don't go anywhere without it. I also have something else that could prove useful—the night-vision goggles we took off those two. And one more instrument of comfort." All three of them got out and went back to Bursaw's trunk. He held up an MP5 submachine gun. "When you called today, I took this from the gun vault. Not that I expected any problems with you along."

Vail handed Kate a pair of the goggles. "You and Luke wear these." He helped her put them on and adjust the straps. "Keep them flipped up until we get off the road, or the headlights along here will blind you."

Vail took the shotgun, and all three of them started loading extra ammunition into their pockets.

They turned up the winding dirt road, and Vail checked the phone screen to make sure the two men they'd been following were still stationary. "Evidently they're at their destination." He reached over and pivoted Kate's goggles into place. "All right?"

"Wow, yeah, I'm good."

As quietly as possible, Vail chambered a buckshot round. Then he checked the phone and pointed up the road. Quietly but quickly they started walking. There were some stands of trees, mostly hardwoods, now bare. A few minutes later, they followed a turn in the road, and in the distance both Kate and Bursaw, through their goggles, could see a stone cottage sitting on a small rise about seventy yards away. Thirty yards from it was an old-fashioned water well. It had a waist-high wall around it, constructed of the same type of stone as the cottage. The car they had followed was parked next to the well, and the two men were taking Radkay's body out of the trunk.

Beside the well was a small, newly constructed shed. One of the men carried something from it that looked like a bag of cement. Through his goggles Bursaw could see that the man had taken out a pocketknife and was cutting open the top of the bag. He then went to help carry the body.

Bursaw described everything to Vail in whispers.

"That's probably lye. It'll eventually destroy all traces of the body. Let's go."

When they got to the top of the rise that the old house sat on, Vail glanced over at Bursaw, who because of the goggles didn't notice the red laser dot on his own chest. Vail jumped into him just as a rifle shot came from the house, which was now at their ten o'clock. At the same time, Kate dove to the ground. Quickly Vail crawled next to Bursaw. "Are you hit, Luke?"

"Left shoulder."

Vail pulled his friend's coat open, and after finding the bullet hole in his shirt, he carefully tore it open. "It's not bad." Another shot came from the house. Vail called over to Kate. "You all right?"

"I'm okay."

There was a small amount of cover provided by the uneven terrain, so Vail crawled forward a couple of yards to find a firing position but immediately started taking handgun fire from the two men at the well. He came back to Kate and Luke's position. "This is an ambush. They were expecting us."

"How?" Kate asked.

"Probably my call to the club. Radkay would have used a code name."

From a second window in the house, a barrage of automatic-weapons fire ricocheted around them. "I guess we had a wrong head count. There are at least four of them. And they've got us pinned down in an L-shaped crossfire. Right now they can't hit us. If they had waited another ten yards before springing this, we'd all be well-diving by now. In a minute they're going to figure out that if the two in the house can keep us pinned down, the two at the car can start moving up to our position and pick us off."

"So?" Kate said, with a little more urgency than she intended.

"When your position becomes indefensible, there's only one option. You have to—"

Bursaw said, "Don't say it."

"Attack." Vail picked up the MP5 and handed it to Kate. "You know how to use this, right?"

"I fam-fired it at the range a few times."

"Well, you're about to get a lot more familiar with it." Vail started ejecting the buckshot rounds from the shotgun and replacing them with deer slugs. "Luke, you think you can fire this into their car, one round every ten to fifteen seconds? It'll sound like a howitzer when it hits and keep their heads down so Kate can move."

"Sure."

"I'll go after the two in the house. Once I start shooting and moving toward them, Luke, you fire. Kate, you're going to have to move when we shoot and get down when we stop. If you don't, that rifle probably has a night scope along with the laser, and they'll be able to find you. Even though your two targets are at our twelve, you should flare off to like one o'clock so you're not coming straight into them. Then, when you get there, you'll be on their flank rather than head-on." He could hear her breathing. "You ready for this, Kate?"

She chambered the first round and flicked off the safety. "This is getting close to being worse than our last date in Chicago, but I'll be fine."

Vail said. "Luke, you set?"

He rolled onto his side and passed Vail two more of his Glock magazines. "Hands down, this is the worse date I've ever been on with you."

Vail crawled around Bursaw and watched the cottage that was to their ten o'clock. Then he was up, running and firing. Behind him the shotgun exploded, the massive slug thudding into the car that the two LCS men were using as cover, causing them to squat further down. Kate was off at a dead run in the one o'clock direction Vail had suggested.

Keeping low, Vail used the same slightly indirect route, approximately toward nine o'clock, that he had suggested to Kate, running to the stone house in an arc that swept away from both Bursaw's and Kate's positions. That would force the two gunmen in the house to shift their points of aim away from the other agents, so they could fire at Vail. If the sniper rifle that had hit Bursaw was resting on something to keep it steady, Vail's path would completely disrupt its accuracy as it tracked him.

The front of the house had a single door with a window on each side. The scoped rifle was being fired out the right window and the assault rifle the left. When Vail got to within twenty yards of the house, the automatic weapon opened up on him.

Inside, Alex Zogas said in an urgent whisper, "Karl, did you get him?"

"I think so."

Outside, Bursaw's shotgun boomed again, followed by the thud of the slug hitting the car. Within the house the two men's focus shifted back to Bursaw and Kate, trying to reestablish them as targets.

Suddenly Zogas noticed the doorknob turning. He snapped his fingers to get Karl's attention, pointing at the door. Karl nodded and backed up a few steps from the window and toward the door to establish a better angle to shoot through it. Then he opened fire, expending the entire clip into the door. Zogas had taken the rifle off the window rest and stepped back himself, ready to fire.

A single shot came through Karl's window, hitting him in the face, throwing him back into the wall, where he crumpled to the floor. Zogas could see that he was dead. He backed up a few more steps with the rifle held on his hip, waiting for Vail.

Kate got up from the ground where she had found cover in what looked like a deep wheel rut. She could see one of the men through her night goggles. She was far enough off to his left that he hadn't seen her yet. She was hoping that Bursaw could track her through his goggles.

As quietly as possible, she walked toward the gunman. But somehow he sensed her movement, turning quickly and firing blindly. She was in the open now and had no choice but to be aggressive. Flipping up her goggles so as not to be blinded by her own gunfire, she quickened her stride, walking steadily toward him, firing two- to three-round bursts. She wasn't sure exactly where he was, so she would have to fire out the clip in hopes of hitting him. If not, she still had her handgun.

The killer fired back, and now she knew exactly where he was. She adjusted her fire with the next couple of bursts. Then, with a sickening clank, the gun's bolt locked back, indicating that her MP5 was empty. But the final burst had found the gunman, at least one of the last three rounds hitting him in the stomach. She dropped the submachine gun and started to draw her sidearm when the second man came around the car and leveled his gun on her. *"Kale,"* he spit out at her in a guttural foreign tongue, a derogatory term every woman recognized no matter the language. Her only option now was to try to finish drawing.

Then a single shot rattled through the cold night. The Lithuanian fell to the ground dead. A head shot had blown out a good portion of his left temple. She had the presence of mind to flip down her goggles.

The first man she'd hit in the stomach got to his knees and raised his gun. Kate took careful aim and fired three rounds into him. He fell back, his legs at impossible angles under him. She went over and checked him for a pulse. He was dead.

The adrenaline vanishing from her body, Kate started shaking and sank to her knees. She replayed in her mind what had happened. At the time, because her life was about to end, it hadn't registered. Now, in slow-motion memory, she watched a tiny red dot settle onto the right side of the gunman's head. And then the shot. "Luke!" she yelled down the rise to Bursaw. "They're both dead! Hold your fire!"

She worked her way back to Bursaw's position, keeping her Glock in her hand, watching the stone house. "You get them both?" he asked.

"Just one. Steve must have shot the other one," she said. "Hold on, let me see if he needs any help."

She moved quickly but cautiously to the cottage. There was a small light on inside. When she opened the door, she immediately saw the sniper rifle sitting on its firing stand at the window oriented toward the car. Vail was kneeling over Zogas's body, searching his pockets. The Lithuanian lay on his back, his chest and abdomen covered with blood. She walked up to Vail's side. "You all right?"

"Fine, you?"

"I assume that last shot was yours."

"Can you go get Luke out of the cold? I'll turn up the heat in here."

"Sure."

By the time she got back with Bursaw, Zogas's body had been rolled over and Vail had turned on more lights. He was searching the other man's clothing. Kate sat Bursaw in a chair. Vail came over and helped him off with his coat and shirt. Examining the wound, he said, "How's it feel?"

"I don't know whether it's the cold or the endorphins, but not bad."

Vail prodded it a little more roughly now. "Looks like just meat, no bone."

Kate found a couple of clean towels and gave them to Vail. He pressed them against the wound. In the distance they could hear what sounded like a single siren. "Luke, I think your ride is here," Vail said. "Kate, can you hold this in place? I'm going to make sure the ambulance finds us."

Vail hurried down to the road and was surprised to see John Kalix getting out of his car. "Put on your flashers so everyone will know where we're at," he told Kalix. "Where'd you come from?"

They started back to the house. "Everybody all right?"

"Luke got dinged, but he'll be okay."

"When Kate called Richmond, she told them to call me. I've had this thing up over a hundred. I don't ever want to do that again. How about the bad guys?"

"Four dead, including Zogas."

"I'm sorry, who's Zogas?"

"He's the leader of the Lithuanians."

"The Lithuanians?"

"They're tied in to the Russians. I'll explain everything when we get Luke taken care of."

As they reached the house, more sirens could be heard in the distance. Kalix went inside. "Luke, how you doing?"

He said to Kalix, "I'm begging you, John, make Vail go back to Chicago."

Kalix said, "Kate, how about you?"

"You should have seen her," Bursaw said. "Charging the enemy, taking them out with that MP5. It was definitely ladies' night out there."

"One of them anyway," she said, looking at Vail.

"Well, Bannon," he said, "if you think you've had trouble getting a date up until now, wait until the guys hear about you machine-gunning men who cross you."

"Actually, I'm thinking about reloading right now."

THIRTY-SEVEN

THE BLURRY LIGHT OF DAWN HAD COME UP JUST AS VAIL AND KATE STARTED back to Washington. Bursaw had been taken to a local hospital, and the doctor had said he would be fine but that he wanted to keep him for twenty-four hours to preclude the risk of infection. Agents from the lab had been brought in to supervise the crime-scene investigation and the excavation of the well where it appeared that multiple bodies had been dumped.

Vail was unusually quiet during the drive. As they crossed into D.C., Kate said, "You're going to make me ask?"

"About?"

"About searching Zogas's body?"

Vail said, "Yes, I searched his body."

"And you don't want to tell me if you found anything." When he didn't answer, she said, "Apparently that isn't what's really bothering you."

"You're right, it's not. My real problem is that your first instinct was to call Kalix."

"He's the assistant director in charge of counterintelligence. Remember, the director wanted him in the loop. You know, the director, the guy who keeps calling me every time something goes wrong. What's the big deal? The entire Richmond division was on their way—do you think it was going to be kept a secret?"

"For once let's look at this from my perspective. Six months ago I told you that under no circumstance would I work for the FBI. And then again two weeks ago, I made it quite clear I did not want to get involved in this. But when the director told me what had happened to you, I agreed, for no other reason than . . . well, since I don't know how you really feel about me—let's call it loyalty. And never once did I back off my commitment to you. The only thing I asked in return was that no one at headquarters be told what we were doing. Apparently even after all this time, you don't understand that's how I get things done. I knew they would find out soon enough, but I'd have enough time to figure out the next step before they got in the way. As they did when Dellasanti was killed at the drop. And, even worse, the next day, when they somehow figured out I was going to the park to look for more evidence. I don't know how they figured out what I was doing. I didn't think they were smart enough. But you were."

"You think I told Langston?"

"After this call to Kalix, I'm starting to wonder."

"Why would I do that?" she asked.

"I don't know. I hope it's not because of your career, but that is the one thing that keeps getting in our way."

"So you think—" She stopped herself and fell silent for a moment. "All along, you didn't really care if the director or Kalix found out what we were doing. Your telling me to keep it quiet was just a test of my loyalty, wasn't it?"

"If it was, do you think you passed?"

She laughed sarcastically. "You do understand that the real problem here is your inability to trust anyone. I understand that, because I'm the same way. At least I was. But I'd like to think I've made myself change. And do you know why? Because I thought there was a chance for us. The first time I came to Chicago, that was one of the most difficult, most open things I've ever done. I was hoping that my trust would be contagious. But it wasn't. That's why our last date was a catastrophe. That's why I told you not to come here for New Year's. You can't trust anyone or anything. I understand now that it's because of what your father did. The other night when you told me about him, I thought you were finally letting me inside your life. The problem is that deep down inside, you don't want to let go of what your father did to you. You think it gives you an edge, and I suppose it does. Nothing gets by you. While that makes you a great agent, it's the reason there'll never be any hope for us. You absolutely will not allow yourself the vulnerability that is necessary if two people are going to trust each other. You keep trying to make your life failureproof, and you believe that the only way to do it is to cut everyone out of it."

"You don't think I've tried to trust people?"

"I don't think you've even tried to trust yourself."

"That's ridiculous."

"Is it? You're even afraid to let anyone see your sculptures. Your pieces are good, really good, but you don't trust yourself enough to put them out there. You're one of the bravest men I know, but I seriously doubt that you have the courage to ask yourself why that is."

Vail stopped at a light, and she got out, slamming the door. The light changed, and he sat there, watching as she hurried away.

VAIL STOOD IN ALEX ZOGAS'S HOUSE, unable to stop thinking about his argument with Kate. She, of course, had been right. He was incapable of trusting anyone. But that was hardly a revelation for him. It was something he had reluctantly accepted about himself long ago. And she was right about its giving him an edge, especially when it came to resolving complex situations like going after the LCS. And also, there couldn't be any argument that he was unwilling to do anything that would take away that advantage.

If asked twenty-four hours earlier, he would have said unequivocally that the one person in the world he did trust was Kate Bannon, but, as she had demonstrated, that wasn't true. Since there was no longer an investigation to camouflage his flaws, he wondered if he hadn't picked the fight with her so he wouldn't have to complicate his life by committing to a relationship with her. Maybe that was why he was now standing in Zogas's house—to prolong the investigation, to delude himself with the possible repair of the impossible rift between them.

There had not been anything in Zogas's pockets except his wallet and keys, which Vail used to get into the house. He turned on the computer, which sat on a living-room table. While he waited for it to fully load, the image of Kate's face, twisted with anger and, even worse, disappointment rose up in his memory. He blanked it out halfheartedly, knowing that it would be back.

To suppose that the FBI had uncovered every single double agent in Washington, at least those recruited by the Lithuanians, would have been naïve and shortsighted. They had given up their inactive sources to further the Calculus scheme, but there still had to be individuals currently supplying them with information. If the entire Calculus matter had proved anything, it was how susceptible the government had become to counterintelligence. Espionage was no longer about one country trying to gain an upper hand militarily or politically; it was about the global marketplace—technologies and trade secrets to be stolen and sold.

Raymond Radkay had existed completely undetected, so why not others? If there were others, their names, addresses, and contact points had to be kept somewhere. Vail started checking the files on the computer. There weren't many documents stored, but he would have been surprised if Zogas had been that obvious.

Next he checked the Internet history. It looked as though the last Web site that Zogas had visited was something called American Business News. Vail clicked on it. At first glance it appeared to be a generic business site, as uninteresting as its bland graphics.

He clicked on the "About Us" link, and again the description was uninteresting, except for one fact—although it tried to make the reader think otherwise, it wasn't American. The syntax, possessive pronouns, and vocabulary contained a few small errors that indicated that someone whose first language was not English had written the copy.

There was a freshly posted article that had been cut and pasted from some unattributed publication. It described a new chemical process for supersynthetic motor oil that was being developed by a company in Maryland.

Off to the right side of the home page was the heading "For Our Clients." Vail couldn't access it because there were user-ID and password windows that had to be filled in to open it. What was this site? Vail pushed back from the table and stared at the screen, trying to make sense of it. He dug the heels of his hands into his eyes, reminding himself how little sleep he'd had in the last two days. To distract himself he got up and walked around the room, settling onto a recliner in the living room. He turned on the television and started running through the channels, using the rhythm of the changing images to hypnotize himself into a brief period of thoughtlessness.

After five minutes he went back to the computer. Looking at the page again, he suddenly realized its purpose. It was how the Russians and the LCS communicated. Both of them were able to access and upload onto it. The Russians sent their "orders" to it in the innocuous form of business articles, and the LCS could send coded e-mails through its "Contact Us" link. But what was the "For Our Clients" section used for, and why was it protected by a password?

Vail started searching through the house for anything that might have a password written on it. When he didn't find anything, he returned to the living room. On the wall next to the recliner were three large picture frames. Each contained twelve postcards forming a large rectangle. On all of them were depictions of chessboards with pieces in the final stages of a match. But there were things that weren't right about them. Of the thirty-six cards, each one had four white pieces and four black pieces remaining. The second thing was that even with Vail's limited knowledge of chess, he could see that their positions of play were not logical. The only reason someone would go to the expense of turning a postcard into a wall display would be to recall the last position of the pieces before a checkmate. As he scanned the cards, he could see that none of the games were in check.

And why were there so many of them? Taking out his knife, he slit open the back of the frames and then slid his knife between the cards and the backing until they came off. All twelve had been mailed from Washington, D.C. The return address was a post-office box. Why would two people play a game of chess by mail within the same city?

Then he compared the dates. Each was marked on the second of the month, unless it was a Sunday. Of course, he thought, the second day of the month was when the passwords were changed. Zogas had mounted them and put them in plain sight as trophies, proving, as so many sociopaths needed to, that he was smarter than the rest of the world. And shoving it right in everyone's face was part of the rush. There was no way any of them could hurt him once the passwords had been changed.

Quickly, Vail peeled the other cards from their backings and checked the dates. The last was dated December. That meant that if they contained the code for getting into the Web site, there was a card with this month's password on it. But where was it? Vail started tearing the house apart but then realized where it was. And that he had actually seen it, in a different form, without realizing what it was.

He drove to the Lithuanian Chess Society, trying not to think about Kate. He could have called and invited her along as an apology, but it would probably have been too little too late. And if he didn't give her a chance to say no, he could make himself believe there was hope, at least a little longer.

Using Zogas's keys, he let himself in and headed back to the office. The computer was still on from the night before. Vail checked the Internet history and found that the last entry was the American Business News. He clicked into the user-ID window and then looked over at the chessboard next to the desk that Zogas had claimed was for his mail game. The last postcard could be anywhere, maybe even destroyed since Kate's and his visit there. But Zogas had probably used the actual board setup as a quick reference to the codes. Once it became apparent that the FBI was starting to focus in on the LCS, he would have been able to kick it over quickly should there be a raid.

On the board there were eight pieces—four white, four black—and, as on the postcards, the degree of their engagement was illogical.

A chessboard has sixty-four squares designated *a* through *h* along the top and bottom rows, left to right, and *1* through *8* vertically as you face the board. So the top left corner is a8, the bottom left corner is a1, and the top right is h8. Then the rank of the piece is added in. If the white queen was sitting in its beginning position, it would be designated Qd1. If it was moved straight ahead three spaces, it would be Qd4.

To test his theory, Vail had to decide whether black positions were to be used for the user ID or for the passwords. The site could have been protected by a system by which if one wrong entry were made, access would become permanently denied. He took out the postcards he had taken from Zogas's house; they all had the black pieces at the top of the boards. Since the user-ID space was over the password window, he decided to use the black pieces as the user ID. Carefully, he typed into the password box the twelve numbers and letters designated by the four black pieces and then did the same with the four white pieces into the password box. He clicked on "Log In."

A page opened, and a list of seventeen names, addresses, and phone numbers scrolled down. Vail still wasn't sure what they were until he got toward the bottom. Number eleven was Raymond Dante Radkay. Radkay's middle name didn't seem right to Vail. He would have remembered "Dante." He looked at the other middle names, some of which were Houston, Spain, and Opus. They didn't seem right either. Most likely they were a quick reference to the moles' code names.

Sixteen more spies, and no one in the FBI had any idea they existed. Until now.

THIRTY-EIGHT

IT WAS THE MIDDLE OF THE NIGHT, AND KATE COULDN'T GET HERSELF TO SLEEP. IT had been a day and a half since she'd jumped out of Vail's car. She got up and opened a bottle of wine, turning on the television. Scanning through the channels, she found a Spanish soap opera, which she couldn't understand a word of. It was the perfect distraction, as it took her complete concentration to try to figure out the relationships between the characters by the expressions on the emotive actors' faces. After an apparent series of arguments over a sisterly affair and the help of half a bottle of wine, she finally dropped off in the chair.

Although she woke up early the next morning, Kate didn't get to the office until late afternoon. She'd sat around her apartment thinking about Vail and what he'd said. By now he was probably gone. The Calculus case was over, and everyone was accounted for—or would be as soon as they finished the DNA analysis of the bodies from the well. She did some housework, vacuuming carpets that didn't need it and pulling weeds in her garden.

After finally arriving at the office, she turned on her computer.

Feeling-sorry-for-herself time was over. Back to the Bureau's business. She checked her e-mails, and there was the usual overnight bureaucratic avalanche of meaningless memos and directionless directives. But there was one sender she didn't recognize. It was simply entitled "A Favor." She opened it.

> Kate,
>
> Leaving my gun and creds here at the off-site, plus a few other things, if you wouldn't mind.
> Also check www.americanbusinessnews.com
>
> Stan

That he'd signed the message "Stan" caused her to smile.

She felt a tear run down her cheek. He had risked his life to clear her, and she continued to expect so much from him—too much, she supposed. Instead of trying to understand his side of things, she'd lost her temper as quickly as he had. Maybe, deep down, she didn't want to have to take any more chances, which was the exact thing she'd accused him of. She wondered if there was any chance that he was still in Washington. The time on the message was 5:14 A.M. Knowing him, she was sure he would have sent it just as he was heading out the door. As much as she wanted to race over there and find out, she had a late meeting. It was the only reason she'd come to work. Maybe it really was time to move on.

She clicked on the link and found the site's generic quality curious. Since Vail had sent it, she suspected that there was more to it than met the eye. It was probably part of "plus a few other things" he'd referred to. There was something waiting for her at the off-site. She packed up her briefcase and headed for the garage.

IT WAS PAST FIVE THIRTY and already dark when Kate let herself into the off-site. The alarm was set, so she knew that Vail wasn't there. She punched in the code and went upstairs to the workroom. Vail's credentials and his Glock were on the desk in front of the computer. She checked the room that he had used for a bedroom and found that one of his suitcases was still there. She opened it and found his winter clothing. That's right, she reminded herself, he was going to Florida.

Back in the workroom, she noticed that the computer was on. She turned on the monitor, and the Web page for American Business News appeared. The only difference was the "For Our Clients" windows for user ID and passwords were filled in. Carefully, she clicked on. When she saw the list of sixteen names, she half collapsed into the chair. She immediately spotted Radkay's name and knew what she was looking at. Vail had pulled one last rabbit out of his hat, and his message was obvious: He was trusting her with this unprecedented trove of counterintelligence information.

After printing out everything, she picked up his gun and credentials. Taking one last look around the room, she noticed some new writing on the wall.

Walking over to it, she read:

> *The Sixth Why*
> *Why would the CIA agent Rellick have to*
> *meet with Calculus three times in exactly the*
> *same place and in such a short period of time,*
> *knowing that the Bureau was tracking his*
> *movements?*

What was that supposed to mean? Did it mean anything? Was it one of those philosophical or hypothetical questions that Vail had written for no one but himself? Or was he throwing something cryptic at her, just trying to show that these things were impossible to decode without him?

If there was something to it, Kate was not going to let Vail end this case being one up on her. She walked over to the wall and started reading Calculus's itinerary, trying to find the answer to the Sixth Why.

She spent two hours making notes and cross-checking dates and locations. Writing theories on a pad and then angrily scratching them out as additional facts eliminated them. When she was done, there didn't appear to be an answer to Vail's last question, at least not one that she could find. Kate looked down at the list in her hand and decided that it had to be the priority now.

THE CIA AGENT WALKED into the airport bar and spotted the man he thought he was looking for. "Vail?"

Vail gave him an appraising glance. "Sit down."

The agent took out his identification and flipped it open. "Where is it?"

"You want a drink?"

"What I want is the list of our European sources that Rellick stole. That is why you called, isn't it?"

"I never said anything about just *giving* it to you."

"How much?"

"I would imagine right about now there's quite a panic over at Langley, so it's got to be priceless."

"Then why do I get the feeling you're about to put a price on it?"

"It's nice to see that the agency didn't send an idiot."

"How do I know you have it?"

"Do you really want me to read it so I can give you a name? Why would I say I had it and risk being arrested if I didn't?"

"Maybe we need to arrest you to sort this out."

"Then I'd use the list to get free, plus get what I want, so why don't I just tell you what I want?"

KATE KNOCKED on John Kalix's door. When he opened it, she said, "John, sorry to bother you at home, but Vail, believe it or not, has come up with another whole list of moles. And since that's your division, I didn't want to waste any time getting it to you."

"Really? Come on in."

She walked into the living room and sat down, opting for a chair by the window.

"Can I get you a drink?"

"You know, I think I could use one. Any kind of whiskey and water, if you have it."

A few minutes later, Kalix brought her the drink and sat down in a chair opposite her. She took a sip and pushed the list of spies across the coffee table between them with a touch of drama.

He opened a drawer and took out a pair of glasses. "Wow," he said. "And how do we know these are spies?"

She explained about the Web site and that Radkay's name was on it.

"Yes, of course, how obtuse of me." He continued to look at the list. "Wow. This is going to keep us busy for years. Where is Steve?"

"Scuba diving in Florida—I think. He's turned in his creds, so as far as he's concerned, he's done. I don't think we'll see him again. At least I won't."

"Really? I thought you two had a little more going on than work."

"Very briefly. But I guess it wasn't meant to be. He left the list along with his Bureau property and cleared out of the off-site."

"No explanation, no good-bye?"

"We had a discussion of each other's character flaws that got kind of vicious," she said, smiling sadly. "The only other thing he left was something he wrote on the wall. 'The Sixth Why.'"

"What's that?"

As briefly as possible, she explained the Japanese inventor's process for getting to the root of a problem and how they had used it to discover the LCS's role in the spy ring. "It's called the Five Whys. In this case I guess Vail felt there was one more that needed to be answered."

"What was the question?"

"'Why would the CIA agent Rellick have to meet with Calculus three times in exactly the same place and in such a short period of time, knowing that the Bureau was tracking his movements?'"

"That is an interesting question. Maybe Calculus had to keep checking with him to make sure that whatever clue he was leaving wouldn't cause Rellick any exposure."

"The little bit of experience I've had with counterintelligence would indicate the opposite. Besides, we tracked down Rellick by the phone that he and Calculus used to contact each other. They didn't need to meet. Meeting with your handler too often is probably the easiest way to be discovered. Hasn't that been your experience?"

"Yes, I suppose you're right. I guess I was just trying to play the devil's advocate. Do you think there's anything to this question, or is Vail just messing with you?" Kalix chuckled. "It's no secret how much he loves management. From what you've said, I'm guessing that's kind of how he sees you now."

"At first I thought it might be just that. But once I started driving over here, the validity of the question sank in. If you think about it, why weren't the Russians afraid someone would figure it out? I mean, they met near CIA headquarters at the same park all three times.

Almost regimented. Wasn't that the reason you were able to narrow it down to those nine agents whose photos you showed me?"

"Yes, I guess it was."

"It's almost like they wanted us to figure out who Rellick was."

"What advantage would that be for the Russians?" Kalix asked. "Giving up such a highly placed source would be completely counterproductive."

"Maybe that's the real Sixth Why. From all the copies of the documents they recovered at his house, it looks like Rellick's information had dried up a couple of years ago. If they were giving up Rellick, it changed only one thing: Bill Langston was removed as head of counterintelligence because he failed to chase down the connection between Rellick and his handler, Nikolai Gulin."

"Why is that an advantage for the Russians? Langston wasn't exactly dismantling the Russian SVR single-handedly."

Kate laughed and let her voice shift from a tone of curiosity to one of accusation. "Would you say that the assistant director of the Counterintelligence Division is privy to a lot more classified information than his deputy?"

Kalix took off his glasses and set them on the table. He opened the drawer again and drew out a small silver automatic, pointing it at her. "Nicely done, Kate. You walked me right into it."

She stiffened in reaction. "So this was all about you getting to the top of the intelligence chain."

"Sorry about having you locked up, but I had to rescue you and at the same time show how Langston's incompetence was the cause. Nothing personal, Kate. It was all to make me the hero and the heir apparent."

"And that included killing one of the LCS men in that shoot-out when you saved Vail?"

"Unfortunately, Vail saved himself. The guy behind the false mirror was supposed to kill him, and then I was supposed to shoot the second LCS man and switch guns with the one who shot Vail, having it look like I killed the lone gunman who killed Vail. I was outside and assumed that Vail had been killed when I heard the initial shooting. I just opened up on the second man. When I came in, they were both dead."

"The LCS was willing to give up one of theirs to make you a hero?"

"He was the one who tried to kill you at your house by trapping you in the garage with your car running. He told Zogas, who was waiting outside, that you were in fact dead. Alex didn't like incompetence, so someone had to be held responsible. The whole Calculus gambit was his plan. Quite ingenious, actually."

"Except that it is about to fail also," Kate said.

"Yes, I guess Alex wasn't as smart as we thought he was. But he was quite a businessman and recognized an opportunity when it came along. Because of the Bureau's ever-increasing scrutiny of the Russian SVR, it had become almost impossible for them to recruit spies. So Zogas started providing the service. He thought the Russians would be his customers for life. What he and I planned to do in the future was that when one of his moles stopped producing, I would be given the name so I could 'uncover' him, enhancing my reputation. Which in turn would give me access to more and more information, not only within the Bureau but also from the other agencies. I would have become the great American hero."

"How about Sundra Boston? How did you know she was onto the LCS?" Kate asked.

"Every morning I checked the Bureau computer system to see if anyone was querying the LCS or any of the moles they were willing to give up—or myself, for that matter. When she requested tolls on Longmeadow, we knew we had to get rid of her."

"How about the guy in the tunnel in Chicago?"

"He knew that Vail was coming, because Vail had me wire the funds to the account. Vail was getting to be a real thorn in our side, so our man in Chicago was told to take him out. He knew there was no real money on its way. As soon as Vail killed him, I told Zogas, and he came up with the ambush that was supposed to make me Vail's savior. Zogas was brilliant at visualizing and planning for contingencies. Off of the ambush, he had set up the CIA involvement with that phone number that would lead you and Vail to Rellick. I came up with the idea that the Russians were protecting a CIA agent. Then if Vail didn't figure out the three contacts between Calculus and Rellick, I would have. I knew about the video with Gulin and him, and Langston's inability to see its importance. And I knew that you knew Rellick. The other eight photos were men I was pretty sure you didn't know, so you'd have to pick out Rellick. Funny thing was, Rellick had no idea about your being framed to *protect* him. In the end he just thought the government had finally caught up with him."

"Why didn't you kill Longmeadow when we first heard him on that tape?"

"Zogas liked to profit from every death. Longmeadow was in the air force and technically bright. He had the potential to be of use later. There was no need to kill him when you missed him the first time around. The only reason they put him on the list was that when Zogas was putting this together, Longmeadow was becoming demanding. I always knew where you and Vail were because of the GPS in Vail's car. I was the one who was monitoring it."

Kate said, "That's how you followed him to the Maryland park when he found the flash drive."

"Yes."

"And what about you? What did you do it for? Idealism? No, that's never really the case, is it? Was it to make fools of everyone else?"

"I suppose that was part of it, but ultimately it was about one million dollars a year, tax free."

"And now?"

"I'll have to defect. I will be looked up to in Russia—not that it's a big deal, but at least I won't be spending the rest of my life in prison. And I have three million dollars in an account there. It's like an SVR 401(k)."

"More likely you'd be looking at the death penalty."

"If you're trying to get me to surrender, Kate, your salesmanship could use a little work. However, the point is moot, since I'm holding the gun," Kalix said. "But I do have one question: How did Vail break the Web site's code? I have a different access code than Zogas did, but they're the same number of digits, twenty-four. The Russians said they're uncrackable. There are over eighty million combinations. And they change the codes every month."

"I have no idea, but maybe that's who Vail is, one in eighty million."

"Too bad he's not around to save you this time."

"So what are you going to do, John?"

"You don't think I would have given you all the answers and then let you live, did you?"

"Then I've got some bad news for you." She unbuttoned the top two buttons on her blouse, revealing a transmitter mike taped under her bra.

Kalix tightened his grip on the automatic. "How do I know that's not a bluff?"

"Why do you think I sat down in front of the windows? There's a SWAT team out there with a sniper locked onto you."

He smiled cautiously. "You've learned a lot of tricks from Vail. This feels like one of his bluffs."

"It could be."

"Then I assume there's a green-light word or phrase for him to fire. What is it?"

"Think about it for a second. If I say it, you're dead."

Kalix took a moment. "Kate, one of us isn't walking out of here alive. If you're bluffing, you're dead. If you're not . . . well, I'm not going to prison or to death row. So let's have the word and find out which it is." He raised the gun up to where he could aim it more accurately.

"The word is . . ." She stopped, looking uncomfortable.

After a few seconds, Kalix said, "You *are* bluffing." He thumbed back the hammer.

" . . . John Kalix is *Agent X*."

The window exploded as the shot caught Kalix fully just above the ear, ripping him sideways out of the chair.

AFTER

VAIL WALKED UP TO THE FRONT DOOR OF THE SIXTEENTH STREET OFF-SITE AND, knowing that it would be the last time, took a moment to admire the exterior construction of the old mansion. The weather had gotten warmer, almost springlike. He stuck his key in the lock and was a little surprised when it opened. After turning off the alarm, he took his time walking up the black marble staircase, listening to the echo of his steps remind him of what he was leaving behind. The door to the workroom was closed, and, not knowing what to expect, he took a moment before opening it.

Everything had been taken from the walls, which had been patched and painted. The furniture and other pieces of equipment were in their original places. In the back room, the cot he'd slept on was gone. His suitcase with the clothes he'd left behind was on the floor in its place.

Back at the former workroom, he called the CIA agent he'd met at the airport before taking off for Florida and made arrangements to meet him.

Then he dialed Bursaw's cell. He had called him from Florida after reading about Kalix's death and the subsequent news releases regarding the Lithuanian spy ring. Vail told him he'd be back to Washington in five days and asked if they could have dinner before he took Vail to the airport. "Luke, I'm back. At the off-site."

"Forty-five minutes, okay?"

"We've got one other stop to make, if you don't mind."

When Bursaw pulled up, Vail walked out with his suitcases and put them in the trunk. "How's the shoulder?"

"I can tell when it's going to rain, but that's not such a bad thing."

"That's good news," Vail said. "Do you know where the Oceanic Grill is?"

"I thought I was picking the restaurant."

"You are. This is the stop I told you I had to make."

"That's okay then, because I made reservations at this Thai restaurant that has the cutest hostess."

"This shouldn't take more than ten or fifteen minutes. Did you bring Rellick's phone?"

"It's in the glove box. Why have I been the custodian of that thing? It's kind of creepy, since I'm the one who had to shoot him."

Vail put the phone in his pocket. "All in good time, my friend."

Fifteen minutes later they pulled into the Oceanic Grill's parking lot. Vail spotted the car he was looking for and told Bursaw to park next to it. Once he did, the CIA agent got out of his car and into theirs. He handed Vail an unmarked folder. Stapled inside the front cover was a photograph. "We had a hard time tracking down that phone number you gave me at the airport. Where did it come from?"

The number was the one that had called back on Rellick's phone right after Luke killed him, the man Rellick had called "Tanner." Vail looked at the photo. "This is who it came back to?"

"Believe me, it wasn't easy tracing it back. His name is Viktor Bran-ikov. We call him 'The Mosquito.' "

"The Mosquito?"

"Yeah, from *Dr. Zhivago.* The character Viktor Komarovsky, who seduces Lara and sucks the blood out of everyone no matter which communist regime is in power. The root of the name, *komar,* is Russian for 'mosquito.' That's this guy, Branikov. He actually survived the KGB purges and has prospered. According to our source at the embassy, he's the *rezident.*"

" '*Rezident*'? What's that?" Bursaw asked.

Vail said, "The head of the station in Washington for the SVR."

"Supposedly he worked his way up through the ranks by making difficult problems disappear permanently."

"What about the dust?" Vail asked.

"Like you wanted, we had the same source at their embassy start the rumor that Branikov was doubling for one of our agents, a Donald Winston. Of course there is no one by that name with us, but we had someone play the role. We also had our source spread the word that Winston went to the same gym five days a week. Three days ago, when Winston got back to his car, there was dust all over the passenger side." He handed Vail a common-looking pen. "Just point and click."

Vail showed Bursaw the photograph. "Luke, go in there and get a table near this guy. I want to make sure he's completely alone. I'll be five minutes behind you. If you spot anybody else, give yourself a tug on the ear when I come in."

Bursaw entered the restaurant and immediately spotted the big Russian alone at a table in a side room. He was just finishing his meal and looked hard into Bursaw's eyes as the black agent came into the room, without an employee seating him, and sat down a couple of tables away. Bursaw watched him carefully, because he knew that if someone was watching Branikov's back, it would be at that moment that the Russian would signal him to be suspicious of Bursaw. Instead he resumed drinking his coffee.

Five minutes later Vail walked into the side room. Bursaw didn't look up, letting him know that his target was alone. Vail sat down at the Russian agent's table. "How are you?" Vail said, reaching into the bread basket.

"I'm sorry, do I know you?"

"Sure, you know, Steve Vail. You tried to kill me a couple of times."

"I'm sorry, you must have mistaken me for someone else," the Russian said. "Someone who doesn't sound very nice."

"You're not Viktor Branikov? Or would you prefer 'Tanner'?"

Branikov set down his coffee cup and leaned back, a smug grin forming on his face. "Mr. Vail—I assume it's no longer Agent Vail—I have to wonder why you're here."

"You must be pretty pleased with yourself. The Lithuanians had no idea that they were your fall guys. If they'd been successful killing Kate at her home, then you would have been able to have Kalix 'solve' the murder, naming the Lithuanians as responsible, and he would have gotten promoted that way. That was your original plan, wasn't it? Then, of course, you would have had to kill Zogas, so he couldn't involve the Russians."

"If that's true, then you have done my organization a great service."

"That would have been true if one of our snipers hadn't killed your boy Kalix. I don't imagine they're planning any parades for you in Moscow."

"That's an awful lot of supposition, Mr. Vail."

"You're right, and you can call me Steve if you like. Actually, I'm here because it occurred to me that you might have other American double agents left in your stable."

"And if that were the case, do you think I would just turn their names over to you?"

"You just lost a bunch of your assets, not to mention the services of the Lithuanians. I imagine Moscow is not pleased at this point. Let me give you some words of advice—'political asylum.'"

Branikov threw his head back and laughed. "*Steve,* I've come to expect more from you. That's a very weak tactic. One that assumes there are no other options at my disposal."

"Then how about you being charged with the attempted murder of an FBI deputy assistant director and one regular old street agent?"

"I am disappointed. I know this is not your usual profession, but certainly you've heard of diplomatic immunity. If you could prove anything, which I don't see how you can, at most I would be sent back to Moscow. And that is kind of an honor for a man in my field."

"Unfortunately, I believe you're right." The waiter brought the check, and Vail grabbed it. "Allow me. Never let it be said that I'm not a gracious loser." He gave the waiter a credit card.

"You're too kind." Branikov sipped his coffee in silence, studying Vail until the waiter brought back the charge slip and the card.

"I guess you'd better hope that nothing happens to the rest of your sources, because Moscow might start to wonder if you turned."

"I'll try to be careful," Branikov said, his tone amused and patronizing.

Vail looked at the bill and then took out the pen the CIA agent had given him. As he started to write in the waiter's tip, the pen slipped from his hand and fell to the floor. Vail bent over and picked it up. Outside the Russian's line of vision, he pushed the clicker, silently discharging a mist of the ultraviolet powder, covering Branikov's shoes. Vail straightened up and attempted to write with the atomizer pen and then took the waiter's pen and signed the receipt.

"Thank you, Steve. You know, it's too bad you don't do this for a living. It would have made life infinitely more interesting to have you around." Branikov got up and walked out, giving Bursaw a last hard look.

A few minutes later, Vail and Bursaw walked out into the parking lot and over to the CIA agent's car. Vail took out Rellick's phone and handed it to him.

"That's it? He loaded it into his phone?" the agent asked.

"The list is in there."

"And you didn't read it."

"It's no longer any of my business, so no."

"We appreciate it," the agent said, and got back into his car. The two men watched him pull out of the lot before getting back into theirs.

Bursaw said, "Okay, I'm just a common street agent, incapable of understanding the subtleties of counterintelligence. What just happened?"

"Branikov was responsible for everything. He's the one who contracted the LCS to carry out Kate's 'suicide.' But between our being unable to prove it and his diplomatic immunity, he was going to get away with everything. You know how I feel about that. So before I left for Florida, I asked the CIA to identify the phone number that called Rellick's phone that night in the park. I knew that they had a source in the Russian embassy, because they gave us some information from him early on in the Calculus case. So when they identified Branikov as Rellick's handler, they had their source in the embassy leak it out that Branikov was a double agent and that he was being handled by a fictitious CIA officer named Donald Winston, and that he went to the gym every day. A technique they commonly use is spy dust. When they know their suspected man's contact—in this case Winston—they find a way to put dust in his car and then discreetly keep checking Branikov's clothing to see if it shows up. If it does, they know that he's been in the car and doubling. Three days ago the CIA found the dust in *Winston's* car. So they collected it and loaded it into the pen, which I just used to spray Branikov's shoes with."

"So they're already suspicious of him, and when they find the dust on his shoes, they'll start putting him through the grinder."

"I can't speak for Russian bureaucracy, but that's the way it looks on the drawing board. And as soon as the Bureau starts making arrests off the lists that were in Zogas's computers, Branikov's looking at some serious gulag time. At best."

Bursaw laughed. "It does have a nice symmetrical irony to it, since the dust was part of Kate's frame. Like the Bible says: 'Dust to dust.' "

"I think the thing I like best about you, Luke, is you appreciate just how flawed an individual I am."

"That's very flattering—I think—but you're still buying dinner."

"Let's go meet your Thai hostess."

They drove for a while before Bursaw asked, "Well, how was wreck diving?"

"It was okay, you know."

"I never really take vacations, but aren't you supposed to look at least a little bit happy when you come back?"

"Sounds like I'm about to be the recipient of well-intentioned but pointless meddling," Vail said.

"As a friend it's my job to stick my nose in your business."

"Right now that would be a good way to end our friendship."

"Okay, what do you want to talk about?"

"Catch me up on what's been going on since I left."

"We found six bodies in the well. They've only been able to identify two of them—Sundra and that missing air force sergeant. The lye had been working on the others for a while, so we may never know who they are."

"And what are you doing with all your free time now?"

"I do have one fairly large bone to pick with you. They've got me working counterintelligence because I know all the players, and thanks to you they figure I can keep my mouth shut."

"Glad to help."

"Actually, it's not that bad. We're going after guys we know are spies. It's not like the rest of the time where you're guessing and hoping. And if I get bored, I'll do something not so surprisingly stupid and be sent back to WFO. You know me, whatever way the wind blows."

"For someone with a degree in philosophy, you have an extraordinary lack of it in your personal life."

"Said the bricklayer with a master's degree."

Vail smiled. "It's like that old Bureau adage, 'If you want something done right, go find yourself a misfit.'"

Bursaw watched the street in front of him for a few blocks before saying, "So you're not going to ask?"

Vail looked at him and then went back to staring out the windshield. "Okay, how is she?"

"Was that so hard?" Bursaw demanded.

"Don't press your luck. How is she?"

"You would think with all the press she's gotten for taking down the LCS and cleaning up the little problem inside our own hallowed halls, she'd be on top of the world, but I think her face is at least as long as yours. You should try to see her before you go."

"I gave that a lot of thought when I was gone. I think we're both too comfortable with being mildly unhappy. It precludes unhappiness on a larger scale."

"And you talk about my personal philosophy being misguided."

"Ironic, isn't it? The thing that brought Kate and me together is what ultimately keeps us apart. We're a great match working together, and the little time spent completely away from the job has been very good, but invariably her work creeps back in and that's the end of it."

"She told me how this case has gotten in the way. Not that she had to tell me how you are. But it's over now. I don't have all the particulars, but knowing you, I'm going to guess it's long past your turn to blink."

"I said some things that would be hard for her to forgive. She'll be better off if I just get out of here."

"And how would you be?"

Vail stared at him for a few moments. "You're a good friend, Luke."

Bursaw pulled in to a parking space. "In all the time I've known you, I've never seen anyone change your mind, so I'm done trying." He turned off the engine. "Let's eat."

As Vail got out of the car, he realized that they were in the section of Georgetown where he and Kate had gone to dinner the night they'd arranged her escape. He and Bursaw walked into the same small courtyard where they had window-shopped. It was late enough that all the stores were closed but one. Vail glanced into the window of the art gallery where he and Kate had stood that night when he told her about his father.

There were four new sculptures, a series, depicting the same woman in varying poses, all draped with sheer fabric that was somehow more sensuous than if she'd been nude. Three of them had Sold signs placed next to them. "What the—" Vail looked back for Bursaw, hoping that his friend could answer the incomplete question, but he had already gone inside the gallery. Vail looked at the sculptures again to see if he was imagining things. They were his.

He looked past the display and could see some of the people inside, glasses of wine in their hands, Bursaw now among them, shaking hands with an older woman and accepting a drink from a server.

Vail took a step back and, with attempted objectivity, judged the pieces. Were they good enough? He went inside to find out.

The gallery was deceptively large, consisting of three rooms. Other pieces of his were exhibited on pedestals, more than a dozen. He started over to Bursaw and was about to pull him aside when his friend held up his hands, indicating it wasn't his doing. He then pointed back at the office door. It was open, and Vail could now see Kate sitting alone. When she spotted Vail, she stood and smiled with a hint of uncertainty.

He entered the office, and all he could say was "How?"

She took his hand. "A Bureau plane. Your building manager remembered me and let me in. A lot of bubble wrap. It wasn't really that hard. The only difficult part was taking the chance that you wouldn't hate me for doing this."

"As far as surprises go, this isn't bad."

"Then you're not mad at me?"

He smiled reflectively. "I haven't gotten that far yet."

"The gallery owner thinks I'm your manager, so don't tell him what I really do. He loves that you're a bricklayer. He keeps telling everyone that you're just like Rodin. I suppose you know he was a bricklayer before he became famous. Some of them have already sold. I let him set the prices. I hope that's okay."

Vail, looking as confused as she'd ever seen him, turned around and watched the people examining his work. He turned back to her, still unable to answer.

"*Is* it all right?" she asked.

"I don't know what to say."

"Just say it's okay."

"I'm talking about you. The way I was to you—why would you do this for me?"

"I'll leave the obvious answer to that limited imagination of yours, bricklayer. And let's not forget the way I was to you. I accused you of not being able to trust anyone, and then you left me all the answers. And never once looked back. Of the good and bad we've traded, I'd say I got the better of the deal." She took a sip of her wine. "That last why had me for a while. Only after I left the off-site and was on my way to give Kalix the list of spies did I realize that you were pointing at him. But you evidently had enough confidence in me that I'd figure it out. Thank you."

"I'm the one who should be thanking you. For the first time since I was a kid, I feel like I'm connected to someone."

She put her arms around his waist. "And now I believe I owe you one New Year's Eve."

Vail glanced out into the gallery and closed the office door quickly.

Kate said, "Actually, I was thinking more like at my place."

"Do you know who just walked in?"

"Who?"

"Mike, the director's driver, and he doesn't look like he's here for the art."

"Oh, he's probably—"

Vail went to the back of the office and opened an exit door. It led to an alley. "Remember what happened when I let you answer that phone on the real New Year's Eve?" He grabbed her by the wrist. "Let's go."

"They know where I live."

"We're driving straight to the airport."

"Where are we going?"

"Yeah, like I trust you enough to tell you."

She grabbed his arm. "You always did know just what to say to a girl, Stan."

*I'd like to thank the following people, without whom
Noah Boyd would never have been born:*

*My agent, Esther Newberg,
who never allowed me to consider failure a possibility*

*My editor, David Highfill,
who is the best possible person
to be with in the literary trenches*

*And the rest of the good people at William Morrow:
Danielle Bartlett
Mike Brennan
Lynn Grady
Tavia Kowalchuk
Shawn Nicholls
Gabe Robinson
Sharyn Rosenblum
Liate Stehlik*